BROKEN COMPASS

BOOK 1 OF THE TRUE NORTH SERIES

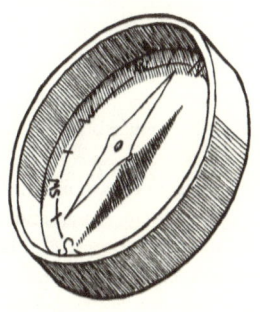

R. E. CROSS

ISBN: 979-8-9901474-0-9 (Paperback)

Author: Rachel E. Cross
Cover and Book Design: Eduardo Gonzalez Ripoll

First Print Edition: 2024

Rufosia Publishing
r.e.cross.author@gmail.com

Dedicated
to my wonderful students:
The too-often-forgotten kids
who need
more than anything in the
world
to be told
Vanyalida.

Table of Contents

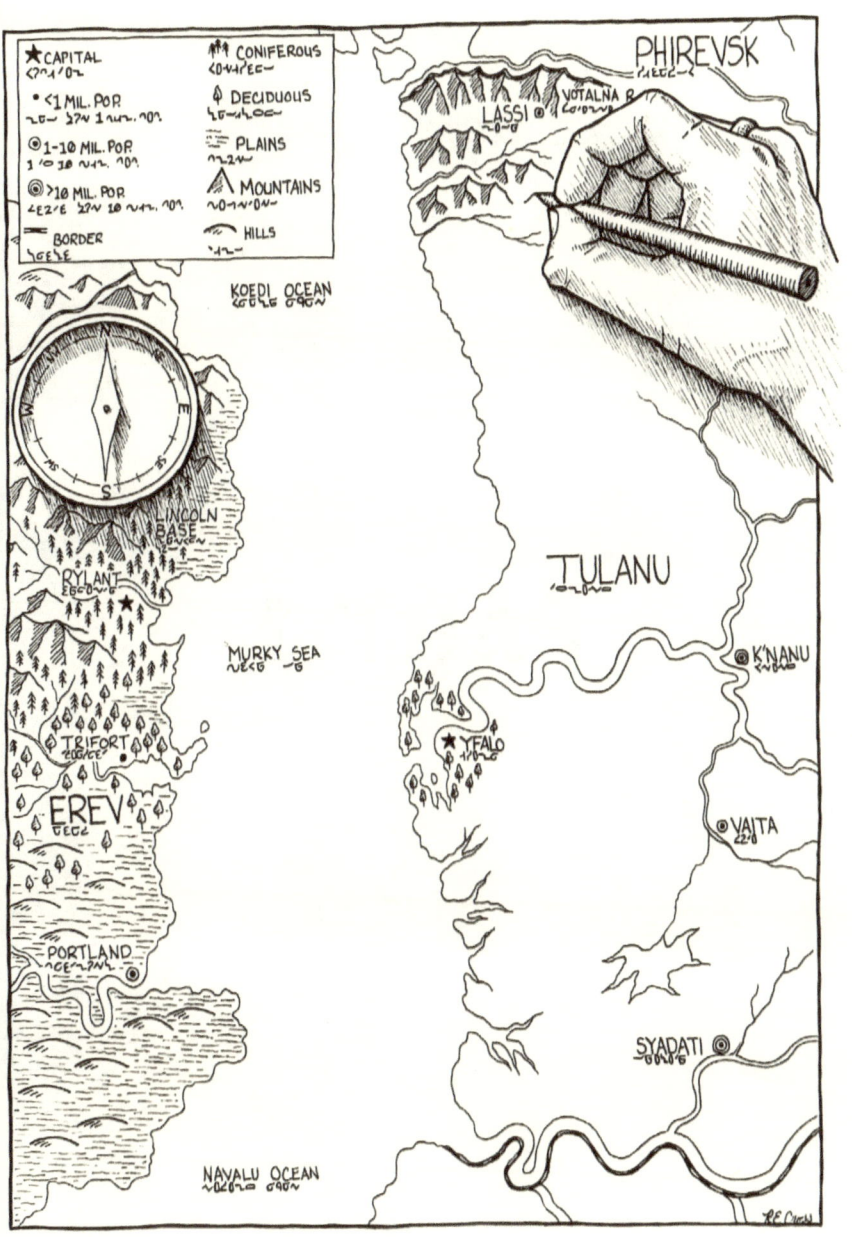

PART 1

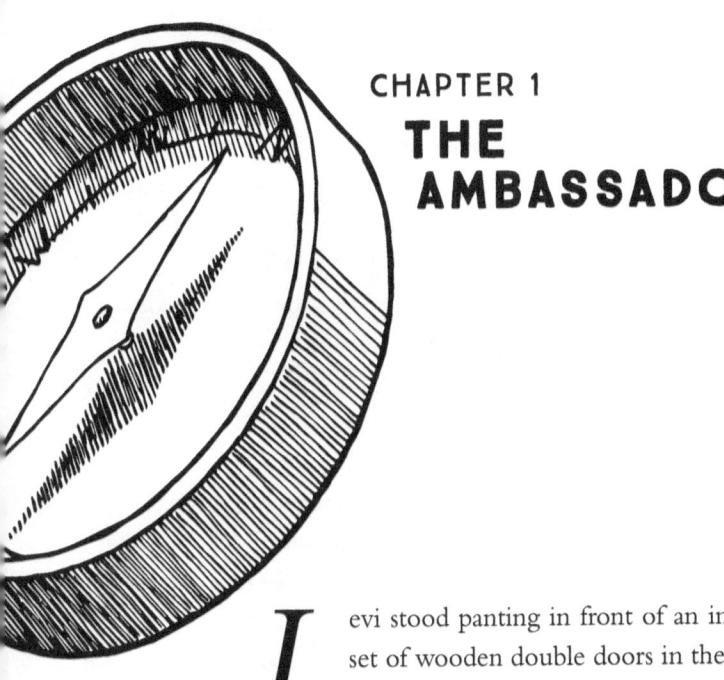

CHAPTER 1

THE AMBASSADOR

*L*evi stood panting in front of an imposing set of wooden double doors in the middle of an empty hallway. The lanky nineteen-year-old glanced at his watch. He was one minute early. His khaki undershirt was soaked from three quarters of what would have been his daily five-kilometer run. He wiped away the sweat threatening to drip into his pale green eyes with the sleeve of his camo uniform.

The unexpected call away from the monotony of his solitary routine left the young soldier anxious. He hurriedly buttoned his shirt and straightened his collar before fighting his hair for cooperation. His thick, brown locks were the perfectly wrong length—too short to tuck behind his ears, but too long to stay out of his eyes.

Levi blew air from his cheeks and stared at the simple gold band on his right middle finger. Disdain was the only emotion the nicked metal induced in him, but he shook it off and straightened his posture. He took a deep breath, stepped up to the doors and knocked.

"Enter."

The heavy doors swung open, revealing the owner of the solemn voice. A man in his early forties sat at a round table in the middle of the large room. President Jake Feyer was a trim, tidy man with dark hair and even darker eyes. His formal and immaculate appearance was accentuated only by a single gold ring on his right middle finger. He thumbed through a sizable document while furiously taking notes in a journal, paying no heed to his surroundings.

Levi silently closed the door behind him, walked towards the center of the room, and stood at attention a meter from the table. No information had been provided about his summons. He resisted the urge to fidget, but anxiety clung to him like his damp shirt. His eyes darted about the room.

Sparse furnishings did little to rid the president's expansive office of its sterile and intimidating air. Crackling flames were at risk of spilling from the marble fireplace while a large, gold framed oil painting of Feyer in regal attire hung over the mantle. It leered down on the room's occupants. A few couches and a coffee table cowered under the painting's icy gaze and huddled dangerously close to the fire.

Feyer sighed and set his pen on the table with a clatter. His gaze narrowed on the boy. "Levi."

The young soldier stiffened, and his attention snapped to the president. "You called for me, sir."

Feyer closed his notebook and flipped through the large document with a scrutinizing eye. "Ambassador Grenard Alsh will be arriving shortly. I need you to meet him at the docks in an hour and escort him here."

Levi had heard the ambassador's name before, and it was not one of which he was particularly fond. He hesitated and shifted his weight. "Permission to speak freely, sir."

"Granted."

The soldier's brow furrowed. "I thought it was dishonorable to interact with the Tulku. Why allow them to come here? And isn't the ambassador supposed to arrive two months from now?"

Feyer turned to the last page as he glared at the boy. "I'm humoring the animal. He requested an earlier arrival due to, quote, 'rising tensions between our nations.' Your orders are to keep him alive until he arrives here. You're the only one I can trust to deal with him." He picked up his pen and began to scribble a few notes on the document.

For a brief moment, Levi stood just a little taller. But another comment Feyer had recently made slithered into his mind and deflated his spirit. He dropped his gaze. "I thought you said I was too young and too inexperienced to handle a mission involving the Tulku." A lock of Levi's unruly hair slipped out of place.

Feyer slammed his pen down. "When did I say that, boy? I've been training you since you were five. You know enough." His eyes were as cold and hard as stone. "Get cleaned up before you leave." He halfheartedly waved the soldier away. "Someone of your status should not look so disheveled."

"Yes, sir."

———iii———

Levi's olive dress uniform was stiff, making the drive through the pine forests and foothills of Erev rather uncomfortable. He futilely blew at a few defiant strands of hair that had slipped out from under his cap. His hands wrung the steering wheel as his

watch screamed at him for his tardiness. That, and the antagoniz-
ing thought of having to host a Tulku made his stomach churn.

The jagged pines and rolling hills gave way to an angular
skyline framed by the Murky Sea. Rylant, the capital of Erev,
was neat and collected by the tree line, but the closer Levi came
to the water, the older and more dilapidated the brick buildings
became. The harsh breeze that blew across the sea had beaten
the eastern edge of the city until it came crumbling to its rusty
knees. The ruggedness of the coastal area seemed to attract a
similar crowd; eastern Rylant was at best unpleasant and at
worst criminal.

A steep sea wall defended the city from the cruel winter
waves. The sandy bottom of the bay had been dredged to provide clearance for small watercraft, and a docking area had been
constructed for safe landing, or as safe a landing as the weather
would permit. A staircase led from the docks to a thin strip of
abandoned beach that separated the sea from civilization.

The remnant of humanity had initially settled in the city
of Rylant after Earth had been destroyed more than a century
before. Everything about the planet Rufosia bore a striking resemblance to the pictures that survived of the old and irradiated
globe humans had narrowly escaped.

Except for the natives.

Levi parked at the edge of the sea wall and stepped out,
nearly losing his cap to a violent, salty gust. Annoyed, he tossed
it inside the car, sure that the Tulku would be ignorant of his
incomplete ensemble. He headed to the gangway and squinted
into the setting sun.

His nerves gathered into an unbearable knot as a small
motorboat approached the weathered dock. He had never seen
a Tulku in person, let alone talked to one. They had been fre-

quently described as animals with fur and fangs and tails. They were bad tempered and cunning, able to swindle their way out of any unpleasant situation.

As the boat came to a standstill, a tall, thin, vaguely human figure carrying a case and a satchel stepped onto the dock. The watercraft pulled away, forcing Levi to walk down and greet the newcomer. He swallowed hard and stood at attention. "Ambassador Alsh?"

The creature faced him and bowed. "Indeed."

The Tulku did, in fact, have fur. It was a deep, rich, rust color. Golden symbols and lines decorated the animal's entire body, shimmering in the fading light. He had black, pointed ears and a voluminous, white-tipped tail. He was tall—taller than Levi, who was more often than not the tallest in the room. As the ambassador stood on the weathered planks, his slender face reminded Levi of a photograph he had seen of a fox in an old Earth book.

The Tulku's apparel was exotic compared to Levi's uniform. The ambassador wore a skirt that came to the ground, but it was separated into three overlapping pieces that blew apart in the strong breeze. The skirt was held in place by a thick band of bright purple fabric wrapped tightly around his waist.

Ambassador Alsh cocked his head to one side, his ears standing on end in a curious fashion. "You must be Levi." He spoke without the slightest accent.

The soldier half nodded. "Yes, sir. I—I presume your journey went smoothly."

The Tulku smiled. "It did. Thank you for asking."

Levi wrung his hands behind his back. He didn't like that the Tulku already knew his name, but he assumed Feyer must have intended for him to retrieve the ambassador long before Levi had been informed of the task.

"I'll grab your belongings." Levi started for the ambassador's case, but the Tulku cleared his throat. The soldier paused and looked up at him.

"If you don't mind, I would like a moment to stretch my legs. A quick walk along the beach should do the trick."

The hair on the back of Levi's neck stood on end. Evening had arrived, and more than a few unsavory characters would have begun to wander the streets by now. He awkwardly met the Tulku's gaze. "Sir, you don't know what Rylant is like at night. We really should be leaving."

"I understand and appreciate your concern, soldier. However, my mind is still made up. You may make a recommendation that I may choose to ignore. And I am more familiar with Rylant than you might realize." The Tulku remained calm and smiling as he watched the boy. "I might also add that there is nothing safe about a Tulku in Erev to begin with." The ambassador raised one eyebrow, waiting for Levi's response. There was a curious twinkle in his eye.

It was not the reaction Levi had expected. He frowned, hoping the Tulku would change his mind. When the ambassador's resolve remained constant, the boy sighed. "Very well, sir."

Levi stashed the ambassador's satchel and case in the back of the car. He turned and found the Tulku patiently standing at the top of the stairs that led down to the waves and the beach. After he joined the ambassador, they descended the stairs to the coarse sand.

A few cottony clouds floated lazily above them, glowing in the last blazing drops of sunlight. The surprisingly calm winter waves caught fire as the sun set in the far east. Whistling wind and crashing water drowned out the sound of cars driving on the narrow streets above. The tall skyscrapers had crept dangerously close to the sea wall, on the verge of toppling into the shallow waters.

Levi matched the ambassador's slow and deliberate pace while constantly glancing at the city above. The Tulku let out a contented sigh and smiled peacefully. The soldier tore his gaze away from the streets and peered at the slender-faced creature walking beside him.

"Permission to speak freely."

The ambassador eyed him curiously. "You don't need my permission to talk, my boy."

Levi paused for a brief moment, his breath caught in his throat. "May I ask what you are smiling about, sir?"

"I'm simply enjoying the fresh air. What is not to enjoy, hmm?" His smile grew to a grin.

A trio of drunkards lurched and tripped their way towards the edge of the sea wall, instantly drawing Levi's attention. He prayed they wouldn't notice the Tulku, but all too soon one of the gray, grizzled men pointed and started shouting at them.

"Wha's th'animal doin'ere? Go back to th'ole y'crawled outa'!"

The two other men with him joined in, jeering at the ambassador. Levi was sure that one good gust of wind would be enough to send all three flailing over the edge and onto the sands below.

Feyer's orders rang in the boy's mind like the tolling of a large bell. He had only been with the ambassador for a matter of minutes, and he was already at risk of failing his mission. His heart pounded in time to the alarm ringing in his head. "We should have left earlier."

"Leave them be."

Levi snapped around and found the ambassador already walking back to the docks at the same pace as before, as if nothing but the direction of the wind had changed. The soldier rushed to catch up. "Isn't it my job to protect you, sir?"

The Tulku glanced at him. "What real danger are they?" He continued before Levi had a chance to collect his thoughts. "They're drunk. They hardly know what they're saying. Even if they did, I have thick skin. You don't need to waste time protecting me from meaningless taunts."

The ambassador eyed the drunkards warily then pushed forward. By the time he and Levi had made their way back to the car, the slobbering trio had clamored their way to the docks, vehemently declaring their hatred of the Tulku. Levi shoved the ambassador inside the vehicle and slammed the door shut. His heart raced as he turned and found himself pinned between the car and the surly drunks.

The most vocal of the graying slobs came right up to Levi's face. His hair was greasy and scraggly, his chin covered by silver stubble. His teeth were yellowed and crooked. He spat on the ground next to Levi's boot and pointed a grubby finger at the Tulku safely behind glass. "If 'e didn't leave, I'ma skin 'im alive, him an' all 'is kind."

Levi blinked as the man's rancid breath washed over his face. "You're threatening an ambassador and guest of President Feyer." He instinctively reached for the holster that usually occupied his hip during training, but he felt only air. His heart stopped.

"I don' care who 'e is! 'E's an animal tryin' t' take wha's ours! An' who put you in charge?"

Levi's fists balled at his side as the pressure in his chest mounted. "I report directly to President Feyer. You need to back away now."

The man laughed, and a crooked sneer slid onto his face. "A boy like you? Repor'in t' Feyer?" He brushed some invisible speck of dust from Levi's shoulder. "I don' give a damn abou' Feyer. He can go f—"

Levi swung hard and landed an uppercut to the man's jaw, sending him flailing to the ground. The man lay on his back, gaping like a fish as the other two turned tail and ran as fast as they could in their incapacitated state.

Levi stared down at the drunk. "Feyer's your leader. You should give a damn."

The soldier stepped over the bleary-eyed man, disgusted by his blatant disrespect. Levi knew better than most that Feyer was not to be trifled with. He slid into the front seat, breathing heavily, hands shaking. He started the car and pulled away from the docks, only glancing in the ambassador's direction as he checked his mirrors.

Ambassador Alsh cleared his throat. "Was that truly necessary?"

Levi frowned. "Excuse me?"

"You didn't need to hit him."

"I have my orders."

The Tulku chuckled. "Your orders are to hit anyone who gets too close to you?"

Levi huffed. "No. I'm supposed to protect you until you arrive at President Feyer's home."

"Then my comment is still relevant."

Levi rolled his eyes, avoiding the Tulku's gaze. "Alright. How would you have handled that situation, sir?"

"You could have simply called the authorities. No one would have been injured, and all three men likely would be off the streets by now. You might have put yourself in a potentially difficult position by assaulting him."

Levi sneered. "I am the authorities, sir. That's what the uniform is for."

The Tulku huffed and shook his head as he looked out the window. "You still have much to learn about life, my boy."

"I think I know enough." Levi ground his teeth. He struggled to keep his voice steady. Imitating Feyer's earlier comment gave him no comfort as he tried to believe what he had spoken. Despite his lack of belief in his own words, he doubted the Tulku really knew more than him. Who did the animal think he was to freely critique the human keeping him alive in a place where everyone wanted him dead?

The rest of the drive was steeped in silence. Levi repeatedly played over the interactions with the drunkard, evaluating, recalculating, and critiquing himself. The Tulku kept his own counsel, gazing at the passing city lights. Neon signs and cracked concrete gave way to wrought iron lamp posts and perfectly manicured lawns as the grunge of eastern Rylant submitted to the glamor of western Rylant. Eventually the lamp posts turned into pine trees as Levi drove up the winding road towards Feyer's compound. He hoped his time with the ambassador would soon come to an end as the walls around Feyer's property came into view.

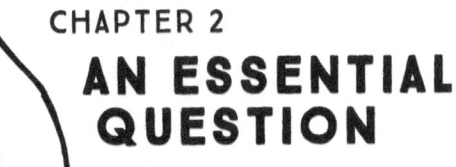

CHAPTER 2
AN ESSENTIAL QUESTION

President Jake Feyer's home was less a home and more of a castle protected by a stone wall. Levi's turn through the gate revealed the pompous, three-story chateau, illuminated like a beacon. The house was surrounded by perfectly manicured gravel pathways and gardens. Every detail of the estate screamed intentionality and aristocracy.

"Welcome to the West." Levi parked in front of the perron and stepped out into the crisp night air. He grabbed his cap, hoping to mask his windblown hair, and straightened his now creased uniform.

The ambassador had let himself out of the car and stood staring at the house with his hands clasped behind his back. Levi couldn't tell if he was in awe or if he was disgusted by the sight in front of him. The Tulku's perpetually calm and regal disposition was one Levi had begun to dislike.

The ambassador marched up the stairs to the grand entrance with the soldier in tow. The large double doors swung open before them, unveiling the main foyer. A large chandelier hung from the ceiling, partially obscuring the equally lavish staircase that led to the second floor. A luxurious ballroom stood on their right, but Levi led the Tulku into the dining hall on their left.

Feyer rose from his chair at the head of the table as they entered. "Good evening, Ambassador Alsh. I trust your journey went smoothly."

The Tulku bowed slightly. "Thank you, President Feyer. It went flawlessly. I appreciate your willingness to indulge me on such short notice."

The ambassador was seated on Feyer's left by an attendant as several dishes were brought out. Levi hung back behind the president, his mouth watering as the steaming food filled the air with savory aromas. It had been hours since he had last eaten, and his interrupted run had only made him more ravenous. But the soldier had not been invited to dine with them, nor had he been dismissed so he could rummage through the kitchen.

Feyer brushed his suit coat out of the way and sat. He took his silverware and picked at the food in front of him. "I have prepared accommodations for you to stay here while you work. I would like for one of my men to accompany you at all times. I hate to admit it, but my people are not particularly fond of the Tulku at the moment." The president offered Alsh a half smile.

"I am not unaware of our distaste for one another. Erev and Tulanu have been at odds for decades." The Tulku dabbed around his mouth with a napkin, setting it down gently beside his plate. "With all due respect, I do not wish to become more of a burden by occupying one of your soldiers. I am grateful for the generosity you have already shown me, but it seems as if a soldier constantly at my side might be counterproductive to my work. It will likely draw more attention than I would prefer."

The shallow grin fell from the president's face. "Ambassador Alsh, I insist. Your extensive absence has left you at a disadvantage. You do not know my people as I do."

"I would never claim to know them half as well as you. May I ask who my companion will be?"

"Levi will be assigned to you."

The soldier's eyes grew wide as he glanced towards Feyer. He struggled to maintain his composure as he processed the news. He had not been informed of this assignment, nor did he want it. Interacting with a Tulku was disgraceful. But babysitting a Tulku for any length of time was utterly humiliating. From previous conversations he had overheard, Levi suspected the ambassador would be working in Erev for several months.

Alsh eyed the boy and seemed mildly pleased. "Very well. I would like to make a request."

Feyer said nothing and watched the Tulku.

"I would like for Levi to assist me as I make my observations. Four eyes are certainly better than two, and a bit of human perspective on this conflict will surely not go to waste."

Levi's face contorted without his permission.

Feyer carefully placed his silverware on the table and clasped his hands together, tapping his fingers. "What exactly are you proposing Levi do?"

The ambassador sat thoughtfully for a moment before he smiled. "I expect I will want help conducting interviews, researching recent events, and occasionally performing behavioral analyses."

Feyer's shoulders lowered as he sank back into his chair. "Levi can help you make your observations while you are in Erev."

"Speaking of having a human perspective on my work, would you consider letting one of your men help me make observations in areas of Tulanu with a significant human population?

My work would not be complete if it was also not cohesive in methodology."

"Levi is not to leave the country under any circumstances."

The ambassador nodded. "I understand perfectly. Thank you for such a splendid first meal in Erev." He set his napkin on the table and scooted his chair back.

Feyer cleared his throat as the Tulku stood to leave. "Ambassador Alsh, I would like to host a ball in your honor."

Alsh's collected composure cracked. His ears flattened. "It was my understanding that my presence in the West was not to be broadcast to the media. Why host such a large event?"

"It would only be among my closest officials. I figured it would be important to celebrate the progress we will be making towards a more peaceful world."

"When were you intending on having the ball?"

"In two months' time. I hope you will consider attending."

Alsh gave Feyer one solemn, unsmiling nod. "I shall."

Feyer grinned. "Excellent."

Levi's head was still swimming from his new assignment as he started towards the ambassador.

Feyer grabbed the soldier's sleeve. "Meet me once you get him settled."

"Yes, sir."

———···———

A luxurious suite with two bedrooms, a sitting area and kitchenette had been reserved for the duration of the ambassador's stay. The far wall of the central commons area was floor-to-ceiling glass, showcasing a stunning second-story view of Rylant and the sea beyond. A few couches and a long, low table gazed out at the treetops peeking over the estate's protective wall. An attendant had already brought the ambassador's case and satchel up and placed them squarely on the small kitchen table by the time Levi showed the Tulku upstairs.

Ambassador Alsh stood with his hands on his hips, surveying the area. "I assume you will be occupying whichever bedroom I am not."

Levi kept his gaze fixed on the floor. "I will clarify that with President Feyer."

Alsh sighed. "Well, I suppose I'll take the room on the right. Whether or not you are to stay here, you will have the room on the left."

"Yes, sir." Levi grabbed the ambassador's case and satchel and carried them to the dresser in the right room. He set them down and stood at attention. "Is there anything else you need for the time being, sir?"

The Tulku's ear twitched, and his brows furrowed. "Just one thing. Call me Grenard. At least when it is the two of us. I'm not particularly fond of the ambassador title."

"Yes, sir."

Grenard eyed him quizzically with his ears perked forward. "Do you ever lighten up, my boy?"

"No, sir."

He chuckled. "I see." Ambassador Alsh began to pull various books out of his satchel and pile them on the dresser.

Levi started to walk out of the Tulku's room, but a question jumped into his mind. He froze, debating whether to speak or hold his tongue. The ambassador hadn't minded him asking a question earlier, so Levi turned back to him. "Are those the only kinds of observations I will have to make?"

Grenard flicked an ear towards him. "Pardon?"

Levi hesitated. "The request you discussed with Feyer at dinner. Are those the only things you will want me to help you with?"

"That will depend on many things."

Of course it did. Levi took a deep breath and pushed down his growing frustration. He watched the Tulku unpack for a moment. The shimmering golden lines in Grenard's fur were mesmerizing. Each symbol was unique, and many contained a flamelike design.

"What are the symbols on your fur?" Levi wanted to kick himself for blurting it out.

Grenard paused and looked up at him. "Mighty curious for a soldier."

Levi's face scrunched. "Don't you want me to be curious? It seems like that is a prerequisite for the work you want me to help you with."

"Indeed. I just had not anticipated someone like you knowing how to ask good questions."

The young soldier folded his arms across his chest, standing taller than before. "I was taught to gather enough information so I can make well-informed decisions. I believe that involves asking good questions."

Grenard pulled out yet another leather-bound book and inspected it. "It is always challenging to know when you have collected enough information to make such decisions. I suspect you and I both will have several difficult decisions to make in the near future. What decision are you trying to make right now, my boy?"

Levi opened his mouth to speak, but no sound came out. He searched his thoughts, then started again. "Can you be trusted?" The thought had been haunting him ever since he had learned that the ambassador would be coming to Erev weeks ago.

The Tulku smiled. "That is an essential question that needs to be answered for both our sakes. I have had a similar question on my mind. Unfortunately, time is needed to procure that answer, and time is not on our side." Grenard set the books down and considered the boy. "But let me answer your previous question. The lines on my fur are called syamta. All Rufosians are born with them. Each symbol possesses a different meaning. The collection of syamta you have represents who you are capable of becoming."

"That seems like a lot of pressure, to be born with those kinds of expectations."

Grenard shrugged. "Not everyone makes the choice to try to live by their syamta, but I have found it to be more hopeful than burdensome. I know who I am becoming, and that certainty is a blessing and an encouragement."

Levi's stomach churned. Something about the concept left him feeling unsettled. He shook it off. "I know what I'm supposed to become. I wouldn't want some special lines to dictate my life."

The Tulku gazed at him, head tilted, tail swishing slowly from side to side. "Let me guess: Feyer wants you to become some special soldier of his with lots of responsibilities."

Levi turned towards the door. "Something like that."

"A soldier is not who you are."

The boy stopped and glanced back at Grenard.

"That may be your occupation, but who you are is something much different, something much more profound." There was a warmth in Grenard's amber gaze.

Levi watched him for a few lingering seconds before he looked away. He shook his head and left the suite.

The ambassador's final comment burned in Levi's thoughts as he absentmindedly meandered towards Feyer's office. He didn't know who he was if he wasn't a soldier. It was all he knew. What would be left of him if that was taken away?

He shoved the thought aside and knocked on the door. Feyer's muffled response slipped past the doors. Levi stood tall and pushed his way inside.

Feyer paced in front of the fireplace with his hands behind his back and lips pursed. The flames cast long, ominous shadows as he walked.

"You wanted to meet with me, sir."

Feyer glanced up at him "Yes. Do not trust Ambassador Alsh. I want you to report everything you discuss with him, everything you do with him, every movement he makes. I don't care how insignificant the detail may seem."

"Does this mean I will be staying with him during all hours of the day?"

"And the night." Feyer stopped and stared at the soldier intently. "Remember that he is only an animal that we are entertaining. Don't fall prey to whatever lies he tells you." He resumed his pacing. "The Tulku can be very convincing."

CHAPTER 3
SOCIALLY ACCEPTABLE

*A*mbassador Alsh had a strict daily routine that started well before dawn. Levi would wake to him sitting on one of the couches having already spent several hours poring over dozens of news articles on a glass tablet and taking notes in one of his journals. Grenard would continue doing that until lunch.

After lunch, the Tulku would drag Levi around the mansion, searching for someone to interview back at the suite. Grenard would often prioritize visitors to the mansion: government officials that had finished meetings early, or soldiers who had been ordered there on minor business. When no visitors could be found, he would snatch away one of the mansion's many staff.

Post-interview, Grenard and Levi would spend the latter half of their afternoons strolling through the gardens. By the time the sun hit the edge of the sea, the ambassador was ready to retire to one of the couches and end his day with leisurely reading—primarily fiction.

Levi was more than happy to leave the Tulku to his research and reading. He never asked what Grenard was diving into, and the Tulku never asked him for help. It was a relief, in many ways, to still have solitude throughout the day. Feyer had mandated that Levi continue his studies; the endless hours of sitting provided an excellent framework for the soldier to cram information into his mind. The kitchen table was often littered with textbooks, his digital notebook, and loose sheets of marred paper.

Being assigned to guard the ambassador was tolerable, but there were two things that Levi dreaded on a daily basis. The first nerve-grating gripe he had was with Grenard's humming habit. The Tulku had a strange device called a tevet. It looked like an ordinary silver bracelet until Grenard pulled it apart into three pieces. Two of the pieces were thin crescents that he would place around his ears. The remaining piece was just a thinner version of the original object. Whenever the Tulku had the silver pieces on, he would inevitably begin humming. And it was always the same three songs.

The ambassador didn't have a bad voice. In fact, he could sing quite well. But it was a constant reminder that Levi had been relegated to a glorified babysitting position instead of training or a more engaging assignment.

The second thing Levi dreaded was the daily hunt for a new interviewee. He had no choice but to follow Ambassador Alsh around the compound until another target had been sighted. Once they had ensnared their prey, they would go back to the suite where Levi would try to keep to himself as Grenard drained his victims of their answers. Depleted of information, they would glare at the soldier as they retreated from the suite.

As time progressed, Levi received an increasing number of foul stares from any human that frequented Feyer's mansion whenever he dared venture beyond the safety of the suite. It had not been his choice to be joined at the hip to the Tulku. He couldn't help but wonder if his assignment was some cruel joke Feyer was playing on him to test his resolve; it was certainly wearing on him.

Weeks passed with each day progressing just as the previous one had, until one late winter morning brought more than the usual heavyset clouds, constant drizzle, and bitter breeze.

Levi rubbed his eyes and yawned as he trudged out to the table where his stout textbooks waited begrudgingly for him. He stared blankly at the work he had completed the night before. His eyes struggled to focus on his notes and decipher his own handwriting, but something more than his grogginess was off. He looked about and found the ambassador standing in front of the window, watching the gray, bleak morning. The Tulku's tablet sat on the coffee table, off, next to a closed journal. Levi craned his neck to see Grenard's unusually somber reflection in the glass. When the Tulku took no notice of him, he picked up his pen and forced himself to work through another problem.

"Is there a restaurant you like to frequent?"

Levi glanced up from his notebook. "Pardon?" His diction was, annoyingly, beginning to mimic that of the ambassador.

Grenard turned towards him. "Is there some place you would like to eat lunch today?" There was something in his eyes that the soldier didn't recognize, something akin to sadness.

Levi returned to his studies, shaking his head. "I've never eaten at a restaurant before." The boy had spent most of his life training. Luxuries, even small ones, had often been denied him. But ignorance was bliss; he didn't know what he was missing out on, and he didn't have much time to dwell on such things. He had far bigger problems than seeking out so-called common experiences.

Alsh tilted his head to one side. "No? That's something we should change. If you don't mind taking a break from your studies to humor an old Tulku, there is a place I would recommend we go."

Levi glanced over his math assignment. The incomplete problems mocked him and shamed him, but sleep had done little to help his numb mind recover from the hours of practice the day before. He glanced at his watch. He had slept well past his alarm. By the time he got ready and they drove into Rylant, it would be noon. The opportunity the ambassador offered was mildly tempting.

Levi huffed. "What did you have in mind, sir?"

A half sly, half sorrowful grin slid over the Tulku's face. "Are you familiar with French cuisine?"

"No, sir."

"No longer shall you miss out on it, my boy. It was an Earth experience I was introduced to early on in my career that I quite enjoy. We don't have much that is similar in Tulkish cuisine."

Levi stuffed his loose assignments into his textbooks and returned to his room to finish getting ready for the day. When he came out with laced boots and halfway manageable hair, Grenard was waiting in the common area. The ambassador had his usual weird skirt on, but he also wore pants and shirt, all in a vibrant purple color. His brown leather satchel was slung over his shoulder.

Grenard looked at Levi expectantly. "Are you ready to go?"

"Yes, sir." Levi ran his fingers through his hair as he stared at his mandatory companion. "Why the sudden outfit change?"

Grenard smirked. "Tulkish formal apparel is a little more socially acceptable in Erev than what we normally wear in Tulanu."

Levi nodded slowly. "Where is the restaurant located?"

"If memory serves me well, I believe it is on the southwest corner of Washington Avenue and Tolstoy Street."

Levi's shoulders slumped. "If you don't mind me being blunt, sir, that isn't a place where good society spends any considerable time." The soldier's knowledge of Rylant was limited, but that part of town he knew. Tolstoy Street ran only a few blocks from the sea and was notorious for a high crime rate.

The ambassador grinned slyly, and his ears perked up. "Sometimes the unsavory places are where the best treasures are found."

————iii————

Tolstoy Street consisted of dilapidated brick buildings packed together like sardines. What little color existed was faded, and the sidewalks were riddled with cracks. On the southwest corner where Tolstoy Street intersected with Washington Avenue sat a tiny cafe. Levi parked on the curb in front of La Boulangerie. A sagging red awning hung over the establishment's single, large window. Under the main window sat a man, huddled against the brick in a ratty blanket and grungy hat.

Levi frowned and began to wonder about the Tulku's sanity. There was nothing appealing about this place, contrary to what the ambassador had stated. *Unsavory* felt like an understatement for a place harboring society's useless beggars.

The soldier scanned the area for any other suspicious characters. "Are you sure this is a good idea, sir?"

"I never said it was a good idea, but I do enjoy the food." Grenard took a deep breath, then stepped out onto the deserted street.

Levi gripped the steering wheel tightly. He double and triple-checked the mirrors for any other living creatures, then ducked inside the shabby cafe to join the ambassador.

La Boulangerie was tired. A worn podium squatted just inside the door with a dozen or so tables crammed together beyond it. A few of the tables were occupied with similarly exhausted customers, each consumed with their own problems. The only redeeming qualities of the establishment were the savory aromas that wafted throughout the whole place and the soft music that drowned the already muted conversations of the other patrons.

A stringy waitress, smacking a piece of gum between her chapped lips, plodded up to the podium, gave the ambassador a double take, then grabbed a few menus. "Just the two of you?" Her voice was as flat as a pancake.

"Yes." Grenard smiled pleasantly at the woman. "Would it be possible for us to have that table?" He pointed towards a small square table with two chairs situated directly in front of the main window.

Levi's breath caught in his throat. It was bad enough that the quiet restaurant had as many occupants as tables, but to sit where the entirety of Tolstoy Street could see them seemed like a recipe for disaster.

The lady shrugged. She led them to the table and handed them the menus. "I'll get your orders in a minute."

Grenard draped his satchel over the back of his chair before seating himself and scanning the plastic sheet. Levi copied the Tulku. The menu was covered in strange names of dishes he had never heard of or seen before. The words contained far too many vowels and an absurd number of Qs. Levi didn't understand how a language like French was, at one point in time, spoken fluently by millions of people when he could barely manage to read the name of a soup. He rested his face in his hands as he attempted to decipher everything.

"If I might make a suggestion, their boeuf bourguignon is quite hearty. But if you are in the mood for something a little lighter, try the quiche lorraine."

Levi glanced up at the ambassador, but Grenard's gaze was firmly fixed on his own menu. The soldier found the two items the Tulku had recommended and read their descriptions. He sat back in his chair and crossed his arms. "What makes you think I would like either of those dishes?"

Grenard looked over the top of his menu, unenthused. "I have been dining with you every day for several months now. I figured those would be safer options than, say, escargot."

"What's escargot?"

"Snails."

Levi wrinkled his nose. The thought of eating the small slimy creatures was revolting.

A gust of wind rattled the window, blowing tiny white flecks across the face of the glass. Levi gaped at the snow. It rarely snowed in Rylant, being so close to the sea. But with the heavy clouds having grown noticeably darker since he had woken up, the soldier suspected it would be more than a flurry. A cold and unfeeling draft snuck under the door, making Levi shiver.

The waitress plunked two glasses of water and a plate with two croissants onto the table. "Do you know what you want?"

Grenard handed her his menu. "Yes, I'd like an onion soup and a cheese souffle."

Levi tore his gaze from the snow and fumbled with his menu. His mind went blank. He stared at the Tulku, eyes wide. "May I have the boeuf bourguignon?" The name clattered across his tongue and spilled out in a jumbled mess, but the Tulku gave him a small nod and a smile.

The waitress grabbed the soldier's menu, tucked it under her arm, then scribbled on a stained, yellowing notepad. "Anything else?"

Grenard cleared his throat. "Two chocolate mousse, please. And would you mind bringing them out after our main course?" He smiled politely as she finished writing and meandered to the back of the restaurant without saying another word. The Tulku turned his gaze to the window and watched the steadily increasing snowfall cover the gray city in a blanket of white. He rested his chin in his hand. That strange something in his eyes that Levi had noticed earlier was still there, robbing the ambassador of his usually optimistic disposition.

Levi squirmed and shuffled his feet under the table. "You've been to Rylant before?" It was a half question.

The ambassador's eyes darted to the boy. "Many times, my boy. Most of my early career was spent here, working with President Feyer's predecessor. Tensions were still high back then, but much has changed in the decade that I have been gone." Grenard sighed heavily, then turned and scanned La Boulangerie. A smile crept to the corner of his mouth. "But this place has hardly changed in thirty years, and that I am grateful for."

Levi fiddled with the ring on his finger. "You knew Anton Feyer?"

Grenard eyed the boy, a glimmer of mischief easing back into his downcast demeanor. "Yes. I had quite the relationship with Anton. He was not the most logical person, but he was better to us than most, Vanyani and me, that is." He chuckled to himself. "We had some interesting, though rather unproductive conversations. He was good humored."

The Tulku's grin faded once more. He resumed staring at the snow. "It was tragic when he passed. I cannot say that my relationship with his son can quite compare, try as I might."

"I was too young to remember him." All his life, Levi had heard that Anton Feyer was a great man, leading his people with a firm hand. A desire to have known, or at least to have remembered seeing the man lingered in Levi's mind, but he knew it would always remain unfulfilled.

They were silent for some time as the snow outside the window slowly obscured their vision of the city.

"Do you have any games that you like to play?"

Levi eyed the ambassador and scoffed. "No. They're a waste of time. I don't have any to spare."

"That's a shame. Games are one of life's small joys, and they can often be quite useful."

The soldier rolled his eyes and scanned the restaurant. A few older couples sat about, contentedly sipping on hot beverages, while a group of three youngsters bickered about the weather and packed up. All minded their own business except for a man who sat at the table closest to the door. A scowl was plastered across the salt-and-pepper haired man's face as he watched Grenard intently, slouched behind an old laptop and a plain, white mug. He and Levi locked eyes. The man's eyes grew wide for a split second before he fully tore his gaze from the ambassador and sunk further behind his computer, typing with fervor.

Levi watched the man as nausea mounted in the pit of his stomach.

The waitress set their food on the table unceremoniously, breaking Levi's concentration and making him jump in his seat.

Beef, potatoes, and carrots swam in a thick gravy-like sauce. Aromatic steam rose from the bowl, flooding Levi's senses and making his mouth water. He had had stews before, but upon the first savory bite, this stew was by far the richest one he had consumed. It was challenging to not scarf it down as the food warmed him from the inside out. When every morsel was gone, Levi scraped the gravy off the side of the bowl with his spoon, savoring every last drop.

Grenard had pulled out a journal from his satchel and filled one of its pages with a script Levi did not recognize. The ambassador's food remained largely untouched. He glanced up, and seeing Levi's empty bowl, pointed with his pen to one of the pastries the waitress had brought out earlier. "Take one of the croissants, if you're still hungry."

Levi grabbed one and examined it carefully. As he inspected the flaky, buttery pastry, the graying man once again caught his attention. The man had resumed glowering at the ambassador as if staring long enough would make the Tulku spontaneously burst into flames. Levi returned the glare. The man noticed and dropped his gaze.

The soldier shook his head and continued studying the croissant. It wrapped around itself in a curious fashion. He thought he had maybe seen them once before, likely at one of Feyer's many dinner parties. The boy unraveled the layers, tearing off pieces and enjoying each bite.

It wasn't long after Levi had finished his croissant when the waitress, in her undignified manner, returned with two bowls filled with a brown custard and topped with whipped cream. She cleared away the soldier's empty bowl and Grenard's half-eaten food.

Levi started to dip his spoon into the dessert, but hesitated as he glanced up at the ambassador. Grenard's amber eyes were swimming in that strange, sad look. But it was deeper and more profound than mere sadness. The Tulku's ears drooped as he stared at the dish in front of him.

Levi set his spoon down. "Is something wrong, sir?"

Grenard took a shaky breath and rapidly blinked back tears. "Many things are wrong in the world, but that doesn't answer the intent of your question." He sat back and sighed. "The first time Vanyani and I came here, we were sitting in this exact spot. We ordered chocolate mousse." He paused. "That's when I found out we were having our first child."

"Wouldn't that be a happy memory, sir?"

Grenard nodded. "It is. It's one of the happiest moments of my life, but I cannot share that memory with her anymore."

"Did she leave?"

"In a sense, yes. She passed away ten years ago today." The fur by the corner of the Tulku's eyes grew dark.

Levi sank into his chair. "My condolences." He had heard someone say that once. The expression left a strange churning in his heart as he realized the look that had settled on Grenard's face was grief. Though he had never lost anyone that he could remember, the significance of the date made the rest of the strange morning suddenly make sense. "How did she die?" As soon as the words escaped his mouth, Levi wished he could take them back.

"That is a story for another time. We must answer our ultimate question of trust before I am willing to share that with you." There was an inkling of hope in the Tulku's eyes. He gave the soldier half a smile then took a bite of the dessert.

Levi took his cue from the ambassador and tasted the custard. It flooded his mouth with an earthy sweetness just as rich as the stew, but it could not shake the heavy weight that settled on his mind. It was a weight he did not fully understand. It bothered him that the Tulku was unwilling to share what had happened so long ago. What was so horrible about his wife's death that Levi couldn't be trusted to know?

He stopped himself. He didn't need to know.

But he wanted to.

They finished eating in silence until the waitress came by with the check, which Grenard immediately snatched up. Curiosity got the better of Levi as he peeked at the amount Grenard had tipped. The service was far from exceptional compared to what was standard practice in Feyer's mansion, and yet the Tulku had tipped what seemed to Levi to be an exorbitant amount of money. Grenard stuffed his journal in his satchel, threw it over his shoulder, and carefully wrapped the remaining croissant in a paper napkin as Levi stood to lead the way out.

The salt-and-pepper-haired man stuck his foot out into the narrow passageway before Levi had a chance to react, sending him flying. His hands slammed into the dirty floor, and his forehead throbbed from hitting the edge of the podium.

The man spat at the soldier. "Animal lover."

The ambassador firmly grabbed Levi by the elbow and hoisted him up. The other patrons had all turned in their seats to see the commotion. Levi could feel the heat and embarrassment flooding his face. He started towards the smug man, blood boiling and fist balled, but Grenard kept a hold on him. He glanced back at the Tulku, wrenched himself free, and stormed out into the swirling snow.

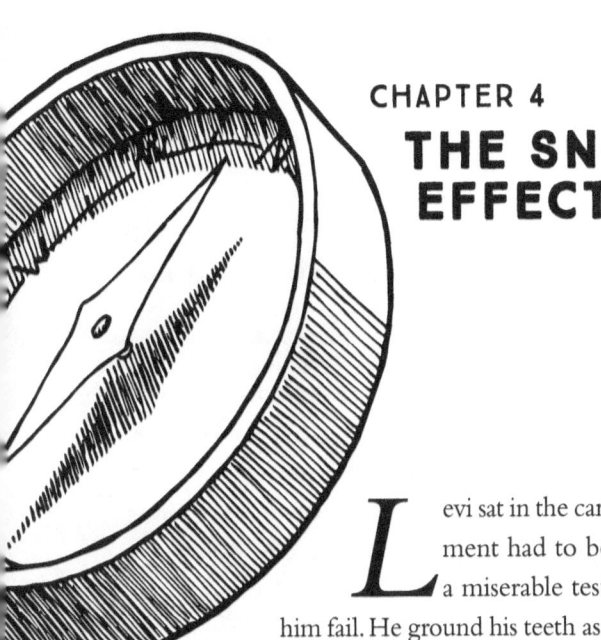

CHAPTER 4
THE SNOWBALL EFFECT

*L*evi sat in the car, fuming. His assignment had to be a test from Feyer,
a miserable test designed to make
him fail. He ground his teeth as his white-knuckled
grip tightened on the steering wheel, but out of the
corner of his eye he still watched Grenard.

The ambassador had stopped to talk with the homeless man
now shivering in the snow. Grenard handed him the croissant
before joining Levi. He had barely closed the door when Levi
peeled away from the curb and tore down the street, racing to
return to the safety of the president's mansion. A mild panic
settled in the soldier's mind as he fought against the wind and
drifting snow to keep the car on the road.

A lock of Levi's hair fell into his face. He angrily brushed
it back into place, then glared at the ambassador. "You shouldn't
have lingered. You shouldn't have given the bread to the homeless
man. We never should have gone there to begin with."

Grenard maintained his composure. "Why should I not have
given the croissant to him?"

"He didn't deserve it. Neither did the waitress deserve that tip."

The Tulku frowned. "Why do you care what I do with my money?"

Levi froze.

"Maybe they didn't deserve it, but keep in mind that I did not have to buy you lunch. You don't deserve it any more than they do."

"But I'm protecting your life!"

A ghostly silhouette stepped onto the road. Levi slammed on the breaks, sliding precariously across the icy pavement. His heart pounded in his ears, overtaking the sound of the howling wind.

A massive, hoofed beast stood motionless, fading in and out of the swirling snow with its white coat. Its grand, crescent-shaped antlers pierced the falling flakes. It had ice-blue streaks in its fur, much like Grenard's syamta, only wilder. It watched the car for a moment, then shook its head violently and stepped back into the storm.

"Beautiful." Grenard smiled. "One does not see a vyanda beast every day."

Levi eased off the brake pedal and drove more carefully than before. He had never seen a vyanda beast in all his years living outside of Rylant. Their existence was almost mythical. They were so rare that when someone reported seeing a vyanda beast, they were either called a loon or attention-seeking.

"Levi."

The soldier glanced at the ambassador, still furious.

"There is little you can do to protect me from all the humans on Rufosia and their hatred of me. I have willingly put my life in danger by simply existing on this side of the Murky Sea."

"So my being here is pointless."

"I did not say that." Grenard's voice was short and firm. He sighed and shook his head. "I hope to make your assignment more meaningful than you only being a bodyguard. I also don't want to make you miserable."

"You already are. And I will continue to be miserable as long as you stay."

The ambassador sighed. "I'd like to teach you how to play a game, if you'll indulge me."

"Feyer has never seen any value in playing games. He says they're useless."

The Tulku scoffed. "Feyer plays plenty of his own games, my boy. I can assure you that we are both pieces in his game that he is constantly moving and manipulating to accomplish what he wants. I strongly recommend that you do not believe everything any one individual says. No one knows all truths, including myself."

Levi hated every claustrophobic second he had to exist next to the ambassador. The Tulku was an ignorant fool to think Feyer would use and manipulate them, childish and small-minded. The longer they sat in silence, the longer the soldier stewed in his growing frustrations.

As soon as the president's mansion peered through the snow, Levi raced to park the car. He slammed the door behind him and left the ambassador to fend for himself. He ran to the president's office and pounded on the door. Without hearing a response, he burst into the room.

"Fuck the Tulku! I want to be reassigned."

Several officers sat with Feyer at the central table. They all turned and glared at the boy. Levi's eyes grew wide, and the blood drained from his face. He immediately collected himself and stood at attention.

Feyer dismissed the officers. When the door had closed behind the last one, he scowled at Levi. "You don't get to pick and choose what you want to do and when, soldier!"

Levi looked up at Feyer, unable to contain himself. "He sees me on the same level as a homeless man. He doesn't think I'm capable of doing my job. He says I can't believe anything you say. He says you're manipulating everyone. And of course, no one goes after the Tulku, but everyone loves targeting the soldier forced to babysit the animal! Is this some kind of joke or test?"

"Do you believe him?"

Levi paused. "What do you mean?"

"Do you believe anything that he has said about me?"

"No! No, of course I don't believe him. You said I can never trust a Tulku."

Feyer's scowl darkened. "Then stop letting him get under your skin."

"I would still like to be reassigned, sir."

"Absolutely not." The president stood and slowly approached the soldier. It felt as if the air was being sucked from the room. "I have given you your orders. I expect you to fulfill them with excellence, not be a coward and run away crying like a child after the first unpleasant moment. That is not who I trained you to be."

Levi sneered at Feyer. "Fine." He turned and stalked to the door.

Feyer grabbed his shirt and yanked him back. The president's gaze churned like a late summer thunderstorm, paralyzing Levi with strikes of anger and drenching him in terror. "I did not dismiss you, soldier."

Levi's heart raced, and his voice wavered. "May I be dismissed, sir?"

Feyer held on a few seconds longer. A sickening sneer spread over his face, and he let go. "Yes."

Levi stormed into his temporary room. He paced about frantically, pulling at his hair. The walls began to close in around him, confining him to an unbearable state of frustration. He needed more air. He needed more space. He needed to run.

Levi burst into the common area. "I'm going outside."

Grenard closed his journal and stood from his usual spot on the couch. "I'll join you."

Levi rolled his eyes and balled his fists at his side. "I have no choice but to keep an eye on you anyways."

The soldier raced from the suite, down the stairs, and out into the heavily falling snow without bothering to see if the ambassador had kept up. Frigid air swirled around him and froze his misery. The open space felt freeing compared to the stuffy interior of the president's office and his claustrophobic room. There was a gate at the back of the compound that let out into the secluded foothills and vacant forest. It called his name, pleading with him to run for his life.

A sudden, cold wad struck Levi in the shoulder. He whirled around. The Tulku was staring off into space a few paces away, minding his own business. Grenard's gaze darted towards the soldier. A mischievous glimmer in his eyes removed any hint of innocence.

Levi brushed his uniform off, still stunned. "Did you just throw snow at me?"

Grenard looked about. "I see no one else enjoying this lovely weather." He bent down and pressed the wet snow into a compact ball. "I bet you can't hit me." He smirked before throwing the snowball and hitting Levi square in the chest.

The soldier stared down at his uniform then glared at the Tulku. "Why are you doing this?"

Grenard was already working on a third snowball and circling him. "You need an outlet, and I want to play a game. Hit me with a snowball."

Levi shook his head but crouched anyway and stuck his fingers in the frosty, white substance.

Grenard's next snowball hit Levi in the head, making his bruised forehead throb.

"Knock it off!" He took the partially formed projectile and launched it at the ambassador, jaw clenched. It broke apart midair, showering the Tulku in flakes.

"Be faster." Grenard took aim and fired his snowball. "Hit me, Levi."

The soldier narrowly dodged out of the way and scooped up more snow, packing it tighter than before. He focused on the Tulku and threw as hard as he could. The release of the snowball felt good. Levi watched it arc through the sky.

It hit Grenard right on his nose.

Levi froze, wide-eyed and terrified.

The ambassador stood with his eyes squeezed shut and his mouth open. He sneezed then brushed the snow from his muzzle and smirked. "Do it again."

The next snowball landed right between Grenard's eyes, knocking him backwards into a snowdrift. The Tulku looked ridiculous sprawled on the ground. Levi started laughing at the sight, but he stopped himself. He wasn't supposed to mock Feyer's guests, even if Alsh was a Tulku.

The ambassador propped himself up on his elbows and gave a belly laugh. Levi felt his breath creep back into his lungs.

Grenard rolled onto his knees. "That was an excellent shot, my boy, but I think my age is starting to show. Those snowballs hit differently at fifty than when I was your age." He stood and slipped on a patch of ice, barely staying on his feet.

Levi rushed towards him. "Are you hurt, sir?"

Grenard stabilized and brushed himself off. "I'm quite fine, my boy. Shall we continue?"

Levi hesitated. He looked into the windows of the mansion and glanced around the grounds. No one was there. Surely, he wouldn't get in trouble, but the fear that there was something terribly wrong with this game filled his mind.

"Come on. Does it matter if anyone sees?" Grenard smiled at him reassuringly.

Levi took a deep breath. "I guess five more minutes wouldn't hurt."

"Excellent!"

The ensuing battle lasted far longer than five minutes. What little daylight had penetrated the clouds had faded significantly, but neither party minded. They danced around each other and wrecked the pristine snow around the entire mansion, dodging snowballs, slipping into drifts and laughing boisterously. Levi's anger gradually slipped away. It wasn't running, but it was more than an adequate substitute, and all the laughing warmed his soul more than running ever could.

A side door opened, illuminating the snow where Levi and Grenard stood. A well-decorated officer with silvery hair and a portly figure emerged with a cigar in hand. Levi immediately dropped the snow in his hands and brushed the powder from his uniform.

The silver-haired man did a double take. He stared at the soldier and the Tulku in the fast-approaching darkness, then walked over. "Good evening, gentlemen. Enjoying the unusual weather, are we?"

Levi stood at attention. "Yes, General Thomason."

"At ease, Levi. I hope I wasn't interrupting anything." He smiled and held out his hand to the Tulku. "I presume you are Ambassador Alsh. I'm very pleased to have finally made your acquaintance."

The ambassador shook his hand. "General Thomason, it is good to have met you. After several weeks of being promised a formal introduction, I suppose meeting you outside in a snowstorm will have to suffice. I can't say I mind, though."

The general's chuckle was full and jolly. "I am looking forward to helping you with your work. It has been far too long that we have needlessly been at odds, and I am all for preventing a formal war. It isn't good for either of our nations."

"I wholeheartedly agree."

Thomason gave Grenard an indecipherable look. "I believe we both remember what it was like when Anton was governing Erev."

Grenard nodded.

"If I may be so bold, Jake is not so easily humored."

"I am aware. Nevertheless, I look forward to our future conversations."

Thomason's smile returned. "Indeed. I expect we will have some time to coordinate our efforts. Feyer has a few handpicked soldiers arriving in the next few days before we all head to Lincoln Base. I expect my time will not be fully occupied between now and then."

"Excellent."

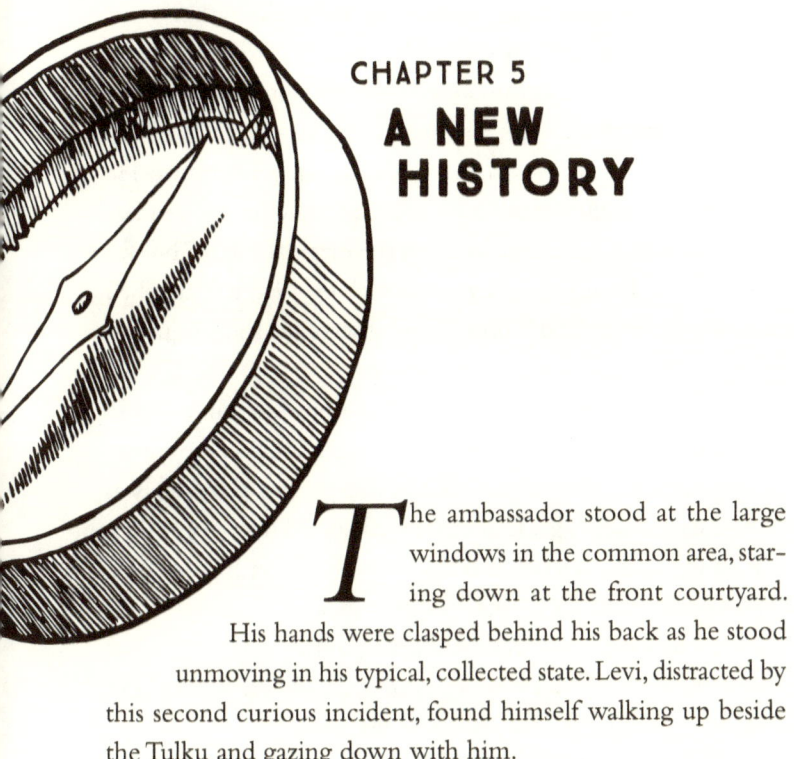

CHAPTER 5
A NEW HISTORY

The ambassador stood at the large windows in the common area, staring down at the front courtyard. His hands were clasped behind his back as he stood unmoving in his typical, collected state. Levi, distracted by this second curious incident, found himself walking up beside the Tulku and gazing down with him.

The freak snow from a few days before had completely melted away and had been replaced by a drizzle. Ten young men in uniform were lined up just beyond the bottom step of the perron, standing straight and tall with their chests puffed out in the rain. General Thomason and President Feyer greeted them. Levi couldn't hear what Feyer said as he addressed the troops, but they swelled with pride as the president's muffled voice echoed emphatically around the courtyard.

Grenard's ears were perked forward, and his head tilted to the side as he watched the soldiers march into the house behind their leaders. "Keep an eye on the second-to-last one, Levi."

There was something slightly off about the rather average-looking fellow. His shoulders slouched. The toe of his boot caught on one of the steps, sending him stumbling forward until the last soldier caught him and steadied him.

It was the last soldier that Levi couldn't help but notice. He was noticeably taller with blond hair and something green behind his ears. Levi tried to focus on the original soldier, but his curiosity had been piqued by whatever the blond had attached to his head. The boy's opportunity to observe the soldier quickly ended as they disappeared out of view.

"Curious indeed." Grenard turned from the window and grabbed one of the leather-bound journals that sat on the couch. He paced back and forth, scribbling furiously. Just as suddenly as he had started writing, the ambassador snapped the journal shut, stuffed it into his satchel, and threw the bag over his shoulder. "Shall we go to Rylant Public Library today?"

Levi furrowed his brows, still staring at the courtyard below. "Why the library? And why focus on that soldier? What about the blond with the weird device on his head?"

"I would like to do some research and find a few books to read. You also need a good excuse to get more studying done with that exam coming up."

Levi swiveled around and eyed Grenard. "How did you know I have a test?"

"You don't exactly clean up your schoolwork at the end of the day. It does make for some lovely reading in the morning."

Levi's gaze dropped to the ground. He hadn't realized the Tulku looked through his work and the materials his tutor had given him.

Feyer had always insisted on Levi's education and had done everything in his power to ensure the boy's highest achievement.

Levi's weekly debrief with the president also frequently included his comments on the young man's academic progress. Perfection was what Feyer expected and what Levi strived for but often failed to attain. The boy's tutor, Mr. Miller, had set the date for the next math test, but triple integrals in polar coordinates had refused to permeate Levi's mind.

"I am teasing you, my boy. Slightly." Grenard's smirk had faded and had been replaced with an expression Levi rarely saw from anyone. The Tulku's gaze was intent and soft.

"I don't understand, sir."

"If you would like, I'll help you study. I know you've been struggling a bit." Grenard paused. "But first, we should go to the library."

Levi was taken aback by the creature. He doubted the Tulku's ability to help, but he distractedly gathered his textbooks and notes into his rucksack and followed after Grenard.

———ɪɪɪ———

Ambassador Alsh grinned as they pulled up to the strange building in the heart of the city. Rylant Public Library appeared to be an earthen structure that defied the laws of physics. It was a round three-story building without a single straight line. Its exterior was decorated with arches, curves, and organically shaped windows. Even the main doors were rounded and whimsical in nature.

"It is good to see a bit of home now and again." The Tulku smiled contentedly.

"What do you mean, sir?" Levi stepped out of the car and studied the building. He had been there a select number of times when he was younger, but he had never truly noted the oddity that it was compared to most of Rylant. As he glanced at the surrounding buildings, most of them, too, were strangely shaped and not the standard cardboard-box, brick buildings he was used to.

"It's Tulkish architecture from the original city." Grenard practically skipped as he rushed forward. "Just wait until you get inside!" He beamed as he glanced back at the boy.

Levi chased after the ambassador as dozens of questions began bouncing around his mind. "Wait! Why are there Tulkish buildings in the middle of Rylant? I thought humans built Rylant."

Grenard stopped with a hand resting on the door handle and raised an eyebrow. "Is that what you think? My boy, I'm afraid you have your history all wrong. There was a city here long before humankind ever left Earth."

The soldier's heart pounded in his chest. His mind struggled to juggle the new information with what he had always known. "Then how did humans end up living here? And why would the Tulku have a city on this side of the Murky Sea? This isn't even part of Tulanu."

"It is not a part of Tulanu anymore, my boy. The city used to be a joint military base between the Tulku and the Phirin to guard the northern borders against attack from the Deku and the Havaj. As time passed, it became more of an expense than an asset to maintain the city. By the time humans arrived on Rufosia, it had been all but abandoned, so we gave it to the humans. Your people have added to the city since settling here, but the heart of Rylant still remains Rufosian."

"Has it always been called Rylant?"

The Tulku chuckled. "No. It used to be called Riyanti."

The soldier's mouth turned sour.

Grenard waited for another comment from the boy, but when Levi stayed silent, he opened the strange door and walked inside.

Levi stood outside, trying to sort out the swarm of thoughts that collided in his mind. Long had he been raised to think that humans, in their great ability to adapt, had created such wondrous and artistic buildings after a long voyage in space. But that vision had been cracked by an animal he was told to hate. He eventually entered the library, remaining deep in thought. He didn't know if he should be convinced that what the ambassador told him was true. Feyer had told him to never trust the Tulku. Still, what if it was true?

"Levi."

The soldier's focus snapped to the Tulku.

"Why don't you go find a place to study while I wander. I'll come find you in a bit."

"Yes, sir." Levi shifted the sack that rested on his shoulder and instinctively looked for the stairs.

The library was torus-shaped with a circular atrium in the center of the building. A tree Levi had never noticed before grew in the small courtyard. It looked as if it could have been a pine tree, but its branches drooped towards the ground. It was an exceptionally frosty blue color. The soldier thought it was strange to grow a tree in the middle of a library and wondered about its significance. But it wasn't by his choice that the tree had been planted, nor was it his responsibility to think about such things, so he redirected his focus.

The large entryway that Levi stood in exposed all three stories using geometric supports. The beams crossed in a mathematical pattern and connected seamlessly with the curved roof and walls of the outer structure. As he wound his way up, Levi noticed that every timber was intricately carved with geometric designs akin to Celtic knots. The railings were well worn with use over the past several decades, if not centuries, the building had been standing. Levi fully expected it would remain standing for centuries to come.

There were very few patrons visiting the library. Even so, Levi found himself retreating to the most remote nook on the third floor. The small space had an impressive view of the city. There was a distinct difference in the roof outlines that defined what was supposedly Rufosian and what was definitely human. He gazed at the city he realized he knew so little about. Conflicting notions of Rylant's history battled for his attention, but he shoved them aside and sat at the nearest table. Did it really matter who built which buildings?

No.

Levi dropped his bag on the floors and pulled out his textbooks. The heavy schoolbooks nagged at the soldier as he worked up the courage to open their covers. A few loose papers containing his previous failed attempts slipped out and floated across the table. His tutor had left them bleeding with dozens of corrections. Levi stared at the pages hopelessly for a couple minutes before he trudged through more problems.

It must have been an hour or two before Grenard found Levi on the third floor. The soldier's textbooks and papers had consumed the entire surface of the table. Several more problems had been completed, but whether they were completed correctly, Levi had no clue.

The ambassador plopped a stack of books in a nearby chair, startling Levi. Grenard began pacing back and forth in front of the window, blocking Levi's light as he reread a page in his textbook. Levi buried his face in his hands and tried to block out the ambassador, but the repeated change in lighting broke his concentration. Levi glared at the Tulku.

Grenard's tail was bristled and curled into a corkscrew, and his ears were pinned flat against his skull. A silent snarl twisted his lips. His hands fidgeted behind his back as if baffled by the absence of something to do.

"Is something wrong, sir?"

The Tulku glanced at Levi without breaking stride. "There are quite a few titles that the library ought to have, yet they have disappeared from both the shelves and the minds of the librarians."

"The library got rid of a few books. What is the problem with that?"

Grenard huffed. "I am familiar with both this library and Earth literature. There are a few books that I would like to re-read, but they don't exist anymore. They aren't on the shelves, or the catalogs. More than that, the librarians that I have known for decades and who know my reading habits are denying the existence of the books."

"Sir, it has been ten years since you were last in Rylant. You're sure they aren't Tulkish books? I know Feyer discourages distribution of Tulanu's literature."

"I am quite sure. These are pieces of classic literature from Earth. They were so profound during the times they were written that they remained in print for centuries and even survived a trip across space. There are many aspects of human culture that do not exist on Rufosia and were presented in those books. Stories with that much power shouldn't just disappear." Grenard waved his hands with enthusiasm, and his voice quivered with passion.

"How do you even know about these books?"

The Tulku finally stopped pacing. "My grandfather was a linguist and historian. His life's work was to preserve the ancient

languages and cultures from Earth, primarily through literature. He spent his life collecting Earth books in their original
languages before they were lost for good. Those books are still
in my library at home. I have Jules Verne in French, Tolkien in
English, and Dostoevsky in Russian, to name a few authors. I
grew up with him teaching me Earth languages and reading me
your people's stories."

Levi sat back in his chair. "I've only studied English, but I
don't know that I've ever read an entire novel in English. I've
only read in Tulkish. The Tulkish we speak now is a combination
of English and Ancient Tulkish, right?"

"Indeed, though there are still significant differences in vocabulary between Tulanu and Erev. The next opportunity I have,
I'll bring you one of the English books from my grandfather's
library. Then, you'll be able to practice if you so desire."

"Thank you, sir." Levi wasn't sure what to make of Grenard
bringing him a book, especially if the Tulku was tricking him into
reading Tulkish literature. But the Tulku's answer concerning the
spoken language of Tulanu and Erev brought more relief than
the young soldier had anticipated. He was glad to know there
was some small amount of consistency between his world and
Ambassador Alsh's world. "What kind of vocabulary differences
are there?"

The ambassador moved the books from the chair and sat in
their place. "A few obvious ones would be clothing. Most Tulku
would not know what shoes or socks are unless they have spent
significant time around Erevian humans."

Levi snorted. "The Tulku don't know about shoes? That's
ridiculous."

The Tulku smirked. "Do you know what vyata and
katoms are?"

The sneer fell from the soldier's face. "No."

"Then it isn't ridiculous. All Tulku traditionally wear vyata and katoms. It would be an incredible feat to find one not wearing them. The closest English words might be belt, or skirt, but they are such poor translations that we always kept the Tulkish words. Erevian humans don't wear them either, so they never made it into Western vocabulary."

Levi tried to imagine what the streets of a Tulkish city would look like with hundreds of Tulku wearing the clothing Grenard had first arrived in and worn every day since among strange, curved buildings. It was such an absurd image that he quickly gave up.

Levi shook his head. "I should get back to studying."

"I did say I would help you study earlier. That offer is still on the table."

Levi stared intensely at Grenard, eyes narrowed. "You're an ambassador."

A mischievous glint appeared in Grenard's amber eyes. "That doesn't preclude me from knowing calculus."

"You shouldn't. You don't need it."

"Where I'm from, all individuals are pushed to achieve their fullest potential. My education involved studying many subjects that do not relate to my current occupation. Calculus happens to be a topic that I don't need to know, but still understand."

Levi deliberated. Additional help couldn't hurt, but he wasn't sure he wanted to face the shame if someone found out that a Tulku had taught him. He rubbed his neck and felt a small scar.

Failure was unacceptable.

The boy looked up at the ambassador and gave him a small, sheepish nod.

It was odd having someone watching over Levi's shoulder as he worked, but as the ambassador gently corrected him and explained the concepts, the math slowly began to make sense. He saw the equations take shape in his mind as the lines became shells and expanded into volumes. One problem in particular reminded Levi of the basic shape of the library. He amused himself with thinking that he could now approximate the volume of the torus-shaped building with this newfound skill.

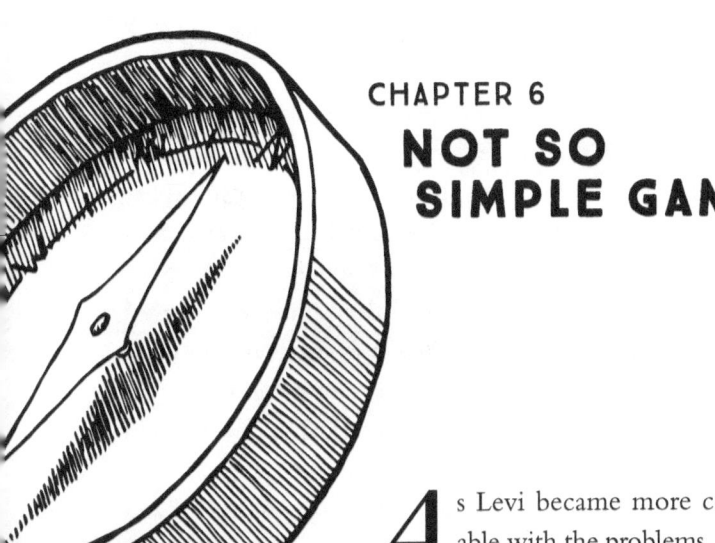

CHAPTER 6
NOT SO SIMPLE GAMES

*A*s Levi became more comfortable with the problems, Grenard backed away to let him try on his own. The sudden success seemed to fall away immediately as Levi's mind failed to retain all the tips and tricks the Tulku had given him during the previous problem set. The soldier finished a problem and handed it over for the Tulku to review. He watched and fidgeted with his ring.

Ambassador Alsh scanned the boy's math, a small grin creeping onto his face. "Much better than before, but you missed a minus sign during one of your algebraic steps."

Levi slammed his stylus down and ran his fingers through his hair. "I'm never going to get this." He shook his head as he scowled at the pages containing an entire world that eluded him.

Grenard sighed and handed the sheet back. "You're grasping it just fine. You simply made an algebraic mistake. How long have you been studying triple integrals?"

Levi glanced at the Tulku. "A week."

"And in polar coordinates?"

Levi hesitated, already annoyed at the answer he suspected he would receive. "A few days."

Grenard smiled. "Let's take a break. Then we will address the material again in a little while."

The soldier threw his hands up in the air, exasperated. "Why? That's not going to help me learn this any better. I can't afford to take breaks."

"Actually, it does help." The Tulku's deep amber eyes pierced Levi. "Just as your stomach needs time to digest food, your mind also needs time to digest and process new information."

Levi sighed and shook his head. He tucked the loose papers into his textbook and shoved everything into his rucksack. He focused on the rust-colored Tulku with his arms crossed and waited. "What now?"

"How about a game?"

The boy groaned and rolled his eyes. He slumped in his chair, strongly disliking the troublesome glimmer in Grenard's eyes. He reminded himself that all he had to do was humor the animal. He looked out the window. The clear skies indicated little chance of it snowing again, making the only game he knew and knew he liked out of the question.

Grenard sat opposite him. "I propose we play a simple word game."

Levi glared at the Tulku.

"One person says a single word, then the other person responds with the first word that comes to mind. Only one word, though. You go back and forth for a bit and that's the game." Grenard paused and eyed Levi. "I'll go first. Book."

It was a purposeless game, but a word popped into Levi's head anyways. He sighed and unfolded his arms. "Studying."

"Education."

"Expectations."

"Failure."

"Not an option."

"That's a phrase." The reprimand was gentle and calm.

"I know it's a phrase. I'm not an idiot!"

"The only rule of the game is that you can only respond with one word. It's part of the challenge. Try again. Failure."

Levi's blood boiled over. "What's even the point? There is no way to win and no objective. What do you gain from it? At least with the snowball fight it was exercise, and I know who lost by who was hit first or who tired first or who was knocked to the ground."

Grenard chuckled. "One could argue that you lost by breaking the one rule of the game."

The boy's cheeks flushed, and he dropped his gaze. How could he have been so careless as to break a rule?

"You know, there is much more to the game than meets the eye. I have learned that you do not think failure is permissible. You have learned that I believe some expectations are associated with failure. It may be simple, and indeed rather mindless, but I expect it might help us both answer our grand question."

Levi sat perfectly still, thinking. It was an odd game. Uncomfortable. Maybe there was more that he and the ambassador had in common than he had previously thought possible.

"Shall we return to Feyer's?"

Levi pulled himself away from his thoughts. "Yes, sir."

The drive was accompanied by the usual quiet of their companionship. Grenard read in the car as Levi regularly glanced over at him, pretending to check the mirrors. The young soldier mulled over everything the Tulku had said that day, chewing on the gristly material.

Grenard closed his book. "Levi?"

"Yes, sir."

"I would like to go on our usual walk through the gardens when we get back."

"Yes, sir."

———— ··· ————

A few winter-blooming trees and flowers brought bright pops of color into the mansion's landscaping as they walked. The ambassador, by habit, stopped every few feet along the gravel paths to enjoy the scent of the blossoms. Brilliant green vegetation countered the bleakness that often accompanied February's lengthening, but still dull days.

While Levi had begun to appreciate taking the time to admire the beauty of each bud, they were insufficient distractions from what plagued him. He fidgeted with his ring as he waited next to the ambassador. "May I ask you a question, sir?"

Grenard had his face in a bush covered in bright pink flowers. "I have told you before: you do not need my permission, Levi. You may always ask me anything you like, though I may not always choose to answer."

"Thank you, sir." Levi opened his mouth and froze. Hundreds of questions had been piling up, all demanding answers, but the boy knew not to ask them all. He took a deep breath and settled on one. "Why did you come to Rylant so early?"

Grenard glanced up at the soldier and straightened his posture. His expression hardened. "There was an attack on my people. It did not seem right to linger while they continue to suffer. That, and the guilt of waiting so long to come back, forced me to reconsider many things."

"Why come alone?"

Grenard sighed. "Politically speaking, I did not want to draw much attention to myself, and I did not want to pose a threat. The truth is…" He paused and shook his head. "Vanyani was the only one who would work with me."

"Why come at all? I mean, we're essentially at war, aren't we?"

Grenard shook his head. "Not quite. Your government and my government are still tolerant of each other. From a public perspective, the attacks that have occurred were instigated by radicals and isolated extremists. I don't fully believe that, so I'm trying to figure out what the true roots of the conflict are. This started when I was a child and despite so much effort, it has gotten worse.

"It becomes even more of a curious situation when you compare Anton's leadership to Jake's leadership. During Anton's era, the cost of food was extraordinarily high because he stubbornly refused to reduce tariffs. Jake has reduced tariffs while still developing Erev's agriculture. By all accounts, Jake has been a good leader, bringing stability to Erev, and in some cases to Tulanu as well. So why, if things are measurably better, are they getting worse?"

Levi sighed. He had no answer for the ambassador. "You said it had been ten years since you were last here. Why?"

"I could not bring myself to come back after Vanyani's death. I did not want to risk finding good in humanity, but things will never have a chance to get better if I don't give your people another chance."

Levi frowned. "What have humans done? All I've seen or heard about is violence from the Tulku."

Grenard gave him a curious look. "How many attacks, on either side, are you aware of from the past month?"

The soldier recalled the events of the past few weeks. "There were two attacks in Erev: one in Trifort and another in

Portland. I believe the total number of casualties from both attacks was seventeen."

"Yes, five passed away in Trifort and twelve in Portland. And in Tulanu?"

Levi met the Tulku's gaze for a moment. "I haven't heard of anything going on in the East."

Grenard's ears pinned back. "The event that drove me to come so early involved the deaths of forty-three of my people."

The boy ran his fingers through his hair, avoiding looking at the ambassador. "How do you know it was a human and not some Tulku with a major grudge?"

Grenard frowned. "Have you heard of a device called a camera?"

Levi didn't dare respond.

"There were four humans, and they all shouted, 'Death to the Tulku!' before wreaking havoc on the streets of Syadati."

"Isn't that one of the major trade cities?"

The Tulku nodded and clasped his hands behind his back. "Simply stated, if anything catastrophic happened to Syadati, Tulanu's economy would likely collapse, and Erev would starve."

The news sat uneasily with the young soldier, though he didn't know what he had originally expected to hear from the ambassador. As the sun drifted towards the horizon, another question bubbled to the surface, but Levi wasn't sure he truly wanted to know the answer. "How many attacks have there been in Tulanu?"

"Four or five alone in the month before my arrival."

"Why haven't I heard about any of this?"

Grenard sighed. "That is one of the many things I am trying to figure out, my boy. I have not been able to access

Eastern news sources since I arrived, and I fear that Erev's media may not be reporting international affairs properly, if at all."

Levi let his feet drag across the gravel path as he pondered all the ambassador had told him. Why couldn't Grenard access his own news sources? Why would Erev's media report events incorrectly? Was Levi's world truly that interconnected with the ambassador's world? Was it all really that fragile?

"Tell me about your family."

Levi shoved his hands in his pockets and avoided the Tulku's amber gaze. "I don't have one."

"You're a terrible liar, my boy."

Levi rolled his eyes and turned back to the ambassador, glaring. "Why do you even care?"

Grenard shrugged. "I'm curious."

The boy huffed. "I'm not supposed to talk about it."

The Tulku raised an eyebrow. "That's a bit peculiar. You can't tell me anything?"

Levi kicked at a rock. "No."

"Any siblings?"

"Wouldn't know even if I did."

"Mother?"

The soldier gritted his teeth. "You're going to keep pushing, aren't you?"

Grenard grinned slyly. "It's just a question. You don't have to answer every time I ask something of you."

Levi began twisting his ring. "She died when I was born. That's what I was told, anyways."

"That leaves your father. Is he involved?"

Levi shoved his hands back in his pockets.

"Do you even know who—"

"Yes, I know exactly who he is!" Levi sent several pebbles into a nearby bush.

"I'm sorry."

Levi looked up and saw a deep softness in the Tulku's eyes.

"Do you mind if I ask about your association with President Feyer?"

The boy froze. "He's my uncle."

Grenard smiled. "It's your turn to ask me questions, if you wish."

The soldier searched his mind for the one question that had been bothering him like an itch that couldn't be scratched. "Will you ever tell me what happened to Vanyani?"

The ambassador's gaze dropped to the ground. "I expect I will give you that answer soon, my boy."

Levi smiled to himself. "How many children do you have?"

"Thirteen sons and one daughter."

The boy's jaw dropped. "That's a lot."

"Maybe by human standards, but the few of us who do get married tend to have large families. Granted, adoption has added to the size of my family."

"Will you tell me about them?"

Grenard grinned. "Arden, my firstborn, is twenty-four. However, Zev, my adopted son, is twenty-six. My youngest son, Kido, is nineteen. Beka, my daughter, is the youngest at eighteen. She is not someone to be trifled with."

"Why is that, sir?"

"She's as stubborn as ever, and usually right, though you didn't hear me say that. I expect you would get along with them quite well. I hope you get to meet them someday, if tensions ever dissolve." There was a tinge of sadness in his voice.

"Maybe I will."

It seemed hopeless that Levi would ever leave Erev, but, until the ambassador had shown up, he had never even considered leaving. A spark of desire started worming its way into his mind, but he snuffed it out immediately. He wasn't supposed to like the ambassador. He wasn't supposed to be interested in the Tulkish world. He was just supposed to keep the animal alive for a few months. Then, Levi's life would return to normal.

But the thought kept coming back. He wondered what Grenard's family was like, how different Tulanu was from Erev, what Tulkish cities looked like, what their food was like. The spark had ignited a flame.

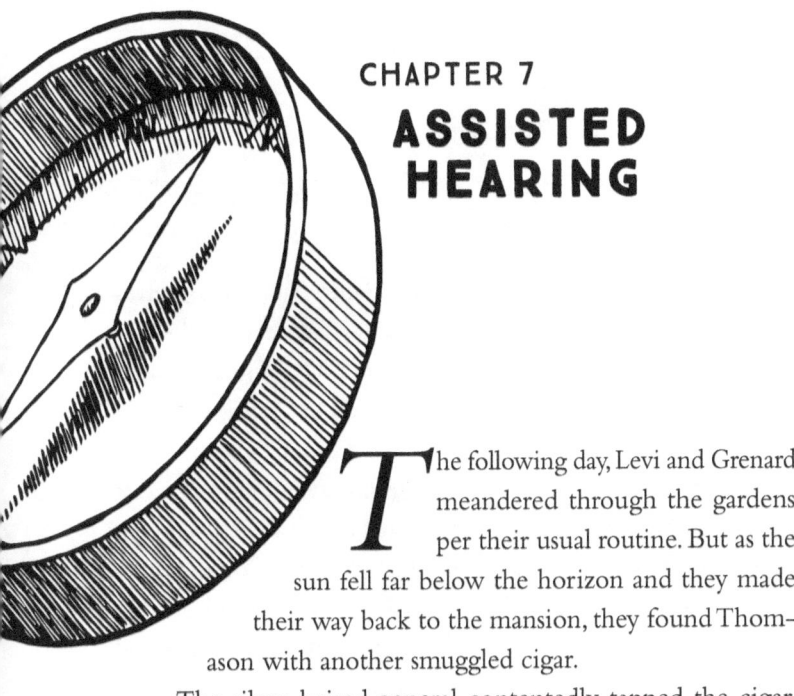

CHAPTER 7
ASSISTED HEARING

The following day, Levi and Grenard meandered through the gardens per their usual routine. But as the sun fell far below the horizon and they made their way back to the mansion, they found Thomason with another smuggled cigar.

The silver-haired general contentedly tapped the cigar, flicking ashes to the ground. As he glanced up and noticed the pair, he grinned and waved them over. "Ambassador Alsh, what a pleasure it is to run into you once more."

"Indeed, General Thomason." Grenard bowed politely.

Thomason breathed out smoke. "I have a proposal for you. I'd like for you to come up to Lincoln Base in a few days to discuss a few matters. President Feyer has already given his blessing."

"I would be delighted to take you up on your offer."

Thomason beamed. "Wonderful. I'd also be curious to know your opinion of Feyer's little project team."

"Oh?" The Tulku's eyes widened. "Would I be permitted to interview them briefly?"

"My dear ambassador, you have a reputation to uphold. They have already been informed that their personal time won't entirely be theirs next week."

Grenard smirked. "Excellent."

———— ııı ————

The young soldier and the ambassador found themselves at the southern gate of Lincoln Base four days later as the sun was slipping towards the horizon. It wasn't very large compared to some of the military bases farther south, but it was still large enough to have a rigorous training program and sufficient air, land, and sea-based defenses for the northernmost border of Erev. It was half an hour north of Rylant, situated on a flat plain hemmed in by steep peaks on two sides and the Murky Sea on the third.

Levi had only been to the base a handful of times. He glanced at Grenard, who was absorbing the sunset as if it was his last, and wondered if the Tulku had been there before. It would not have been surprising if the Tulku had and this trip was simply another visit to a place with a handful of memories already attached to it.

Dozens of monotonous, tan, square buildings passed by until they pulled up to—though still largely a shade of beige—a more modern construction. Snowcapped peaks rose up behind the four-story building. Large windows framed the main entrance and reflected the vibrant colors of the eastern sunset.

Levi parked and stared at the structure. His heart rate slowly sped up the longer he watched men and women in uniform walking in and out.

"Everything alright, my boy?" Grenard eyed him carefully.

"Hmm? Yes, sir." Levi put on the camouflage cap he rarely wore.

General Thomason hovered just beyond the front doors with a spent cigar in hand. As Levi and Grenard approached him, he grinned and snuffed out the butt with the toe of his shoe. "I'm glad to see you've arrived! I've already let them know you were coming tonight."

The duo trailed behind the general into the barracks. The lobby spanned the entire depth of the building, with a security desk at the front and the mess hall beyond it. To either side were a series of pristine conference rooms, glassed in like fish tanks. Suspended walkways connected the left and right wings on each floor above them. There were surprisingly few scuff marks on the polished floor and a certain new construction smell about the place.

Thomason led them down one of the wings where some soldiers were roughhousing. The general cleared his throat, and every individual immediately fell in line, standing at attention.

Levi followed closely behind Grenard, watching the disgusted glances of the strangers he passed. Every uniform he saw displayed the rank and name of its owner. Except his. A strand of his unruly hair fell into his eyes, and his cheeks flushed. Every other male had neatly trimmed hair that didn't touch their ears. Even the women had their hair pulled back out of their faces. Levi avoided making eye contact and trudged forward.

General Thomason stopped at the very end of the corridor and called out the ten young men that formed Feyer's hand-selected team. They piled out into the hallway, quickly sorting themselves into a single-file line.

The faintest of smiles flicked across Thomason's face. "Men, this is Ambassador Grenard Alsh. He is an esteemed guest of President Feyer and will be meeting with each of you over the course of the next few evenings. You will be civil. Is that understood?"

"Yes, sir!" Ten voices rang loud and clear.

Grenard bowed towards Thomason, thanking him, and lost no time picking his first victims. He accompanied two of the men into their room. The room was decorated with a few crooked posters. Two beds leaned against one wall and two desks sat opposite them. A holographic screen on one of the desks was illuminated with a pause screen from some video game Levi had never seen before.

One of the two men shot the Tulku a menacing look. He was twenty-five or thirty centimeters shorter than Levi, stocky, and had black, curly hair. "You don't mind if we continue our game, do you?"

Grenard smiled. "Not at all. I realize you only have so much time to yourselves."

Both men rushed to grab their controllers and flopped on their beds, resuming the game as the ambassador pulled a journal from his satchel.

"Who would like to go first?"

The short soldier shrugged. "Why the hell not? What do you want to know, Tulku?"

"What is your name?"

"Derek Smith." He pitched forward, pounding the buttons on his controller furiously.

Grenard gazed at the game. "How did you end up on Feyer's team?"

"I'm the best in my class, and I'm no fucking pushover."

"Why did you choose to join the military?"

Derek smiled. "I like a good fight, and I can't stand the likes of you getting in my way." He pummeled the buttons again. "Shit!" The screen read *Game Over*. Both men groaned and restarted the level.

Grenard watched Smith silently for some time. "Do you like the Tulku?"

Derek glanced at the ambassador, unenthused. "Should I have a reason to like you?"

"Do I understand that to mean 'no' then?"

The soldier rolled his eyes. "No shit."

"Were you explicitly taught to dislike the Tulku?"

Derek scoffed. "Who wasn't? You're pathological liars and aggressive animals. You kill my brothers without reason. You try to steal what is rightfully ours."

Grenard froze, his pen hovering above the paper. His ear twitched before he resumed writing. "Have you ever been directly harmed by a Tulku?"

"No."

"Have you known someone personally who has been harmed by a Tulku?"

"No! But I can look at the fucking news and see how many you've killed." Derek glared at the ambassador.

"Have you ever questioned the accuracy of the information you receive from your media sources?"

Smith laughed. "That's funny." He paused the game and stared at the Tulku. "Look, the only reason I'm answering your fucking questions is because Thomason will beat my bare ass if I don't, and I kinda' like my ass the way it is."

Grenard smirked. "I appreciate your cooperation, Private Smith. Do you ever question your media sources?"

Derek growled. "I don't have to answer any of your questions."

"Very well. Thank you for your time."

The ambassador plowed through three more interviews that evening, and four the second evening. There was nothing particularly fascinating about any of the men's responses.

Most attended some military academy and had differing special abilities. Feyer had been impressed by their promise and that was the end of the story. They weren't fond of the Tulku, and they weren't afraid to make it clear the ambassador was stealing their precious free time, however civil they attempted to be. The ambassador, at the end of each interview, thanked them for their time and cooperation before bowing and swiftly moving on.

As the third evening came round, Grenard pounced on the last two soldiers. Levi immediately recognized the pair as he followed the Tulku and entered their room. The first, Private Peyton, was the average-looking, out-of-sync soldier Grenard had pointed out from their suite's second-story window. The second, Private Brown, was the curious blond with the green earpieces.

Private Peyton, up close, looked exactly as Levi expected. Brown hair, brown eyes, a slight slouch, average height. He wore a sorrowful expression, even when smiling. He breathed heavily and slowly as if he was carrying an invisible load.

Private Brown was just barely taller than Levi. He had straw-blond hair and primarily light gray-blue eyes. His left eye had a striking patch of brown mixed into the blue. The green devices, upon closer inspection, were made of two pieces. The largest part hung just behind his ears and was attached by a wire to a circular disk that seemed to magically stay in place towards the back of his head.

Peyton and Brown's room was quieter than the rooms of the other soldiers. There was no music, no games, no roughhousing. They didn't talk much and instead used hand motions to communicate with one another.

The room itself was in a bipolar state. One side was spotless. All surfaces were cleared of debris and were minimally decorated.

But the other side contained haphazardly displayed knickknacks and a few piles of paper splayed across the desk.

Brown offered the ambassador the chair belonging to the cleared off desk. He then sat cross-legged on his bed, waiting. Peyton began fussing with the objects on the messy desk. Levi stood by the door, always keeping an ear towards the hallway.

Grenard pulled out his journal and immediately began scribbling. He didn't look up for some time. "Private Peyton, would you like to go first?"

Peyton stilled for only a moment before shoving a stack of papers into a desk drawer. "I guess."

"What is your name?"

Peyton glanced at the Tulku. "First name?"

The Tulku smiled pleasantly and nodded.

"Quinn."

"I'm pleased to make your acquaintance. Would you mind telling me a little about yourself?"

Quinn shrugged. "There's not much to know. I did well enough in school and came here to support my mother."

"Is it just you and your mother?"

"Yes."

"Brave soul. Was that your only reason for joining the military?"

Quinn nodded.

Grenard watched the soldier with a certain softness in his eyes. "How do you feel about politics?"

"I know you're going to ask what I think about the Tulku."

The ambassador nodded. "That is why I'm here."

Quinn sighed. "I don't really care about what happens with the Tulku. I try to not pay attention to the news. I've got enough on my mind as it is."

"I appreciate your honesty." Grenard jotted down a few notes. "May I ask why you stay?"

"Starting over is harder than staying put." Quinn closed one of the desk drawers. "And my contract isn't up yet."

The ambassador bowed. "Thank you for your time. I believe those are all the questions I have for you."

Quinn didn't respond as he continued to straighten his side of the room.

Grenard flipped to a new page in his journal and turned his attention to the patiently waiting Private Brown. "What is your name?"

"Prifa'e Liam Nathaniel Brown." His voice sounded as if cotton had been stuffed in his mouth.

The Tulku cocked his head to one side, ears perked forward. "May I ask if you are deaf?"

"I am, sir."

Quinn waved at Liam, then began rapidly signing. Liam seemed to brush him off.

Grenard pointed behind his ears. "I am guessing that is what these are for."

Liam nodded. "They help me hear, yes. Bu' i's har'er than you migh' thin'. Some'imes i's easier to rea' lips since I'fe been doing tha' my whole life. I'fe only been able to hear for abou' eigh'een months now."

Quinn waved at him for a second time and seemed to sign the same message. Liam quickly replied, leaving Quinn shaking his head and walking out the door.

Liam's answer to Grenard's question struck Levi as odd. How could someone so defective end up on Feyer's hand-picked team?

"Can you read the Tulku's lips?"

Liam nodded enthusiastically. "I grew up in Por'lan' and hafe in'erac'ed with lo's of Tulku. I probably pu' more effor' in'o learning how to rea' Tulku than humans."

Grenard took a few more notes. "I'm curious to know your thoughts on this remarkable situation, Levi."

The boy collected himself. "I don't have any thoughts to share, sir."

The ambassador smirked. "I doubt that, my boy."

Levi shifted from one foot to the other. "I don't understand how someone would end up here without being able to do everything a normal person can."

Liam chuckled. "I'm hafing a normal confersation with you righ' now. Unless being able to iden'ify music no'es suddenly becomes a mili'ary requiremen', this should be proof enough tha' I can manage. I can hear commands jus' fine and I hafe sufficien' sishuational awareness. And I can play poli'ics in my fafor."

Grenard grinned as he wrote. "You are quite blunt."

"Thomason seems to like tha' charac'eris'ic more than Feyer. I'm sure I'm only here because of his recommendation, no' because Feyer wan'ed me." Liam watched Grenard for a moment. "Wha' exac'ly is the poin' of this in'erfiew, sir?"

The ambassador set his pen down and crossed his arms. "You're the first person to ask. I am trying to discern the factors that are exacerbating the tension between our two nations. President Feyer and the Tulkish Council are wanting solutions to reduce the number of casualties and ease trade."

"I migh' be able to add to your theories if you hafe any leads. When you spend your whole life wa'shing the world, you no'ice more than the aferage person."

Levi glanced sideways at the Tulku, holding his breath. Did the Tulku have any hypotheses? How much of the blame would he put on humankind, and how much would he claim ownership for?

Grenard's tail began to flick from side to side. "I don't believe all my theories are fit to share, but I would like to know how you were raised to perceive the Tulku. I suspect you were taught that the Tulku were a threat, just as the Tulku teach their children to be wary of humans."

Liam nodded. "My paren's taugh' me to afoid your kind, bu' I don' see the Tulku as a threa'. Growing up in Por'land, I would jus' wa'sh people on the s'ree' and I nefer saw any aggression from your people, only hos'ili'y from mine."

Grenard's brows furrowed. "Why join the military then?"

"To defend peace. The nation we came from on Earth swore to defend freedom, no' jus' for their people, bu' the res' of the nations under their pro'ection. I don't care if you're human, Tulku, green, or purple. If your freedom is being threa'ened, then i's my job to res'ore tha' to you."

Levi winced. Somehow it seemed both right and contradictory to the mentality he had grown up with. It had always been, "Defend humanity at all cost." But what if humanity was in the wrong?

He quickly shoved the idea aside. Humans were actively being harmed by the Tulku. That was an indisputable fact.

Grenard stood and bowed. "I admire your efforts, Private Brown. Those are all the questions I have for the time being. You have given me much to think about." He began to usher Levi out of the room, then paused and turned back to Liam. "Actually, I do have two more questions, more out of personal curiosity. Why does your roommate know sign language?"

Liam hesitated. "His younger sis'er was hard of hearing."

Grenard nodded.

"And your second queshion?"

"Did you ask Private Peyton to leave earlier?"

"I did. I wan'ed to answer your queshions hones'ly withou' someone lis'ening in. I trus' Quinn…" Liam's voice trailed off.

"But it isn't always advantageous to speak your mind for all to hear."

"Yes, e'sac'ly."

Grenard thanked him again and left with Levi. The Tulku stood in the middle of the hallway, switching his tail back and forth, deep in thought. A pleasant smile spread across his face before he finally strode towards the front of the building.

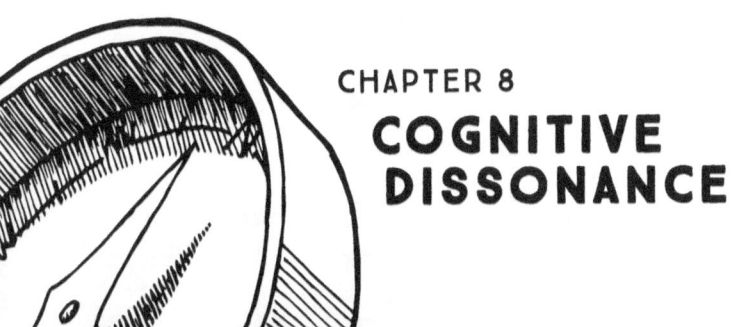

CHAPTER 8
COGNITIVE DISSONANCE

The following morning was their last at Lincoln Base. General Thomason had the ambassador wrapped up in a meeting just between the two of them all morning in one of the conference rooms off the barracks' lobby. Levi waited outside the door, pacing back and forth, then leaning against the wall, then sitting on the floor.

The special unit had come in from their various unexciting activities and had all sat down for lunch. Levi worked up the courage to join them. He grabbed a tray of food and took a seat at the far end of their table. He positioned himself with a direct line of sight to the conference room door.

Before long, Derek Smith slid his tray in front of Levi and sat down. He picked up his sandwich and took a large bite out of it. "Why're you hanging around the Tulku so much?"

Levi scooted a few centimeters over to keep an eye out for Grenard and General Thomason. "President Feyer assigned me to be Ambassador Alsh's bodyguard."

Smith raised his eyebrows. "Huh." He took another massive bite. "He seems weird."

Levi grinned. "You have no idea."

A few others had sidled over and were listening in on the conversation. Levi nervously glanced at them.

Smith smacked his lips. "Does he growl?"

His question earned a few laughs.

"No." Levi picked at his food, his appetite suddenly diminished.

"Does he... Does he howl? Or bark?" Derek mimicked the sounds, clearly amused with himself.

Levi shook his head. "He does neither."

Smith's smile fell. "What the hell does he do, then?"

Levi shrugged. "He reads articles, interviews people, listens to music, and goes for a walk every afternoon. That's about it." He took a sip of water and scanned the room. No one was out of place or looked suspicious. Private Brown still sat at the far end of the table, minding his own business. Levi nodded towards him. "Does he like being by himself?"

Smith growled. "He pisses me off. All high and mighty over there with his fancy fucking hearing devices." He set his half-eaten sandwich down and cupped his hands, speaking loudly and slowly. "*Li-am. Eat your damn lunch over here!*"

The blond's demeanor didn't change at all. He didn't even flinch.

Derek frowned and slammed the table three times, but still managed to solicit no response from the other soldier. "Damn it, Liam! I know you can hear me. How can you still be both deaf and dumb with fucking cochlear implants?"

Liam smiled and looked over. "I'fe tol' you before, Derek. I'll respon' when you speak in'elligibly, no' when you're talking like you're re'arde'." He stood and joined the rest of the group.

Smith moaned. "Glad you could come down from your self-righteous tower and join us. Shaggy here was telling us about the animal he's stuck pet sitting."

"My name's Levi." He was beginning to dislike the character that sat across from him.

"That's what I said. Shaggy." Derek gave him a hard stare.

Levi didn't argue. Instead, he shifted the topic back to the Tulku. "What else do you want to know about the ambassador?"

"How long has he been here, and how long is he going to stay?"

"Almost two months. I don't expect he will leave until he's accomplished his mission or until something more pressing pulls him away."

Most of the soldiers exchanged nervous glances.

Liam shoved his tray back a few centimeters. "If a human adul' was going to a'ack a Tulku chil', woul' you pro'ec' the chil'?" He looked around the group, waiting for their responses.

"What the hell have you been smoking?" Smith glared at him. "No! There's five of them to one of us. Who cares about one of their offspring. If they want more, they can just go fuck around. They have ten of them at a time anyways."

Levi's gut reaction to Liam's question was also no. But as he stopped and thought, he truly didn't know what he would do. After all, his job was guarding a Tulku from humans. But those were his orders. Would he choose to protect a defenseless child without orders? His heart was torn.

Smith scoffed and rolled his eyes. "What I don't understand is why we don't kill them all now. They've already killed a ton of humans and have been restricting trade with us for decades."

Grenard walked out of the conference room with Thomason and bowed politely.

Levi hurried to clear his tray and approached the Tulku and the general.

"Feyer informed me and a few others of the masquerade ball next week." A bubbly smile took over Thomason's face, and his jolly laugh was scarcely contained. "He invited the team and I to join for the evening. I couldn't say no. It will be an evening to remember, I'm sure. Feyer is an exceptional host."

"Yes, he certainly is." Grenard smiled, but it was a nervous grin. Worry and concern were barely masked as the Tulku continued the conversation. "It has been many years since I have attended one of his parties. He has excellent taste from what I can remember."

Levi understood the ambassador's hesitation. He assumed Grenard didn't want to draw much attention to himself. A grand ball held in his honor with lots of people did precisely the opposite. He had said himself that there was nothing safe about a Tulku in the West. He wasn't wrong, even with Levi's protection at Feyer's mansion.

Levi wasn't sure he was liking the news much either. It would make his job exponentially harder. Keeping an eye on the Tulku in a crowded space with potentially hundreds of people wanting to see Grenard dead sounded like a nightmare, and Levi could not risk failing on his first major assignment. With Smith's most recent comment, it made the boy even more wary. None of the soldiers the ambassador had interviewed seemed like they wished him direct harm, save Smith, but Levi knew they were all more than capable killers.

"Thank you for such a splendid experience here, General Thomason. I look forward to reconvening in a couple weeks." Grenard bowed.

Thomason's tone grew somber. "I'm curious to see what you dig up, Ambassador." He gave a curt nod as Grenard and Levi left the building.

The Tulku didn't say a word as they drove back to Rylant. And he didn't look out the window like he usually did. He simply sat with his eyes closed and his ears drooping on either side of his head. His satchel lay in his lap, protected by a fierce grip.

Levi felt worry as cold as ice suck the warmth from his soul. "I think Feyer scheduled for a tailor to come tomorrow so you can have a suit for the ball."

"Thank you for telling me, my boy." The Tulku still did not open his eyes.

They continued on in stale silence, until Levi couldn't stand it. He tapped the steering wheel. "Are you alright, sir?"

Grenard slivered one eye open. His amber eyes were worn and lacked their usual luster. "Yes, I'm a little tired, but otherwise fine."

Levi bit his lip. "Do you want to play a game?" His knuckles turned white against the steering wheel, scarcely believing the words that had just come out of his mouth. He wanted the ambassador to say yes to bring some kind of relief to the invisible weight that was smothering them.

"What kind of game did you have in mind?"

Levi's shoulders slowly dropped. "There's a simple word game I learned recently." He glanced at the Tulku. "There's only one rule: you can only say the word that first comes into your head in response to the other person's word." He hesitated. "I can go first."

Grenard finally smiled. "That sounds like a fine game."

It pleased Levi that he had been able to make the ambassador smile, though he didn't know why. "Tulanu."

Grenard sighed. "Home."

"Unknown."

"Life."

"Freedom."

"Family." Grenard grimaced, and Levi thought he saw a tear escape the ambassador's eye.

Family. Levi felt as if he knew nothing of family, but it supposedly started with something people called love. "Romance."

The word left a sour taste in his mouth. He instinctively touched the ring on his middle finger, hating every little ridge and scratch on its surface.

"Dancing."

"Ball."

"Worry."

Levi felt his heart sink in his chest. "You aren't the only one. And, yes, I know I just broke the one rule of the game. It might be a bad habit starting to form, I guess."

Grenard sat up and cleared his throat. "What makes you worried about the ball, my boy?"

"I don't like thinking that I may not be able to keep you safe." It dawned on Levi that maybe he didn't care so much about his orders. Of course, he wanted to obey his orders as best he could, but there was something else. He wasn't sure he liked the idea of seeing the ambassador get hurt. In fact, he didn't want Grenard to get hurt at all. "Why are you worried, sir?"

"I would rather not make the target on my back any larger than it has to be. I would like to make it home to my family." He sighed. "Thomason hinted at a few things when I was meeting with him, and I need time to research. I'm not sure I can sufficiently do that in less than a week, but I'm afraid going beyond Feyer's walls after the ball will suddenly become much more dangerous than it is now."

"You may not be wrong. Feyer's parties can be a bit eventful." Levi had attended dozens of Feyer's fancy gatherings. The media liked to get ahold of whatever drama had unfolded on those evenings and twist it into a mangled mess. What could be more dramatic than a disaster involving a Tulku at the president's mansion? It was the perfect fuel for an already raging fire.

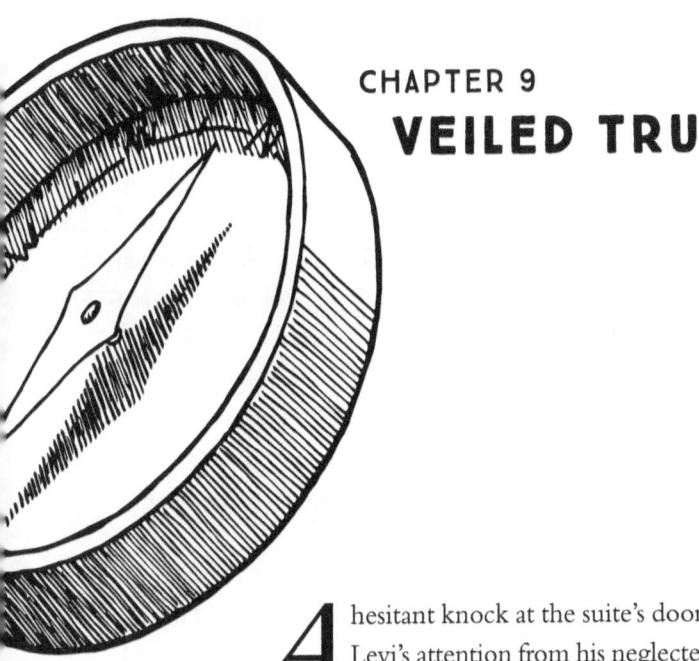

CHAPTER 9
VEILED TRUTH

A hesitant knock at the suite's door dragged Levi's attention from his neglected studies. A small twig of a man dressed in a navy suit with a neat mustache and slick black hair stood just outside. He carried only a small briefcase to match his suit, and a white handkerchief was neatly folded in his breast pocket.

The man peered nervously past Levi. "I believe I'm here to see Ambassador Alsh."

Levi waved him in. "You must be the tailor."

The man nodded quickly, shaking as he stepped inside.

Levi cleared his belongings off the kitchen table to allow the man to set up. He ended up sitting across from Grenard, who was finishing his usual morning deep dive into current events.

"Ambassador Alsh, if I may…" The man's voice trailed off. He had a tape measure curled in one hand and tablet next to him on the table.

Grenard tore his gaze from his reading. He stood and stretched. "Tell me what you need me to do, good sir. I am at your disposal."

The tailor awkwardly took a few measurements of the Tulku's torso, then handed Grenard the tablet and told him to pick out what style and details he wanted for his suit.

Grenard scrolled through the pictures on the tablet, chuckling to himself. "Well, I suppose I could always go as myself. What do you think, my boy?"

Levi glanced at the picture the Tulku was showing him. It was a black fox-like mask with gold detailing. He tried to suppress a smile. There was an uncanny resemblance the Tulku shared with the now extinct Earth creature. "Doesn't that defeat the purpose of a masked dance?"

Grenard laughed. "I suppose it does, my boy. I suppose it does." He continued scrolling through the options. "I can't decide. Ten years of being away doesn't help much for remembering how these events are supposed to function."

Levi set his work down and walked over to the Tulku and the tailor. "It's black-tie apparel. How much of a statement do you want to make?"

The Tulku smirked. "I'm already enough of a statement. I don't think I need to intentionally amplify that."

"Then pick a black tux and whatever accent color you like." It seemed like a no-brainer in Levi's mind until he saw the ambassador's face.

The Tulku seemed lost. "I forgot that suits are generally black. I don't know why that escaped me." He narrowed the selection, but he still seemed hesitant.

"Don't the Tulku wear black?" Levi's curiosity was piqued. Black seemed like such a standard color to him, but he realized he had never seen Grenard wear anything other than bright colors, particularly purple.

"No. We don't wear black. Not anymore, anyways." He sighed and stared at the tailor's tablet. "Oh, why not? It is only for one evening. It wouldn't be so inappropriate if the world was how it ought to be."

Levi desperately wanted to ask why Grenard wouldn't normally wear black, but the tailor seemed to be growing frustrated. He watched the small man measure and re-measure Grenard's leg several times.

The ambassador looked down at the flustered tailor and grinned. "I perceive there is a problem. Might it have something to do with differences in anatomy?"

The man refused to look Grenard in the eye as he stumbled over his words. "I—I've never had a client with a tail as voluminous as yours." He swallowed hard, and his face grew red.

Grenard chuckled. "I would not expect you to have ever had a client with a tail. But trust me, my friend, when I say that my tail is far from its full volume."

The poor man shakily took one last set of measurements before completely giving up. He coiled up his measuring tape and pointed to the table. "Have you ma—made your decisions?"

Grenard lost his smile and refocused, sighing. "I'm hopeless. Levi, will you pick? I trust you won't make a fool of me."

The boy was caught off guard by the comment, but he took the tablet and picked a mask and style that he thought would agree with the ambassador. "What do you think, sir?"

"Perfect." Grenard returned the tablet to the tailor.

The man rushed to pack everything up. "Do you have dress shoes?"

The Tulku glanced down at his short, padded feet. "I believe I have that covered. Thank you."

The tailor huffed and dashed towards the door. "I will have your suit delivered before the masquerade. Have a good day, Ambassador." And with that, he was gone.

Levi tried to keep from snickering. "I think you frightened him."

"That certainly wasn't my intention." Grenard smiled and clasped his hands behind his back. "You can't blame him, though. I am absolutely terrifying, especially with my voluminous tail."

"Exceptionally." Levi returned to his study materials, smiling. Maybe he didn't dislike the ambassador as much as he thought he did. The Tulku's presence was calm and comforting. Conversation came easier than before. Levi wondered how much longer he would be assigned to the ambassador. Life before Grenard had been solitary, and he had liked it, but he missed it less and less every day.

"Levi, I have a favor to ask of you. Do you have access to the Presidential Library?"

He shrugged. "It's open to the public. What are you wanting from there?"

Grenard walked to the windows and squinted out at the sea. "Thomason has me thinking that I need to read through some of Erev's early legislation. He seems to think that there is something there I would find interesting."

Levi stared down at the math problems he had barely managed to touch that morning. He sighed and closed his textbook. "Let me get my boots on."

The Presidential Library was located in the midst of stately two and three-story buildings lit by wrought iron lamp posts and framed by perfectly manicured lawns. It housed all the original legislation and documents from every presidency, and a myriad of other information. Recordings, photographs, and videos of historical significance also lived there.

Levi and Grenard stood gazing up at the square, temple-like building before walking through the doors that were dwarfed by the front colonnades. The interior was no different. Grand pillars formed a corridor flanked with two stories of impossibly tall bookshelves, groaning under the weight of knowledge they bore. Light from the slim windows beyond the bookshelves streamed in, casting deep shadows. Dozens of tables piled with manuscripts were strewn about the building.

Grenard set his satchel down on one table and immediately began searching the call numbers listed at the end of the rows. He frowned and skipped several rows at a time, repeating this action several times over before he migrated to the other side of the aisle.

Levi watched curiously. "Can I ask what you're looking for, sir?"

"There are two particular documents I am hoping to find. They both date back to 04 Ko'ne Humankyi."

Levi eyed the Tulku. "That's the year humans settled on Rufosia. I know where those documents would live." He led the ambassador up a flight of stairs and to the back of the massive building. "They have all the legislation organized by date. This would probably be a good place to start." Levi pointed to a small section of shelves at the back of the library packed with thin books protecting copies of the oldest and most fundamental laws.

"Thank you, my boy." Grenard smiled and wandered in.

The soldier left the Tulku to search so he could finally sit down and study for his test. His miserable textbooks almost seemed to pout in the sack Levi had them in, so he freed them and scattered them across the table next to where the ambassador had placed his satchel. He forced himself to begin the mind melting task of mathematics.

It didn't take long for Grenard to make his way back with two files in hand. After an hour of quietly reading, he growled and leaned back in his chair, crossing his arms. He frowned as he stared down at the two documents. "Levi, what do you know about Erev developing weapons?"

The boy looked up at the Tulku, mildly shocked. "Why are you asking?"

"Come read these." Grenard waved him over and pointed at two specific places in the documents.

Levi peered over Grenard's shoulder. The first document was the *Creed of Erev*, a paper that outlined the basic laws and philosophies humanity was supposed to abide by after their laborious journey through space. The clause Grenard had pointed out said: *We shall not develop nuclear devices for the use of mass destruction, for risk of repeating history that resulted in the end of Earth's habitability.*

The second paper was the *Treaty of Riyanti: In order to maintain peaceful conduct between the nations of Erev and Tulanu and Phirevsk, Erev will be prohibited from extensive weapons development, including but not limited to weapons of mass destruction.*

Levi knew of both the creed and the treaty, but he had never read either of them. He swallowed hard. "If I told you Erev wasn't recreating nuclear weapons, would you believe me?"

The ambassador held his gaze, searching the boy's eyes for the truth. He didn't answer. Eventually he stared down at the documents, deep in thought.

Levi knew Grenard knew he was lying, but there was no point in either of them saying more. His comment had more than answered Grenard's unspoken questions. He perceived the

Tulku recognized his asking more questions would only put Levi at risk for receiving Feyer's wrath.

The ambassador sighed heavily. "I have my work cut out for me." He stood abruptly from the table and left.

Levi didn't see the Tulku for an hour after that, until Grenard came back with a massive pile of documents and dozens of recordings. He deposited the heap on the table and pored through them for several more hours. The ambassador took hundreds of notes, quickly filling one journal and taking out a second from his satchel.

Grenard brought over an unmarked recording. "Tell me what you think of it."

Levi took the small, finger-sized black box and connected headphones to it.

"Hayden, where are those import reports?"

"Just here, Anton. "

"Well?"

"If we continue to apply pressure, Erev's economy might collapse. There is already considerable unrest about the prices of food—"

"Yes, but who do the people blame?"

"Tulanu."

"Good." Anton cleared his throat. "As long as we can continue to direct the human populace's rage towards the Tulku, we can slowly cripple Tulanu without the military ever lifting a finger."

Hayden sighed. "I'm not sure the people are inclined to take matters into their own hands yet."

"Then let's create a reason for them to. Frame the Tulku for an attack and see if the spark from that catches."

Hayden mumbled something under his breath.

"Speak up, man!"

"How are we supposed to get the Tulku to attack first? They're pacifists."

"Create a Tulku! Given the right circumstances, I'm sure no one would be the wiser to an imposter."

When the recording finished, Levi set his headphones on the table and glanced at the Tulku. He fidgeted with his ring. "It sounded like Anton was trying to start a war with Tulanu."

Grenard smirked. "I'm glad he didn't succeed, but I'm afraid your uncle might have resumed Anton's efforts after he died. I just have no proof. Yet." The ambassador took the device back to his table.

Levi tried to sort out what was happening. What he had just learned wasn't just a Tulku trying to convince him that humans had started everything for the sake of pushing off blame and pointing fingers. It had come from an authoritative source, from Anton Feyer himself. He looked at Grenard. "You're going to try to expose Jake, aren't you?"

"I have to put an end to this, either by stopping Jake, or by convincing the Tulkish Council that we are in greater danger than we suspected. War is a horrible thing, and my people are not prepared for it. If Feyer decides to launch an attack…" Grenard stood hunched over the edge of the table, looking over the open documents. He burst. "They are fools! Blinded by their naivety and their ignorance!" He pounded his fist on the table and sat back in his chair, snarling and stewing in his frustrations.

Levi leaned back in his seat and furrowed his brows. He couldn't imagine saying such things about Feyer. He was a just man, leading humanity with a strong hand and defending her valiantly. Or at least, that was what Levi had been taught to believe. But the Tulku spoke freely of his government's faults. "You don't support your own leaders?"

"Supporting and agreeing with are not always interchangeable concepts. I support my leaders by doing what they ask of me, but I can still believe they are making poor choices. It seems General Thomason may have a similar view about your president."

The few times Levi had spoken out against Feyer, he had paid more dearly for those comments than anyone truly knew. "Can you tell the Tulkish council you disagree with them?"

"Yes. And I very frequently do. That does not mean they heed my advice." Grenard blew out a breath.

Levi kept his eyes focused on his textbooks as another question sidled into his head. "Do you ever get punished for speaking out against them?"

"No, my boy." Grenard looked at the soldier. "Why do you ask?"

Levi avoided the Tulku's gaze and shrugged.

Grenard narrowed his eyes and shifted in his chair. "Are people punished for voicing a dissenting opinion in Erev?"

"I was just curious how other governments respond to things like that." He could not fathom being able to disagree with Feyer so freely. Nor did he want to. Feyer had given him a good life. He had purpose and never wanted for anything.

The ambassador stared for a long while. Levi feared he would ask more questions, but the Tulku silently returned to his work. Levi breathed a sigh of relief as the icy tension melted within him and settled back into pounding calculus into his thick, non-absorbent skull.

After an extended period of quiet, Grenard stood and stretched. He fiddled with his satchel and pulled out a book. He approached Levi's table, holding it close. The Tulku glanced at the boy, then held out the book to him. "I would like you to have this."

Levi took the book. It had a beautiful, embossed leather cover with green-colored foil stamped into some of the crevices. He opened it to empty, creamy white pages. It still had that new book smell.

"I did mention that I wanted you to help me make observations. I find journals are good places to store ideas so one can revisit them later." Grenard lingered a moment, his tail swishing ever so slightly. "The journal is for your eyes only, by the way. I won't go snooping through your thoughts, but I wouldn't mind listening to some of them if you do choose to share."

Levi nodded solemnly. "Thank you, sir." He felt over the intricate design, absorbing every detail.

Grenard returned to his table.

"Sir, is there something in particular you would like me to record my thoughts on?"

The Tulku shook his head. "Anything you wish will suffice. But I am curious to know what you think of Private Brown and his teammates."

"The deaf one?"

"Yes." Grenard picked up a document and scanned it. "I quite like him. He has a good head on his shoulders and a strong moral compass, but that's what I think of him. I want to know what you think of him."

Levi took a deep breath and opened the journal to its first, flawless page. He had a lot of thoughts about the deaf soldier.

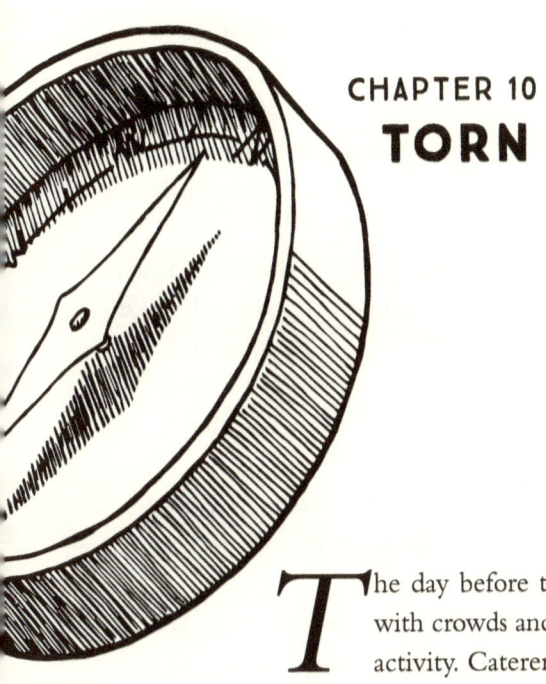

CHAPTER 10
TORN

The day before the masquerade came with crowds and an unusual thrum of activity. Caterers, florists, and bakers swarmed the mansion like bees to a newly blossomed flower. They piled up at the front of the mansion, barking and narrowly dodging dagger-like glares from each other when someone else stepped in their way.

It was Levi's turn to stray from his typical morning routine and stand at the window, staring at the chaos unfolding below. He fidgeted with his ring, twirling it around and around until his skin was sore. There were too many new and unfamiliar faces. Too many people Levi could not trust. The thought of the evening to come was almost nauseating when he tried to think about how to keep the ambassador alive from any number of unknown dangers. He wished he had had more training to prepare him for this, but it was far too late to do anything about it now.

"You don't like new people, do you, my boy?"

"No. You have no idea who they are and what their intentions may be. You can't trust them until you know them, and even if you do learn to trust them, they can still stab you in the back." Levi tore himself away from the window and joined Grenard on the couch. He sat with his elbows on his knees, wringing his hands.

The ambassador set down his tablet. "If it is any consolation, I do not intend to leave your sight tomorrow night. I will do my best to make your job easier."

"I don't need easy, sir."

"Maybe not. You are incredibly sharp, my boy. But dealing with an aging and stubborn Tulku is difficult enough as is. I know I frustrate you at times, and I will likely continue to frustrate you. However, I am not so selfish as to intentionally get you into trouble. I hope you know that."

Levi looked at him. There was an overwhelming amount of kindness in Grenard's amber gaze. It had always been there, but the young soldier had been too preoccupied to appreciate it. He prayed that tomorrow would not be his last day with the Tulku.

"Can I ask a question, my boy?"

Levi stared at the ground. "You don't need my permission to ask a question, sir. I can always choose not to answer." He lifted his eyes and smiled.

Grenard grinned. "How well do you feel you know me?"

Levi scoffed. "I've been living with you constantly for over two months. You like humming the same three songs over and over again. You usually wear purple, and you stop to smell pink flowers every time we go outside for a walk."

Grenard crossed his arms. Mischief glimmered in his eyes. "Yes, but what of my character?"

Levi had to pause. What had he learned about Grenard's character? He thought back over the past weeks. "You're always calm, even when things may be stressful. You're generous, even if people don't deserve it. You aren't afraid to correct people, but you're kind when you do it. You like playing games." He smiled. "You have a habit of going to unsavory places."

Grenard smirked. "That's not what I meant by 'character.'"

"It's a character flaw, is what it is." Levi grinned wildly.

"Character flaw by your definition. Not by mine!"

They laughed together.

"Levi, you seem much happier now than when I first met you. What changed?"

The boy sighed, stood, and made his way back over to the window. He shoved his hands in his pockets. "I don't hate you. I don't even dislike you." It felt strange saying it out loud, admitting it not just to the ambassador, but to himself. He saw Grenard smile in the reflection of the window.

Just then, Levi spotted a figure in the gardens below. Feyer was sitting on a bench, watching the hustle and bustle. No one else seemed to notice the president, but the sight of Feyer suddenly flooded Levi with guilt. The blood drained from his face. His legs felt like they might collapse underneath him. He wasn't supposed to like the Tulku. But worse than that, he realized he resented Feyer. It was criminal. Even traitorous. A strangling sensation squeezed the air out of his lungs. Levi slowly backed away from the window and sat down. He clasped his shaking hands together, hoping Grenard hadn't noticed.

"Is something wrong, Levi?"

The boy turned to Grenard, eyes wide with fear. "Feyer can't know that I don't hate you. He'll beat the shit out of me if he ever finds out."

"That seems a little dramatic. He's your uncle."

Levi didn't answer him. There was nothing between him and Feyer. It was as if he was naked and all Feyer had to do was turn around to see Levi's blatantly exposed treason. He fumbled towards the table and grabbed his schoolwork. He picked up his stylus and shoved his nervous energy into his studies.

The afternoon continued in fragile silence until Grenard yawned. He stretched, and his tail curled behind him. "Shall we go see what preparations have been made, my boy? Or do you advise against it?"

Levi peered out the window. Most of the unfamiliar cars had left. "It should probably be fine. It doesn't look like there are that many people here anymore."

They crept down a back staircase and wandered towards the front of the mansion. The few remaining stragglers stopped dead in their tracks when they ran into the Tulku. Most were speechless, turning tail to escape the ambassador's presence. The usual staff roaming about didn't bat an eye as Levi and Grenard snuck around.

Dozens of large flower arrangements were posted as sentries about the ballroom and foyer. Their overly sweet fragrance wafted throughout the entire mansion. A few ladders and feather dusters had been left out under the chandeliers, and empty tables had been adorned with decorations and pushed to the sides of the ballroom. Everything shone. Every surface had been painstakingly polished, leaving the rooms sparkling with an eerie glow.

Grenard gazed upon the scene with his hands behind his back. "Might I ask what you think Feyer meant by a small gathering of close officials?"

Levi frowned. The extent of preparation was not in their favor. "If even Feyer's project team will be here, then at least a hundred. Maybe more, based on all this."

"It seems being inconspicuous is no longer a possibility."

"Was it ever a possibility to begin with?"

The Tulku grimaced and sighed. He glanced at Levi. "Let us enjoy being unnoticed and unknown for this last evening."

CHAPTER 11

DANCING AROUND

The tailor finally came!" Levi laid the new garment bag at the foot of the ambassador's bed. "But he was terrified to come in."

Grenard stood at the sink, furiously brushing the back of his head. Fur was flying everywhere as he attempted to tame an out-of-control tuft. "Not a moment too soon." He swore under his breath. "Tof!" His ears were pinned flat to his skull, and the corner of his mouth was raised in a snarl. "If only I could get my coat to cooperate before we present ourselves to the growing number of precious few individuals that are near and dear to the president."

Levi stood by, feeling the weight of the coming evening settle on his heart. "Is there anything I can do to help?"

Grenard set the brush down and leaned against the counter. He took a deep breath and looked at his reflection. "No." He smiled. "If Beka were here, she would say, 'Ba, you already look nicer than freshly fallen snow. Stop fussing so much.'" He sighed. "So much like her mother." He straightened and turned towards the boy. "How much longer do we have?"

Levi glanced at his watch. "Just under two hours."

"Go get ready, my boy." Grenard shooed him out of the room. "We mustn't be late or unkempt."

Levi had already brought down his tuxedo from his neglected and dusty room on the third floor. He stood in front of the mirror attempting to tame his own locks. His fine, brown hair managed to stick out in strange places, even when plastered with gel. He meticulously combed his hair, knowing that it was bound to be messed up from wearing a mask for the entire evening. It just had to stay out of his face.

He eventually gave up and changed into his tux. His suit jacket was starting to show signs of wear at the cuffs from years of attending similar events. Levi's dress shoes had a few scuffs, which he diligently buffed and polished out. His vest and bowtie were a bright crimson. He had always worn red to these events, though he couldn't remember if he had chosen the color or if it had been dictated for him. It didn't really matter since it was his only option for the evening. He had been fitted for the suit when he was sixteen, and though he had not grown much in the three years since, the shoulders were a little snugger than he would have liked.

He waited to put on his mask. It was nothing special. Just a plain, black mask without much detail or decoration. He wasn't supposed to stand out at these events anyways. Levi carried the mask to the couch and waited for the ambassador to emerge from his room. He didn't have to wait long.

Grenard came out wearing a black suit coat, a black and gold vest, and a gold bowtie. The gold fabric matched the Tulku's syamta perfectly. The tailor had certainly done a fantastic job, even with differences in anatomy. It looked quite flattering on the ambassador. He fidgeted with the buttons on his jacket. "Levi, can you remind me of the silly little rule about suit coat buttons?" His was a three-button jacket, the same as Levi's.

"You only need to button the middle one."

Grenard fixed his jacket and looked up at the young soldier, smiling. "You look spectacular, my boy." He twirled briefly. "What do you think of the tailor's work?"

"I'm impressed. You almost look like a human, sir."

"Ha!" Grenard smirked. "It'll take a little more than a properly fitted suit to fool anyone. Is it time?"

Levi checked the time. They had a few minutes before guests would start arriving. "It won't hurt to be early."

As Levi and Grenard approached the foyer, the scent of perfume and flowers assaulted them. Light sparkled and glistened around the eerily glossy room, bouncing off the crystals hanging from the chandelier, and casting strange geometric patterns on every surface.

Feyer was poised in a dark red suit under the chandelier orchestrating last-minute preparations. Various staff flitted around, attending to the finer details under Feyer's keen eye and finding their assigned posts for the evening. Levi and Grenard descended the stairs, masks in hand, and joined him.

"President Feyer, I hope we are not underdressed." Grenard bowed deeply with a forced smile.

"Ambassador Alsh." Feyer nodded at him. "I appreciate you being willing to join me tonight. I see the tailor pulled off a small miracle."

The glimmer of mischief appeared in Grenard's eyes as his ears perked up. "I am very thankful for your generosity. Your boy was instrumental in helping me decide what style to go with. Do you mind if I take a look around?"

Feyer held out his hand, inviting the ambassador to bask in the pompous surroundings. As soon as Grenard's back was turned, he shot the young soldier a deadly glare.

Levi paled. His heart felt it might pound through his chest, and he dropped his gaze.

Grenard ambled back towards them. "It really is fantastic, President Feyer. I expect tonight will be a night to remember."

Feyer smiled. "That is my hope."

Levi watched the president apprehensively. There was a darkness that hung over him like a cloud threatening to rain, but the doors opened, and his esteemed guests came flooding in. Emerald, sapphire, and ruby-red countered the white and gold of Feyer's mansion.

Levi donned his mask and stayed by Grenard's side, scouting suspicious characters as Feyer introduced each of his esteemed guests to the ambassador. The more people that came in, the more Levi felt oxygen leave the room. The foyer and ballroom both began to fill rapidly with far more people than the soldier had anticipated.

General Thomason came in with the ten special soldiers trailing behind him. He greeted the president with an emphatic handshake. "President Feyer, it's an honor as always." He glanced over at Levi. "I'm glad to see your nephew could attend." He caught Grenard's attention as he returned to smiling at Feyer.

"I'm glad you could join us, General Thomason."

The general moved to shake Grenard's hand. "Ambassador Alsh, it is good to see you again." As he left to join the rest of the guests, he winked at Levi.

"You as well, General Thomason." Grenard bowed respectfully, then cast a glance at the boy.

As the flood of guests turned to a trickle, the Tulku made his way into the ballroom and was soon invited to join the dancing. Ladies dressed in shimmering, jewel-toned evening gowns swarmed him, enthralled with the scandalous idea of having danced with a Tulkish ambassador.

Levi found an isolated place against one of the walls to keep watch. He was flanked by two pillars topped with gaudy vases stuffed with far too many roses. Feyer's decorations always bothered him. So much glamor and vanity had been poured into what was likely an intricate coverup for someone's murder. Or at least every previous ball had been that way.

The crowd had begun to settle into a pattern. The older participants had taken to the chairs along the edges of the room, chatting with one another about politics or whatever other useless topic came to mind, while the younger individuals twirled in the center of the room. Servers carrying trays of refreshments dodged the dancers and floated about the room silently.

"Do you efer ge' a brea'?" The unmistakable blond soldier with green cochlear implants came and stood next to him, surveying the scene. Liam's outfit was accented with rich emerald-green, which Levi assumed was to help disguise the hearing devices.

"No. At least not in the past two months."

"I' doesn' seem qui'e righ'. You shoul' hafe a nigh' off efery once in a while."

"I'm not sure I want to take tonight off." Levi glanced over at the blond. "Are you not going to dance?"

"Musi' is har'. I know people li'e i', but the noises mis together too mush. I don' en'oy i'."

Levi nodded. "Why come, then?"

Liam frowned and shrugged. "You can' say no to Feyer. Tha' and i' seeme' ru'e to pass up an infi'ation from the presi'en'."

A group of young ladies had congregated nearby, talking in hushed voices as they eyed the two soldiers. Levi dared glance over, and amongst the group was a woman in a navy-blue dress. She held Levi's gaze and gave him a flicker of a smile. But her attention was wrenched away as another girl broke away from the group.

The lady now approaching Levi and Liam was a pretty thing in a soft, shimmery, rose-colored dress with a billowing skirt. She had soft features and a graceful air about her. Her round face was framed in platinum curls, and her lips were perfectly plump.

Levi watched her approach, holding his breath, hoping she would walk past him and yet knowing she wouldn't.

She curtsied in front of them and blushed. "I know it isn't customary, but would one of you care to join me for a dance?"

Levi smiled politely. "I'm sorry. I'm actually on duty right now, otherwise I would."

She turned expectantly to Liam, eyebrows raised.

Liam blushed. "I can' dance."

The girl in pink feigned a smile and curtsied. "Have a good evening." When she rose and turned from them, her infuriated muttering could be heard until she rejoined her companions.

Levi noticed Feyer walking from the opposite side of the room towards him. He must have noticed the interaction with the girl. The boy dreaded Feyer's deliberate and focused approach. Levi stood tall and avoided looking at the president.

Feyer straightened his suit coat and surveyed the room next to Levi without making eye contact. "She was quite pretty. Why aren't you out dancing with her?"

Levi took a deep breath. "I believe I'm still Ambassador Alsh's bodyguard. I can't just leave my post and let myself become infatuated with a girl."

"I want you to be considering the young ladies here."

"How would you like me to consider them, sir?"

"You know exactly what I mean."

Levi huffed and scowled. "My primary objective is to protect the ambassador, so unless someone will relieve me of my duties for the evening, what you ask of me is impossible." Levi knew he was in the right, but his palms grew sweaty. Liam had not moved from his side, something Levi hoped would be to his advantage.

Feyer frowned at Levi. "Private Brown, would you consider relieving Levi for the evening?"

Liam stood tall, eyes wide with excitement. "Yes, sir. I woul' be honore'."

Feyer finally removed his frozen gaze from Levi. "What's wrong with your speech, boy?"

Liam took half a step back, his eyes frantically darting around as he searched for an answer to appease the president. "I—My hearing difficul'ies affec' my speesh pa'ern, sir."

"Fix it, Private."

"Yes, Presi'en' Feyer." Liam dropped his gaze and shifted his weight between his feet.

Levi cleared his throat. "I will inform Ambassador Alsh that I will be otherwise occupied this evening." He skirted the edge of the room to where the Tulku was sitting, sipping on a glass of water. Levi stood next to him as nausea crept in. "Do you remember Private Liam Brown?"

"Yes."

Levi instinctively ran his fingers through his stiff, overly gelled hair. "He is going to be your bodyguard for the evening. Feyer wants me out dancing."

Grenard eyed him curiously. "You don't seem particularly enthused about that."

"No." He scanned the room and saw Feyer staring him down. He tried to shake the creeping feeling away.

"Not particularly talented at dancing?"

"No. I'm alright at it."

Grenard grunted. "Do try to enjoy yourself for at least one dance, my boy. It isn't every day that you get to enjoy the thrills of masked adventures that last only one evening. Besides, I can handle myself for a few minutes while you satisfy Feyer." He nodded respectfully towards the president.

The boy hesitated.

"Levi."

He looked at the Tulku.

"Romance, while it isn't always everything it's cracked up to be, can still be fun if you give it a chance."

Levi took a deep breath and scouted the group of young ladies, occasionally glancing at Feyer as he crossed to the other side of the room where they stood. He cleared his throat, gaining the attention of the girl in pink.

She turned and looked him up and down, her arms crossed.

"I have been temporarily relieved of my duties. Are you still wanting to dance?" He offered his hand to her.

She sneered. "That depends. Are you a good dancer?"

"I would like to think so, but I will leave that to your judgment."

The girl in pink huffed and took his hand.

Levi was a good dancer, even exceptional. The pair twirled about the floor with elegance as envious eyes followed them. The girl in pink seemed to thoroughly enjoy herself as she followed his lead. They didn't talk much, but when the song ended, she lingered, holding onto him.

Levi took her hand and kissed it gently. "Thank you for the dance." He glanced over at Feyer, who was frowning at him. Levi turned back to the girl. "Are any of your friends also in need of a partner? I would hate to leave a young lady without an opportunity to dance this evening."

"I'm sure they do, but they'll have to do their own grunt work." The young woman's smile was arrogant.

She tried to pull Levi into the next dance, but he hesitated only to see the president scowling. Levi gave in.

As the next song ramped up, Levi noticed a man talking with Grenard. He watched their interaction intensely. The man wore a black tuxedo with no colorful accents and had a scar along the base of his neck. Something wasn't quite right about him, but the young soldier couldn't put his finger on it. He tripped on the girl's shoe. "Sorry."

Levi knew the girl had muttered something to him, but the man had stopped talking with Grenard and picked up a glass from one of the tables covered in refreshments. The man took something out of his suit coat and poured it into the glass, making his way back to the ambassador.

Levi barely glanced back at the girl. "I'm sorry, I have to go." He left her suspended on the dance floor as he weaved his way through the crowd. By the time Levi made it to the ambassador, Grenard already had the glass in hand, and the man had vanished from sight.

"Don't drink that!" Levi put his hand on the glass before Grenard had a chance to sip at it. He scanned the room for the man with the scar along his neck, but he had disappeared.

Liam rushed up beside him, relieved when he saw that the ambassador was safe.

Grenard stared at the glass for a moment, swirling the liquid around. "I suppose it is a good thing I am not much for drinking. I might see if I can get another glass of water." He calmly stood and sauntered around the room. As he approached the table with various beverages, he stopped at one of the flower bouquets standing sentry and poured the glass out. He set it with a few other half-emptied glasses then picked up a new glass as if nothing had happened. He casually took a sip, eventually rejoining the pair of soldiers. "It has certainly been a refreshing evening." He raised his glass cheerfully and once again took his seat. "Levi, go enjoy yourself. Private Brown is perfectly capable of keeping me safe."

Levi frowned, but the Tulku subtly pointed behind the boy. He turned and noticed Feyer strolling towards them. He ducked in the opposite direction and sought out the girl in pink before being chastised.

She sat in one of the chairs along the edge of the room with her nose upturned and her arms crossed.

Levi took a deep breath. "I'm sorry I left so abruptly."

"A few of my acquaintances might want a partner to dance with."

Levi bowed towards her, slightly relieved. "Thank you for the one and half dances. It has been a pleasure, miss."

Most of the other young ladies had been picked for a dance by the rest of Feyer's project team. Only one young woman remained standing along the perimeter of the room, the one wearing royal blue. The dress was sleek and flattered her figure. Her mask was feathery and elegant. She stood awkwardly with her hands clasped together, staring out at all the dancing couples.

Levi approached her, wary of Feyer's watchful gaze. He stood next to her, debating how to strike up a conversation. He wiped his sweaty hands on his pants as subtly as he could and took a deep breath.

"I noticed Juliette turned you down after your little stunt."

Levi glanced at her. "I'm not exactly used to not being on guard all the time."

"I think I can understand that." She smiled and held out her hand. "I'm Callie, by the way."

"Levi." He shook it.

Callie had a surprisingly strong grip. "Do you normally look after the Tulkish ambassador?"

"Yes. Well, except for tonight." Levi stared down at his shoes. "Feyer had Private Brown take my place for the evening."

They stood silently, watching the crowd. Levi tried to keep from staring at her, but she was gorgeous. The long-sleeved gown she wore had an open back, exposing flawless skin. Her raven hair was pulled into an intricate updo and cascaded down to her shoulders.

Callie turned to him. "Do you want to go for a spin?"

"Yes." Levi smiled and blushed. "Sorry. I guess I should have asked."

She shrugged. "I don't really care. I generally don't like dancing, but I would rather do that than stand here awkwardly with you staring at me and us saying nothing at all."

"Again, sorry."

Callie grinned and rolled her eyes. "Come on."

Levi offered her his arm and beamed. When she took it, he escorted her onto the dance floor and pulled her in. There was something intoxicating about her presence. She smelled like mint, and her eyes were an intricate tapestry of green and amber. He almost didn't notice beneath her makeup, but there was a thin, delicate scar just under her eyebrow. It was a miniscule imperfection, but it drew Levi in. It was as if this perfect, dreamlike woman was now somehow real and tangible.

"Do you talk while dancing? Or are you a purist?"

Levi laughed nervously. "I talk. I just don't always know what to say, I guess."

Callie nodded, eyeing him. "You're not very good at this whole conversation thing."

"No. Not with most people. I'm good at talking with the ambassador, but I've also been stuck with him for two months straight."

"Do you like him?"

Levi watched her carefully. "Which answer do you want?"

"I don't care if you like him or not. I'm just curious."

"You don't hate the Tulku?"

Callie shrugged. "I'm open to some differing and unique opinions."

"Then yes, I like him."

The song ended, but they lingered on the dance floor, waiting for the next one to begin.

Levi looked into her eyes. He wanted to say something, anything, hoping that he wouldn't make a complete fool of himself. "Can I ask about your scar?"

Callie frowned and looked away. She let go and took a step back from him.

"Please." Levi reached for her hand. "I didn't mean to pry." The music started back up. "May I at least have the next dance?"

Callie stared at his hand for a moment. "Come get a drink with me instead." She held onto his hand and pulled him away.

She grabbed two flutes of champagne and gave one to Levi as they tucked away in a more remote corner. They watched the ballroom churn with life. Grenard was back on the dance floor, enchanting everyone he interacted with.

Callie cleared her throat. "Why do you want to know about my scar?"

Levi shifted from one foot to the other. "I think it's beautiful. I wanted to know the story behind it."

The young woman scoffed. "No one likes scars."

"I'm a terrible liar. You can ask the ambassador."

Callie smirked. "So you're telling me you can only tell the truth?"

"No." Levi smiled. "I can lie, just not well. It also wastes fewer words to go with the truth the first time." He stared deep into her hazel eyes. "You know, I don't have to like scars or what they mean to still think you're more beautiful with it."

"You're strange, Levi." She shook her head and sighed. "Let's just say that I got it from a fight with some older boys when I was younger. It's how I ended up in the military."

Levi stared at her, shocked. "Enlisted or officer?"

She smiled, holding her head high. "Officer."

"How did you end up here? At the masquerade?"

Callie finished her champagne. She rolled her eyes. "Something about being picked out to potentially court Feyer's nephew. I have no idea, but you don't say no to Feyer, so I showed up. You don't happen to know who the spoiled snot is that can't win his own girl, do you? The guy must be completely, socially inept."

Levi held his glass to his lips, but he paused. "You might have already danced with the completely socially inept, spoiled snot."

She scoffed. "How? I've only danced with you." She froze. Callie gawked at Levi, but her gaze was drawn away by something behind him.

Levi turned and found Grenard standing just behind him. "Ambassador Alsh—"

He glanced between Callie and the ambassador and dropped his gaze.

The Tulku smiled politely at Callie. "Forgive my intrusion." He looked at Levi. "I expect I will be retiring for the evening after the next dance."

"Thank you for telling me, sir."

Grenard started to walk away, but he grinned at Levi. "I was right, wasn't I?"

"About what, sir?"

"Romance can be fun." Grenard raised his eyebrows and darted off.

Levi's cheeks flushed, and Callie chuckled.

"I like him." Callie folded her arms. "Now what was I about to say?"

"You were about to ask Feyer's socially inept nephew for one last dance before he has to resume his duties." Levi waited with mounting anticipation.

Callie grinned at him. "Alright."

Levi took her and led her onto the dance floor until a piercing shriek filled the room and stopped them in their tracks. The music died a horrible death as the pair froze. A crowd had begun to gather a few paces from where the ambassador stood. Levi rushed through the masses and pulled Grenard away from the hoard. Liam was right there at the Tulku's side.

Levi grabbed the blond soldier. "Take Ambassador Alsh to his room and make sure the door is locked. Now!"

"Yes, sir." Liam positioned himself between the ambassador and Feyer's remaining guests, rushing the Tulku out of the ballroom.

Levi turned to address the panicked throng of people. He shoved his way through, only stopping when he saw the body.

CHAPTER 12
REMOVING MASKS

The girl in pink, Juliette, lay motionless on the floor. Her eyes had glazed over, and a sickening foam had started to creep from between her perfect pink lips. A broken champagne flute rested between her fingers.

Levi's mind raced. The man who tried to poison Grenard came to mind, but he didn't have time to think about it. He and the other soldiers in the room cleared the crowd away from the body and dismissed them for the evening. Levi only barely caught a glance of Callie leaving, and he wished he could have said goodbye.

It wasn't long before crime scene investigators showed up and began taking photos of Juliette. Levi stood at the edges of the room, watching General Thomason and Feyer's special team clear out. He looked back at the lifeless body on the floor as guilt crept into his mind. He should have kept more tabs on the man who tried to poison the ambassador, but he hadn't, and now someone had died. He hated the idea of what the media would do with this story. Even private balls managed to make it into the public eye.

Feyer walked up beside him. "It is a shame, really. I was hoping she would catch your fancy, as pretty as she was. She would have made a fine mother, I'm sure."

Levi swiveled towards Feyer, fists balled at his sides. "She was poisoned, and all you're thinking about is that?" He rolled his eyes and tore off his sweaty mask. Strands of his hair immediately fell into his face.

A few investigators glanced at them. Feyer grabbed Levi's arm and pulled him into the empty hallway just off the ballroom. Levi's veins turned to ice. He dared not flinch or open his mouth again.

Feyer scowled, his grip tightening painfully. "Meet me in my office in twenty minutes."

Levi trembled before him and grimaced. "Yes, sir."

Feyer let go, straightened his suit and tie, then walked back into the ballroom to answer the officers' remaining questions.

Levi raced upstairs and into the suite. Liam stood guard in the kitchen while Grenard read on the couch, both waiting for him. Levi stormed past and slammed the door to his room behind him. The tight suit jacket now felt constricting. He tore it off, leaving it in a crumpled pile on the floor. He paced back and forth, trying to steady his shaking hands. When that didn't work, he flung himself on his bed and yelled into the pillows.

"Levi, can I come in?" It was Grenard.

"No!"

"Thank you, Private Brown. Have a good rest of your evening." Grenard opened the door.

"I said I didn't want you to come in."

Grenard sighed. "We both know I'm terrible about taking your recommendations."

"It wasn't a recommendation!" He sat up and flung a pillow at the Tulku. "What the hell do you want?"

Grenard folded his arms over his chest. "What happened?"

Levi flopped backwards and groaned. "It doesn't matter! You can't do anything about it." He grabbed another pillow and buried his face in it. He wanted to shut the world out, to avoid existing if only for a moment.

"I can listen."

Levi pulled the pillow off. "The first girl I danced with was killed, and all Feyer cares about is me having kids with her! She was probably killed by the same person who tried to poison you, but I didn't catch him, so now someone's dead, and it's my fault." He tried to take a deep breath and rein his feelings in. "I'm supposed to meet with Feyer in a minute. I need to change."

Grenard started to leave but looked over his shoulder. "Do you want me to stay up until you return?"

"Not unless you really think it's that important." Levi waited for Grenard to close the door, then changed out of the rest of his suit and donned his uniform. The fancy black and red clothes were left in shambles. He would deal with it later.

All of the lights in the upstairs hallway had been turned off. Levi crept forward in the dark, feeling the carpet with his bare feet. He was too angry to be bothered to put shoes on, and he didn't think that small details like that would make Feyer any angrier than he already was.

Levi peered down into the foyer from the top of the grand staircase. Everything was dark here, too. There were no dead bodies, no officers, no staff. All was eerily quiet. He continued towards the president's office and knocked on the door, waiting for Feyer's call.

"How dare you challenge my authority, let alone in front of another soldier!"

Levi had barely stepped inside. "It won't happen again, sir."

"It sure as hell won't. And why did Ambassador Alsh refer to you as 'my boy'?"

The young soldier swallowed hard and finished closing the door. He faced the president and stood at attention. "It's a habit he has. He's been calling me 'my boy' since the day he came here."

Feyer wasn't enthused. "He seemed very intentional when he spoke. Why did you tell him?"

"I swear I didn't! I haven't told him anything, even when he asks questions." Levi regretted his word choice immediately.

Feyer rushed towards him, fire blazing in his dark eyes. "What kinds of questions has he asked? Why didn't you tell me this before?"

Levi desperately wanted to step back, but his feet remained planted where they were. "We were talking about family, and he asked if I knew my father, and I told him I didn't!" Levi fiddled with his ring.

"Liar. What did you actually tell him?"

"Nothing! I said nothing. What do you want me to do? I can't lie to him. Every time I do, he calls me out on it. Refusing to answer his questions only gives him answers through my silence!"

"Become a better liar!" Feyer pointed his finger in Levi's face. "Someday you're going to take my place, and you will need to be able to tell a convincing lie, or else you will lose everything."

Levi stood silently, trying to maintain his composure.

Feyer took a step back. "There is the other matter that we need to discuss. I will give you until your twentieth birthday to figure out who the girl of your dreams is and fall madly in love. If you can't do that, I will choose for you."

"Why can't I wait until I'm older?"

Feyer grabbed Levi's shirt and pulled him forward. "I didn't get to wait until I was twenty. You're lucky you get a choice at all. I've been more than fair." He let go.

Levi thought about Callie. He wanted to get to know her more, but the idea was colored by her being picked to come for the sole purpose of meeting him. "But you don't really let me choose for myself. You set up every interaction I have with every girl that walks into this house. You have to approve of them before I can even lay eyes on them."

"Someone has to maintain the bloodline. I've already done my part. Now it's your turn."

Something broke within Levi. He clenched his fists, loathing the man that stood in front of him. There was no freedom as long as he lived with Feyer breathing down his neck. "Maybe I don't give a damn about carrying on the Feyer bloodline or being your successor. I don't want to be a leader like you. I don't want to be a father like you!"

Feyer raised his hand. Levi squeezed his eyes shut.

It was better to hold his ground than flinch. Flinching showed weakness and weakness was not tolerated in Feyers. A sharp, stinging sensation washed over the right side of Levi's face. A warm something dribbled down his cheek, but he held firm. He slowly looked up.

Feyer took a handkerchief out of his pocket and cleaned the ring on his right hand. "I have given you shelter, food, and an education like none other. I have disciplined you so you can become the greatest man alive and set you up to succeed where no one else has. I have given you everything you have ever wanted. and this is how you repay me. You lie to me. You challenge me. You deliberately defy me. What kind of a son do you think you are?"

Levi could say nothing. He was sure that half the world would have jumped on the opportunity that he had been born into. He knew there were people who could claim to have none of what Feyer had freely given him. He should be grateful. Feyer was right.

"If Ambassador Alsh asks how you injured yourself, you will tell him that you walked into a corner of a piece of furniture, fumbling through the dark, like the imbecile you are."

"Yes, sir."

"You're dismissed."

As soon as the door closed, Levi let out a single, barely audible sob. Silent tears slipped from his eyes and stung his throbbing cheek. He gingerly touched his face. One light at the end of the hallway shed a dim light on the deep red liquid now covering his fingertips.

"Shit." Levi wanted nothing more than to collapse to the ground then and there, but he knew he would get in trouble if his blood ended up staining the carpet. He ran back to the suite, thinking about the microscopic chance that Grenard would believe any of what he could say, truth or lie. He just hoped the ambassador hadn't stayed up for him.

He quietly opened the door and found a lamp on. Grenard was sitting on the couch, reading over notes from one of his journals. Levi almost turned back into the hallway, but he knew the Tulku would keep waiting for him no matter how long he took. Levi covered his cheek and darted towards his room.

"What happened?" The spine of the journal crackled as Grenard set it down.

Levi grimaced. "Nothing."

"That is not nothing, my boy."

"I'm fine!"

"Levi, sit down and let me see." Grenard's voice was firm and powerful.

Levi squeezed his eyes shut and took a deep breath. He pulled a chair out and slumped into it, blinking back tears. He avoided looking at the ambassador.

Grenard turned on another light and dragged a chair directly in front of the boy. He gently pulled Levi's hand away from his face and tilted his head back so he could better see the injury. "How did you get this?"

"I ran into a piece of furniture."

"The truth, Levi."

"He hit me." He fidgeted with his ring, now slick with blood.

Grenard simply stood and rummaged through various cabinets until he found a first aid kit. He grabbed a few rags and a bowl of warm water, setting them on the table. He sat and carefully began to wash away the blood from Levi's face. "Why did he hit you?"

Levi gripped the chair tightly. His cheek stung furiously. "He thinks I told you something I shouldn't have."

"He's your father."

"How did you know?"

Grenard grabbed a new rag. "I have suspected for a while now. Was that the only thing you said?"

"I told him I didn't want to be a father like him."

"I can understand his anger, but there is still no excuse for him to act this way." He spent several more minutes patching Levi's face back together before sitting back and examining his work. "It's stopped bleeding, but you'll need to ice it." He sighed, then peeled Levi's fingers from the chair and continued his work. Anger and sorrow, like distant thunderstorms, churned in the Tulku's eyes as he diligently cleaned.

Levi sat unmoving. Who was this creature who would tend the wounds of his enemy? And what had Levi done to earn favor in the Tulku's eyes? He had been snotty and arrogant, short-tempered and impatient. All the while, Grenard stood by, ever calm and kind, waiting for him.

"I don't deserve this."

"What? Feyer hitting you?"

Levi took a deep breath. "You helping me."

Grenard smiled at him. "It's never been about you deserving it. There is a concept as old as time that I believe explains my disposition. It is called Vanyalida."

"What does it mean?"

"Vanyalida means, *I see you, I know you, and I love you*. But it is more than that. It is to see a person for who they truly are, broken and flawed but with immeasurable value. It is to know their struggles and understand their pain. And it is to love them unconditionally. It is how a husband ought to treat his wife, or how someone ought to care for a friend, or how a father should love his son." He finished cleaning the boy's hands.

Levi finally met Grenard's gaze.

"I, too, have been stuck in the same room with you constantly for the past two months. I have been forced to see you and to know you. What I have seen and what I have learned have helped me make one particularly well-informed decision. I have chosen to love you as one of my sons."

The boy began to cry. He wanted to be embarrassed. He had never broken down like this in front of someone, but Grenard had already seen the worst of him. "Why?"

The ambassador rested a hand on his shoulder. "Do I need a reason to love you?"

Levi shook. "*I* need a reason! Why the hell does a Tulku say he loves me when my own father can't?" Rage and confusion ravaged his body. He buried his face in his hands, gasping for air between ragged sobs.

"I'm afraid I don't have an answer for that question, son."

They sat there for what was the better part of an hour while Levi vented all the pent-up emotions from the past nineteen years of his life. There was nothing refined, or dignified, or beautiful about the tears and snot oozing from his face. But Grenard never moved from his side and never judged him. He simply grieved with the boy.

When Levi finally managed to come up for air, his eyes were bloodshot, and his cheeks flushed. He was utterly spent, but some invisible weight had slipped from his shoulders. Grenard offered him one of the clean rags.

The boy took it gratefully and wiped his face clean. He took a deep breath and laughed to himself. "I've never cried like that in front of anyone before."

Grenard chuckled. "Then I'm honored. Vanyalida, son."

Levi smiled.

PART 2

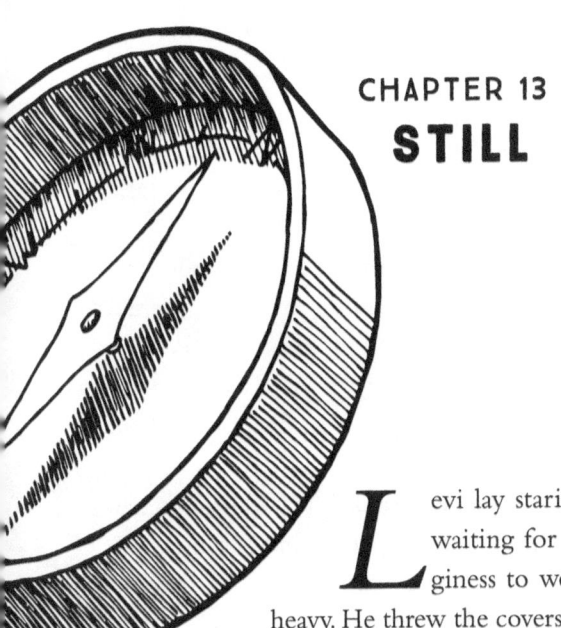

CHAPTER 13
STILL

*L*evi lay staring up at the ceiling, waiting for sleep-induced grogginess to wear off. His chest felt heavy. He threw the covers off and slowly sat up, finding his cheek had swelled considerably and partially obscured his vision. Brisk air hit him as he tugged the cuffs of his black, long-sleeved shirt over his marred forearms. His head complained about the sudden change in altitude.

A glass of water and an ice pack covered in condensation lay on the bedside table. Levi's head complained a little less once the glass had been emptied; the pain in his cheek dulled as he held the ice to his face.

The hem of Levi's gray sweatpants dragged on the ground as he meandered towards the bathroom mirror and examined the cut. What skin wasn't covered with glue and gauze was a sickly blue color tinged with purple.

Every time he had to look at himself now, he would be plagued with the memory of his defiance. Nothing could be done to change that.

Levi gave up on his reflection and wandered to the common area, seeking out Grenard, but the Tulku wasn't in his usual spot. Nor was he standing at the window.

The boy's heart rate accelerated. "Ambassador Alsh?"

Only a faint whispering of what might be wind met his ears. "Grenard!"

"In here, son." The Tulku's voice floated in from his room.

Grenard was sitting on the floor in front of the bedroom's open windows. A strong, early spring breeze blew into the room, ruffling the Tulku's fur. His golden syamta danced brilliantly in the morning light. The pages of an open journal by his feet rustled.

Levi peered into the room. He padded forward and joined the ambassador on the floor. He brought his knees to his chest and rested his chin on his folded arms. The ice pack quickly turned his fingers numb and dripped onto the ground.

He knew the night before hadn't been a dream, but it was still hard to believe it had been real. He wanted to say something, to ask if he remembered everything correctly, or see if Grenard had only said those things to comfort him in the moment, but his voice refused to work. He resolved to be content with the Tulku's silent presence.

Grenard sat cross-legged with a firm grip on his ankles. His eyes were closed, and his ears flat. His nose twitched occasionally in the breeze. Levi watched him out of the corner of his eye. For the first time, he noticed a small scar on the Tulku's graying muzzle. Just like with Callie, he wondered how the ambassador had acquired it and what it meant.

Grenard sighed heavily and opened his eyes. "Levi, I need your help."

The boy lifted his head.

The ambassador flipped a couple of pages over in his journal and revealed a folded packet of paper. "I need help reestablishing contact with my family. I haven't been able to talk to them since I arrived." His amber eyes were flooded with deep sorrow.

A horrible sinking feeling dragged Levi's heart into the pit of his stomach. There was only one person in Erev who had the authority to shut down communication lines. "Have you been able to contact them on your previous visits?"

"Yes."

"Do you have a plan in mind?"

Grenard gave him half a smile. "It involves my unfortunate tendency of going to unsavory places."

———— ''' ————

Levi pulled up to the docks, already on the lookout for unpleasant individuals. Dull clouds had obscured the midday sun and cast everything in a gray haze. The drunken rabble they had run into on that first day did not seem to be out and about, but Levi couldn't help but stay on high alert as the ambassador walked directly down to the wood pier.

A few fishermen tended to their old, rickety boats, checked their nets, and cleaned their catches from the night before. The last boat along the pier, *Serenity*, seemed far older but far better taken care of than the rest and perfectly matched the grizzled, white-haired man in a bright yellow raincoat that was hunched over some electronic device on her panel, muttering to himself.

Grenard stood next to the boat. "Good morning, Monroe."

The man barely looked up from his work. "Alsh, this is no place for ya'." He banged the panel a few times and grunted before he disembarked. He stood in front of the Tulku, frowning.

"I am fully aware, dear friend. But I have a favor to ask." He revealed a packet of paper tied together with string. He clutched it close to his chest for a moment, then held it out to the man in the yellow coat. "I assume Beka still stops by every week?"

Monroe took the paper in a rough, weathered hand and tucked it into an inside pocket of his coat, patting it to reassure the Tulku of its safety. "Aye. She buys fish as usual. They've been askin' if I'd seen ya'. Had t' tell 'em no, but I'll be glad t' give 'em a different answer now." The fisherman eyed Grenard. "Are y'in trouble, Alsh?"

"I'm in Erev, Monroe."

He grunted. "You've just never had t' resort t' this before."

Grenard nodded. "I know. How have they been?"

Monroe smirked. "Oh, I saw 'em playin' in th' waves th'other week. Th'ole crew was splashin' and causin' a ruckus. O'course, Arden was standin' there barkin' orders at 'em 'til Kido snuck up behind 'im an' dumped a bucket o' sand on 'is head."

Grenard chuckled. "I assume Arden didn't take kindly to that." He took a deep breath. "I'm glad to hear none of them have lost their spirit. I miss them."

Monroe nodded and patted Grenard on the shoulder. "I'd expect nothin' less, Alsh. I'll keep an eye on 'em when I c'n spare it. Make sure they don't get int' too much trouble while yer away."

"I appreciate it."

Levi stood by patiently and silently.

Monroe nodded over Grenard's shoulder. "Who's 'e?"

The Tulku waved the boy closer. "This is Levi. Feyer assigned him as my bodyguard when I arrived."

The old fisherman examined the boy with a deter-mined scowl. "Ye' ne'er had a bodyguard before, Alsh." His

eyes were a blue as deep as the sea, framed by leathery creas-
es that had seen many days of harsh sun and many nights of
tumultuous storms.

Levi felt as if he might melt under Monroe's stare.

"Do ye' talk at all, boy?"

"Yes, sir."

Monroe gave a satisfied nod. "Take good care o' the ambassador, ye' hear me, boy? I ne'er met a better Tulku, or a better
man, f'r that matter."

Levi nodded vigorously. Monroe's words weighed heavily
in his mind.

"We must be off. Take care, Monroe." Grenard bowed.

"Same goes f'r ye'."

Levi and the ambassador walked back up to the street that
hovered over the edge of the sea.

Grenard paused as they got back in the car. "I would like to
spend the rest of the day at the Presidential Library since we are
already in town, if that's alright."

"Yes, sir." Levi started the car and wound through the streets
of Rylant. "How do you know Monroe?"

"He sells fish at the docks outside Lassi. He had the best
prices, so I started buying from him. After a while, we began to
talk and struck up a friendship. He's practically part of the family
after all these years."

"Where exactly is Lassi?"

Grenard glanced over at him. "It is located at the northernmost point of Tulanu. It sits between the Great Divide, the Koedi
Ocean, and Votalna Rayne, the volcano."

"Does Monroe live in Lassi?"

Grenard chuckled. "No. He technically lives here, though
he might as well live on his boat."

"Oh." Levi sighed. "Why are you having Monroe deliver letters for you?"

Grenard grimaced. "I would normally just call my family, but my tevet hasn't been able to get any signal through."

"That bracelet thing is a communication device?"

"Yes. Among other things. I can manage my finances, play music, use it as a digital key, track and analyze certain kinds of data, to name a few functions." Grenard held out his wrist and showed Levi the small holographic screen hovering above the silver band. He flicked through various applications.

Levi sat, perplexed at the technology. Humans had never managed to solve the transistor problem. Transistors, the basic component of electronics, could only become so small before quantum tunneling of electrons began to take effect and defeated the function of transistors. Humans had begun research on different materials to prevent electrons from teleporting from one part of a transistor to another, but the research stopped when war broke out on Earth. The past couple hundred years had been spent simply surviving and rebuilding the human race. Technology hadn't changed much for humans in a long time other than what had been borrowed or stolen from the Tulku. And even that technology had limited uses without Tulanu's extensive infrastructure.

The technological gap between Erev and Tulanu was a silent threat that Levi had only ever heard discussed within the walls of the president's office. Feyer feared it, but as Levi watched Grenard's demonstration, he was more impressed than he was frightened.

———— ııı ————

The rest of the day was spent sifting through dry and unimportant legislation. Levi found nothing related to the *Treaty of Riyanti* and nothing related to weapons development. That didn't surprise him though. By the time the sun was casting a rich orange light into the library, he was ravenous, and his mind was numb. His eyes only glossed over the pages and refused to register anything meaningful. Levi yawned as he refocused on the documents in front of him.

Grenard looked up from his work and rubbed his eyes. "Would you like to eat at a restaurant this evening?"

"Are you wanting to go to the French place again?"

"I have another place in mind, but it is in a similar part of town."

Levi shook his head and tidied up his table. "Alright. I'm too hungry to care right now."

Rylant was exceptionally busy that night. The streets were lined with vehicles, and crowds waddled along the sidewalks. Grenard pointed out the tiny hole-in-the-wall restaurant with a flickering sign hemmed in by other, nicer looking establishments. Levi parked at the edge of a sketchy alley and anxiously scanned the streets for characters to match. Most of the folks roaming didn't seem to match the profile. Grenard left the car without a second thought and meandered towards the tiny establishment with Levi on his heels.

A small bell rang as they opened the door to Cafe El Jardin. Unlike La Boulangerie, the restaurant's interior did not match its exterior appearance. Spice swirled about the brightly colored space. Every wall was painted in a different hue, and dramatic art hung on the walls. The chairs and tables were painted with similar, eye-catching artistry.

Most tables were filled to the brim. Two older women were bickering in the kitchen that could be clearly seen from the front door as they worked. A kid waiter with bronze skin and black hair sat on a stool behind the counter. He rested his head in one hand and swung his feet in boredom, staring at the projection of some sports game on one wall. He straightened as the Tulku and the soldier walked up to read the menu, written in chalk on the wall.

The kid's jaw dropped. "You're tall! Are you tall for a Tulku?"

Grenard smiled at the boy. "Yes. Most Tulku are shorter than him." The ambassador pointed at Levi.

Once again, none of the names on the menu were anything that Levi remotely recognized, but they were at least readable and there were far fewer Qs smashed between a hundred vowels. He nudged Grenard. "You're going to have to tell me what to get again."

The Tulku nodded. "Do you like spicy food?"

Levi frowned. "Not much."

The ambassador chuckled. "You'd do fine in Tulanu, but not here." He looked at the young boy. "I'll have the molca jete, and he'll have the huaraches, mild."

The boy pivoted on the stool and addressed the women. "Molca and huaraches guero style!" He spun back around, putting on his best business face. "Is that all?"

"Yes, thank you." Grenard smiled pleasantly.

The ambassador paid for the meal and directed Levi to a table in one of the corners. A soccer game, one of the few sports that had survived Earth, was displayed on the projector. The other patrons were fully engrossed in the event, cheering when their favorite team made a successful pass and booing when the other team got the upper hand.

Their food came out in a matter of minutes, piping hot. Levi's plate had a long, flat piece of bread mounded over with beans, chicken, cheese, cabbage, tomatoes, pickled onions, and radishes. Grenard's dish was a large, black stone bowl filled with rice and several kinds of meats and peppers. Purple-tailed shrimp and a strange green vegetable hung over the edge of the entire bowl surrounding what Levi guessed was a mound of cheese or sour cream.

The soldier readily took to scarfing down his food and absentmindedly watching the game. He didn't particularly understand the appeal of kicking a ball around some people, passing it to others, and ultimately trying to hit it in a net over and over again. It did involve a lot of running, but that was about the only redeeming quality Levi saw that it had.

The game came to a halt as a few commercials began playing. A propaganda reel began playing, but a banner at the bottom of the display read, *Juliette Arthur dead from poisoned champagne at President Feyer's mansion. Police investigation underway.*

Levi sat up as his veins turned to ice. "I think we have a problem."

Grenard glanced up from his meal and read the news banner, then returned to his bowl. "Indeed."

Levi kept his voice low and tried to not draw any attention. "What do we do?" He picked up his fork and forced himself to eat another bite, though he had lost his appetite.

"We stay calm and finish our meal. Then we head back to Feyer's. There is nothing to do but stay alert." The Tulku's demeanor didn't change as he continued to chip away at his meal.

The propaganda reel ended, and a woman in a formal blouse appeared on the projection, tapping a set of papers together in a sophisticated manner. "Good evening. I'm Bailey Fletcher with a shocking story still unfolding. Last night, eighteen-year-old Juliette Arthur was poisoned while attending a masquerade at

President Feyer's mansion. Initial police reports indicate traces of cyanide were found on the glass she was drinking from. One set of fingerprints was identified as Tulkish. While it has not been determined who the Tulku was, witnesses have divulged that there was only one Tulku present in President Feyer's home yesterday evening."

"Shit. I hate the media." Levi's fork clattered against his plate.

Grenard tapped Levi's shin with his foot. "Maintain your composure, my boy."

"Sorry." Levi picked up his fork.

By that time, the other patrons had quieted significantly. Their conversations had died down to whispers as they cast worrisome glances between each other and the Tulku. The hair on the back of Levi's neck stood on end as he tried to ignore the news and focus on his surroundings.

The soldier pushed his plate away. "I don't think I'm hungry anymore."

"Shall we head back?"

The young boy came up to their table with a pitcher of water. He eyed the Tulku curiously. "You're the Tulku in the news, aren't you?"

The room fell silent. Even the two women in the kitchen had wiped their hands on their aprons and stood just behind the counter, watching cautiously.

"Why do you want to know, my boy?"

The kid shrugged. "I need to know if I should call the police on you."

Grenard smiled. "Brave soul, you are." He fiddled with his satchel for a moment. "If President Feyer was concerned about my being guilty of Juliette Arthur's death, I expect he would have already had me arrested. Instead, he has allowed me to continue my work in peace. If he truly is a good leader, I wouldn't expect him to want a suspected murderer to roam his streets. Does that answer your question?"

"Yes."

Grenard counted out a few bills and handed them over to the boy. "The food was delicious. Tell your abuela thank you."

The young boy took the bills and nodded silently.

Grenard redirected his focus to Levi. "Shall we?"

"Yes, sir."

CHAPTER 14

INJURIES

L evi and Grenard stepped out into brisk night. A harsh breeze stole their warmth as they trudged down the street. A select few streetlights illuminated the road, creating intermittent patches of pavement out of the darkness. Most flickered, casting strange shadows in deep corners. Dark alleyways and dimmed store fronts stood at their right. A few late-night stragglers and their buddies huddled in doorways, smoking and drinking. They glared as the pair passed by. Levi hated the inconsistent lighting. Haunting figures loomed in the shadows, and he wanted a mental account of every one of them.

A few shapes peeled out of the night and followed behind Levi and the ambassador. The soldier could hear their worn shoes scraping against the concrete. The last dark alleyway was just up ahead, and Levi hoped, if they made a mad dash, that they could outrun their pursuers.

"Grenard, we should ru—"

Sudden pain shot through Levi's head. The world spun around him, and he felt someone grab his arm roughly. The last few lights along the street disappeared around a corner. He barely managed to keep his feet under him. He yanked his arm free and came face to face with a heavyset, bearded man. The man swung a boulder-sized fist at the soldier's head and narrowly missed as Levi ducked out of the way.

An inhuman cry pulled the soldier's attention back to the street.

Two others had gone after Grenard and knocked him off his feet. One was pulling the Tulku into the alley while the other smacked a metal bar in his hands and grinned cruelly. Levi started for the man with the bar, but gnarled hands threw him backwards to the ground.

Levi's lungs froze. He tried to make them move, to expand, but they refused. He scrambled forward and grabbed the pant leg of the man with the bar.

A boot made vicious contact with his side, but Levi only held on tighter, pulling the man with the bar off balance. The bar clattered to the ground. Levi clambered forward and grabbed it. He swung hard and clocked his first attacker in the head. The heavyset man fell to the ground, unconscious. Levi felt weak. His lungs still wouldn't work.

A second set of hands pulled Levi up off ground and slammed him into a brick wall. There was still no air. The soldier's chest was paralyzed. He couldn't breathe! Panic slowly sank in as the second man wrapped calloused hands tightly around his throat. Levi dropped the bar and clawed at the hands that blocked his airway. He tried desperately to pry the man's fingers off, but his vision was starting to blacken at the edges.

Glass shattered on the pavement beyond Levi's sight, and a strangled cry rose behind the man with calloused hands.

"Let go of the boy." Grenard pressed a shard of glass against the man's throat, teasing a drop of blood from his neck.

Fear flooded the attacker's eyes, though his facial expression remained hard and cruel. "Why would I do that?"

"You risk having your artery severed and bleeding out before anyone would be able to call for help. That, and if you do not take this offer, you would not be likely to survive hand-to-hand combat against me. I was the top fighter in my class in the military."

The man slowly released his grip, holding his hands up and stepping back carefully. As soon as Grenard removed the glass from his throat, the man bolted from the alley.

Levi slumped to the ground, gasping and coughing. He could barely keep himself stable on his hands and knees. The world refused to stay put. Everywhere Levi looked, everything moved. A firm, but gentle hand grabbed him under the arm and pulled him to his feet.

"Come on, son. We have to go." Grenard's calm voice was comforting in the confusion.

Levi let the Tulku guide him back to the car with the world jolting uncontrollably around him. The cool metal of the car soon greeted his hands. Grenard opened the door and deposited Levi in the passenger seat.

"I need the keys, Levi."

The soldier patted his pockets and pulled out a hard device from one of them. He handed it over to the Tulku. Grenard slammed the door shut, then took the driver's seat. The car started instantly and peeled away from the curb.

The passing lights made Levi nauseous. He gripped the door handle, trying to not hurl. He opened his mouth to talk, but his throat ached terribly and denied him words. He coughed violently instead, doubling over with pain.

Several minutes passed before Levi's head settled down enough that he could think again. He slowly sat up and made a second attempt at vocalization. "Injured?" The word came out somewhere between a croak and a whisper.

Grenard glanced at him. "I'll be fine."

"Thank y—" Levi fell into another coughing fit. He grimaced and clutched at his swollen throat. Tears squeezed from the corner of his eyes.

"Stop trying to talk, Levi. You might cause more damage!" Grenard's voice was riddled with concern.

"Learn…drive…whe—" The boy's throat ceased to function.

"I mean it, Levi! Please just wait until we get back to Feyer's."

The soldier nodded and tried to keep from hacking again.

The rest of the drive was silent. Levi resorted to staring out the window. All three of Rufosia's moons floated in the sky, peeking out from behind the clouds that had hidden them earlier. They doused the ground in eerie, silvery light.

Grenard parked outside the mansion, breathing a sigh of relief and opened the door. He swung his feet out and stood, only to collapse to the ground. "Tof!"

Levi tore out of the car and rushed to the Tulku's side. Grenard lay on the gravel holding his left leg, growling in pain. The soldier put the ambassador's arm over his shoulders and hauled Grenard up to the suite. He helped the Tulku to the couch, where Grenard clutched his leg and squeezed his eyes shut. There wasn't any obvious bleeding, but Levi feared the damage was extensive. He filled a bag with ice and dragged a chair over to the ambassador. The Tulku painfully, and gratefully, propped up his leg and covered it with ice.

"Talk yet?" Levi's throat throbbed.

Grenard scowled. "No. Grab your journal. You'll have to write everything out to me for the time being."

Levi sighed and went to retrieve his journal. He knew the Tulku was right. He begrudgingly turned to the first new page and scribbled out a message. *Only injury?* He pointed to the ambassador's leg.

Grenard nodded. "The only major one, thankfully." He sighed. "We should get some medical attention—"

Levi glared. "No."

"Why not, my boy?"

"I said no!" He began coughing violently.

"Very well." Grenard wore exhaustion like a thick blanket. There was no more fight in him for the night.

Levi tossed the journal on the coffee table, melted into the sofa next to Grenard, and let himself feel the full brunt of his injuries. His head, face, and neck were raging fires. His ribs refused to expand. Where the bearded man had gripped his arm was tender. Everything ached. Every single little muscle. He let his eyes close and let his chest fall with his energy level.

"I have a story for you."

Levi pried his eyes open and looked at the ambassador.

Grenard readjusted his leg. "I probably should have told you a while ago." He started to speak, then hesitated.

Levi had never seen the Tulku unsure of himself.

"The Council was sending Vanyani and me to the southernmost part of Tulanu for work. I don't remember why they were sending us to Syadati. It was probably for some trade related issue…"

Grenard paused, then shook his head. "It takes a full day to travel from Lassi to Syadati on the velo-train, so we had gotten up at five in the morning, boarded the train by six, and were well on our way. It was just going to be a standard day of traveling for us. We arrived in K'nanu around four in the afternoon, where a few humans boarded. It wasn't anything unusual. There are several groups of humans throughout the south that have been there for generations, since your ancestors first came here. They use public transportation like the rest of us…"

Grenard began playing with the edge of his katom. "We only had about five hours left with one stop in Vaita. I was sitting in the aisle up until that point, but Vanyani offered to take it so I could enjoy the sunset."

His voice broke, and his lip trembled. "I should have never switched with her."

The Tulku wiped the tears from his eyes and took a deep breath. "It was the most incredible sunset I've ever seen. There were raging forest fires in the east, and the smoke had covered most of Tulanu. It made the sky a disgusting gray color until evening hit. When the sun touched the horizon, the entire sky lit up with the most brilliant red for several minutes. I wanted to live in that moment forever. It was awe-inspiring to think that something so destructive as fire can create something so beautiful. It still is."

Grenard glanced at the boy as tears stained his fur dark. "I'm sorry, my boy. I shouldn't be putting this on you."

Levi shook his head and grabbed his journal. *I want to listen.*

Grenard took a shaky breath and continued. "I fell asleep listening to music… One of the humans shouted, 'Death to the Tulku!' and woke me up. When I looked at Vanyani… I didn't even see him stab her." The Tulku sobbed. "She was beyond helping. We both knew it. But I still tried to save her. I tried to stop the bleeding, and I couldn't. She was gone long before we arrived in Vaita."

A tear slid down Levi's cheek. He felt powerless. He could do nothing to comfort the ambassador. There was nothing he could do to bring Vanyani back. Anger and shame seethed inside him. He hated the man who had taken Grenard's wife from him.

What happened to the human?

Grenard read the note and hesitated again. "The other pas-
sengers restrained him and disarmed him. He was arrested as
soon as the train stopped in Vaita. I had to testify against him.
Anthony Pearson was his name. He was convicted for first-degree
murder. I condemned him to death in that trial. I stole the rest
of his life away from him because he stole everything from me.
He stole everything from my children, and he destroyed Tulanu's
most respected leader."

Levi thought about the story for a long time. He watched
silently as grief and fury washed over the Tulku. He couldn't
blame Grenard for hating humans, but the Tulku had given him
a chance, taken him in, and saved his life.

I understand why you waited to tell me.

Grenard nodded and sniffled.

They sat in complete silence until the three moons had
fallen into view and the clouds had cleared, revealing a heaven
flooded with stars. Grenard turned off the lights from where he
sat, and the two stared out the window. There was some strange
peace that filled the room as they digested the events of the day.

The Tulku groaned as he slid his leg off the chair. "I'm off to
bed, my boy. You should be, too." He stood on one foot and limped
to his room, clinging to everything within reach for support.

Levi sat a moment longer, listening in case the ambassador
fell again. When he didn't hear anything, he trudged to his own
room and got ready for the night. He peeled back the sheets
of his bed but stopped. A faint glow still came from the Tulku's
room. He walked to the ambassador's door and peered in.

Grenard was fast asleep on top of the covers with the lamp
still on. A blanket lay draped over the end of the bed. Levi took
it, spread it over the Tulku, and turned the lights off.

CHAPTER 15

SECRET IDENTITIES

*I*t was less than five minutes between when Grenard requested a medic and when a petite woman in scrubs showed up at their door carrying a bag much too large for her short stature. Her mousy hair was pulled back in a tight ponytail. She marched into the suite with outright determination and made a beeline for the lame ambassador with his leg propped up, covered in ice packs.

Levi breathed a sigh of relief that the medic hadn't taken much notice of him. He snuck into his room while the woman was looking away and began tidying needlessly. He straightened his bedding three times over while he listened in on the medic's conversation with Grenard.

"You don't have a fracture. The bone is just bruised. Give it one to three weeks to heal. Keep it elevated and ice it, and don't walk on it. You should be fine."

"Thank you."

Levi heard her shuffling things around and passed by his door to confirm that she was packing up. Grenard looked up at the boy. Levi immediately ducked out of view, bracing himself.

"Excuse me, would you mind tending to my friend who is hiding out in the other room?"

"Sure."

Levi peeked out of his room and regretted it. The medic spotted him and came after him like a bloodhound on the scent of a rabbit. Wide-eyed, he backed away from the woman.

The woman studied Levi closely for a moment. "What injuries do you have?"

"I'm fine." He was barely audible.

"You clearly aren't. Would you please sit so I can examine you?"

Levi shook his head and withdrew deeper into his room. She chased after him, trapping him in the far corner.

"Sit down already!"

Her fingers were icy against his skin as she pulled at the collar of his shirt. He batted her hands away repeatedly, leaving them both flustered and scowling. After one final attempt, Levi grabbed the woman's arms and pinned them to her sides and pushed her back a few steps. He let go and crossed his arms.

The woman's cheeks had grown bright red, and her hands rested on her hips. Her lips were pursed in utter distaste for his lack of cooperation. "Would you stop fighting me? I'm trying to help you!"

"I'm fine." He barely managed to squeak out the words without sending himself into a coughing fit. He tried to move past her, but she stepped in his way.

"You were strangled. I can clearly see the bruising on your neck. That can be a serious health risk. You need to let me examine you."

"No!" Levi broke out coughing after his nearly silent outburst. He shoved past the medic and slumped on the couch, flipped his collar up on his uniform, folded his arms across his chest, and scowled. He avoided the Tulku's unenthused stare and looked out the window. He didn't want to be touched. He didn't want to be poked and prodded. He didn't want to be exposed.

The medic followed him with an equally foul glare. She stood in front of him. "Are you done yet?"

Grenard cleared his throat. "I will keep an eye on him. Thank you for trying."

She huffed. "He really should go to the hospital. Both of you should have gone to the hospital last night."

Grenard nodded. "I understand."

"No, I don't think you do."

"Madame!" Grenard scowled fiercely. "You will have to forgive me, but I was not thinking perfectly logically after having been attacked by three men and nearly losing both our lives to them. My immediate thought upon pulling both of us out of that alley was to head for a safe place, and I didn't think that a Tulku going to an Erev hospital with a half-conscious soldier would be the best decision. Maybe I was wrong, but I didn't feel like risking my life or his more times than necessary last night."

She paused and threw her hands up. "Fine. But if he dies from a stroke or a heart attack in the next couple of days, it is not my fault." She grabbed her bag and left the suite.

Levi's heart pounded as he watched her leave. He didn't think it was that serious. He returned to gazing out the window. He didn't even have to look at the Tulku to feel the frustration oozing from his companion. The soldier didn't budge. He just stewed in his exasperation.

"Why didn't you let her examine you?"

"Don't like being touched. Don't like being seen." Levi's raspy voice sparked a fire in his swollen throat.

"I'm not sure I fully understand, my boy. I can see you just fine right now."

Levi propped his elbows on his knees and held his head in his hands. How could he make the Tulku understand without giving everything away? He glanced at Grenard and was met with a compassionate, though still frustrated gaze. Levi sighed and ran his fingers through his hair. He looked at Grenard's clothing. He couldn't fathom how wearing so little didn't bother the Tulku. "Vyata, katom, too exposed. Don't want to be seen." He wheezed out a terrible, dry cough.

Grenard's curious expression didn't change much with Levi's expanded explanation. The soldier crossed his arms as he sank deeper into the couch. He just wanted the Tulku to stop asking questions.

Grenard started to speak, but an unexpected rapping at the door barely saved Levi from having to explain himself a third time. He breathed a sigh of relief until he opened the door. His eyes went wide. It was his tutor.

Mr. Miller was a silver-haired shrimp of a man and heavy-handed when it came to lecturing Levi. His round glasses did little to disguise his beady eyes, and he had an air about him that told everyone who saw him that he expected nothing less than perfection and sophistication. He was Feyer's ideal tutor.

He took a poised step into the suite with his nose upturned. He frowned at the wounded Tulku. "You must be Ambassador Alsh."

"You presume correctly."

"I'm afraid I must ask you to leave. Levi has a mathematics examination, and he can't afford to be distracted."

Levi had completely forgotten about his test until that moment. The past two days had wiped all concern for studying from his brain. He was in no way prepared or in a mindset to think about triple integrals.

Grenard smiled politely. "I cannot move of my own accord at the present moment. Doctor's orders. And President Feyer has made it very clear that I am not to leave Levi's sight. But I can promise that I will not be a distraction. Education is highly valued by the Tulku, and the importance of being able to accurately demonstrate one's knowledge and understanding cannot be understated."

Levi grinned at Grenard. He figured having the one person who had managed to teach him effectively in the room with him would be to his advantage.

Mr. Miller sneered. "Very well." He cleared off the kitchen table, haphazardly piling all of Levi's belongings on the coffee table.

Levi eyed Grenard anxiously. The Tulku smiled and gave him a reassuring nod as the tutor laid out the test. Once Mr. Miller was satisfied with the setup, he gave Levi the all-clear. The boy sat down, took a deep breath, and flipped to the first page, hoping his mind had managed to retain any sense of three-dimensional shapes and their volumes.

There were six problems. Of those, only three were in polar coordinates. Levi attempted to refresh himself on the three problems that didn't involve radians, theta, beta, and whatever other absurd variables that existed. All that he had learned slowly came back to him as he trudged his way through the first problem.

"Feyer expects you will do well on the test." Mr. Miller paced back and forth in the empty space between Levi and Grenard. He wasn't even looking at Levi as he strutted about.

Levi rested his head on his hand, but the squeaking of Mr. Miller's leather shoes and the *click-clack* of his pacing were impossible to block out. He tried to refocus on the exam, but his concentration had been shattered and his train of thought derailed. He backtracked and tried to interpret his own algebra.

Squeak. "I hope you studied like you ought to." *Click. Clack. Click. Swivel. Squeak. Clack. Click. Clack.*

Levi scowled and ran his fingers through his hair. He clapped his left hand over his ear, desperately trying to reduce the sound waves entering his brain. But a horrible sinking feeling wedged its way deeper into Levi's mind with each of his tutor's steps. He hadn't studied like he should have. In fact, he hadn't managed to study more than an hour in the past several days. It would show in his grade. He rubbed his eyes and tried to finish the first problem for the third time.

"Fey—"

"Pardon the interruption, good sir, but I'm afraid I am having a hard time focusing on my work. I hate to be rude, but would you mind not talking or pacing for the time being?" Grenard smiled at the man, tablet and journal in hand.

Levi couldn't help but smile as he watched his tutor gape like a fish out of water. After a moment's hesitation, Mr. Miller deflated and seated himself on the couch opposite the Tulku without another word. Grenard winked at the boy, then returned to his work.

The rest of the test went smoothly and silently. Levi set his pen down, optimistic that he had, at a minimum, not failed. Mr. Miller scooped up the materials and exited the room in a flustered hurry.

Levi sighed and slumped in his chair. The test was over. He glanced at the messy pile of papers, notebooks, and textbooks on the coffee table. He tidied them and moved them back to the table.

"Your tutor is certainly interesting."

Levi nodded as he smoothed out several creased papers and situated them neatly between the pages in one of his textbooks.

Grenard set his tablet aside. "Why don't you get your journal?"

Levi complied and had already written out a question for the Tulku by the time he sat on the couch next to him. He showed the message to Grenard. *Why don't the Tulku wear black? You never told me.*

The ambassador huffed. "It's a bit of a long story."

I'll listen. Levi faced the ambassador and sat cross-legged, eagerly waiting for the answer.

Grenard grinned at the boy. "About one thousand years ago, the Tulku were engaged in Ka'i'veta Kizo, the War of Bitterness. It lasted a hundred and seven years. During that war, King Zhebon had two children born with Hjaniyalu, the syamta of the Tulku kings. K'thanu was Zhebon's firstborn and Bek'en was his last-born. Because no generation before or since had seen Hjaniyalu appear in multiple siblings, there was a bit of chaos. K'thanu and Bek'en both took the throne, but K'thanu found ways to limit her power and influence. There are many theories on why he did it, though none of us will ever truly be certain.

"As the war progressed, K'thanu made several critical mistakes that nearly cost my people everything. Bek'en went behind his back and intercepted several of his messages and orders that likely would have ended Tulanu. She then made her own orders and changed the tide of the war. When he found out what his sister had done, K'thanu grew resentful towards Bek'en, he tried to cast her out, saying she had been a traitor to her people, but by then, most of the Tulku with any influence knew better than to trust K'thanu.

"After the war ended, a council formed to decide the fate of Tulanu. They were divided between restoring Bek'en to her rightful throne while removing K'thanu, or simply getting rid of the monarchy altogether. Bek'en pushed to abolish the monarchy and instead be governed by elected leaders."

Grenard paused. "I'm sure you're wondering what all this has to do with the color black."

Levi smiled and nodded.

"Black was only ever worn by the royal family and those who advised the king. When the monarchy was abolished, black was more or less banned from being worn, partially out of respect for what once was but mainly to reject K'thanu's corrupt ways.

"My people, in many ways, still fear having only one leader. They don't want to give history a chance to repeat itself. But most do not realize that King K'thanu was never meant to rule by himself. The syamta had dictated that he was always meant to rule with his sister, not rule over her. That was his biggest mistake that ultimately cost him everything."

The concept of the syamta still seemed strange to Levi. He scribbled furiously in his journal. *How does the syamta choose people to rule if they are just lines? Is it just by chance?*

Grenard read over Levi's questions. "The syamta are not just lines that show up because of genetics, if that's what you're asking. There are certainly patterns that it tends to follow, but everyone can be surprised by the syamta. Zhebon having two children with Hjaniyalu is just one example. Generally, Hjaniyalu only shows up once in a generation, if that. It has skipped up to four generations at a time, but it has only shown up twice in a generation one time."

Can they ever be wrong about someone?

"No, the syamta can never be wrong about someone. They tell us who we are capable of becoming, not who we end up as. K'thanu was always capable of being a good king, but Bek'en was supposed to be there to balance him out. When he denied that, the scales tipped, and he failed."

I still don't understand how they work.

The Tulku laughed. "Neither do I, my boy. No one really does."

What does the king's syamta look like?

Grenard studied Levi for a minute, then slowly pointed to the swirling, golden design above his heart. It looked as if a flame rested there and spiraled outwards, extending across his entire chest and over his shoulder.

Levi's eyes grew wide.

The Tulku gave him a nervous half smile.

Levi's mind swarmed with thoughts, questions, and emotions that he didn't know what to do with. He ran his fingers through his hair, trying to make heads or tails of everything that had happened during the past three days. It was outrageous. He slowly pieced together all he had learned in the last two months. His reality had become perfectly absurd in a matter of moments. He wondered if he was walking through a strange dream or hallucinating, because something about being taken in by the Tulku's rightful king as a son just seemed more fantastical than plausible.

Regardless of what was true and what was fiction, Levi knew that the Tulku cared for him, just as he cared for Grenard. If that wasn't the case, Levi figured he would have been left for dead the night before in the rank back alleys of soggy, downtown Rylant.

"Levi?"

The boy looked up.

"Do you think Feyer would mind if we borrowed a few books to read? I don't expect either of us will want to get out much after last night's incident. And I'm not sure I want to wrangle any interviewees until suspicions have died down."

Levi grinned. He knew of several books he thought might entertain the ambassador.

———— ··· ————

Levi came to the end of a rather dark hallway on the third floor and stopped in front of the second-to-last door. It felt strange to approach his own bedroom. It was his, and yet, as he stood there, this room was no longer his sanctuary. He had had no desire to return here in weeks, no reason to seek complete solitude. He grabbed the handle and entered.

The room was a small space compared to the suite he had been sharing with Grenard. It contained all he had ever really needed. Bed, dresser, desk, and chair were all exactly as he had left them, with the exception of being covered in a fine layer of dust. The light that seeped in through the window was cold and lifeless, leaving everything some variation of gray. The air was stale and stuffy.

Something about two months of distance suddenly made the once familiar and safe space now feel like a prison. Levi eyed his desk where several novels were stacked neatly from largest to smallest. He had read those stories over and over again, entranced by the worlds they contained. They had been a glorious escape for years.

Levi approached the books and blew the dust from their covers. There was still some life left in them, some color and feeling. He grabbed them all and left his room without looking back.

Levi plopped the books on the coffee table within Grenard's reach and sifted through them, pulling one out to hand to the Tulku.

"*Robin Hood?*" Grenard eyed him curiously.

Levi smiled and nodded. "My favorite."

He then grabbed the first book from the stack, not caring which novel it was, and flopped onto his stomach across from the Tulku. He glanced over at Grenard, who eyed him suspiciously and opened the book to its first page.

Levi submerged his mind in the adventures, only coming up for air during meals. There were times he found himself at the bottom of Earth's ocean for hundreds of kilometers at a time, or on the surface of Mars, the fourth planet in the Sol System. He flew through skies on winged beasts called dragons and traipsed through rainy jungles with all manner of strange creatures.

It was during meals and in between books that Levi found himself jealous of the characters he read about. He envied their exciting lives, their widespread travel, and the changes to the course of their histories that they caused. He felt his own life had been anything but exciting, being perpetually stuck in Rylant, subject to Feyer's demands.

However, the ambassador was beginning to change that idea. There was some hope that life would somehow be different, somehow more than it had been, though Levi didn't know what exactly he hoped for.

CHAPTER 16

SECOND CHANCES

The following day, Levi found himself standing in Feyer's office, anxiously awaiting his test results.

Feyer sat in his chair, hands folded neatly on the round table. His disgruntled gaze rested on Levi's neck. The bruises had gone from red marks to purplish-black splotches under his chin. Levi expected no sympathy. If anything, he anticipated a lecture on not having acted fast enough. He prayed Feyer wouldn't make any comment at all.

Jake's expression remained tinged with disappointment as he painstakingly flipped through each page of the exam. Levi feared he had horribly misjudged his performance. Had he failed after all? Feyer eventually closed the test and slid it across the table. The soldier quickly stepped forward and snatched it up.

"Your performance was unacceptable."

Levi carefully turned through his work, scanning for the bleeding pen that usually slaughtered his attempts. But his work had only been nicked, not massacred. He glanced up at Feyer. "I don't understand." His voice struggled to produce sound. "I got eighty-nine percent. Is that not a good score?"

Feyer stood, straightened his jacket and strolled towards the fireplace. "You are incapable of arriving at the correct answer because your execution is poor and you cannot be bothered with small but critical details. Those kinds of mistakes are fatal, boy."

"Yes, sir." It didn't seem fair in many ways. He had been so occupied with keeping the ambassador alive that he hadn't had enough time to study. And to be forced to take the test after having been attacked the night before felt like a cruel injustice. Feyer would not have turned a blind eye to Grenard requesting a medic.

"You will not always get a second chance."

"I understand, sir." Levi's throat blazed miserably, but the mention of a second chance caught his attention.

Feyer growled, staring into the caged flames. "You won't be able to afford making such mistakes in the future. I grow concerned because even after all these years, you still have failed to learn to pay attention. You have failed to recognize how essential diligence is. You will never succeed without it." He faced the boy and looked him in the eye for the first time that evening. "I expect better next time. I expect perfection."

"Yes, s—" His lungs heaved into a coughing fit, enraged at the use of too many words.

Feyer's scowl deepened. "Why did you let yourself get injured?"

Levi returned the frown. "I was entertaining the animal like you ordered." His response burned in his mind. The words. Grenard was no animal, but he dared not give away his opinion of the ambassador to Feyer.

"You should know better."

The soldier dropped his gaze. What could he do? He couldn't protect the ambassador and maintain his studies at the same time.

"May I ask a question, sir?" His heart pounded in his chest.

Feyer hesitated but said nothing. He simply watched the boy.

Levi swallowed hard. His palms grew sweaty. "May I resume my studies after Ambassador Alsh returns to Tulanu?" His brain scrambled for a reason Feyer would not be able to say no to. "I would like to focus on learning as much as I can about the Tulku and politics. Opportunities like this don't occur every day, and I can't study them from a textbook." He hoped he sounded convincing, but his raspy voice made him sound weak and pathetic. He fought back another violent cough, but it sputtered out.

Feyer didn't move. He only stared at the boy as he processed the request. "I will agree to this only if you manage to retake your test and earn a perfect score."

Levi's heart sank like a heavy stone.

"Prove to me that I'm wrong about you." Feyer waved him out.

———'''———

Levi haphazardly dropped his test on the coffee table and collapsed on the sofa opposite Grenard. The jolt made him hack up a storm, squeezing all the air out of his taxed lungs. How would he ever manage to catch all his mistakes? It was a second chance, and Feyer rarely gave him those. But the criteria for success seemed unobtainable. Would he never be good enough in his father's eyes?

Levi picked up the novel he had been forced to part from and tried to reenter the magical world it contained. He read the same page three or four times, his vision glazing over halfway through each attempt. No matter how hard he tried, his focus denied him entry. He slammed the book shut and tossed it on the table. He fell sideways, staring aimlessly about the room as a thousand thoughts assaulted his mind.

He had two courses of action with three possible outcomes: he could try, or he could give up. Giving up was certainly the easier option, but it seemed unlikely he would score better on his retake, and he would have to still continue his studies. If he tried, there was a slim hope he would catch all his mistakes and the prize would be his. He could also still fail.

All Levi wanted was to spend as much time as he could with the one creature on Rufosia who seemed to give a damn about him. He lay on his back and stared up at the ceiling. A tear that had been clinging to the corner of his eye lost its grip and slid down his cheek. He rushed to wipe it away.

Grenard peered over the edge of his book.

Levi sneered. "Don't wanna' talk." His throat screamed.

"Very well." The Tulku set his book down and awkwardly reached for the boy's test.

Levi watched the ambassador out of the corner of his eye. Grenard readjusted his injured leg on the chair and slowly flipped through the exam. A small, pleasant smile slid over the Tulku's face.

Grenard set the test down and looked at the soldier. "That is quite the accomplishment, son. I'm impressed." He resumed reading his book.

The Tulku's comment was only mildly encouraging. Grenard's opinion of Levi would ultimately have no impact on the soldier's life. It was Feyer's opinion that would determine the course of Levi's life and determine his happiness. The thought weighed heavily on his mind. He didn't want to think anymore. He sighed and let his eyes close.

———— ··· ————

Levi found himself covered with a blanket when he woke. A gray, apathetic light seeped in through the windows. 6:19 a.m. His book was where he had left it, askew on the table just out of arm's reach. Levi didn't care. He didn't want to move.

His whole body felt like lead, cemented in place under the warmth of the blanket. He wanted to do absolutely nothing. He didn't want to live. He didn't particularly care to die, either. He just didn't want to exist for a time. He wanted to stay in the detached void until he was ready to come out.

Grenard appeared in front of him holding two plates. "Sit up."

Levi passively obeyed and immediately had one of the plates shoved into his hands. Eggs, sausage, and breakfast potatoes taunted him. As delicious as the food smelled, he had no appetite for it.

Grenard limped as he sat beside the boy. He grimaced as he propped up his leg on the coffee table.

Levi set the plate down and proceeded to wrap himself up in the blanket with his knees to his chest.

Grenard's fork hovered above his plate as he stared at the young soldier before he, too, set his plate on the table. He folded his arms. "What did Feyer say to you yesterday?"

Levi looked away and frowned. He didn't want to think about it, but Grenard had a glint in his eyes that conveyed he wasn't afraid to push. He took a deep breath. "I am incapable. I'm a failure."

Grenard frowned. "I don't see that at all."

"It doesn't matter what you see in me." Levi cast off the blanket and trudged to the windows, staring out at the cloud covered horizon. "It only matters what Feyer thinks. That's the only opinion that has an impact on my life."

"I would not be so sure about that, my boy."

"What happens when you've finished your job?" Levi swiveled and glared at him. "You'll go home to your family, and we'll never see each other again! I'll be stuck here still following Feyer's orders, and if I don't do a good enough job, then I pay the price for it. Just because you think I did fine on something doesn't mean Feyer thinks the same way. He hates you. Do you think that anything you say to him will change him? Because I've never been able to say anything to change him. I can't change him!" Levi doubled over as his chest spasmed and his throat throbbed.

Grenard took a deep breath. His brows were furrowed. "You are right. I cannot do anything to make him change. I understand how difficult the situation is."

"No." Levi gritted his teeth. "You will never understand. No one has ever expected you to be king of Tulanu, but Feyer expects me to become the greatest man in Erev's history. He expects complete perfection. And if I—" Levi hacked up a lung, shaking. "If I can't do that…" He pulled at his hair and paced back to the window before bursting and rushing to his room. He slammed the door shut and sank to the floor. He wished he didn't have to exist, but here he was, existing whether or not he wanted to.

The door clicked. Grenard limped over to him. He lowered himself to the ground, groaning, and raised his arm. Levi flinched away, hiding his face.

Grenard paused, then rested his hand on the boy's shoulder. "I have sixty million people depending on me to prevent war from breaking out." The ambassador squeezed Levi's shoulder gently then removed his hand altogether. "I know how frustrating it is not being able to change Feyer."

Levi unfurled himself and glanced at the Tulku. He sighed. "There are still some things you can't understand."

"What am I not understanding, Levi?" There was a deep kindness in the ambassador's eyes.

Levi hugged his knees to his chest and dropped his gaze. He didn't want Grenard to know. He didn't want Grenard to see. He didn't want Grenard to find out because if the Tulku did find out, he was afraid Grenard would turn tail and run, so he remained silent.

Grenard sighed. "Whenever you are ready to tell me, I'll listen, son." He waited to see if Levi would respond, and when the boy didn't, he pushed himself up onto his feet and hobbled to the door.

"Grenard?"

The Tulku stopped and looked back at the boy expectantly.

Levi's heart pounded in his chest. He deliberated, but as the nausea rose, he gave up on trying to tell the Tulku. "Will you help me study for my test retake? If I get a perfect score, I can take a break from my studies until you go back to Tulanu."

Grenard smiled. "Of course."

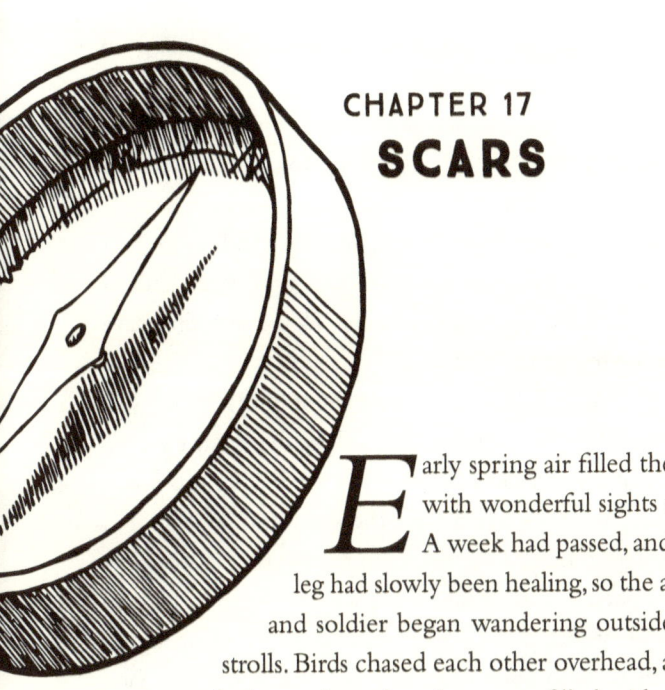

CHAPTER 17

SCARS

*E*arly spring air filled the outdoors with wonderful sights and scents. A week had passed, and Grenard's leg had slowly been healing, so the ambassador and soldier began wandering outside for short strolls. Birds chased each other overhead, and Feyer's perfectly manicured gardens were filled with all manner of colorful flowers. The sky was a brilliant blue, and though the wind blew cold, the sun warmed them to the core as they basked in its glory.

Levi breathed in as deeply as his aching ribs would allow, taking in all the fresh air he could. The urge to run had been plaguing him for days.

"How are you feeling about your test tomorrow, my boy?" Grenard stooped over to smell a pink rose just entering full bloom. Its petals delicately kissed the ambassador's face.

"Nervous." Levi's voice was stronger, and the bruising had faded to a sulfurous yellow, a great improvement from the black and blue hues they had previously taken on. He no longer coughed after speaking at length and the rasp was starting to disappear. He shoved his hands in his pockets as he waited on the ambassador.

Grenard raised his brows and moved on from his rose. "Nervous? That doesn't seem very fitting for the young man who has managed to save my life not once, but twice."

Levi smiled. A gust of wind blew his hair into his eyes, but he didn't mind. "I can't help but think this is all your fault. If you hadn't pulled that guy off me in the alley, I wouldn't have had to take the test in the first place."

Grenard chuckled. "You are quite right, but I prefer you breathing. I can't say that I'm upset about taking the blame for that."

"Does that mean I get to blame you for having too much spare time on my hands when I ace the test tomorrow?"

"Absolutely, though I expect I can readily fill that time."

They laughed as they strolled along a path framed by blooming hedges. They rounded a corner and found Feyer sitting on a bench with an open book in hand. Levi's grin slid off his face. He took his hands out of his pockets and stood at attention. His hair was a mess, but it was too late to do anything about that.

Grenard bowed, maintaining his smile. "President Feyer, what a pleasant surprise! I am glad to know we are not the only ones enjoying this fine weather."

Jake seemed startled as he looked up from his book. "Ambassador Alsh." He closed the book and straightened his jacket as he stood. "I heard you had been injured. I trust you are feeling better." There was a softness to his voice that Levi had only heard a handful of times. His dark eyes seemed light and almost kind.

Levi watched his father curiously. He wondered if the ambassador had managed to work some kind of magic on Jake, just as Grenard had done on him, or if the president had merely been caught off-guard.

The ambassador considered his leg. "I'm still a little sore, but it could have been much worse. You've done a fine job training Levi. I should have been more readily receptive to your suggestion for a bodyguard when I first arrived."

Jake nodded, then glanced at his watch. "You will have to forgive me. I believe I have a meeting I am late for. Please, enjoy the rest of your day." He grabbed his book and strode past them, avoiding any further eye contact.

Grenard watched Feyer disappear into the mansion. He tore his gaze away then took Jake's spot on the bench. "I need a minute to rest, my boy." He surveyed his surroundings and massaged his leg, grimacing.

Levi mulled over the curious interaction in his head, digging the toe of his boot into the gravel. "I don't understand him."

Grenard turned his attention to him. "What don't you understand?"

"You're saying you do understand him?"

"No."

Levi sighed. "I never know how he's going to react."

"Hmm." Grenard sat back, stretching his legs out in front of him.

"If you worked with Anton, you must have known my father when he was younger. What was he like?"

"Standoffish. Bitter. Lonely." Grenard's shoulders slouched, and his ears drooped. "I don't believe Jake had a very pleasant upbringing."

"What makes you say that?"

Grenard frowned and sighed. "Anton was very neglectful, or at least what I saw of him. Jake would constantly ask for attention from him, but Anton would always push him away. The one person Jake was attached to died very suddenly when he was only a couple years younger than you. I don't think he ever really recovered from that."

"What happened?"

Grenard stared off into space for some time. His brows were furrowed, and his ears were flat. He took a deep breath. "I would have been seventeen when I first met Jake. He was nine or ten. Vanyani and I were studying under Ambassador Jeda G'nali and had come with him to Erev to start learning the wonderful game of politics." Grenard gave Levi a sarcastic glance.

"I distinctly remember the first time I saw Jake. We were in Anton's office, and G'nali was introducing Vanyani and me to him. Jake had snuck into the room and was hiding behind some of the furniture. He eventually came out, and you could tell that he was not happy with Vanyani and me being there. He went up to Anton and tapped his shoulder. 'Dad, can we play after this?' Anton told him no. He drooped like a wilted flower and started to sulk away, but G'nali called him back and gave him a small, wrapped box. Jake stood a little taller after receiving the box. He thanked G'nali, then raced out of the room. We quickly learned that G'nali always brought a gift for Jake whenever we came to Erev to meet with Anton.

"I don't think we ever had a meeting with Anton that Jake didn't interrupt at one point or another. He progressively became more troublesome and rasher as time passed, but Anton never really reacted to him. I think the most I ever saw Anton do was escort him out of the room and lock the door.

"During our longer stays, Anton would host the three of us here. G'nali, Vanyani and I would frequent the gardens to discuss matters and be out of doors. Jake, when he wasn't causing trouble inside, would be outside, usually up in a tree. If we ran into him, G'nali would approach him and call him down from his leafy towers. He always listened to Jeda. He would clamber down and stand proud in front of G'nali."

Grenard smiled. "Jeda was not exactly spry, but sometimes he would go find Jake and climb up into the trees with him. They would talk for hours at a time." He paused. "I truly believe Jake loved Jeda and Jeda loved him. Jake was always well-behaved and incredibly respectful towards Jeda.

"About three years after Vanyani and I started training under G'nali, he became incredibly ill during one of our visits. His health deteriorated so quickly that it left him bedridden. He was unable to travel back to Tulanu. We were supposed to go back and attend to a few issues that had come up, but I ended up staying back with Jeda. Vanyani returned to Tulanu.

"Towards the very end, I went into G'nali's room to check on him and found Jake sitting beside him, crying. He must not have heard me come in. I put my hand on his shoulder to comfort him, but I startled him. I don't remember exactly what happened, but I ended up on the ground. My muzzle was bleeding, and Jake was running out of the room swearing up a storm."

Grenard sat in silence, his face twisted in sorrow. He fiddled with the edge of his vyata.

"Is that why you have the scar on your muzzle?"

Grenard froze. "Yes."

Levi now knew the story, and it wasn't what he had expected. He had never known his father to be anything but stoic and strict. To hear that Jake had once wept for a Tulku... The thought was absurd.

"G'nali didn't have any close family, so when he passed, there weren't many to grieve for him. I decided it would be most appropriate for his tyam to go to Jake, figuring it could be the ambassador's last gift to him. When I gave the tyam to Jake, he threw them on the ground and spat at me. I'll never forget what he said. 'The Tulku are no better than humans. You're just animals trying to win my favor, but I can see right through you. You don't really care. You've never cared.' He started to walk away, but just before he completely turned his back on me, he glanced at the tyam, and I could tell he regretted not taking them, but he was too prideful to take back what he had said. I ended up leaving them in his room when he wasn't there. I never learned what he did with them, if anything."

"What are tyam?"

Grenard gave the boy a half smile. "It's one of those vocabulary differences between Erev and Tulanu. Tyam are two long pieces of special fabric that one wears if they are a Vey. Do you know what a Vey is?" Grenard raised an eyebrow at him.

The soldier shook his head.

"A Vey is someone who either holds a position of authority or is born with one of a select number of syamta. Most Veys only ever have one tyam set. For a Vey to have both authority and a syamta, and have two sets, is extremely rare." Grenard sighed. "When a Vey dies, someone in their family is supposed to receive their tyam. Who receives them depends on the kind of Vey the deceased was. If a Vey held an authoritative position, their oldest child, or closest relative, would receive them. But for a Vey who inherited their title through the syamta, the next person with that specific syamta would wear the tyam."

"So, if one of your children had the king's syamta, they would receive your tyam?"

Grenard nodded. "That would be Kido, my youngest son."

Levi thought through the information several times. "You gave my father the tyam because he was the closest G'nali ever came to having a son."

The Tulku nodded again. "I know Jeda loved Jake. He despised Anton for being a terrible father, and I didn't disagree with his assessment, but you can critique your adversary on personal matters only so much when negotiating for international peace."

Grenard dropped his gaze and wrung his hands. "Jake might have ended up being a different man if I had held out a little longer and not given up on him."

Levi's brows furrowed. "What do you mean?"

"He was very trying, and I lost my patience with him after Jeda died."

Levi stared at the Tulku, trying to sort out the story in his mind. He had often wished for a better father, but history had already been written. There would be no revising or rewriting of Jake's or Levi's story. He had often imagined what life could have been like. Maybe Grenard could have made some kind of difference, but none of them would ever know, and daydreaming about a different reality wouldn't help the soldier get through the day.

"I am sorry, Levi." Grenard's amber eyes were downcast.

"It's not your fault." The words slipped from Levi's mouth without second thought.

"Why are you referred to as Feyer's nephew?"

Levi shrugged. "I don't know. He sent me away for a while, and when I came back, he insisted that I was his nephew. No one was ever supposed to know the truth, and if I did tell anyone... there would be consequences."

"Does Thomason know?"

The boy nodded. "He helps maintain my cover and makes it look believable."

"Hmm." Grenard's tail flicked to the side. "Do you ever want him to be your father again? That's a poor way to phrase the question..."

"I think I know what you mean. I don't really know. Most of the time it's easier to think of him as my commanding officer.

He doesn't care about me, and I don't care about him. I just have to do as he says and that's the extent of our relationship." Levi sank into the bench and fiddled with his ring.

"Do you not want his approval?"

"No, I do. I just—it's something I'll never have."

Grenard gripped Levi's shoulder and grinned. "Maybe the test tomorrow will change that."

"Maybe."

After Grenard had rested a moment longer, they returned to their suite, where Levi dedicated the rest of the evening to a few final hours of desperate studying. By the time the sun had set and the sky had grown dark, Levi felt as if there was nothing else he could review. Even so, he forced himself to complete one last math problem.

Grenard set his work aside and turned all the lights off, save the one Levi was still using. He limped to the window and stared into the darkness. He looked over his shoulder at the boy seated at the table. His usual mischievous grin was plastered on his slender face. "Stars."

Levi glanced up. He didn't feel like finishing the problem. He set his stylus down and turned off the remaining light, joining the Tulku by the wall of glass.

Stars rose from the sea in the north and streaked towards the southwest. The moons were all hidden, and the darkness revealed a cone of stars that fanned out from a point about thirty degrees above the horizon from the main band that defined the bulk of the Alu'evan Galaxy, an elliptical galaxy with unusual spiral arms.

"Night." Levi wondered if he could see the Milky Way from this point in the universe. Even if he could, it would be nearly impossible to figure out which galaxy his people had come from. It would take years to compare the map of the universe from

Earth's and Rufosia's perspectives. And even if it was possible to find some similarities, there was no telling if the Milky Way even still existed as they had known it. For all humans knew, the Sol System might not have formed yet, or it might have been destroyed long ago. The physics-breaking wormhole that had carried humans to Rufosia had left many scientists with questions that would likely never be answered.

"Darkness."

"Fear."

"Feyer."

Levi froze. He didn't know what to think of his father. There wasn't only one specific emotion that bounced around his mind when the name came up. He bowed his head and rested it on the cold glass. "Conflicted."

The ambassador rested a gentle hand on the boy's shoulder. It was warm and reassuring. "Uncertainty."

"Grenard, I really don't know what to think of him. I want to hate him, but I can't afford to hate him." He fiddled with the gold ring on his middle finger and watched the faint starlight bounce off its ragged surface.

"Why do you say you can't afford to hate him?"

"I'm not willing to suffer the consequences for hating him."

"Hmm. I suspect you've already suffered the consequences."

"For not keeping my mouth shut when I should have, or not doing something to his standards..." Levi's voice trailed off.

"Is wanting to hate Feyer new?"

"No."

"But something's changed to make you think about it now."

Levi thought for a minute, then looked up at the Tulku. "I don't know what's changed other than you coming here, but that doesn't feel like a sufficient explanation."

"Maybe it is in its own way." Grenard's amber gaze was reassuring even in the darkness. He glanced at Levi's cheek. "That cut should be healed by now." He let go of Levi's shoulder.

The soldier followed the Tulku to the small table and sat down. Grenard turned a light on, then carefully removed the bandage. Levi's cheek was noticeably less painful than a few days prior, but the Tulku frowned as the bandage came off.

"Is something wrong?"

Grenard tilted the boy's chin up. "It's scarring." He sighed and let go, sitting back in his chair. "I'm sorry, my boy. I thought I had done a better job to prevent that from happening."

Levi retreated to the mirror in his room. The new pink skin formed a sharp, rippled line just under his eye. It would still take a while to determine just how significant the scar would be, but it was definitely there. It would always be there.

CHAPTER 18

FROM TULANU

The test flew by quickly the following morning. An hour hadn't even passed from the time Levi finished before Feyer summoned him. The soldier stood in the president's office, praying that he had done even a little bit better than his first attempt. His hands grew clammy at his sides as Feyer painstakingly flipped through all his work.

Jake finally handed Levi the graded exam. "One instance is no indication of a trend."

Levi looked down and saw his perfect score.

"This proves nothing, but you have met your end of the deal. Your studies will resume as soon as Ambassador Alsh leaves Erev."

The soldier grinned from ear to ear. "Thank you, sir."

Feyer strolled towards the fireplace and fiddled with a small wooden box on the mantle. "I'm going to Kilivar for a few weeks. I expect a detailed report when I come back."

"Yes, sir."

Kilivar was an uninhabited island in the southernmost part of the Murky Sea. It was the tail end of an archipelago that spilled out into the Navalu Ocean. While Levi had never been to the island, he knew enough to be wary of it. It was a volcanic island. The volcano had been dead for a hundred thousand years, but because of the unique geometry of the mountain, it had not collapsed in on itself. Feyer had set up a secret military base on the island, using the magma chamber and network of lava tubes to hide his activities. Feyer had never directly told Levi about the work being done there, but after eavesdropping on so many conversations, the boy had his suspicions.

"You're developing nuclear weapons there, aren't you?"

Feyer turned and glared at him. "I didn't give you permission to ask questions."

Levi dropped his gaze. "I'm sorry, sir."

"Go back to the animal, boy."

Grenard was pacing wildly about the suite. When Levi came in, he stopped and stared intently at the boy. His ears were perked forward, and his tail swished back and forth. "Well?"

Levi smiled. He held up the exam and showed the Tulku his score. "It seems like you're going to have to fill all my newfound free time." He was relieved both about the test and Feyer being out of town for an extended period of time. It was as if dark clouds had rolled back and revealed a warm summer day.

"I have a place in mind."

———— ···————

Monroe stood at his boat in his bright yellow raincoat just as he had before, toiling over some broken component. It was still early enough in the day that the streets were empty, and it would be several more hours before the bars would open. Even so, Levi kept an eye on the entrance to the docks.

Grenard strolled up to the old fisherman. "Good morning, Monroe."

The grizzled man looked up from his work. "Alsh, I have somethin' for ye'." He climbed over various nets and snatched a package from the helm. He worked his way over the ropes and handed it to the Tulku.

The package was a small box wrapped in brown paper and a pile of letters all tied together with string. Grenard took it lovingly. "Thank you, Monroe. Would you mind delivering another letter for me?"

The fisherman grunted. "Ye' don't need t'ask, Alsh." He held his hand out, motioning for Grenard to hand it over. He took the second letter and tucked it into his coat, just as he had with the first. "I expect t' see ye' in a few days."

Grenard smiled and nodded. "Indeed, dear friend." He took the package and dragged Levi back up to the car. "We're going to the beach."

Levi eyed him. "We're already at the beach."

"Different beach. There is one a few kilometers south of here that is quite nice and secluded."

Levi followed Grenard's instructions and found himself parking at the end of what could barely be considered a dirt road. Tall brush concealed most of their surroundings, but Grenard scrambled through until the vegetation suddenly disappeared and the sea opened up below them. The sunlight sparkled and glittered on the calm waters. Levi stood at the cliff's edge and stared down, straining to listen for the quiet waves lapping against the sand.

"Levi!"

The boy looked towards the Tulku, who was motioning for him to follow. A steep trail led down the precarious slope to a sunny cove, perfectly isolated from the rest of the world. Levi's boots sent pebbles cascading across the sloped ground as he raced to join the Tulku.

Grenard situated himself against a boulder that faced the sun and began to carefully untie the strings around his parcel. Levi wrenched his boots off. He shoved his feet through the still cool sand and took in the salty air. The breeze was invigorating.

Grenard had set aside the letters and opened the small box. He chuckled to himself. "Why am I not surprised?" He held out the box to Levi. "Do you want to try one?"

Levi stuffed his socks in his shoes. "What is it?" He leaned over and peered inside. There were dozens of blue-tinged cream-colored balls in the box.

"They're called Tsevateni, otherwise known as Tseva root-covered geyser berries. They are one of the finer delicacies of Tulanu and my favorite snack."

Levi took one and examined it curiously. "If it's a delicacy, doesn't that mean it's rare?"

Grenard grabbed a few and popped them in his mouth. "That depends on where you live. Zvateni, commonly known as geyser berries, grow in abundance around geothermally active areas. They are incredibly fascinating plants. Given the right conditions, they will fruit twice a year, which is fortunate for me. I would guess that this is the first crop of the year."

"What about the root?"

"Tseva plants are high-altitude dwellers. Given I live in a place that is both at a high altitude and geothermally active, Tsevateni is relatively easy to procure twice a year."

Levi bit into the berry. The cream-colored exterior was crunchy and had an earthy sweetness, but the inside was bright blue and amazingly tart. He had never tasted something so vibrant. He popped the rest of it in his mouth eagerly, savoring the flavors as they melted on his tongue.

"Have you ever tasted anything so delicious?" Grenard smiled blissfully.

"I don't even know how you would begin to describe that." Levi spent a few more seconds enjoying the berry before picking himself up and strolling down to the water's edge. "I'm going to go for a run."

"Enjoy yourself, my boy." Grenard smiled and waved him off.

Levi grinned as he trudged towards the waves. He unbuttoned his shirt and rolled up his pant legs. Cold waves wash over his feet. He looked up at Grenard, who was completely absorbed with reading his stack of letters, then bolted down the shoreline.

Water splashed up around him and the wind blew freely through his hair. The wet sand gave his feet traction as he flew along the beach. He could have run forever. His lungs, which had felt shallow and constricted from being inside for so long, now felt alive.

He felt free. Free to laugh. Free to smile. Free from expectation and worry. It was the kind of sensation that bubbled up inside him and couldn't be contained. It was invincibility and power and unexplainable happiness.

Levi thudded into the sand next to the Tulku, panting and perfectly content. He lay back and listened to the waves come in and out. The sun warmed him to the core. He wasn't sure he had ever felt so at peace before. No studying, no tests, no Feyer. There were no expectations on him other than whatever minor things Grenard asked of him.

When he opened his eyes again, he glanced at the letters Grenard had received. They were written with an alphabet Levi didn't recognize. He stared for a long time, trying to decipher even one word. He glanced up at Grenard briefly, unsure if he should ask a question.

The Tulku set one of the letters down and picked up the next. "Who are the letters from?"

"My family. This one is from Arden, my firstborn. You're welcome to read it if you like." Grenard held out the letter he had just set down to the soldier.

Levi took the series of papers and studied them closely. The characters still made no sense to him. "I don't know how to read it." He held it, deliberating. "Will you teach me?"

"Yes, my boy." Grenard looked around and retrieved a stick from the sand. He began to write out the alphabet Levi was familiar with. "The Tulkish language functions a little differently than English in a few ways. One key difference is that Tulkish is a true phonetic language, which means we have several more letters, but it is easier to read."

Grenard diligently taught Levi for well over an hour. Eventually, the soldier felt he had a solid grasp on the new alphabet. The Tulku briefly quizzed him, and having done relatively well, Levi picked up Arden's letter again. He began trudging his way through the strange characters, slowly picking up speed as he practiced.

Ba,

You have no idea how relieved we all are to hear from you. I'm glad things have been going well so far and that you have been able to learn a lot. I'm also glad to hear that President Feyer and his people are civil if not agreeable.

Monroe told us that you looked well and in good spirits.

It won't surprise you, but I have several dozen questions for you when you get home. I want to know about Erev's culture and society and all the adventures you've been on the past few months. I want to be solving the greatest problem of our time with you, but I can't. I have been continuing my studies under Ambassador Trevanu, but international politics interests me far more than affairs at home. I would much rather be with you in Erev, learning at your side, but I have to trust that the Tulkish Council knows what is best, though I don't like it.

On another note, things at home have been on the verge of being chaotic without you here to keep everyone in line. Zev and Beka, of course, are the main ones helping me maintain some amount of order at the house, but with spring soon to arrive, we are all itching to get outside more and begin enjoying the warmer weather-

I take the previous statement back. We aren't on the verge of chaos. We are fully in a chaotic downward spiral. I'm about ready to tear my fur out. A couple of the brothers just got in a fist fight over who was going to help Beka make the Tsevateni and a plate was broken in the process. (I hope you enjoy them if they ever make it to you.) Why, again, did you and Oma decide to have fourteen of us and then go and adopt more kits into this family? I'm questioning your judgment right now.

I'm sorry, I'm just stressed, and I can't seem to find enough excuses to send everyone out of the house. Except, I need Zev to not be teaching and to be home more to help me manage. He and Beka are the only ones I can seem to handle and not blow a fuse at.

I take that statement back, too. Beka and I butt heads. Constantly. But that shouldn't surprise you. And she is usually right, but don't tell her I said that. I don't need it going to her head. Who knew that being the oldest and having the youngest be right all the time would be so infuriating?

Speaking of blowing a fuse, I can't seem to even sit down and write this letter to you in peace for more than five seconds without something going wrong. Ailu can't find a book in the library, Marko and Kenaz are fighting over wood for the fireplace, Kido is being, well, Kido.

When are you coming home?

I give up. The house is too crazy. I'm finishing this letter in the old tree fort that Beka likes to hide out in. I can see why she likes it up here.

The reality is, we are all safe and haven't killed each other. Yet. We are still keeping up with our studies, and Kido hasn't burned the house to the ground. Oshi has been planning out the garden, which will hopefully be planted by the time you come home. I think we will easily get another meter of snow before things really start to warm up, but I suppose that is just more opportunity to build a few more snow forts and have the last few snowball fights.

We all desperately miss you. I can't wait to get your next letter. I'm going to try to get them all to sit down and write something to you for at least five minutes. Time will tell if I'm successful.

Vanyalida,

Arden

Levi let the letter rest in his lap. He stared at the waves ebbing and flowing as he let Arden's words float around in his mind. He fidgeted with his ring, spinning it around his finger repeatedly.

"Is something on your mind, my boy?"

Levi glanced over at the ambassador. "Did you tell them I was agreeable?"

Grenard grinned. "More or less."

"Isn't that lying to them?"

Grenard scoffed. "No. I have a very high opinion of you, Levi. That may not be your opinion of yourself, but no one ever said we had to agree on how we perceive one another."

Levi sat a moment longer, collecting his thoughts on the letter. "My life is so different from theirs."

Grenard held out the box of Tsevateni to him. "In what ways?"

Levi took one, but he didn't eat it. "Arden makes it sound like it's crazy having brothers and a sister, and maybe he doesn't like it, but I would expect that it would never be lonely. Having people around you to do things like snowball fights sounds like it would be fun, but it's too warm now for it to snow again here, and you won't be around until next winter. I will have had only one snowball fight in my life." Levi smiled halfway. "It's your fault that I wouldn't mind participating in a few more. I just can't afford to get my hopes up." He rolled the Tsevateni between his fingers. "I also don't have a father I can write to." He popped the berry in his mouth, letting it explode in his mouth.

Grenard flipped through a few of the letters, pulled one out, and handed it to Levi. "When we get back to Feyer's, I would highly recommend writing down your thoughts in that journal I gave you." He set the box of berries between them. "And these have to disappear before we go back. We can't have

Feyer finding out we have a Tulkish delicacy with no reasonable way to obtain it."

"I don't think you'll have to worry about that. Feyer's out of town for a few weeks."

Grenard tilted his head to the side. "He's not in Rylant?"

Levi shook his head. He took the second letter and began reading, hoping the Tulku wouldn't ask any more questions.

Dear Ba (otherwise known as the esteemed Vey Alsh),

I'm sure Arden has already thoroughly informed you of the state of our collective insanity, so I will spare you the details from my own account of the events of the past several weeks. But I will say that I am not intentionally trying to "butt heads" with Arden. I just happen to think that there are some things that should be done differently from my very limited but always humble (and correct) opinion.

Just kidding.

Well, only slightly.

In all seriousness, we need your help. I'm sure there are a few things that Arden neglected to mention because he thinks he can handle it on his own.

The Tulkish Council has been asking if we have heard from you recently. Until about a day ago, we have been forced to say no. They think you're either dead or hiding, so your paycheck hasn't been coming in. With all the violence in the south, it has been harder to get materials shipped up here, and prices have skyrocketed. It will be a few months before the garden can produce anything, and we can't live on Kido's hunting abilities alone. I don't know why this trip has been different from all the other ones, but it does worry me that you haven't been able to contact us this time around. Can we share your letters with the Council as proof that you are still alive?

The next issue on the agenda is Zev. I took a break from studying to help him out with his class last week. He's been fighting for Ren to be moved into a more advanced class where he can be academically challenged, but it has gone nowhere. His co-workers think he is giving preferential treatment to Ren because they're both different. Except Seri. Seri is for the change. She wants to move Ren up into her class, but everyone seems to ignore her input. It infuriates me how racist everyone is. You would think that people would respect Zev for being raised by you and Oma. I don't know how to encourage him, and I don't know how to change others so that they see him as an equal.

Lastly, Kido. I feel like there isn't much I need to say on that one. Not hearing from you has not sat well with him. We've hardly seen him the past several weeks with him constantly running away into the woods. When he is home, fights break out almost constantly, especially between him and Arden. Arden gets mad that Kido isn't taking on more responsibilities, and Kido loses it because he doesn't want to think about you not being here.

I don't know what is actually going on over there. Word has reached us that you might have been involved in a human's murder, which I don't believe for one second, but it makes me worried. Tensions continue to escalate, and it doesn't seem like you've been able to make much progress with President Feyer, as civil as he may be. With you not being able to contact us, how can I know that you'll make it back?

We all look forward to your next letter.

Vanyalida,

Beka

Levi let the letter slide to the sand. His heart ached. "I can't promise you'll make it back."

"Nor should you." Grenard smiled at him sorrowfully. "I knew there were risks when I came here. There is nothing safe about a Tulku in the West."

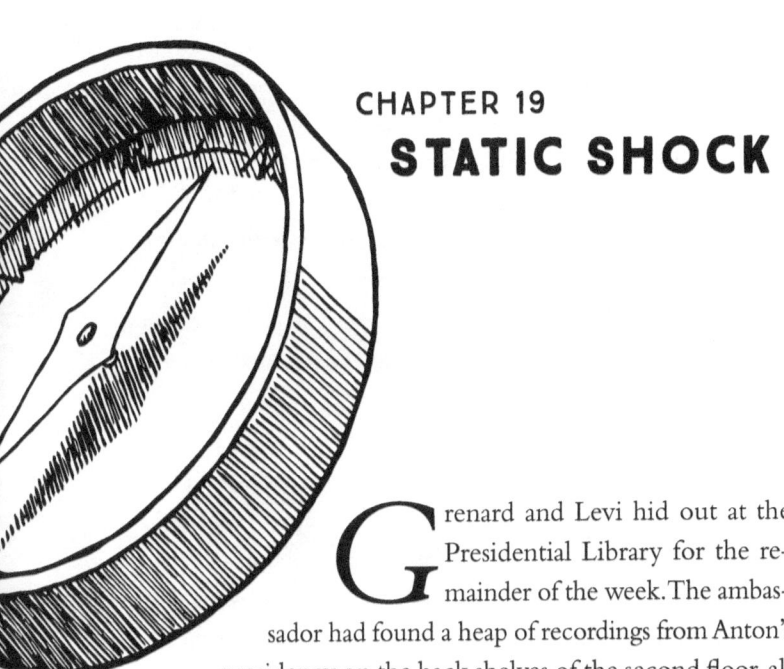

CHAPTER 19
STATIC SHOCK

renard and Levi hid out at the Presidential Library for the remainder of the week. The ambassador had found a heap of recordings from Anton's presidency on the back shelves of the second floor, all contained on finger-sized black drives. Each was haphazardly labeled with the approximate date of the conversation and where the conversation was believed to occur. The Tulku left a few at Levi's table for him to listen through.

The soldier had his journal open to his poor attempts at writing in Tulkish. The letters, while seemingly less complicated than the Earth alphabet he was used to, had to be written out in a specific way and in one stroke. Grenard had hounded him on learning to write properly from the get-go, but the boy didn't have very good handwriting to begin with.

Levi picked up one of the recordings, connected them to his borrowed set of headphones, and turned to a fresh page.

"Good morning, Ambassadors Alsh. It is always wonderful to see you both."

"Thank you, President Feyer. We are grateful for your hospitality as always." The younger Grenard in the recording spoke with more energy and enthusiasm than Levi was used to, but it was the Tulku's voice without a doubt. Levi sat up in his seat, listening more intently to the conversation.

"Just call me Anton. Jeda always did. We don't need to be so formal." Anton's laugh was full and deep.

"Very well, Anton. Then it would only be right for you to call us by our first names. You know I don't particularly like being called *ambassador*, anyways."

"You've convinced me, Grenard."

A third person cleared her throat. "Anton, we would like to discuss a readjustment of some of the tariffs you have in place. Your people are paying a very high price for fundamental agricultural goods, and our people are forced to raise their prices to counter such a high rate." The feminine voice could be none other than Grenard's beloved Vanyani. Her voice was smooth and melodic, yet her tone conveyed no-nonsense determination.

Levi glanced over at Grenard. The Tulku was listening to his own set of recordings and scribbling down notes.

"Ah, Vanyani. Straight to the point as always. I agree, the tariff is too high, but I'd like to get an opportunity to ask you how you've been these past few months. How far along are you?"

Vanyani sighed. "We've been doing just fine since our last visit a few months ago. I don't believe we have much news for you."

"Yes, but shouldn't you be resting?"

"President Feyer, I appreciate your concern, but this is not the first time I have conducted negotiations with you while pregnant. You know that I am perfectly capable of doing my job while in such a state."

"What about the young ones at home?"

Grenard scoffed. "I have my sister watching them, like every other time we've come."

"Doesn't she have a family of her own?"

"No." Grenard huffed. "You know most Tulku don't get married, Anton. Shall we return to the topic at hand?"

Anton sighed slowly and dramatically. "Oh, alright. Tariffs are high, and you think they should be lowered because…"

The conversation droned on for a while with Anton occasionally going off on a tangent and the Alshs redirecting him. The Tulku argued for reduced tariffs because Erev had not managed to get their own farming operations efficient enough to supply food for the rapidly increasing human population. Tulanu could assist in that by providing seed, equipment, and food while Erev's agriculture continued to develop. It was a convincing argument.

They worked well together, Grenard and Vanyani. They would take turns handling Anton's questions and concerns. Vanyani would hound Anton relentlessly until he was on the verge of walking out, then Grenard would step in and humor the president, bringing him back down and seamlessly handing him over for Vanyani to verbally pummel all over again.

There was something mildly enchanting about listening to the duo. It was Vanyani's voice that particularly captivated Levi. She conducted herself authoritatively. She was sophisticated and shot down Anton's constant slights without a second thought. She, much like the Grenard he was familiar with, always maintained her composure. The soldier swore that if he ever ran into a woman that sounded half as confident as Vanyani, he would never let her go. A woman like Vanyani was worth fighting with and fighting for.

The recording with the Alshs ended before they reached any kind of agreement. Levi listened to it a second time, pausing every couple of seconds to write down every question and comment that came to mind using his newly learned alphabet. The primary thing he noted was his distaste for his grandfather's habit to avoid difficult conversation.

When he had finished, Levi began to toss the recording in the pile with the others, but he just couldn't let go of it. He stared at it before shoving the small black device in his pocket. With all his thoughts and hypotheses written down, he picked a second recording from the pile and played it.

"General, I want to start a new military program." It was Anton's voice, but it was not the personable, chatty president he had been in the previous recording.

"I'm all ears, Mr. President."

"I want to start a restricted access program for nuclear weapons development."

Levi immediately stopped the recording and checked the date on the back of the little black rectangle. The writing was smudged and faded, but Levi could barely make out that it was twenty-seven years old. There was no way the information on the recording was declassified, or if it was, it wasn't likely that it was meant to be found by the general public. Levi scanned the library, trying to figure out what to do.

Levi shook his head. If it had landed here, and jumped through all the hoops to be declassified, then it must be. He doubted someone would be so careless as to mishandle information like this. He resumed listening to the conversation, but his stomach still churned.

"Sir, that is against the *Treaty of Riyanti*. That's against our own laws."

"Bah! They're old and outdated. They were put in place to secure a little bit of land. Now that we have that, and Erev's safety is being threatened by the Tulku, it is more than justified. General, we will begin this program, and Tulanu will not know about it."

The general sighed. "Yes, President Feyer. Which base do you propose as the location for the program?"

"I don't want to use an established base. Tulanu already knows where our current military operations are, and they regularly check in on the status of the agreements General Erev foolishly made with them decades ago. No, it needs to be somewhere they won't suspect. I propose an island in the Vutonu Archipelago."

"An island?" The general scoffed. "Sir, with all due respect, you are proposing to start a secret program on an uninhabited island with no resources over two thousand kilometers away. It's insane. How do you expect us to ship massive amounts of materials and personnel there without the Tulku finding out?"

"Fine. I propose Ki—"

A massive burst of static exploded in Levi's ears.

He tore his headphones off as his ears began to ring. The lights flashed brightly overhead then shattered. Glass came raining down upon Levi and Grenard. A putrid, sour, coppery smell filled the air.

Levi rushed to the nearest window. The city stood completely still. All the lights had gone out. Streetlights, stop lights, storefronts, signs. All had gone dark. Nothing moved.

Grenard stepped up behind Levi with a foul glare on his face. His brows were deeply furrowed as he watched small wisps of smoke float up from the city.

"What was that?" Levi already suspected he knew the answer to his own question, but he eyed Grenard carefully.

The Tulku grumbled. "There are only so many causes of an electromagnetic pulse."

"Solar flare?"

"That is one cause, but I doubt it. Tulanu would have seen it coming and warned Erev."

Levi's heart fell into the pit of his stomach. There were two courses of action he could take: he could continue to pretend to be ignorant, or he could admit to what he suspected. Feigning ignorance seemed irresponsible. All the circuitry in Rylant had just been fried. Levi expected it would be the same for the rest of the country.

"Feyer just crippled Erev and Tulanu, didn't he?"

"Why do you say Feyer did this?" Grenard was watching Levi with just as wary a look.

Levi glared at the Tulku. "If it wasn't a solar flare, what else could it be? Tulanu barely has a military, so I doubt your people would be launching an assault like that."

The soldier went back to looking out the window. A hospital a block away was smoking. His stomach twisted into an unbearable knot. He felt powerless. Then he remembered the conversation he had just been listening to.

Levi glanced up at Grenard. "I found a recording of Anton that could be your key piece of evidence." He walked back to the table and picked up the black rectangle. It smelled funny, and Levi deflated. "I bet that EMP just destroyed it. I don't know if it can be salvaged." He offered it to the ambassador.

Grenard took it and examined it. "What was on it?"

Levi shoved his hands in his pockets. "Anton told one of his generals that he wanted to start a secret nuclear weapons program on a remote island in the Navalu Ocean. The EMP went off right as Anton was about to say which island he wanted to use."

Grenard clutched the recording. "Write down everything that you heard as exactly as you can. Then we need to leave."

Levi complied, writing down every detail of the conversation that he could remember. He was grateful to have started learning Tulkish. Feyer wouldn't be able to read anything if he found the journal, making it easier for Levi to hide his betrayal. He only hoped he was doing the right thing. When he finished, he shoved all his things in the rucksack he was beginning to cart around everywhere. The ambassador was rubbing off on him.

They rushed out of the library and found the car. Levi tried to start it. Nothing happened. He tried again. His eyes grew wide as he tried a third time. The engine refused to even turn over.

"Levi, it's no good. We will have to walk."

The boy's chest tightened. "I'd rather not get attacked again."

Grenard grunted. "We don't have much of a choice."

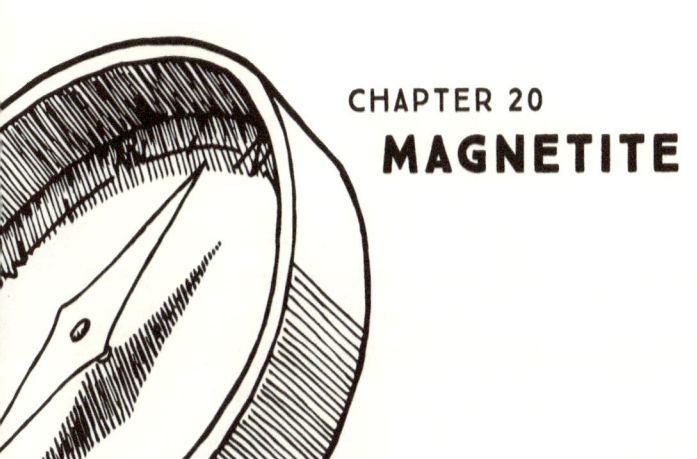

CHAPTER 20
MAGNETITE

Rylant was in shambles as the Tulku and the soldier rushed across the city. Everywhere they went, the air was rank with a sour copper odor. Electrical fires had ignited seemingly inflammable materials on every street corner. Horrible black smoke filled the sky with a miserable, suffocating haze. People poured out into the streets in a hysterical rush, confused and flustered.

Levi stuck to the ambassador's side, keeping himself between the Tulku and the chaotic crowds. His heart pounded harder as more and more people pressed in around them. He felt as if he was going to hyperventilate. "Grenard, I should probably tell you that I was never trained to be a bodyguard."

"I know, son." Grenard stumbled into the soldier to avoid a frantic couple. "Feyer never gave you a weapon to protect me with. That's part of the reason I suspected you weren't just a typical soldier."

"I'm not even a soldier, Grenard."

The Tulku gave him a brief nod as he sidestepped to narrowly avoid crashing into a panicking human.

"You're not mad?"

"Levi, you have managed to still protect me even without proper training or weapons. As far as I'm concerned, you've done your job exceptionally well."

Levi relaxed slightly. "I still might fail you."

"Let's just focus on getting out of the city. Then we can discuss this further." Grenard grabbed his shoulder reassuringly and plowed through the churning and crying crowds.

No one bothered them. No one even looked in their direction.

When they finally hit trees, Levi wanted to faint out of relief that they were both still alive and in one piece. They found the road that led to the mansion and began the long trek uphill. The sun was well on its way to the horizon, and long shadows extended behind the pines.

With the crowds far behind them, Levi's thoughts returned to the hospital by the library. "How many people died because of the EMP?"

"Electromagnetic pulses cannot directly kill people."

"I know that. I'm talking about the people in the hospital: the people on life support, or the people who were just shocked to death because they were attached to medical equipment, or electrical fires causing explosions. How many people were just killed in Tulanu and Erev?" Levi stopped and glared at the Tulku. His heart throbbed.

Grenard paused. "Tulanu's power grid is protected from EMPs. We have been hit by solar flares before. We manufacture our electronics so they are not as susceptible." His ears drooped. "I would expect Erev just lost several thousand people based on how Rylant's power grid held up."

Levi grappled with Grenard's words. He pulled at his hair and paced back and forth on the empty road. "It doesn't make any sense! He goes on all the time about being threatened by the Tulku because there are so many more of you than there are us, but he just killed thousands of our people in a split second. All for what? So he could test a stupid bomb that already destroyed our home planet?"

He grabbed a rock from the ground and threw it into the trees as hard as he could. It failed to relieve the rage he felt deep within his soul. "What am I missing, Grenard? Does he really hate the Tulku so much that he's willing to throw away innocent human lives so he can pursue whatever the hell he wants? Why the fuck would anyone do that?"

He threw his rucksack down and picked the nearest tree. He funneled all his wrath towards it, his knuckles meeting the bark with all the force he could muster.

"Ah! Shit!" Levi shook out his hand. The tree had taken skin and left his knuckles bleeding.

"Levi!"

He looked up at the Tulku. Shame flooded him. Punching trees would get him nowhere, but rage still festered within him. He took a deep breath and walked back to the ambassador, head hung low.

Grenard grabbed his chin and lifted it. "You're not in trouble with me, son. We just have limited daylight left and several more kilometers to go."

Levi grabbed his bag and favored his hand as turmoil ravaged his mind and soul. "How could he do something like that?"

Grenard hiked alongside him. "Might I offer a possible explanation?"

"Sure."

"Have you heard of the concept of a moral compass?"

Levi's teeth were gritted. "Feyer doesn't seem to have one."

"Everyone has a moral compass—"

"Then my father's is broken!"

Grenard stopped and frowned at the boy. His ears were flat against his skull. "Let me finish my thought."

Levi's shoulders slouched. "Sorry."

The ambassador took a deep breath as he started back up the road. "Everyone has a moral compass, but that doesn't mean they all point north. How does a compass work?"

Levi rolled his eyes. "The molten iron core of the planet spins and generates a massive magnetic field with two poles, one north and one south. A compass needle is magnetized by the field and points in the direction of the field lines."

Grenard smiled and nodded in approval. "The magnetosphere is powerful. It is so powerful that it can shield the entire planet from several forms of radiation and high energy particles, yet we don't directly feel its effects. What do you know about magnetite?"

Levi shook his head, irritated. "I assume it's a magnetic rock." He kicked at a pinecone and sent it flying off the pavement.

"Yes. It can become a powerful permanent magnet and can be found in almost any kind of rock formation. In large enough quantities, it can affect compasses, pulling the needle away from true north and misguiding the compass' owner. Life is very similar to walking through the wilderness with only a compass in hand. Most of us believe that our compass is pointing north as we go, but life tends to bring along challenges, misguided notions and temptations that behave much like a magnetite deposit. Our compass needle is drawn away from true north, and we turn astray.

"Those who are more in tune with their compass can see the needle wobble and are able to take corrective actions. They make it through the magnetite and are able to follow north clearly again. Others stumble into the magnetite blindly and flounder for a while. They make many mistakes, but they stumble back out of the magnetite and straighten up their act. There are also people who follow their compass through the wilderness until they come across a mountain or a valley that they do not wish to cross and intentionally turn astray.

"But there are some people who insist that their compass is always correct and cannot be swayed from north. When they come across magnetite, they end up walking in circles, forever stuck, believing they've found north. They might suck others in, leaving masses of people stuck at a false north in a barren wasteland, harming not only themselves but others out of pride and stubbornness. Even if someone tries to take them by the hand to lead them back to north, they either run back to the original magnetite deposit, or when they encounter a new one, they remain there."

Levi rolled the analogy around in his mind as they trudged along. "My father thinks he's found true north. I don't think he has, but how do I know my own compass is pointing north and not at magnetite?"

Grenard grimaced. "That is the question we are all striving to answer. Unfortunately, most of us will never agree on what the right answer is."

Levi waited for the Tulku to continue. When he didn't, Levi probed further. "Grenard, how do you decide what is right and wrong?"

The ambassador sighed. "I cannot give you a good answer. I am not perfect."

"Can you at least give me something to think about?" He stared at the Tulku intently. "Please?"

Grenard's tail swished back and forth as he thought. The Tulku spoke sternly as he eyed the boy. "Use conviction to help you read your compass. It is a powerful tool, but I will warn you that conviction will show you a few things you may not like about yourself. Don't ignore it."

Levi and Grenard made it back to the mansion just after sunset. It was bizarre seeing the chateau fade into the coming night. There were no lights, no glamor, no spectacles. It suddenly seemed a little more ordinary and a little less self-righteous. They walked up to the perron and pushed open the doors.

The foyer was completely dark, and the house was strangely silent. Levi's boots crunched across the glass-littered floor. He squinted in the darkness, trying to make out any significant shapes. The toe of his boot rammed into the bottom stair, and he fumbled his way upwards. Grenard mumbled behind him as they crept through the pitch-black towards their suite.

Levi opened every drawer in the apartment, feeling for anything that could provide light. After endless failed attempts, he searched his memory for any nook in the mansion that might aid them. "I'll be back. I'm going to find candles."

Levi felt along the walls, blindly stepping forward to the other side of the mansion. He came up to the large double doors and, having heard no one else coming, fumbled with the handles and ducked inside. He held his arms out, trying to feel for the table he knew was somewhere in the middle of the room. He walked right into the edge of it. Levi felt along the box apron and stepped around the table until his fingers brushed against a groove in the wood. He pushed on it and heard a small click. The secret drawer slid open.

Levi carefully felt the contents of the drawer, making sure to not move anything from its home, until his fingers met cold metal. He snatched up the small box, flipped the lid off and flicked the wheel. Fire burst into existence.

The small flame cast an eerie glow about the mostly empty office. The primary occupants of the secret drawer were condoms and cigarettes. Levi frowned at them. He had discovered the hidden feature when he was quite young. He never forgot the horror that fell on his father's face when he caught Levi trying to figure out what the objects were. He closed the drawer quietly and made his way back to the doors. He put out the flame and stepped back into the hallway.

A few workers with their own lighters or candles rushed past the boy. Nervous expressions consumed their faces as they juggled their light sources with various hand tools. Levi did not envy the long night ahead of them.

The boy's second stop was a storage room in a secluded corner of the mansion he had not been to in many years. The air was stale as he entered the cramped space stacked high with boxes. The shelves along the walls were cluttered with all manner of knickknacks, decorations, and cleaning supplies.

As a child, he had spent many hours hiding behind all the boxes avoiding his tutor or trying to escape Feyer. He had become quite familiar with the untouched contents of the room. Several large boxes were full of candles that had originally been purchased a decade prior for one of Feyer's dramatic parties. They had never been touched, save the few Levi had used when hiding out. They had been stuffed into the room and left to decay in the darkness after the event had been canceled.

He found a candlestick, and with a fresh candle wedged in it, lit the wick and sat in the middle of the floor. Dozens of memories came flooding back to him. This room had long provided him solace and safety from the outside world until Feyer had finally found his hideout and dragged him out, kicking and screaming. He didn't dare come back after that experience.

Fear crept in around him, seeking to paralyze him with venomous memories. He forced himself to move. Levi slid his rucksack off his shoulders and piled candles and candlesticks in. They wouldn't be missed. He closed his bag and stood to leave, but curiosity pulled him away from the door. He crept to the back of the room and peered behind a stack of boxes. Various drawings, books, and a wooden cube puzzle had been stashed in the nook. Levi grabbed all of them and stuffed them in among the candles, then dashed back to the ambassador.

Grenard was sitting on the floor picking at his foot when Levi returned. "Would you mind finding me some gauze, my boy?"

Levi set the burning candle down and noticed the blood dripping from the pad of the Tulku's foot. He set to finding their dwindling stash of medical supplies in one of the cabinets. "Are you alright?"

"I'll be fine. I just stepped on a piece of glass on my way up here." Grenard took the gauze from the boy and wrapped his foot.

Levi lit a second candle from the first and migrated to one of the couches and dumped the contents of his bag on the coffee table. He quickly sorted all the objects into piles. Candles on the left, the various knickknacks from the back of the closet on the right, and Feyer's lighter next to the lit candle.

He grabbed one of the creased and dusty drawings. He smoothed it out and set it down where he could see. Painful memories came flooding back to him, suffocating him in the process. He crumpled it up and carried it over to the sink where he lit it and left it to smolder. He couldn't face it. He couldn't think about it.

"Levi, is something the matter?"

The boy ignored Grenard and flicked through the rest of the drawings. The suffocating feeling evolved to nausea. He shredded the rest of the paper into a hundred pieces. He dumped the torn pieces in with the ashes of the first drawing and set them ablaze. He watched the flame spark and jump into life as it rushed to consume its prey. It fizzled and left the paper in a lifeless, flaky heap.

Levi peeled his fingers off the edge of the counter as the air slowly returned to the room. He trudged back to his seat and picked up the wooden cube puzzle. He pulled it apart and let the pieces fall into his lap.

Grenard quietly approached the boy. "Levi?" He took a seat next to him, waiting for a response.

Levi grabbed the pieces of the puzzle and began fitting them together instinctually. "How do you know true north actually exists?"

Grenard leaned back. "Do you believe science is true?"

"Yes."

"Why is that?"

"You can objectively test and measure how things work and find something to be true every time. There are universal constants."

"Then you agree that absolute truth exists."

Levi finished his puzzle and glared at the Tulku. "Science and morality are not the same thing. They don't behave the same way."

Grenard raised an eyebrow. "No? Tell me why you think so."

The soldier pulled the puzzle apart again. "Not everything is as cut and dry as science. Morality contains gray areas."

"Relativity and quantum mechanics contain a few gray areas. That does not prove your point that morality is any different than science."

"How are they the same, then?" Levi grimaced as the puzzle fell apart in his hands.

Grenard sighed and crossed his arms. "Is it wrong to lie?"

"Yes."

"Then why do people lie?"

"They're probably trying to hide something that they've done."

"Why do they want to hide?"

Levi restarted the puzzle. "They probably did something that they shouldn't have." He set the pieces down and looked at Grenard. "But what about the times when it isn't clear that lying is bad? What if you lied to protect someone so they wouldn't be hurt?"

"Is it wrong to hurt people?"

"Yes."

"The gray areas tend to show up when previous wrongdoings put us in difficult situations. It may not be clear what is right because that magnetite distorts our perception of reality. It always makes it difficult to discern where true north is. Let me ask you this: if the hypothetical person in harm's way was no longer in trouble, would lying about them still be morally ambiguous?"

Levi paused his fiddling. "No."

"If you could eliminate the initial wrong, moral gray areas would disappear. Wrong tends to cause a cascade of gray over everything it touches."

"That still isn't objective like science."

"Maybe not entirely, but how did you know that lying and hurting people is wrong if true north doesn't exist?"

Levi froze. Had he ever been taught that either activity was wrong? No. If anything, he had been taught that that was part of playing the game called life, yet something deep inside him just knew that they were wrong. He couldn't explain it.

Grenard smiled smugly. "I doubt the world could have made it to this point if it were not definitively wrong to murder or steal. We could have no governments, or laws or cooperation because no one would feel guilty for harming another person. Yet society does exist. You cannot start a discussion about what is right and what is wrong without acknowledging that absolute truth must exist. It is inherent to the debate itself. If moral truth didn't exist, we could not feel guilt, or shame, or anger, or even happiness for that matter. We could have no discussions about justice. Our own emotions are proof that true north exists."

The soldier stared at the puzzle in his hands. He knew he needed to think about what Grenard had said, but the flicker of the flame on the lighter caught his attention. He didn't want his father to find out that he had used it. He knew that if Jake ever suspected, Levi would be tempted to lie to hide that he had been snooping through the president's office.

Levi snagged the lighter and walked back to Feyer's office. He opened the drawer and dropped it in after thoroughly rubbing his fingerprints off the metal surface. He was never supposed to know about the drawer. For the first time, he wondered why it was supposed to remain hidden. Maybe there was something about its contents that Feyer instinctively knew was wrong. Maybe his father was trying to hide the fact that he knew his compass was broken.

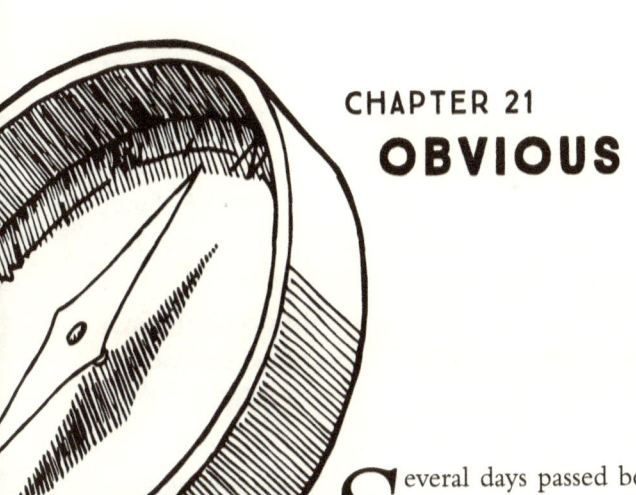

CHAPTER 21
OBVIOUS

*S*everal days passed before limited power was back online at the mansion. Even with power restored, most of the lights had burned out or exploded during the electromagnetic event.

More time passed before Levi looked up from one of his novels and saw his car miraculously parked outside. Someone knocked on the door of the suite. Levi met a gruff, ragged mechanic at the entrance.

The man held a set of keys out to the soldier. "I believe these are yours."

Levi stared at the keys for a minute. "How did you know?"

The mechanic scowled. "I do all the repairs on your car. I saw it sitting in town and figured you might want it back."

"Thank you." The soldier took the keys.

"As a fair warning, about all it'll do is run the engine. I had to tear out all the circuitry and rewire everything. It'll drive differently, too, without power steering."

Levi smiled. "It's better than nothing." He said goodbye to the mechanic then rushed back to Grenard, beaming. "I don't know about you, but I'm ready for a change of scenery." He held up his keys and jangled them.

"Unsavory places, it is." Grenard jumped to his feet and collected his satchel.

The two rushed towards the front of the mansion. A chorus of panicked voices echoed from the foyer. A crowd swarmed around a newly arrived President Feyer, hounding him with dozens of questions. He calmly addressed their concerns for a few minutes before dismissing them. Grenard and Levi weaved through the thinning crowd towards the front door.

"Levi." Feyer waved the boy over.

The soldier obeyed and stood at attention in front of him.

Jake leaned against a table and shifted his weight to one foot. "Meet with me at noon."

"Yes, sir."

Jake nodded solemnly, then limped up the stairs.

Grenard put his hand on the soldier's shoulder, startling him. "Is everything alright?"

Levi watched Feyer disappear towards his office. "I have no idea."

The soldier barely noticed the drive into Rylant. Feyer's request saturated his mind with anxiety. He blindly followed Grenard out onto the docks, stewing in his worry. He fidgeted with his ring and danced from foot to foot.

The old and worn *Serenity* was gently rocking in the waves. Her yellow-coated owner sat in a reclined folding chair with his hat over his face and his clasped hands resting on his chest. Live fish in buckets on deck splashed and fought each other.

"Monroe?" Grenard began to climb on board. He tapped the fisherman. "Monroe, wake up."

The old man grunted and peered out from under the rim of his hat. "Alsh." He cleared his throat and sat up, rubbing his eyes. "Glad t' see you've survived all this madness." He fished in his coat and brought out another packet of letters. "Arden and Kido brought 'em this time 'round."

"Thank you." The ambassador took them and handed over his newest message. "It seems the *Serenity* survived the EMP."

"Is 'at what it was?" Monroe grunted. His white hair flew in every direction. "There's a reason I don't own fancy things. I like bein' able t' fix it myself." He plopped his hat on his head. "She still gave me a good bit o' grief, but she's purrin' now."

"I'm glad. Were they hit in Tulanu?"

Monroe shook his head. "Figured Arden would've mentioned somethin' to me, but no. It seems like everything's still runnin' like normal over there." He stood and patted Grenard on the shoulder. "They're fine, Alsh. I'm keepin' an eye on 'em like I said I would."

Grenard smiled gratefully. "I appreciate it, dear friend." He glanced back at the nervous soldier. "I would stay longer, but unfortunately I don't have the time today."

The fisherman grinned and nodded to the boy. "Most things are a bit more important than an ol' sea dog." He slapped Grenard on the back one last time and settled back into his chair.

The Tulku and the young soldier piled back into the car. Levi gripped the steering wheel with white-knuckled fists. He glanced at his watch. They barely had enough time to make it back before he had to meet with Feyer.

Grenard held onto the letters tightly, playing with the string that bound them together. "Ocean."

"Riptide."

The Tulku looked over at the boy. "Swim."

"Drown."

Grenard paused and sighed. "Cave."

"Trapped."

"Cornered."

"Suffocate."

Grenard frowned. "I expect he just wants to know what has happened while he's been away."

"What if he's found out what we learned at the library? What if he knows you're on to him?"

"If he doesn't already suspect, I expect he will find out sooner than later, but I will not be dragging you into that discussion."

Levi felt sick to his stomach. "I don't want to get in trouble with him. It already feels like I've gone behind his back and betrayed him."

"What have you done that Feyer hasn't already approved in some way?"

Levi glared at the ambassador. "Don't tell me you don't know what I'm talking about." He wrung the steering wheel. "I'm helping you find information on him breaking an international treaty! I'm incriminating him!"

Grenard sighed. "I suppose that is true."

The rest of the ride was deathly silent. Levi deposited the ambassador at the suite and hurried to the large double doors that divided him from an uncertain future. He was two minutes late. He brushed his messy hair into a semi reasonable state and knocked.

A smug officer opened the door and let him in. Levi tentatively walked past him, wary of the extra presence in the room.

Feyer sat at the table massaging his leg. "Levi, Lieutenant Drake will be relieving you of your duties for the time being. He will be stationed outside Ambassador Alsh's living quarters. I have ordered him not to enter."

"Yes, sir." Levi watched as the lieutenant promptly left. It was unsettling. Feyer had rarely given him a break. He didn't like the idea of someone else being responsible for the Tulku's life. He knew nothing about the lieutenant or his moral compass, but there would be no arguing with Feyer.

Jake leaned heavily on the table as he stood. He kept the weight off his right leg as he reached for a cane that had been propped against his chair. His dark eyes were tired and lacked any luster. "Walk with me, boy." His voice was low, but there was no disappointed scowl on his face.

Levi glued himself to his father's side and watched with great concern as Jake limped forward. They made their way out into the fresh air. The gardens were brimming with blooms, and the trees had fully leafed out. They made their way down several manicured gravel pathways towards the back of the property where a grand deciduous tree shaded the lawn. Its leaves rustled in the breeze. Two chairs and a table had been set up underneath. A few attendants quickly disappeared into the vegetation as they strolled up, leaving Levi alone with his father.

Jake seated himself in the nearest chair and rested the cane against the table. Levi stood by, anxiously waiting for further instructions. Jake glanced up at the boy, then pointed to the other chair before dishing himself out food. Levi sat without saying a word. He stared at a silver platter, neatly decorated with fruit and delicate little sandwiches.

Jake took a few bites, then stared at the boy. "You may eat. This is your lunch, too."

Levi swallowed hard before taking one of the sandwiches. He took a small bite. He wasn't sure he had much appetite, and Feyer's lack of comments or criticisms only made the tension worse.

"What subjects would you be interested in studying after Ambassador Alsh leaves?"

Levi swallowed. "I don't understand why you are asking for my input, sir."

Jake stabbed a piece of fruit with his fork. "You are more mature now. I want to give you more freedom to make your own decisions, provided you don't betray my trust. I won't always be around to protect Erev, so you need to learn to stand on your own two feet."

Levi set his sandwich down. There were so many things he had done that would cost all trust Feyer had in him. He dropped his gaze and spun his ring around his finger.

Jake set his fork down and frowned. "Levi, is there something you'd like to tell me?"

"I snuck into your office and borrowed your lighter while the power was out. I couldn't find any matches."

"You know you aren't allowed in there without my permission."

"It won't happen again." Levi waited for Jake to react, but the president just picked up his fork and attacked another bite. The soldier let his shoulders drop. He picked up his sandwich and made himself finish it. When he was done, he looked at his father. "I would be interested in studying Rufosian history."

"Why Rufosian history?"

"A lot of the Tulkish culture seems to have evolved from their past. Knowing where they came from would better help us inform future interactions with them."

Feyer nodded. "A reasonable suggestion." He started massaging his leg again.

Levi opened his mouth but cast a glance at Jake and closed it. Jake eyed him curiously.

Levi took a deep breath. "May I ask you questions until lunch is over?"

Jake nodded. "Yes. You may say whatever you wish."

"Are—are you alright?"

Jake froze momentarily. "What do you mean, boy?"

"Your leg…"

"It will heal."

Levi nodded.

Jake wiped his mouth on his napkin and sat back in his chair. "Have you learned anything interesting from your assignment?"

"Ambassador Alsh is an interesting character." Levi smiled and stared at the grass between his boots. "He's a voracious reader and incredibly observant, almost too observant. He told me some things about Tulkish culture. I hadn't realized Erev and Tulanu were so different."

Jake raised an eyebrow. "What has he told you about the Tulku?"

Levi clasped his hands together. "Well, most of them don't know what shoes are; they don't wear shoes. But they do wear vyata and katoms. Most of them don't get married, but if they do, they tend to have large families. They value education." Levi looked Feyer directly in the eyes. "Did you know that Tulanu used to have a monarchy? They got rid of their king because he nearly cost the Tulku everything during one of their wars."

The president's gaze hardened. "Why would Ambassador Alsh tell you that?"

"He made a comment about the Tulku not wearing black when the tailor came, so I asked him about it. The color was banned from being worn after King K'thanu was removed from the throne because it signified corrupt power and authority."

Jake relaxed only slightly. "Do you know how much longer he intends to stay?"

Levi shook his head. "He hasn't said anything definitive to me, but he's made a couple of off-handed comments that make me think he's finalizing his conclusions and wrapping up his work." A wave of sorrow rushed over the boy, but he stuffed it down. He didn't want Feyer to know he had grown attached to the Tulku.

"I'm curious to know what he's come up with."

Levi twiddled his thumbs as he tried to think of something else to say. "Ambassador Alsh told me his wife used to work with him before she died. They trained under Ambassador Jeda G'nali. He said you knew Ambassador G'nali…" He trailed off. He wasn't sure what he wanted to ask.

"I expect you want me to tell you about them."

Levi nodded.

Jake cleared his throat and settled into his seat more. "I remember Jeda G'nali quite well. He had been around long before I was born and was constantly here on Tulanu's business. He had ugly brownish fur with a lot of gray mixed in. He was quite old when I knew him. He wasn't very tall, and he wasn't exactly trim either. He was a rather unsightly creature. The only redeeming feature he had was the lines in his fur. They were deep green and shimmered whenever he moved or the sunlit hit him just right. It always fascinated me.

"G'nali was usually here negotiating with Father about terms of trade and tariffs. Every time he would come, he would bring me a gift. It was usually something small, like a box of, oh—" Jake snapped his fingers. "Some kind of berry. It is a delicacy of theirs."

"Tsevateni?"

Jake eyed Levi warily.

The soldier avoided his gaze. "Ambassador Alsh said it was his favorite snack."

"Yes. Tsevateni. That was one of the regular gifts. He never forgot, not once. He never disappointed me."

Jake paused and thought. "Father had him poisoned."

Levi's eyes grew wide, and he stared at Jake. His father's statement had been so plain and emotionless, as if he were commenting about the weather or some well-known fact. The boy didn't know what to do with the information.

Jake took a deep breath. "G'nali was pushing for a deal that would save Erev and ease trade with Tulanu. Everyone across Erev was on the verge of starving, and Father was happy to let our people die for his pursuits of power. I never forgave him for that.

"Then Grenard came in trying to save the day and step into G'nali's shoes, so to speak. He knew I had grown attached to Jeda. He told me he would be there if I needed someone, but as soon as I reached out to him, he lost his temper and walked out on me. He chose to waste his days humoring Father. Vanyani, at least, was willing to have an argument with him and fight for Erev and Tulanu, but she never liked me and always gave me the cold shoulder."

He paused. All hint of emotion was replaced with a vacant stare. "People will always fail you, Levi. They will say they love you or they care or they will support you when you need it, but they are always empty words. Don't ever let yourself rely on anyone other than yourself. Don't even rely on me. I will not be there for you."

Levi nodded. Feyer's words hung in the air like poisonous gas and stung Levi's lungs. He knew his father would not be there, but he didn't want to believe what Jake had said. The Grenard that Jake had described did not seem to match the Tulku that the boy had gotten to know. The Grenard he knew had been loving and caring. The Grenard he knew had saved his life. The ambassador's words had not been empty and fruitless. His father was wrong.

Levi looked at Jake. "How many people died because of the EMP?"

"They can't directly kill people."

"I know that."

"Then why ask the question?"

"I figured not having power for an extended period of time would cause a cascade of problems."

Jake considered Levi and sighed. "I don't know the answer to your question." He glanced at his watch. "I have a meeting I need to attend to address the lack of power. You may resume your duties."

"Yes, sir."

Jake grabbed the cane and grimaced as he stood. His leg suddenly gave way, and he frantically grabbed the table to catch himself. Levi rushed to help him, but didn't need to. Feyer glanced briefly at Levi, then let his gaze slip from the boy and started slowly crossing the lawn.

"Do you want me to walk back with you?"

"No. Thank you, Levi."

"Father?" The word tasted strange in Levi's mouth as it forced its way out.

Jake paused and looked back at the boy with tired curiosity.

"Do you love me? Even if you say I can't rely on you?"

Jake frowned. "Isn't it obvious, Levi?" He held the boy's gaze. There was something strange in his eyes that Levi had never seen before. Jake turned away and trudged up the path before the boy could think of a response.

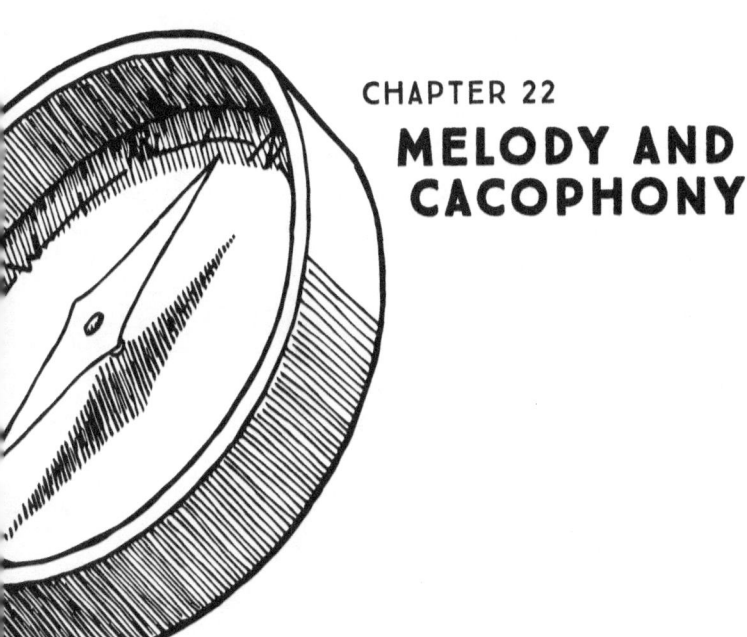

CHAPTER 22
MELODY AND CACOPHONY

*L*evi stood stranded underneath the rattling branches, watching Feyer disappear into the mansion. Was it obvious? Did Levi somehow miss where Feyer's obvious affections for him truly lay? The lunch and additional freedom were nice, but how did that line up with all the times he had been yelled at? How was that consistent with Feyer hitting him after the masquerade? Even Feyer's comment about not being there for him was a double-edged sword. It was meant to be an encouragement to stand on his own two feet, but if Levi ever stumbled, Feyer wouldn't pick him up off the ground. He would tell Levi to figure it out for himself.

No, it wasn't obvious at all.

Levi walked back to the suite with his hands shoved in his pockets and his head hung low. Lieutenant Drake was standing guard outside the door, just as he had been ordered.

Levi stopped in front of him. "Thank you. I have it from here."

Drake nodded curtly then left.

The boy slid into the suite, where Grenard had several letters spread out on the kitchen table. The Tulku set down the letter he was reading and tracked the boy with his ears. Levi sat across from him and slouched.

"Did something happen?"

Levi glanced up and shrugged. "Yes. And no. He just wanted to have lunch and talk."

"Do you want to tell me about it?"

"What's there to tell? He asked a few questions. I asked a few questions." Levi sighed. "It's never easy talking with him. I never know what's going to happen."

Grenard grunted, then resumed reading his letter. There were at least six packets of paper that lay unfolded on the table. One hadn't been opened yet, but as Grenard finished the current letter, he transitioned to the last one. A small black square about the size of Levi's fingernail fell onto the table as the Tulku unfolded the paper. Grenard only briefly glanced down. As he scoured the paper for information, his face went from calm to frowning to scowling to snarling. He slammed the letter down, grabbed the black square, and retreated to his room. He came out with a small, flat circular object about the size of his palm. He put the black square in the device and powered it on.

A crystal-clear image hovered above the device, shaking as Grenard set it down on the table. He began to run his hand through the light and manipulate the image. Levi stared wide-eyed at the technology and waved his hand through the light, messing with the display.

The Tulku raised an eyebrow. "Have you never seen a holograph?"

Levi shook his head. "Since when have you seen one in Erev? We don't have that kind of technology." He flicked his fingers through the light again and made the image move.

Grenard batted Levi's hand away, then navigated to a collection of several video files. He opened the first and sat back with his arms folded.

Hundreds, if not thousands of Tulku appeared in three-dimensional clarity in the middle of a strange city. There were even a few humans sprinkled throughout the crowd. Dozens of trees were strung with colorful lights and floating lanterns were suspended well above everyone's heads. A parade of magically dressed Tulku danced through the street, breaking like water around a beautiful fountain with a white stone statue in the middle. Wild music and singing filled the space.

Levi leaned forward, entranced by the dancers. Their movements were perfectly timed and elegant. The Tulku were paired up by similar looking costumes. Levi watched one particular couple wearing bright yellow ensembles. There was an unspoken understanding between the two dancers. They danced as if they were the only two in the whole world and there was no reason to hide or run.

A loud noise made Levi and Grenard both jump out of their seats. Fire erupted in the video frame, and the dancers fell to the ground, covering their heads. Two more explosions added to the chaos, each one startling Levi just as much as the first. Tulku ran from the city center, crying out. The mesmerizing festival was overtaken by smoke and flame. The video ended.

Levi sat, horrified. The screams still rang in his ears.

"Grenard?" He pivoted towards the Tulku.

Tears hovered in the ambassador's eyes. He slid the last letter across the table. "Arden sent it to me to warn me. He expects there will be massive retaliation in Erev for this."

"Does Feyer know?"

Grenard sneered and shook his head. "I would be surprised if he didn't, but I also would be surprised if he publicly acknowledged that it even happened."

"Because humans did it?"

The Tulku nodded solemnly. He sniffed and looked away.

Levi's chest felt like too small a cage for his lungs. He picked up the letter.

Ba,

I don't expect you to have access to Tulanu's information if you can't even contact us. There was a massive attack in Yfalo yesterday. 157 people were killed in a bombing during the Layano Festival. That number will likely rise dramatically over the next few days. Reports suggest that three human suicide bombers were responsible for the crime.

Tulku throughout the southern cities are already organizing protests. They want to force all humans to leave Tulanu or place massive restrictions on their freedoms if they stay. I don't see why the Tulkish Council wouldn't give in to their demands, but I also know that won't dissolve the tensions. I don't know what will, though.

I would expect massive retaliation from the Tulku in Erev. I am not sure if President Feyer is aware of what happened, but he should be warned. The Tulku want justice. Since they are not getting it from him or from the Tulkish Council, they will take matters into their own hands and exact revenge. Militias have started forming, and some of them are destroying the property of humans who have been in Tulanu for generations. These militias are going to further polarize the situation unless someone can do something.

I sent a collection of videos and newsreels so you can see for yourself. Considering I can't find the hologram, I assume you took it with you.

Please, Ba. If there is anything, absolutely anything you can do, act swiftly. Time is running out for Tulanu and Erev.

Arden

Levi returned the letter to Grenard. "I'm sorry." It seemed a pathetic response, but it was all he could think to say.

"What has happened cannot be reversed. It is up to us to either make a change and attempt to not repeat history, or fall into its ugly habit of destruction." Grenard wiped the tears from his eyes and played the next video.

The next hour was filled with clips of the explosions and chaos from numerous angles and news reports on the incident. Levi hated it. After a few minutes, he moved to the couch and picked up a random book. He tried to drown out their cries, but the silence of words on a page did little to overcome the videos.

Levi gave up on the book and lay down on the couch, covering his ears. He knew the pain in their voices. He could feel their fear as if it was his own. He occasionally glanced at Grenard. The Tulku just sat at the table, watching the videos over and over again. Levi didn't know how he could stand it.

Grenard's people had been massacred, and he stoically watched them die on repeat.

Levi snatched his book and rushed into his room, closing the door behind him. He sat on his bed and propped open the book in his lap. He flattened his hands over his ears and forced himself to focus on anything other than the videos. He glued his eyes to the book and proceeded to skim the same two pages four times over before he squeezed his eyes shut and battled with his imagination.

The sun set before the noise finally ceased. Grenard opened Levi's door. "You can come out now."

Levi peeled his hands from his ears.

Grenard sighed and shook his head. "I need to talk with Feyer in the morning."

Levi started from his bed, but the ambassador cleared his throat.

"You don't need to do anything, my boy. I will approach him myself." Grenard retreated into the commons area.

The ambassador paced for the rest of the evening, simmering in his building anger. He pulled out his journals, flipping through some and taking notes in others as he walked in circles.

Levi quit reading and threw on a long-sleeved shirt and sweatpants. He just wanted to get the screams out of his head. He closed his door and crawled under the covers, beckoning sleep to whisk him away.

He lay staring at the ceiling instead. No matter what he did or how hard he tried to pry his mind away, the sounds wouldn't leave his mind. But it wasn't just the Tulkus' screams that raced through his head. They were mixed in with other miserable pleas from his own memories. He tossed relentlessly, but sleep avoided him.

Levi threw the covers off, frustrated that 1:32 a.m. had come so slowly and miserably. He paced in the dark until he noticed a faint light creep under his door. He peered out of his room.

Grenard was sitting on the couch, cross-legged. His eyes were closed, and he wore his tevet. His hands rested peacefully in his lap. Levi padded to the couch and sat next to the Tulku. He propped his feet up on the coffee table and crossed his arms.

Grenard glanced over at him, then took the earpieces off and sighed. "Having trouble sleeping?"

Levi nodded.

Grenard took the two, thin metal crescents in his hands and held them out to the boy. "I don't know if you like music, but I find that it often helps."

The boy hesitated.

"There's no harm in it."

Levi sighed and took the pieces. He carefully put them around his ears while Grenard messed with the silver bracelet on his wrist. The Tulku swiped through several files before selecting one.

A soft note seeped in around Levi. It grew and began to float across his mind. He closed his eyes and focused on the melancholy melody as it began to dance in his consciousness. The notes embraced his sorrow and tinged them with hope. It was as if someone knew him intimately and knew the chaos that ravaged his mind and heart. His feelings had been delicately crafted into something beautiful and acceptable. His thoughts began to still, and the swirling madness slowed to the rhythm of the music. A strange sense of peace rested on him.

As the song ended, Levi looked at the Tulku and gave him half a smile. "Thank you." He took the earpieces off and held them for a moment. The screams were still there, ringing in his head, but they weren't quite as loud as before. "Can I listen to another one?"

"Yes."

Levi must have fallen asleep because a sharp knock at the door startled him awake. Wonderful music still floated in his ears. Grenard mumbled to himself with his head resting on his hand.

The knock sounded again. Levi removed the earpieces and opened the door. He recognized the soldier at the threshold, but he didn't know from where.

"Feyer wants to see you now."

CHAPTER 23

INTO ASHES

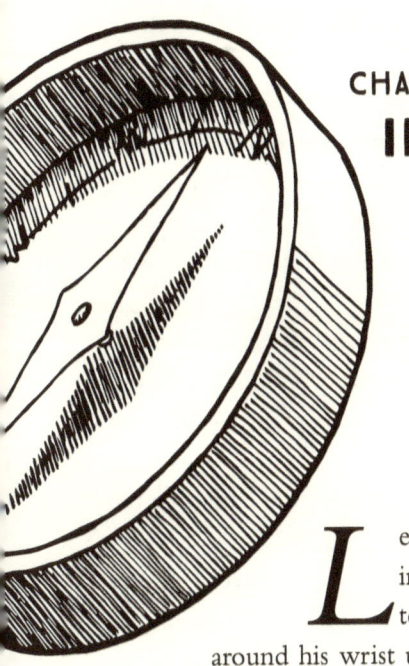

*L*evi stifled a yawn and rubbed his eyes in the middle of Feyer's office. The tevet earpieces were safely hidden around his wrist under the cover of his sleeve. His watch read 3:27 a.m.

President Feyer was wide-eyed and fully dressed. He leaned against the mantle, cane in hand, glaring at the crackling flames. "There was an attack in Trifort less than an hour ago."

Levi straightened at the news.

"Several Tulku were detained for burning buildings down. I need Ambassador Alsh to sort out this mess, or else there will be no chance of peace between Erev and Tulanu." The president limped to his chair, growling.

"We will leave as soon as Ambassador Alsh wakes up."

"No!" Feyer slammed his fist on the table. "You will leave immediately. I will not tolerate more unprovoked violence from the Tulku, and if that means Ambassador Alsh doesn't get sufficient beauty rest, then so be it. I don't give a damn!"

"Yes, sir." Levi watched Feyer carefully. "Why do you think the Tulku attacked?"

Feyer glared at him. "Ask the animal you're watching. Maybe he'll know! Whatever the reason, I'm tired of it. You're dismissed."

Levi left without hesitation. Grenard was still asleep on the couch, face in hand and ears flopped over.

The boy tapped the Tulku on the shoulder. "Grenard, wake up. We have to go."

The ambassador blinked a few times. "What time is it?"

"Almost four in the morning. Arden was right. There was an attack in Trifort." Levi handed him the tevet pieces and went to his room to get ready.

Grenard moaned. "Did Feyer mention the extent of the damage?"

"He just said a bunch of buildings were burned. That was it." Levi paused and stared at the scar on his cheek in the mirror. "He said it was unprovoked."

The Tulku scoffed. "I'll deal with that later." He stood and stretched. "Pack for a few days. I expect we will be thoroughly occupied. This will be a different kind of unsavory place, my boy."

———— ··· ————

The drive south was long and silent. Ghostly shadows of darkened towns slipped by them without a hint of life. Cars had been abandoned in the middle of the road where they stopped when their lives had been stolen from them. Rufosia's three moons shed their eerie light on Erev, guiding Levi south.

As a dull gray broke over the western horizon, they crested a hill and were met with a sickening sight. Thick, black clouds poured from the valley below them, fighting to reverse the sun's effects. The underbelly of the billowing smoke glowed orange. Ash began to flutter around the car and dust the ground in light gray powder.

Grenard leaned forward, eyes wide. His jaw dropped. "This is far more extensive than I had imagined."

Levi tried to focus on the road, but his gaze was drawn to the flame-engulfed city. "The Tulku must be angry."

The ambassador grimaced. "*Angry* is an understatement, my boy. This is no mere act of vengeance. This is an outpouring of misery."

The main road weaved through the city only a few blocks from the fires. Levi drove down the deserted street, seeking signs of life and finding none.

"Turn left."

Levi slowed. "That's closer to the burning buildings, Grenard."

"Yes, I know. Turn left." The Tulku frowned as he leaned forward. His ears were alert as he observed their surroundings.

Levi obeyed and continued towards the wall of smoldering structures.

"Stop here."

The car had barely come to a halt before the ambassador stepped out into the sweltering heat. Levi darted after him, but the thick air attacked his lungs. He pulled the collar of his uniform over his nose and blinked away the smoke that stung his eyes.

Grenard raced around a corner, then froze as his ears twitched from one side to another. His eyes narrowed.

"Is every—"

Grenard ran straight into one of the buildings, jumping over flames and through a broken storefront window.

Levi's heart stopped, and before he knew what he was doing, he too found himself inside.

Rolling smoke clung to the ceiling, threatening to reach down and choke him. He ducked low, trying to make out any Tulkish form in the orange and black haze. Heaps of coals lay scattered on the charred floor, trying to reignite with their dying breaths. In many places, the bare concrete and steel of the structure lay exposed. A loud creaking sound echoed and scraped around the building.

"Grenard!" Levi strained to listen, to see any sign of the ambassador. "Grenard!"

The Tulku burst through the smoke, cradling something in his arms. "Run, Levi!"

They retraced their steps towards the outside world. More pops sounded, followed by gut-wrenching creaks. Grenard and Levi leapt through the broken window and into free air just seconds before the building let out a guttural cry and collapsed to the ground. It kicked up a storm of dust and debris, scattering rubble in the pair's path.

They ran, choking on smoke until two blocks later when visibility finally increased and the air had less bite. They stopped, lungs aching and hearts racing.

Levi pulled at his hair. "What the hell was that? You could've just died!"

Grenard slid to the ground and looked at the thing in his arms. It was a little girl, a toddler, in what might have been a pastel pink dress. The Tulku brushed her long, blond hair out of her face and revealed tear-streaked cheeks.

"I have you, my child. You're safe."

The girl leaned forward and wrapped her arms around the Tulku's neck. Her pudgy, little fingers dug into his fur.

"We should go to the police station." Grenard glanced at the boy. "I thought I saw another Tulku."

Levi simply watched as they walked how the ambassador hugged the girl and whispered constant reassurance to her. He ran his fingers through her tangled hair until she started to settle. Grenard slowly got little pieces of information out of the girl.

Emily had been waiting for her mother in the abandoned building. They were homeless. She was hiding in the stairwell when the flames overtook the building.

When they finally made it back to the car and resumed their trek south, they came upon a mass of people. A police barricade had been partially built as dozens of humans were pulled from the surrounding buildings and herded south. Tear-stained cheeks, angry sneers, and slumped shoulders defined the mob.

Levi rolled down the window and called out to one of the officers. "Where's the police station where they're holding the Tulku?"

The man rushed over, and, seeing the boy's uniform, nearly smiled. "It's another three kilometers south. Has the military finally come?"

Levi paused. "I—I'm supposed to escort the Tulku to where the others are detained."

The man looked past him, and the half grin slid from his face. He refocused on Levi. "Riverside might cause him some problems."

Trifort's Riverside Police Headquarters was a whirlwind of injured, lost, and manic people, searching for loved ones. As soon as Grenard stepped foot inside, angry humans swarmed him, yelling and swearing at him. Levi fended them off as best he could, even shoving them aside when necessary. A few officers, seeing the commotion, aided in dragging Grenard and Emily away from the mob.

Catching her breath, one of the officers brushed a few loose strands of red hair from her face and eyed the strange trio with half-hearted excitement. Her makeup from the day before had begun to smudge. "Are you from the army? We've been waiting for hours for assistance."

Levi frowned. "No. I'm escorting Ambassador Alsh here on President Feyer's orders to help investigate the fires."

"Oh." The officer's shoulders dropped. "I remember hearing that you were coming." She nodded towards Emily. "Who's the kid?"

Grenard cleared his throat. "She could use some medical attention. We pulled her from one of the burning buildings, and her mother is missing."

"Wait, hold on just a minute." She put her hands on her hips. "You're telling me you ran into a burning building."

Levi laughed nervously and fiddled with his ring. "It might be more of a smoldering heap now."

She shook her head. "If you'll come with me." She led them to an office off the main lobby. "I'll be back in a minute." She walked out of view for a moment, then came back with a paramedic. "He'll take a look at all of you."

The paramedic frowned at Grenard but refrained from saying anything as he ensured everyone's health.

The redheaded woman sighed. "If you don't mind watching the girl for another couple minutes, I need to track down Captain Williams. He'll want to speak with you both."

Grenard nodded and smiled. "I don't think we mind. I do have a strange question, though. Do you have a comb or a brush?"

The woman frowned. "What for?"

The ambassador ran his fingers through Emily's matted hair. "I'm sure she will want to look nice for her mother when she comes around."

The redhead understood. She disappeared into the inner maze of the station and returned shortly with a comb.

"Thank you…" Grenard's voice trailed off. "I'm sorry. I didn't catch your name."

"Meg Carlson." She almost smiled.

Grenard sat so that Emily could keep an eye on the lobby through the office windows as he began to pick at the knots in her hair. She never complained about the ambassador pulling on her tangled blond locks. Levi alternated between pacing and investigating the ever-changing crowds.

"Emily, what is your favorite color?"

She spun around and beamed at him. "Lellow!"

"I see." He pointed to his syamta. "This kind of yellow?"

She giggled. "No! Lellow like da sun. Wha's yours?" She poked him in the stomach.

"Purple." He pointed to his clothes.

"Pwetty." She brushed her grimy hands on the fabric.

The Tulku grinned. "Why don't you turn back around so I can finish brushing your hair? You can also look for your mother."

She zipped back around and resumed her scan. "Is she going to come get me?"

"I hope so, Emily." Grenard's ears were trained on the section of knots he was untangling. The tip of his tail occasionally flicked at his side.

The toddler sat patiently for a few minutes before peering back at the Tulku again. She shied away from him and had a silly smile plastered on her face. "Can I touch your tail?"

"Yes, but you must be very gentle."

She nodded, then, with one finger extended, poked the ambassador's tail. She looked up at him and giggled. She poked his tail again, then carefully grabbed it and pulled it into her lap, burying her fingers in his fur. "I's so soft!"

Levi couldn't help but smile at the completely entranced little girl as she continued to exchange little comments with Grenard. The soldier was more than content to listen and keep an eye on the churning crowd. He wouldn't have known where to start if Emily had been put in his hands.

Meg slipped into the office with several sandwiches in hand, holding them out to Levi, Grenard, and Emily. "Figured you might be hungry. You're also welcome to use our facilities to get cleaned up. Captain Williams apologizes for making you wait. He's dealing with some rather difficult people."

Grenard accepted the sandwich with a grateful smile. "I wouldn't mind getting the ash out of my fur, but I don't want to trouble you with this little one. You have more than enough on your hands already."

Emily had already begun happily munching on her sandwich and snuggled into the Tulku. Her hair had been completely detangled.

"They can spare me for a few minutes." Meg scooped up Emily. "Besides, I can get her cleaned up, too."

"Very well."

———···———

Grenard managed to go through five towels and still look like he was half soaked. His fur stuck out in all directions, but he had returned to a rust color instead of the pale gray of soot. He had donned a formal emerald outfit; his shirt, pants, vyata and katom were all subtly different hues.

He grabbed a sixth towel and rubbed it furiously over his face and ears. "There's a reason Tulku don't bathe every day. Miserable!" Grenard continued to grumble to himself until he was halfway satisfied with his appearance.

Levi amused himself with listening as he packed away his dirty uniform as neatly as he could into his pack. A few more muttered comments about what Beka would say and her likeness to her mother escaped from the ambassador, making the soldier smile.

The duo eventually made their way back to the lobby, where Meg was talking to a woman, now holding a clean Emily in a bright yellow dress. They casually approached, but when Meg noticed them, she rushed to them, wide-eyed and nervous.

"Ambassador Alsh, can you wait here for a moment? I need to borrow Levi to talk with Emily's mother."

Grenard bowed.

Meg dragged Levi over to the sneering, ragged woman. Her clothes were stained and covered in dirt. Her hair was a much darker shade of blond than her daughter's.

She shoved a finger in Levi's chest. "How dare you let a Tulku touch my daughter! You're a soldier. You of all people should know they can't be trusted."

Levi scowled. "If it had not been for Ambassador Alsh, your daughter would be buried in a pile of rubble right now. I, of all people, know that he is more trustworthy than most humans and if I thought any less of him, then I would not have let him take care of her."

The woman maintained her frown as she readjusted Emily in her grasp. She ran her fingers through the little girl's hair, halfway surprised. "Who brushed out her hair?"

"Tulku!" Emily threw her arms up with a big smile. "Mama, he's vewy soft."

"We're leaving." The woman started stomping away, but her daughter tugged on her clothes.

"I wanna' say goodbye to Wevi."

Her mother paused, glancing at the soldier, and reluctantly put her down.

Emily walked up to Levi and stuck her hand out. "Thank you."

Levi shook her hand and smiled. "You're welcome."

Emily's mother bent down to pick her up again, but the toddler had run off towards Grenard. The two talked for a minute, then Emily led him over by the hand. Her mother crossed her arms and sneered.

"Mama, you should say thank you, too. Tulku saved me."

The woman pulled Emily away and snatched her up. "I don't thank animals."

The little girl peered over her mother's shoulder and waved one last, solemn goodbye.

Meg eyed the ambassador. "You're not going to change everyone's minds about the Tulku."

"I didn't save Emily to change anyone's mind and make a show of how morally superior the Tulku are, if that's what you're implying. A life is still a life. That should be reason enough." The Tulku sighed. "Shall we meet this Captain Williams you mentioned earlier? I would like to begin the work I was sent here for."

CHAPTER 24

GHOSTS

*C*aptain Williams was a broad-shoul-
dered man with a no-nonsense disposition. His constant frown was
framed by short, spiky hair. He shook Grenard's hand
emphatically. "Rylant notified me of your coming earlier
this morning. I apologize for making you wait. I just received
word that the army is arriving from Portland."

Grenard smiled. "I understand that coordination can sometimes be challenging. I assume they are assisting with evacuations
and putting out the fires."

"Yes. However, putting out the fires will be easier said than
done. The wind has been the major player in spreading the fires.
When we initially got reports, there were only a few right along
the coastline, mostly empty or abandoned buildings. But we've
already lost several emergency responders because of the weather."

Grenard's ears flattened. "I'm very sorry to hear that. President
Feyer has informed us that several Tulku have been detained that
you believe to be responsible."

"We have three Tulku detained. Two of them have already confessed, but this last one has been giving us some grief. She hasn't said anything since she came in, but we have multiple witnesses claiming that she was causing damage throughout the city."

Grenard nodded. "I will start with her. I would like for Levi to watch and take notes. He has been aiding my work for several months now."

Williams only smirked as he led the way to the troublesome Tulku. Levi walked into the dimly lit observation room with Meg and Williams trailing him.

A silvery-black Tulku with golden-green eyes and lime syamta was cuffed and growling to herself. Her gray vyata and katom were smeared with charcoal. Grenard stepped in and quietly closed the door behind him.

The Tulku shot him a venomous glance and snarled. "You're a traitor to Rufosia."

The ambassador sat across from her and waited.

Her tail bristled. "Go ahead. Tell me I've just thrown my life away. I have nothing left to live for anyways."

Grenard said nothing.

Levi watched from behind the glass with his journal open and pen at the ready.

Meg stepped up beside him. "Is your Tulku friend going to do anything?"

Levi shrugged. "He's gotten more words out of her just by walking in that room than you have since you detained her. I'd just watch if I were you."

The black Tulku slowly sank back into her chair.

"What's your name?" Grenard spoke calmly and softly.

"Ko'evu. Yours?"

"Vey Alsh."

Meg scoffed. "I thought his name was Grenard."

Levi glared at her. "It's a cultural thing." He began writing.

Ko'evu immediately bowed her head. "Forgive me, my Vey. I didn't know it was you."

"I'm not here to lecture you. I just want to hear your story."

Ko'evu glanced at the glass. "Aren't they listening?"

Grenard nodded. "They already know you're guilty."

She scoffed. "Then I'm not saying anything! I'm not going to make my life any worse."

The ambassador raised an eyebrow. "If you have nothing left to live for, what is the harm in telling me your story?"

Ko'evu's ears drooped. She chewed on her lip and avoided Grenard's eyes. "My father died ten years ago in a skirmish that broke out in Portland about the time that Vey Alsh passed away. My oldest brother was killed in Vyonu two years ago. He was shot by humans while he was visiting his fiancée. My mother and youngest brother were just blown to bits at the Layano Festival." She looked up at him with tear-filled eyes. "Tell me that you wouldn't want a little justice after all that."

Grenard knelt and took her hands in his.

The captain stirred behind Levi. "I don't like where this is going." He stormed to the door, but Levi blocked his way. "Move."

"No." Levi crossed his arms. "If you interrupt him now, you won't be able to get any more information out of Ko'evu. Ambassador Alsh has rapport with her, something you don't. What's he going to do anyways? Give something to her? He doesn't have anything that will help her." Levi's heart pounded in his chest. He hoped Meg and Captain Williams couldn't hear it rattling against his ribs.

The captain sneered but returned to his seat. Levi didn't dare move from the door.

Grenard kissed Ko'evu's hands. "I do desire justice, daughter. Losing Vanyani cost me everything, so I can only imagine how much more pain you must feel. But killing more people doesn't bring the dead back to life."

Ko'evu burst into tears. "I just wanted to scare the humans! I only burned a few empty buildings so they'd leave us alone. I swear I checked they were empty."

Captain Williams walked up to the glass. "That's our statement. She's guilty."

"Of arson, yes. But not of murder. I'm not even sure you could pin manslaughter on her." Meg folded her arms over her chest.

The black Tulku gasped for air. "I didn't kill anyone, did I?"

Grenard frowned. "I pulled a little girl from one of the buildings just before it collapsed. They weren't all empty."

Ko'evu covered her face with her hands and squeezed her eyes shut.

Grenard backed away from her. "I will arrange with the Tulkish Council and President Feyer for you to have a fair trial, but I would expect that you will have several charges brought against you."

She nodded numbly. "If you go to Yfalo, will you put flowers at my mother's and my brother's memorials?"

"What are their names?"

"Mava and H'nan G'nali."

Levi looked up at the frozen Grenard.

"You don't happen to be related to Jeda G'nali, do you?"

"He was my father's uncle. He died before I was born."

"Your father must have been Drevan. I remember him fondly. I'm so sorry, my daughter." He rubbed his eyes. "Please excuse me for a moment." He stood from his chair and left the room.

Levi rushed into the hallway. Grenard stood in the middle of the empty corridor with one hand covering his face. His tail hung limply, and his ears drooped. The boy walked up to him and put his hand on the Tulku's shoulder. It was something he had never done before, but Levi didn't think words had any true worth in that moment.

Grenard peered out at him from between his fingers and reciprocated the gesture. His chest rose and fell heavily. He sat against the wall, deflated.

Levi sat beside him, fiddling with his ring. "Grenard, there's probably something you should know about Jeda. I should have told you sooner, but I guess I got distracted."

"What is it, my boy?"

"Feyer told me that Anton had someone poison him."

"I suspected as much. Unfortunately, that knowledge doesn't bring Ko'evu and her family any justice. Anton has been dead for a long time. He cannot pay for his crimes."

Captain Williams stepped into the hallway. "It seems you and that Tulku have quite the personal history. I'm not sure how I feel about this investigation continuing."

Grenard grunted as he stood. "I believe I can convince her to share what she knows. She may have let her anger get the better of her, but in many ways, she is still rational. I ask for just a few more minutes with her."

Williams nodded.

"Thank you." Grenard took a deep breath and re-entered the investigation room while Williams and Levi hurried to watch.

Ko'evu straightened and followed the ambassador's movements with her eyes and ears.

The ambassador paced back and forth across the room. "My daughter, can I convince you to share what you know about the fires with me?"

The black Tulku shifted uncomfortably. "Won't that get me in more trouble?"

"Not unless you are responsible for more than what you have already shared with me."

Ko'evu stayed silent, staring at the ground.

"Think about it like this. You desire justice for the loved ones you lost, yes?"

She nodded hesitantly.

Grenard smiled. "The humans who just lost loved ones will also want to seek justice. I think you know as well as I do that the vast majority of humans have never committed a crime against a Tulku, just as most Tulku have never committed a crime against a human. The violence cannot end if we keep wrongfully accusing one another."

Ko'evu sneered, avoiding Grenard's amber gaze. Her ears flattened. "I don't know much."

The ambassador sat across from her. "I don't expect you to know everything, but what you do know may be able to save lives."

She took a deep breath. "I was approached by a couple of distant acquaintances a few days after the Layano Festival. They asked me if I wanted to send the humans a message to not mess with the Tulku. I said yes. They said there was a plan being formed and to watch for a message with more information. Two days after that, I found a piece of paper in my apartment with a note that said to go to a drop point behind one of the towers in the Lo'a district at midnight in five days to receive final instructions. I destroyed the note."

He thought for a moment. "What were the names of your acquaintances, and how did you meet them?"

She grimaced. "Monva and Netka Jeknyi. They're brothers. I know them from when I was in my ninth year in school. We had a few classes together that year. They were always getting into trouble, so I tried to avoid them."

"Why get involved with them now?"

Ko'evu buried her face in hands. "I don't know. I don't know what I was thinking. I was just angry."

"What information was at the drop point?"

Ko'evu sat back up and sighed. "A map of Trifort with specific buildings marked as my targets and the location of where materials were stashed. There were also instructions on how to get there without being caught, how to start the fires, when to start them, and to destroy everything after I had memorized it all."

"Did you destroy the map?"

She nodded. "I'm really good at following instructions, as it turns out."

"If you had another map, could you mark down everything on the previous map?"

She shrugged. "Probably."

Grenard stood and tapped on the glass.

Meg disappeared from Levi's side, racing out of the dark room.

Grenard sat back down. "How long ago was the Layano Festival?"

Ko'evu counted to herself for a moment. "Twelve days ago."

"Do you know how many Tulku were involved in starting the fires?"

She shook her head. "I have no idea, but I do know that Monva and Netka weren't the ones organizing everything. They were just the recruiters."

"What makes you say that?"

"Some of the comments they made to one another during that initial conversation about needing to talk more with someone named Kavo'kido…"

Grenard frowned, but Meg entered the room and laid out a paper map of Trifort in front of Ko'evu and handed her a pen.

The black Tulku took the pen and studied the map before she began to copy down everything from her memory. The map filled up with detailed notes on the buildings she had been instructed to target: which windows or exits, stashes of supplies, how many there were and how much she had taken, the routes between buildings, the dropoff and pickup points along the shores of the bay, and the times of each event.

When she set down the pen, she sat back and sighed contentedly. She looked up at Grenard and waited for a reaction from him.

Meg, still standing in the room, gawked at the map.

The ambassador smiled and nodded. "Thank you, daughter." He grabbed the map and started to escort Meg from the room.

"Vey?"

Grenard turned back to the Tulku.

"Please don't forget my family."

He bowed towards her. "How could I?" He closed the door behind him.

———···———

Williams, Meg, Grenard, and Levi stood in a conference room just down the hallway from Ko'evu's interrogation room. The map was spread out on the table with all four of them studying the Tulku's meticulous notes.

Grenard scowled and peeled away from the others. He began to pace, ears pinned back. "I am quite concerned by what Ko'evu shared, particularly about Kavo'kido."

Williams straightened. "Something we should know about that?"

"The name in Ancient Tulkish means the Great Warrior of Death. It has only been given to a few people over the millennia. They were often individuals who were notorious for causing great destruction for specific causes, but they never gave themselves the name. The name was usually used to describe our nation's heroes. For someone to give themself the name... I fear it is a tactic to pull people in and justify further violence. I need to bring this to the attention of the Tulkish Council as soon as possible." He stopped pacing. "Captain Williams, do you feel you can continue the investigation without me?"

"Yes, Ambassador Alsh."

"Excellent. May I request a copy of the reports for all three Tulku so I can bring their charges to the Tulkish Council? They need to be made aware of these crimes if they aren't already. I will not stand for Erev to suffer needlessly at the hands of my people."

Meg disappeared at Captain Williams' request and returned with several files, handing them to the Tulku.

Grenard thanked her. "Is there anything else I need to address while I am here?" When neither Williams nor Meg responded, he bowed deeply. "Thank you for indulging me."

The ambassador and Levi left the conference room, snaking their way out of the police station.

"I need to go to Yfalo tonight." Grenard looked at the boy. "I need to address the Tulkish Council and attempt to restore some sense of dignity and justice."

Levi's heart pounded in his chest. The only creature he truly cared about was about to leave. Would Grenard be back? Or would this be the last time? It seemed such a pathetic goodbye if this was it.

"Take me with you. Please."

Grenard froze and turned to him. "I'd gladly take you with me, but Feyer has made it quite clear that you cannot go to the East. I won't ask you to disobey orders."

Levi fiddled with his ring. "He doesn't have to know."

The Tulku scoffed. "He's bound to find out, my boy."

Levi's stomach twisted in a knot. "Not if we don't tell him. Feyer won't think to seek out witnesses if he doesn't suspect anything."

PART 3

CHAPTER 25

THE EAST

*L*evi clung to the rails of the ferry as he peered over the edge. Angry waves spewed their fury up the sides of the boat in frothy passion. Levi had seen the Murky Sea every day of his life, and even when he had gone swimming in its usual tides, he could always see the sandy bottom. But there was no telling how deep the dark waters were below him.

The strong, salty wind kept his hair from falling into his eyes as he searched the horizon for his first glance of the forbidden East. His stomach twisted in knots as the sun rose behind him and cast its rays towards Tulanu's shores. His mind was still reeling from his spur of the moment decision, and he had known there would be no turning back once he stepped foot on the boat. He had stepped on anyways. If Feyer ever found out... The boy shut out his own thoughts.

Grenard stood tall and proud next to him. Levi still found it strange to see him wearing a color other than purple. His emerald clothes shimmered strangely in the light. The ambassador also wore two pairs of long pieces of fabric draped over his shoulders, which were neatly tucked into his katom and nearly touched the ground. Levi assumed they were the tyam the Tulku had mentioned before. The more prominent set was made with silky royal purple fabric. Every edge was embroidered with fine golden thread in a pattern that resembled the syamta on Grenard's chest. The second set, mostly hidden by the first, was black with blood-red embroidery in the same royal syamta pattern. The Tulku's presence demanded respect, and Levi was more than happy to give it to him. The soldier amused himself by thinking about how he, of all humans, had been stuck with the king of the Tulku, a Vey of both position and inheritance.

"Levi." Grenard pointed at the horizon. "Yfalo is straight ahead, my boy."

Levi squinted and noticed one tiny blip that disrupted the otherwise perfectly straight horizon. The ferry plowed between two large hills that framed in a large, enclosed bay. At the far end, a wide-mouthed river dumped its contents into the cove. The entire city was nestled in the bend of the river. Yfalo did not sprawl like the cities of Erev. It shot straight up out of the ground, scraping the clouds with the tops of its staggeringly tall buildings, forcing Levi to tilt his head towards the sky.

As the ferry neared the docks, Grenard stepped closer to the boy. "Levi, you must stay by my side. That is the only way I can keep you safe." The Tulku's eyes were unusually intense.

"Yes, sir."

The soldier's heart pounded as he took his first steps on foreign soil. He followed right behind the ambassador as they left the boat behind and made their way into the depths of the crowded city. Thousands of Tulku walked the streets, wearing vyata and katoms of every color.

The Tulku themselves were much more colorful than Levi had anticipated. He had half expected them all to have the same rust-colored fur as Grenard. While they all had black-tipped ears, white-tipped tails, and slender faces, they each had a different fur color. Black, white, cream, purplish-gray. Every shade of red from light orange to mud-brown appeared in the crowds surrounding Levi. Some had random patches of white, and others had streaks of black. They all had shimmering syamta just as colorful as the clothes they wore.

It wasn't just the people that were shocking to see, but the city itself was nothing like Rylant. There wasn't a single brick building within sight; rather, the structures were made from earth, glass, metal, and wood. They twisted and turned as they grew into the sky. Some of the buildings were connected high above the ground by beautiful glass archways. Balconies spilled over with leafy green vegetation and brightly colored flowers.

Even the street wasn't really a street. Or at least, it wasn't made of asphalt, and there were no cars to be seen. Wide pathways divided the buildings from one another. The center of each lane was a greenway, flanked by two rows of trees. Children played in the grass while older Tulku sat on benches enjoying flowerbeds erupting with blossoms. Flocks of birds flew overhead, landing in the tops of the trees. Beyond the trees were paved walkways where the bulk of the crowd wandered.

Levi had to stop to take it all in. He had never imagined anything so awe-inspiring, but his gaze was quickly interrupted.

A stocky Tulku with cherry-red fur shoved him hard. "Why are you here, human? Is Feyer finally sending soldiers here to start a war?"

Levi stuttered as he regained his balance. "No—no, I'm here with the ambassador. Ambassador Alsh." He frantically looked around for his companion and felt his heart sink into the pit of his stomach. A small crowd was circling him, and Grenard was nowhere to be found. "Shit." He looked back at the cherry Tulku.

The Tulku's fists were balled at his sides. His snarl had morphed into a crooked sneer. "You ought to pay for the lives you've taken."

The crowd pressed in around Levi, agreeing with the Tulku.

"No! Wait, I need to find Ambassador Alsh. I swear I'm not here to hurt anyone. I'm trying to stop the war!"

Levi tried to leave, but the Tulku grabbed him and raised his fist high.

The soldier closed his eyes and braced himself. He would not fight back, not against them.

The murmuring of the crowd suddenly died down.

Levi looked about and instantly felt relief.

Grenard had his hand on the Tulku's shoulder and was staring at him sternly. "You will not lay a hand on this human. He is under my protection."

The Tulku studied the ambassador and, seeing Grenard's tyam, slowly released his grip and lowered his hand. He bowed his head and stepped back. "Yes, my Vey."

Grenard stood tall, head and shoulders above most of the Tulku, and addressed the crowd. "This boy is not your enemy. How can you claim to be better than the humans if you turn around and kill them after they have scratched you?"

"How can you say that?" A petite cream-colored Tulku pushed her way forward with tears in her eyes. "How can you say they have only scratched us? My family is dead because of them!" She collapsed at Grenard's feet, weeping. "Are we not allowed to even defend ourselves?"

The ambassador knelt and took her head in his hands. He brushed away her tears. "My daughter, I am not asking you to let yourself be massacred. By all means, defend yourself, but defend yourself from those who intend to do you harm, whether they be human or Tulku. Do not seek to hurt those who are innocent." He took her hands and pulled her to her feet.

She glowered at Levi. "How can I know he won't kill one of us?"

"You can't." Grenard's voice was compassionate and gentle. "You will have to take my word that this human has chosen to save my life on more than one occasion. He has no intention of harming anyone here."

The cream Tulku nodded and took a couple shaky breaths. "Thank you, my Vey."

Grenard dismissed the crowd and put his arm around Levi, steering him away. "Please don't leave my side. I would hate to see anything happen to you."

"I'm sorry. I got distracted."

Grenard smiled and patted his shoulder. "It's quite different from Rylant, I know. I promise I will let you take it all in, but I would prefer to get you to a safer vantage point."

Levi nodded. "That sounds like a good plan."

They walked along the street, making their way deeper into the city. Grenard only stopped to buy two bouquets of flowers from a small stand. As they continued, people spilled out of their way as if they were water. The deeper the pair went, the taller the buildings became, blocking the sunlight. The air became cool and still, nearly breathless. The crowds thinned and quieted as they approached Yfalo's center.

Levi's heart seized.

The large circular area was paved with what would have been pristine white stones, but they were caked with grime and ash. A statue, made of the same white stone, stood in the middle of a broken fountain at the circle's center. The stone figure looked as if it was crying as it stood in agony holding the unbearable weight of its surroundings. The trees that surrounded the fountain were black and no longer bore any leaves. The life of the rest of the city had been drained of its color and replaced with soot.

Levi stumbled and looked down. Broken stones under his feet formed a crater and were marred with black streaks that radiated out from where he stood.

Gray and black were not the only colors present. A dark rust was smeared across the ground. The more Levi looked, the more rust he found.

His crater was not the only one, either. Several other pock-marks scarred the city center, extending their reach even to the buildings they were closest to. Many of the buildings had lost their windows.

Memories of the videos Arden had sent flooded Levi's mind. He could see it all play out in front of him. He could see the dancers dressed in yellow twirling in front of the fountain and the explosions knocking them off their feet. He could see the crowds panic and flee for their lives as fire erupted. He could hear the glass as it shattered and fell to the ground. It was nauseating.

Grenard strode to one side of the plaza where square stones had been placed on top of each other to form well over a hundred semicircular coves. As Levi followed closely behind the ambassador, he saw that each stone wall guarded a picture and a name. Most pictures were accompanied with flowers, candles, and notes from loved ones.

They weren't the soulless animals Levi had been taught to believe they were.

The ambassador stopped at two adjacent memorials, that of Mava and H'nan G'nali. They were barren compared to the rest of the memorials, just pictures and nothing more. Grenard took the flowers in his hands and unwrapped one bouquet from the paper that bound it. Each bloom was lovingly placed one at a time around Mava's softly smiling face. She had the same fearsome eyes as her daughter, golden-green, though her fur was a matte brown color.

"Will you help me with H'nan's?" Grenard looked up at Levi with tears in his eyes and held out the second bouquet to him.

Levi took the blossoms and sank to his knees in front of the young Tulku's photograph. H'nan had the same black fur as his sister and forest-green syamta. The stone was cold and un-forgiving as the soldier carefully picked up one of the flowers. Just as Grenard had done with Mava, so Levi wreathed H'nan in blue and white flowers. When he was satisfied with his work, he stood and took a step back.

Levi, seeing one end of the memorials close by, walked over and began reading every single name. It was exhausting reading in Tulkish, but he wanted to know every person who had died at the hands of his race. He didn't know why, but he needed to know their names. He refused to skip a single one.

The last memorial belonged to a young child. Dozens of photographs were pinned to the stones. The child couldn't have been more than eight. He had a big smile in every picture, where he was running, or playing, or grinning at the camera. There were a few candles burning under the pictures, staining their bottom edges black. Small toys huddled together around the candles, craving the warmth of their owner that they would never feel again.

Levi sat on the cracked pavement as he stared at the photographs of the young Tulku. Kavali Ishna. That was the child's name. Tears silently slipped down Levi's cheeks. He could not understand why someone would choose to end something that had barely begun. This was a child with a family who loved him dearly. His parents would never get to hold him again. He would never play with his siblings again. His smile was forever locked away in these pictures.

The soldier eventually pushed himself up onto his feet and wiped his face with the cuff of his sleeve.

Grenard stood silently beside him and rested his hand on the boy's shoulder.

"This is not the one-sided conflict I thought it was."

"Both sides are a little more engaged than you initially thought, aren't they?"

"No, it's still one-sided. But it's not on the side I thought."

The ambassador sighed. "Most things are not entirely as they seem, son."

The boy looked back on the horrifying scene one last time. He had read a hundred and seventy-eight names.

CHAPTER 26
SPINNING
NEEDLE

Levi followed Grenard back to the land of the living where they entered a building that twisted into the sky a few blocks from the city center. The vibrancy didn't stop inside. A few small trees grew in the lobby, surrounded by flowers, but Levi didn't get an opportunity to gawk at the thriving indoor garden. Grenard had already found an elevator and was holding the doors open for the boy. Levi rushed to catch up. His eyes went wide as the ambassador hit the top button.

"There are ninety-five floors?"

Grenard smiled. "There are a few more than that. You can only get to the first ninety-five floors from this elevator. Take a look behind you, though."

Levi pivoted and stopped breathing. The side of the elevator was glass and looked out upon the city. The ground had already dropped far below them and the street they had walked on only moments before was rotating out of sight as they zipped along the curves of the building. Levi was completely mesmerized as he caught glimpses of the surrounding countryside through the tall structures hemming them in on every side. The higher they went, the more buildings dropped out of view, further exposing the thick sea of forests that shot out in every direction. When the elevator finally stopped, Grenard peeled Levi off the glass and pulled him onto the ninety-fifth floor.

There was a second lobby, though this one had significantly fewer trees growing in it. Several chairs and couches huddled together by the wall of windows on either side of a series of elevators. A few Tulku were quietly working at a reception desk in the middle of the floor.

Grenard patted Levi on the shoulder. "I'll just be a moment." He stepped up to the counter and struck up a conversation that Levi ignored.

The boy was drawn to the view like a magnet. The sun had started to set. Brilliant orange and red hues bounced around the city, illuminating it as if it were on fire.

"Levi."

He tore his gaze from the window. Grenard was waving for him to follow. They made their way deeper into the structure to another set of elevators that flung them even higher. The second elevator spat them out into a room with several hallways branching off of it. Grenard meandered down one such hallway and, having waved his tevet in front of the door handle, opened the only door in the corridor.

"We'll be staying here tonight. You get the room on the left." Grenard grinned in his usual suspect way.

Levi walked into a large domed room with a jaw-dropping view of the dusky city. A long, thin dining table, with tall chairs standing sentry, occupied the back of the room, guarding the various couches, chairs, and side table from intruders as they lounged in front of the view. The walls on either side of the long table wrinkled and twisted, forming strange doorways where no one could see through to the adjacent rooms.

The boy took his cue from Grenard and ambled through the left doorway. The bedroom was easily twice as large as the one he had grown used to at Feyer's compound. Two of the walls were floor to ceiling glass, revealing a wraparound balcony. The two glass walls were joined by a stone fireplace that cast a lovely glow about the room. A bed, two lounge chairs, and a squat table were the only furniture to fill the massive space.

Levi's bag slipped from his shoulders and landed on the short table as he approached the glass wall. One of the panels slid easily to the side and made way for a sharp and frigid breeze to eagerly greet Levi. He stepped out into the fast-approaching night.

The faintly glowing city was only obstructed by a planter box that sat on top of the glass barrier protecting Levi from the thousand-foot plummet to the street below. The box was filled with stiff, trailing greenery that laughed in the face of the wind that bullied it constantly. A sudden gust threatened to knock Levi off his feet and suck all the warmth from his body. Finding he was not as hardy as the plants, he hurried inside and recovered in front of the fire.

A tapping came from the doorway as Grenard poked his head into the room. "May I come in?"

"Yes." Levi stayed planted by the blaze and shoved his hands in his pockets. His fingers brushed against a small rectangular piece of metal.

"There's dinner on the table if you would like some."

"Thank you." Levi stared into the dancing flames. His mind began to wander over the past few days. "Why did I come here, Grenard?"

The Tulku walked up beside him. "I've been wondering the same thing, my boy."

Levi sighed.

"Maybe it has to do with that compass of yours."

The boy wondered what had pulled him to Yfalo. Was it true north? Or was it magnetite?

"I need to contact a few people this evening, but when I am done, we can talk if you'd like."

Levi nodded absently. He waited for the Tulku to leave before pulling the strange object from his pocket. It was one of the little black recordings from the Presidential Library, the one with Grenard and Vanyani talking to Anton. He sat on the ground and stared at it, turning it over in his hands. The recording was ruined. It was now nothing more than fried circuitry, but Levi held onto it. There was something about the memory the object held that prompted him to keep it.

His stomach complained loudly about having missed lunch. Levi shoved the recording back into his pocket and abandoned the fire for sustenance.

Several plain white ceramic dishes heaped with food sat contentedly on the dining table. Levi grabbed a plate and dished himself out colorful vegetables, meat, and a round pink fruit. He scarfed all of it down and served himself seconds. He carried his plate towards the windows and sat, gazing out at the city. He could hear Grenard talking in the other room.

The Tulku wandered in, grabbing his own plate of food. "Arden, I'm glad to hear your voice!" He paused. "Yes. I'm fine, but I need to ask a favor of you." He took his plate and meandered back into his room where Levi could no longer make out what he was saying.

The boy picked at the remainder of his food as his mind drifted. He set aside his half-eaten plate and tried to focus on the starry landscape at his fingertips. His thoughts began to swarm him. Why had he abandoned all sanity to come to Tulanu? Why had he broken direct orders? What had he hoped to achieve by coming here? He knew none of the answers to his questions. He felt overwhelmingly foolish.

This wasn't an act of carelessness he had committed. He was blatantly defying Feyer. And he didn't have an obvious reason for doing it, either. His father would never trust him again, and the consequences of that betrayal would be severe.

Levi's mind flashed back to the storage closet where he had hidden as a child. The images on the drawings blinded him. His lungs constricted, and his arms went numb. His thoughts somersaulted through the day Feyer had found his hideout and mixed with the stinging sensation from the newly formed scar on his cheek. Too much. Too much. Too much!

Levi raced to the bathroom, where his stomach betrayed him and rejected all the food he had just consumed. He shook violently and sunk to the floor until his limbs no longer felt like gelatin. He peeled his boots off and crawled into bed, waiting for sleep to come. His eyelids grew heavy, but his mind refused to settle. Dozens of agonizing scenarios played on repeat.

After several fruitless attempts to calm his raging mind, Levi sat up and rubbed his weary eyes. A faint light crept from the doorway. Levi followed it to its source and, unsurprisingly, found Grenard sitting silently with a journal in hand. The boy slumped into a chair by the windows across from the Tulku.

"I can't sleep either." Grenard closed the journal.

Levi sank even further into the chair and folded his arms over his chest. He didn't know how to express the turmoil in his head. "I think my compass is broken."

"What makes you think that is the case?"

"It doesn't feel like it's pointing in any one direction. It's just spinning."

Grenard sighed. "I'm not convinced your compass is broken, my boy."

Levi scowled. "I've disobeyed a direct order, and I don't even know why. I came here fully knowing the consequences for my actions. If Feyer ever finds out…"

"Every action has consequences. Some are good. Some are bad. Even when we follow true north, there are still valleys we must walk through and mountains we must summit. I don't believe you came here to spite Feyer. But I do think you're trying to distinguish north from the magnetite, and those who may be stuck in the magnetite don't always like it when people leave or tell them they may be wrong."

"When Feyer finds out, it won't just be that he doesn't like me straying from him. He will try to destroy my compass if it isn't already broken."

Grenard's brows furrowed. "How would he do that?"

Levi pulled his knees to his chest and forced the bubbling emotions down.

"I will never be able to understand if you tell me nothing, son."

The boy debated if he dared share, but his throat refused to let his voice pass. All he could do was focus on breathing.

Grenard's ears drooped. "You waited in Trifort for me while I spent a few days here to discuss with the Council how to handle the Tulku who were arrested. You never stepped foot on the ferry. You never stepped foot in Tulanu. Feyer will never know otherwise."

"I thought lying was supposed to be bad."

"Lying usually hurts people, but this seems to be one of those gray situations where I'm protecting someone who is being threatened."

Levi looked up at the Tulku.

Grenard half-heartedly smiled. "Try to get some sleep. We have much to do tomorrow."

Levi made his way back to his room and changed into his usual long-sleeved shirt and sweatpants. He crawled in between the sheets. It took him a few minutes to process what Grenard had said, but with the plan in place for Feyer to stay in the dark, his mind began to calm. His eyelids closed, and his thoughts drifted to a halt.

"Vanyalida, son."

The words barely registered as Levi slipped into slumber.

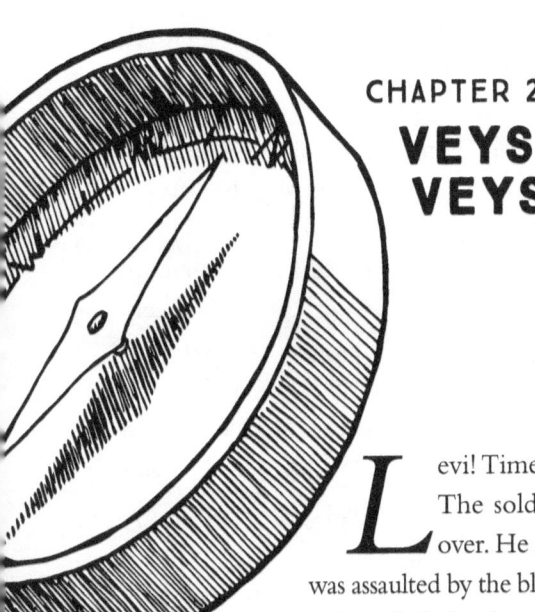

CHAPTER 27
VEYS AND
VEYS TO-BE

L evi! Time to get up, my boy!"
The soldier groaned and turned
over. He forced his eyes open and
was assaulted by the blinding light of late morning. He pulled the sheets over his head, wanting
to go back to sleep.

"Come on. We're going to be late!" Grenard walked into
his room and nudged the boy. "I know you're awake."

"Your yelling woke me up." Levi's voice was muffled by the
sheets. He pushed them down and glared at the Tulku.

"Intentionally so. Get dressed." Grenard was tying his katom
around his waist, holding his tyam in place.

Levi rubbed his eyes and yawned. "Is there a reason for
the rush?"

"The Tulkish Council is expecting us shortly, and they do
not take kindly to a lack of timeliness. I want their full attention
and respect this morning." The ambassador fidgeted with all the
folds of fabric, ensuring they were all perfectly in place.

Levi kicked the sheets off and trudged to his crumpled
uniform and picked it up off the floor. He started to pull his

shirt over his head but froze when he realized Grenard was still in the room. "Can I have some privacy?"

Grenard glanced up. "Yes. Of course."

As soon as the Tulku had disappeared into the other room, Levi changed and, seeing his reflection in the glass, he tried to brush through his wildly out-of-control hair. He could feel it sticking out haphazardly, refusing any sort of cooperation, but there wasn't time to shower and tame it. Or at least there wasn't time from what Grenard had indicated. Levi plodded out to the common area where Grenard stood anxiously at the door with his satchel over his shoulder. The ambassador pushed Levi out the door, barely letting him grab a piece of fruit and his boots.

"Can't I put on my shoes?"

"Do it in the elevator."

Once they had started their initial descent, Levi bent down and laced his boots, frowning at the Tulku the whole time. "When were you going to tell me you were going to meet with the Tulkish Council?"

"Last night, but you had already gone to bed. I didn't think it would be a good idea to wake you then. I just didn't expect to be telling you with thirteen minutes to spare." Grenard glanced at his tevet and frowned. His tail twitched nervously, and his fingers drummed on his satchel.

"Thirteen minutes!" Levi pulled at his hair. "There's something called an alarm, Grenard."

The ambassador huffed, brows furrowed. "Yes, I realize that. I stayed up later than I anticipated and slept through my alarm. It is fortunate we only have to go two blocks down the street."

"Why do you need me there? Isn't it safer for me to stay here than go with you?" Levi bit into the fruit, ravenous.

The doors of the first elevator opened, and they raced to the second one. Grenard hit the first button. "Yes, it would be safer, but I need you to tell them what you've seen."

Levi sucked the juice from the fruit. "Why? What have I seen that they will care about? I'm a human. They're not going to believe a word I have to say."

Grenard sighed. "They might choose to care because you're a human, asking for their help."

The boy rubbed his eyes. "That doesn't make any sense."

"Think about the EMP, Levi. If they knew what it had done to just your people, think how much they might also care about preventing that from happening here. It might appeal to their better nature. That's why they'll listen."

Levi still wasn't fully convinced as they spilled out of the elevator and raced two blocks down the street. They dashed into a stately building and found themselves on the fiftieth floor where a Tulku dressed similarly to Grenard stood waiting in front of a large set of double doors.

The Tulku was still a little taller than Levi, but shorter than the ambassador. He had white fur with a few patches of cream on the lower half of his arms and feet. He wore a navy ensemble and also had two sets of tyam. One set was dark gray with maroon symbols, and the other was royal blue with gold embroidery. His ice-blue eyes pierced Levi, and he carried himself with the same great authority and calm disposition Grenard had on every day except that day.

The ambassador beamed. "Vey Halya."

The white Tulku sighed. "You're late, Grenard."

"My apologies, Kvenu. I'm just grateful the Council was willing to hear me on such short notice." The ambassador bowed then gestured to the soldier. "This is Levi. I would like for him to speak to them as well."

Vey Kvenu Halya's eyes narrowed. "They won't like it." He stared at the boy a moment longer, then sighed and shook his head. "Come on. Let's see if we can't convince them to let him in."

Grenard's ears perked up and his tail swished from side to side.

Kvenu gestured towards a few chairs between the windows and the foreboding doors. "Levi, please wait here while Vey Alsh and I see if we can't convince the Council to hear you."

Levi complied with Kvenu's request and watched apprehensively as the two Tulku stepped inside the dark room. The doors closed thunderously.

Time marched on at a snail's pace. The lack of a substantial breakfast began to gnaw at Levi as the minutes turned to hours. He paced the empty space, occasionally staring down at the crowds as they ebbed and flowed through the streets. Levi was standing at the window when the doors burst open behind him.

"Worthless!" Grenard stormed out with Kvenu right on his tail.

"Grenard, they are still Veys."

The ambassador swiveled and snarled in the white Tulku's face. "Yes, and how many of them have actually been called to lead? How many of them have any kind of syamta that says they should be making any kind of decision for Tulanu or her people? They aren't like you and me. They're foolish cowards!"

Kvenu took a deep breath. "I'm not saying I agree with them."

"Good!" The ambassador paced about wildly. "You had better not agree with them. They were elected by a blind and ignorant people. There's a reason why the syamta choose some and not others—"

"Grenard!" Kvenu grabbed the ambassador by the shoulders and forced him to stop.

The rust-colored Tulku slowly relaxed and looked into Kvenu's blue eyes.

"I know how things ought to be. But that is precisely why you and I are here. We are here to fulfill our callings in life as best we can, knowing the Council will not freely give up their power. Believe me when I say I would much rather be at your side than sitting here every day, arguing endlessly. I know you're right and you've been right for a long time. Give me a chance to discuss with them and try to sway them. That is one battle I can fight for you." He glanced at the soldier. "Go feed yourselves, then we'll listen to what Levi has to say."

Grenard's ears fell back. "Please forgive my outburst."

"Always, my Veyka." Kvenu bowed and returned to the room.

Grenard sighed then turned to the boy. "Come on. I know you're hungry."

Levi waited awkwardly for the ambassador to say anything as they descended to ground level. He shifted on his feet. "It sounds like there's a story between you and that other Tulku."

"Yes. There's always a story, isn't there?"

"Will you tell me?"

The ambassador smiled. "I believe I told you some about the War of Bitterness."

"Yes, K'thanu was removed from the throne."

Grenard nodded. "Before the monarchy was destroyed, there were a few families attached to the kingship. The Halyas were one such family. They served as the commanders of Tulanu's armies. The Alshs and the Halyas have always managed to stay close over the centuries." Grenard scoffed. "Well, with the exception of Kvenu's older brother and my father."

"What did you mean by the other Veys not being like you and Kvenu?"

Grenard's gaze dropped to the ground. "Hjaniyalu isn't the only syamta that has Vey status attached to it. Ka'idonve is one that runs in the Halya family. Just as Hjaniyalu does not choose any random Alsh to be Veyka, Ka'idonve does not choose any random Halya to be Veydon. Those are the only two syamta that indicate leadership over the whole of Tulanu."

"So that's why he has two tyam, as well."

"Yes."

The ambassador led the way to a small shop across the street where they ordered sandwiches. They found a place to sit in the greenbelt and soaked in the noonday sun. The sandwich wasn't much different from what Levi was used to in Rylant, though the bread was heavier, and the contents were much more filling. Levi quickly finished his meal and lay back in the grass. His mind freely roamed.

"Grenard, how did you become an ambassador?"

The Tulku didn't respond.

Levi craned his neck to see the ambassador. "Grenard?"

The Tulku glanced at him. "I ran away from home."

The boy sat up. "Why?"

Grenard took a deep breath. "My father and I did not get along very well. So I joined Tulanu's rather pathetic military to learn how to fight. Kvenu's father saw me and redirected me to train under G'nali thinking my skills would better serve Tulanu in this position than fighting for her directly. I don't know if he made the right call, but my life hasn't seemed to play out too poorly because of it. That is also how I met Kvenu."

A hundred questions sprouted in the soldier's mind. "Why didn't you get along with your father?"

"Let's just say there were several very good reasons why my father did not inherit Hjaniyalu."

Levi knew better than to poke further. The Tulku knew Jake had hit him and had taken the time to mend his wounds. The boy wondered if Grenard's father had committed similar crimes.

A quarrel broke out, disrupting the soldier's thoughts. He looked about and saw a man bickering with a male Tulku a few paces away. Their bickering escalated to yelling as they began shoving each other.

"Get to the back of the line, space trash!"

"I've been waiting, just like everyone else."

Levi bolted towards them without thinking and tore them off each other and put himself between them. "Knock it off! How is fighting over something stupid going to help anyone?" He went from glaring at the man to the Tulku. "We're all civilized here. Figure it out like adults."

The man growled at him and shoved him to the ground. "You're one of Feyer's soldiers! Go back to Erev. All you'll do is make everything worse."

Levi gaped as the man and the Tulku both loomed over him.

"Leave him alone. And I suggest you both go your separate ways before someone calls law enforcement." Grenard frowned and helped Levi to his feet.

They begrudgingly bowed towards the ambassador and scurried off in opposite directions.

"Ba? Is that you?" Another rust-colored Tulku stood a few paces away.

Grenard's ears perked up immediately. He smiled and ran up to the Tulku. "Arden!" He hugged his son fiercely, then stepped back and regarded him with great pride. "You got here rather quickly."

The Tulku shrugged. "I left at 5:30 this morning. The train is fast, but traveling across half the country still takes time."

Levi stood at a distance. Arden looked like an exact replica of the ambassador with the exception of his syamta. The lines in his fur took on different patterns and were a bright orange instead of Grenard's gold.

Arden glanced over at the soldier. "You must be Levi." The greeting was cold and sterile.

The boy smiled and held out his hand. "It's nice to meet you."

Arden stared at Levi's outstretched hand curiously, then looked up at his father.

Grenard laughed. "You shake hands in Erev instead of bowing. Haven't you learned anything from me?" He ushered them towards the grass.

Arden sat across from his father while Levi lay back down and basked in the sunlight that was slipping over the edge of the surrounding skyscrapers.

"There's so much to tell you, Ba."

"Then tell me all."

"Beka started doing three surgery days with Dr. Vealen after she passed her most recent test with flying colors last week. Ailu got another solo. He and Roni are touring with the Lassi Symphonic Orchestra. They'll be gone for a few weeks. Oshi got all the seeds started for the garden and has been looking into potential positions for when he graduates."

Grenard smiled. "That is all excellent news. How is Zev?"

"Beka told you, didn't she?"

"She mentioned that he has been fighting for our dear little Ren to be more appropriately placed considering his capabilities."

Arden sighed. "It still hasn't gone anywhere, and we haven't been able to host him on the weekends as much as usual."

"Hmm. I'm not particularly excited to hear that. Why not?"

"Everyone's been stressed. Zev and I weren't sure it was a good idea for him to be around with everyone acting out and fighting all the time."

"I see. I assume Kido was part of the reason for making that decision. How is he handling everything?"

Arden huffed. "He's not handling anything, at all. If he isn't carving bows, he's out frolicking in the forest shooting them. He's become obsessed with recreating great, great-grandfather's bow. He doesn't do any studying, doesn't look for a job, doesn't do anything except hunt and help Oshi with the garden."

"He's helping feed all of you as you are off pursuing your dreams. That is not nothing."

Arden groaned. "I just wish he was a little more predictable. I never know when he's going to blow up."

"It isn't your job to control him. It's your job to live out Vanyalida and support each other. I know it has been tough with my not being able to reach anyone. I know finances have become tight. Unfortunately there hasn't been much I've been able to do. Even my backup communications were blocked."

"When are you coming home, Ba? I don't like you being over there even if Levi's as good as you say he is."

Levi held his breath as he listened.

"Maybe a week or two. It depends on how the remainder of the council session goes today and how Feyer responds to negotiations. Some complications came up in Trifort a few days ago. That's why I'm here."

A week. That was all the time Levi had left with Grenard, then the ambassador would be gone forever. His heart sunk into the pit of his stomach.

Arden cleared his throat. "I almost forgot. You asked me to bring this from home."

Levi glanced over at them. Arden handed Grenard a large square box wrapped in brown paper. It could have been anything, and it was none of his business, so he resumed watching the birds fly overhead.

"Arden, when will you be needing to leave?"

"The next train leaves in an hour."

"I see." Grenard paused and grinned. "You said you were interested in international politics. Come listen to me debate with the Council for a while. This could be a good start without you having to leave the safety of Tulanu."

"Don't they restrict who has access to the meetings?"

"Yes, but Vey Halya is their gatekeeper today. Kvenu will let you in, I'm sure."

Grenard stood and stretched, giving Levi the cue that it was time to return to the Council. The three of them returned to the fiftieth floor and found Kvenu waiting for them once more.

The white Tulku frowned when he saw Arden. "You're pushing your luck, Grenard."

The ambassador smiled coyly. "I push my luck everywhere I go. You know this already."

Kvenu rubbed his temples. "Yes, I'm afraid I do know that." He opened the doors and ushered them in.

Grenard patted Kvenu on the back. "I appreciate it."

The white Tulku only smirked. "I let you get away with too much."

"Yes, but is it really too much when you know I'm right?"

Kvenu smiled and rolled his eyes, escorting the trio into the expansive room.

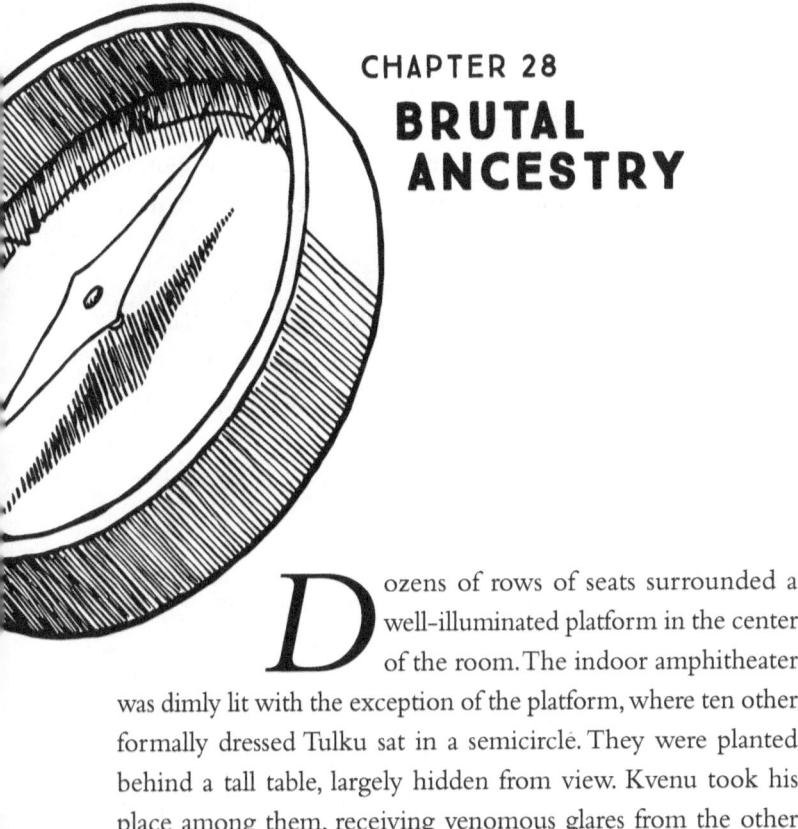

CHAPTER 28
BRUTAL ANCESTRY

ozens of rows of seats surrounded a well-illuminated platform in the center of the room. The indoor amphitheater was dimly lit with the exception of the platform, where ten other formally dressed Tulku sat in a semicircle. They were planted behind a tall table, largely hidden from view. Kvenu took his place among them, receiving venomous glares from the other council members.

One Tulku with dark brown fur and light yellow syamta stood and cleared her throat. "Vey Alsh, what is the meaning of this?"

Grenard stood at the podium in the middle of the circle while Arden sat in the first row. Levi hung suspended between them, unsure if he should sit or stand while he waited to answer the Council's questions.

"Vey Saj, if you are referring to the presence of my son, I say this: I am not growing any younger, and you have refused to let me train a successor. Arden is training under another ambassador who knows nothing of international politics, yet you expect him to take over my role with no training or experience. Let him have some exposure.

"If you are referring to the human, he is the boy I mentioned earlier and requested for him to speak in your presence, which you so graciously accepted."

Vey Saj took her seat, glaring at Grenard. "If I had known Levi was a soldier, I would not have agreed."

"I am well aware of that fact. But it is precisely because he is a soldier who has risked his life in more than one way to come speak to you that you will listen to him."

"If you are so confident in him, let him come forward."

Grenard nodded and bowed to the Council. He stepped down and gave Levi a hopeful smile.

The soldier tentatively approached the ambassador. He kept his voice low. "What do I tell them?"

"Tell them what you've seen, what you've learned. Tell them your concerns about Feyer's actions."

Levi nodded, took a deep breath, and stepped into the spotlight. He looked over the eleven slender faces staring down at him, most with sneers on their lips. He held onto the edges of the podium to steady himself.

Levi collected his thoughts and began, keeping his eyes focused on the ground. "I—I've been raised to hate the Tulku my whole life and—" He swallowed. "And I've been taught to see your people as lesser than my own. We call you animals, and if a human has to interact with a Tulku, they are also seen as lesser than." He looked up at the unenthused Tulku. Unsure, he glanced back at Grenard. Seeing the rust-colored Tulku just behind him nod, he took a deep breath. "I was forced to reconsider that position when I was assigned to guard Ambassador Alsh three months ago.

"Ambassador Alsh has displayed an incredible amount of compassion not just for his people, but also the people of Erev. That is a mindset I have come to appreciate and accept for myself. It has become clear to me that neither of our nations can succeed without cooperation from each other. That has been the case for decades, and I don't expect that to change any time soon. Erev cannot survive without resources from Tulanu, but Tulanu will not be able to survive a full attack from Erev if tensions are not resolved."

Kvenu leaned forward, brows furrowed. "May I ask you a question, Levi?"

The boy froze. "Uh. Yes, sir—Vey Halya." Levi cringed at his mistake.

"What do you mean by a full attack from Erev?"

Levi shoved his hands in his pockets and found the useless black box. "That's why I'm here today. I—I found a recording dating back twenty-seven years. President Anton Feyer was proposing to start a secret nuclear weapons program in full knowledge that he was breaking international treaties and breaking our own nation's laws. I suspect President Jake Feyer has continued that program considering we just survived an EMP. I recognize that Tulanu may not have felt those effects to the same extent as Erev, but I just lost thousands of my people to a high-altitude test of one of these weapons. If President Feyer were to decide to go to war, Rufosia would become an uninhabitable wasteland just like Earth."

"What proof do you have that these weapons really exist?"

Levi frowned, and his hands balled into fists. "Lightning strikes don't cause catastrophic failure of power grids in multiple cities hundreds of kilometers apart. And I have been told Tulanu has the capability of seeing solar flares coming and would supposedly warn Erev if such an event were to occur. Since that has not happened, what else is left but to assume the EMP was created by a nuclear weapon? Humans have had this kind of technology for hundreds of years, and we clearly haven't used it well. Maybe you don't want to admit it's true, but history does repeat itself."

The Council sat, thinking and glancing at one another. Kvenu's expression had grown particularly grave.

Levi anxiously awaited a response. When he received silence, he continued. "I need help protecting my own people— No, I need help protecting the world from Feyer. I don't want to see Rufosia turn into Earth, but I can't prevent that by myself. Rufosia is my home, too, whether or not the Tulku want me here."

Vey Saj looked down upon him. "Why do you put this burden on your shoulders? You're a soldier, and it seems a low-ranking one at that. It shouldn't be your responsibility to keep your president in line."

Levi frowned. "I could ask why you haven't. You have treaties with Erev! You should be making sure Erev is holding up their end of the deal, not putting yourselves in danger by not holding another nation accountable."

"Point taken, but you still haven't answered my question."

Levi dropped his gaze and lowered his voice. "Not every son wants to become like his father."

Vey Saj tilted her head to the side, her ears trained on the boy. "I'm not sure I understand your comment. Who is your father?"

Levi turned to Grenard. He didn't know what he should say, what he could say. He didn't know what was right or what was wrong. He didn't want to hide, but he didn't know how they would respond to the truth.

The ambassador gave him a reassuring nod. "You can choose not to answer, Levi."

"Vey Alsh, you do not get to speak for the Council!" Vey Saj stood with her hands firmly on the table before her and her fur bristling with electricity. "Who is your father, human?"

The soldier looked her directly in the eyes. "My name is Levi Matthew Feyer. I am the son of Jake Feyer and the grandson of Anton Feyer and the great-grandson of Alexander Feyer."

All eleven of the council members shouted out at once. Levi stumbled back from the podium and watched as they bickered among themselves and spewed violent words at everyone in the room. Grenard pulled Levi back and made him sit next to a fuming Arden. Levi didn't dare look in the direction of the Tulku beside him.

The ambassador stepped up and glowered at the Council. "Pull yourselves together!"

The council members quieted and slowly regained their composure.

Grenard stood tall before them and cleared his throat. "You have a choice before you. You can prepare our nation so that it can defend itself. Or you can let this open wound fester until we all suffer the fatal consequences."

Vey Saj pounded her fist on the table. "I will not stand for mutiny, Vey Alsh. Maybe if you had been more effective at performing your duties, we would not be having this conversation."

Grenard scoffed. "Have you ever considered that not everyone can be reasoned with? There are people who exist whose only motive is to satisfy their own desires. I cannot control everyone, let alone change one person's mind, yet you would blame me for being ineffective!"

"Yes, I would blame you. Your sole job is to maintain peace."

"No. My sole calling is to protect my people."

Vey Saj snarled. "Remember your place, Vey Alsh. You are not king, nor will you ever be."

"Whose fault is that? Because it certainly isn't mine."

"Blame your forefather."

Grenard's shoulders bunched. "I am not K'thanu!"

Vey Saj had a sly grin creeping over her face. "No? You seem just as war-hungry as he and just as desperate to be right and just as desperate to have power."

Kvenu cleared his throat. "Saj, you forget that it was your grandfather who ultimately put us in this predicament. It was his pride that lost us our oldest and most valuable ally. We wouldn't be debating if we had Phirevsk providing us with access to the best military in the world."

"I am not my grandfather, Halya!"

"No, of course not. But you did learn your ways from him and became his successor. It seems as if you are just as eager to cling to power and just as prideful and just as blind."

"You always take Grenard's side. It's the Halya obligation to foolishly follow the Alshs."

Kvenu slowly stood, towering over the other council members. "I take the side of defending Tulanu. I take the side of humbly considering that my king may actually be right, even when I don't like it. I take the side of striving for all to live without fear of their lives being taken from them. I take the side of pursuing truth."

Vey Saj sat stewing in anger, her lips curled into a snarl and her ears pinned flat against her head. Her gaze darted towards Grenard. "Alsh, take your son and your space trash and leave."

The ambassador bowed silently and waved for Arden and Levi to follow. Once the doors closed behind them, Grenard sighed.

"What happens now, Ba?"

"We wait."

It felt as if time had slowed to a creeping halt as Levi watched Grenard pace in front of the windows. Hope seemed to be slipping away until Kvenu slipped out of the auditorium. Levi straightened, anxious to hear the update.

The white Tulku approached the ambassador. "They said no."

Grenard stopped. "Did they say why?"

"They do not want to unnecessarily risk innocent lives based on the statement of a boy who should be dead and a Tulku who they perceive just wants power."

Grenard pinned his ears back and stormed towards the auditorium. He threw the doors open. "Your decision will cost you millions of lives. It has already cost you thousands! If it were my decision, we would have never gotten to this place to begin with. I would have stopped it long before Jake Feyer got his hands on nuclear weapons that work!"

"I already told you to leave once, Grenard. I will have you escorted out, and you will never be welcome back in this council." Vey Saj pointed behind him.

Grenard stormed outside and marched in front of the windows, miserably muttering to himself as Kvenu, Arden and Levi watched from a safe distance. Levi peered at the two Tulku next to him, unsure what to do. Arden only sneered at him, but Kvenu's sorrowful gaze was fixed on Grenard. The white Tulku drew near to the ambassador.

"My Veyka."

Grenard brushed him away. "Don't 'Veyka' me, Kvenu. I know you have good intent, but that is not the same as action or outcome."

"I was going to ask what your plan was and how I might be able to help."

Grenard stopped pacing and sighed. "If the Council wants diplomacy, they shall have it, however fruitless it may be. Jake Feyer will not change his ways, and I'm the last Tulku he will listen to."

"Then, let me come with you. Let me talk with him and see if I can't aid in persuading him."

Grenard shook his head. "No. He will only see it as a threat if I bring someone else to help fight my battle with him. Your place is here. Wear the Council down and take every centimeter they budge on so we might have a fighting chance."

"Yes, my Veyka." Kvenu bowed deeply.

Grenard glanced at his tevet, then up at his son. "Arden, your train will be leaving soon."

"I'm not sure I'm ready to go yet."

Grenard smiled and walked up to the young Tulku. "None of us ever truly are, but your brothers will be needing you home sooner than later. I'm sure Kido has started another fight already."

Arden sputtered out a laugh. He threw his arms around his father. "Please come back safely. And I promise I will try to not kill Kido while you're away."

Grenard fully embraced his son. "I'll do my best. Now, don't miss your train, and tell them all Vanyalida."

Arden nodded then scampered off.

"Do you really think you'll make it back after everything you told me last night?" Kvenu eyed Grenard.

"I don't know."

Levi fiddled with his ring. "Vey Halya, I fully intend to do everything in my power to ensure that Ambassador Alsh makes it back to Tulanu."

The white Tulku sighed and looked at the boy. "You worry me, as well, Levi. I'm sure your father will not be pleased to hear you came here."

Grenard's ears flattened. "Feyer won't find out."

"Don't be too sure of yourselves. I'm sure Feyer can find out anything he wants."

Grenard frowned.

Kvenu put a hand on Grenard's shoulder. "When are you heading back?"

Grenard turned to Levi. "Do you think we can make it back to Rylant tonight?"

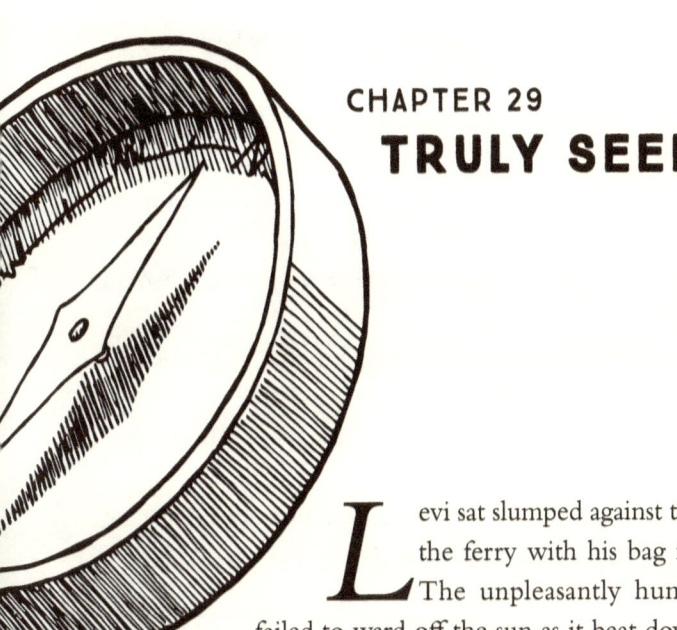

CHAPTER 29
TRULY SEEN

*L*evi sat slumped against the rails of the ferry with his bag in his lap. The unpleasantly humid wind failed to ward off the sun as it beat down on his pale skin. He fiddled with the little black recording from his pocket. Staring down at the nicks and dings in the casing, he felt a strange sort of solemn camaraderie with the object. He studied every scratch and memorized them with his fingers as his mind battled conflicting notions.

Levi's assignment to the ambassador was quickly drawing to an end. While he, at one point in time, had wished for this day to come, now that it was here, he wanted nothing more than for it to have never approached. He had been so used to the quiet of his routine lifestyle that when Grenard showed up, his world had been greatly upset. Yet a sinking feeling now consumed him, one he had never truly experienced before.

Loneliness.

The word rolled around in his head and left a dry taste in his mouth. He sat, contemplating the uncomfortable hollowness. It was exactly like the black box, surprisingly heavy, useless and broken.

Grenard walked up to him, and Levi tucked the black box into his sleeve.

The Tulku sank down beside him. "You don't seem quite yourself. What's on your mind?"

"When were you going to tell me you knew you would be leaving?"

Grenard sighed. "Levi, you always knew I would not be staying forever."

Levi nodded and felt his throat tighten. He bit his lip and turned away from the Tulku.

"I did not know until we met with the Council. They are wanting me to come back to Tulanu."

"But why?" Levi's vision began to blur.

"They are afraid I will make matters worse, I suspect." Grenard put his arm around the boy's shoulders. "I'm not leaving Erev forever, my boy. I will always find a way back."

"We both know Feyer will do whatever the hell he wants."

Grenard grunted. "Yes."

"I don't want things to go back to the way they were before you came."

"Nothing ever truly goes back to the way it was before, for better or for worse."

Levi scoffed. "You're right. Nothing will be the same. When Feyer finds out everything I've done, my life will be ten times worse than it was before you came." He glared at Grenard, tears silently slipping down his cheeks.

Grenard's amber eyes melted, and he squeezed the boy's shoulder. "Will you tell me?"

Levi sniffed and brushed off Grenard's arm.

"You said you trusted me. Why trust me with everything but this?"

The boy's fists balled up, and his voice grew hoarse. "Because some secrets make everyone run away."

"I haven't run yet."

"But you will! It won't even matter because you're leaving, and I'm going to be stuck in Rylant the rest of my life. There's nothing you can do."

"Maybe not, but I would still like to try to help."

Levi shook his head and watched the waves spray along the side of the boat.

"I have something for you."

Levi ignored the Tulku as he pulled out something from his satchel.

"I said that if I had the opportunity to bring you a book in English, I would."

Levi slowly turned to him and gazed at the brown package. He shook his head. "Is this supposed to be some kind of bribe, Grenard?"

"No. As much as I would like you to tell me what's going on, that is your decision and only your decision. However, I made a promise to you that I intended on keeping."

He glanced into Grenard's kind amber eyes, hesitated, then gave in and took the book. He peeled back the paper and revealed a beautiful leather-bound copy of *The Lord of the Rings* by J. R. R. Tolkien. It was a story Levi had always been curious about but had never been allowed to read.

"I think you might fancy this story a little more than *Robin Hood*, if you give it a chance."

Levi brushed the cover delicately. "You didn't need to have Arden travel all that way for me."

Grenard smiled. "I thought it was important enough."

"Thank you." Levi opened the book with a crackle. He flipped through its worn and yellowed pages. Most of the words he recognized, but it would still take some work to read through.

Grenard's kindness confounded Levi. He thought about his trust in the loving creature beside him the whole way back. They arrived in Trifort just before sunset and didn't make it back to Rylant until close to midnight. By the time they made it back to Feyer's mansion, Grenard was dragging his feet along the ground. He let his satchel drop to the floor in a haphazard pile in the middle of his room before collapsing in a pile on his bed.

Levi stood in the commons just beyond the Tulku's view, paralyzed. He didn't know if he could tell Grenard what had been plaguing him for so long. He had never told anyone before.

Could he really trust anyone with his secret? It was too painful to risk exposing, but every other time he had shared anything with the Tulku, Grenard had been gentle and patient. This hidden pain was a burden he was tired of carrying; he just didn't know how to let go of it. Maybe, just maybe, Grenard would know what to do.

He set his bag on the kitchen table. His shaking hands made their way to the collar of his shirt and undid the top button. The second one struggled to come free, but the others soon followed until the shirt hung limp on his shoulders. He yanked at the cuffs, slid the shirt off, and draped it over the back of one of the chairs.

Levi's breath caught in his throat. Was he really doing this? Was he really going to show Grenard?

He pulled the tan undershirt over his head and let it fall to the floor. There, on the ground, lay Levi's walls, his safety, crumpled up and discarded. He knelt and reached out, but he stopped himself. He pulled at his hair and paced back and forth until he finally broke and walked to Grenard's bedroom door.

Levi knocked twice.

"Yes, my boy?" The Tulku looked at him expectantly, but his exhausted pleasantries drained away as soon as he saw the young soldier, leaving only horror on his slender face.

Levi's heart pounded through his chest as he cautiously stepped inside. He kept his gaze trained on the ground. When the boy dared look up, his vision was obscured with tears.

Levi's skin was a battlefield of white, warped flesh. Long streaks crossed his back in a horribly disorganized checkerboard pattern. There were nicks from his neck to his wrists. They lay like dead bodies, memorializing every mistake he had ever made.

Grenard's ears fell limply to either side of his head. He didn't say anything as he stood and slowly circled the boy, taking in every detail.

The boy's hands trembled uncontrollably at his sides. "I'm not supposed to make mistakes. If I do, I'm not supposed to show any weakness." He took a shaky breath. "When I got in trouble for doing something he didn't approve of, he would assign me a certain number of lashes. I wasn't supposed to make a noise while he hit me. If I did, he would add another one for every time I cried out." Tears slipped down his cheeks, and he bit his lip. "There was one time where I remember he beat me until I lost my voice. I—I don't even remember what I did, just that I couldn't scream anymore. He always told me it was for my good, so I'd learn. So I could be great like him. So I could be better than him."

Levi hated the Tulku's silence. He hated being so vulnerable, but he was paralyzed. "You said you chose to love me, but how could anyone choose to love this? I'm worthless and broken.

I will never be good enough. How the hell am I supposed to protect you when I can't even protect myself?"

Grenard stopped in front of him, but Levi couldn't bear to meet his gaze. He didn't want to see the disappointment that he was sure would be smeared over the Tulku's face.

Grenard took the boy's face in his hands and brushed away the tears. Levi looked up and saw the ambassador's eyes welling up. "My son, how could I possibly love you any less?" He wrapped his arms firmly around the boy.

Levi froze as fear flooded him for a brief moment. But the ambassador's touch was soft and reassuring. He slowly relaxed and returned the Tulku's embrace. He could not remember if he had ever been hugged before. He didn't want to let go. He couldn't. He sobbed into Grenard's shoulder and clung to him all the tighter.

The Tulku rested his chin on top of Levi's head and squeezed him, grieving with him. "I will never run from you." He let go and brushed Levi's hair out of his eyes. "I finally see you. And now I truly understand. I love you far too much to simply abandon you." He grabbed the blanket off the foot of the bed and draped it over Levi's shoulders. "I'll listen if you want me to."

The boy nodded and found himself sitting cross-legged on the end of Grenard's bed. He pulled the blanket tight around himself and took a deep breath. "Was your father like mine?"

"In some ways." The Tulku sat in front of him. "There were times when he hit me, but never like that. Can I ask how long this has been going on?"

Levi shrugged and twisted the ring on his right middle finger. "I think I was five. That's when my training started. I don't remember him ever taking an interest in me before then. I actually don't think I really knew who he was because he just didn't exist until I was old enough to start taking orders…"

The boy told his story, and it felt good to finally shine light into the depths of his life. What had been hidden for so long was now exposed, and the hideous form of his pain writhed as it was examined for the first time.

Levi, when he had finished, looked into Grenard's eyes and saw a creature willing to set fire to heaven and freeze hell for him. He didn't understand it, but there was no other being on Rufosia, Earth, or any place in between that he loved more than the ambassador.

"Levi, do you want to stay here?"

The boy sighed. "I can't leave, Grenard."

"That's not what I asked. Do you want to leave?"

"Of course I want to, but where would I go? Where would I ever be free of him? He can find me anywhere!"

"Come back to Tulanu with me. Feyer won't be able to touch you as long as you're with me."

Levi's eyes went wide. "Really?"

Grenard smiled. "I wouldn't suggest it if I wasn't serious."

The boy beamed.

The Tulku grinned and turned his attention to his case, sitting on the dresser. "It's settled then."

"What is?"

"You will no longer be Jake Feyer's son."

"I don't understand. How can you do that?"

The Tulku pulled out a small crystal jar and held it to the light. "Come here." He sat on the ground and pointed for Levi to sit directly in front of him. He fiddled with the lid and opened the seemingly empty container. "Do you still trust me?"

"Yes, but you're starting to make me nervous." Levi sat cross-legged on the floor, blanket still wrapped around his exposed body.

Grenard smiled. "Do you remember what I told you about the syamta?"

Levi nodded. "All Rufosians are born with them, and they each have a different meaning, right?"

"There's something I didn't tell you. It is possible to give syamta to someone who has lost them, or to someone who may not have had them to begin with." Grenard's tail flicked, and his ears perked up.

Levi searched the ambassador's face. "You're joking."

The Tulku shook his head.

Levi dropped his gaze and thought. He had always thought of himself as a soldier, but he realized he didn't want to be only that. He wanted to be more than the uniform he wore, more than the orders he followed, more than Feyer's opinion of him. He wanted to be free. An unexplainable desire to know what he was capable of becoming overwhelmed him. He looked up at Grenard and let the blanket slide from his shoulders.

Grenard dipped a finger in the jar and grabbed Levi's right arm. He began drawing invisible lines on the boy's skin. Whatever the clear substance was, it was oily and freezing cold. Grenard then drew more lines across Levi's chest. When he was done, he closed the container and sat with his ears perked and his tail swishing back and forth.

Levi watched Grenard's growing anticipation as the cold grew to almost painful levels. "How long is this supposed to take?"

"Less than a minute."

A few more seconds had passed, and the oily lines on Levi's arm began to transition from frigid tingling to a burning sensation. His chest soon followed. He clenched his fists tightly. "Grenard, is it supposed to hurt?" Sweat beaded on his forehead.

The Tulku gave him a half smile. "I've been told it isn't the most pleasant experience."

Levi's skin felt like it had been set on fire. "Grenard! What the hell—"

"Look!" The ambassador took Levi's arm.

The faintest blue tinge began to creep over the boy's skin where the Tulku had smeared the oil, and the fiery sensation rapidly dissipated. Grenard pulled him to his feet and steered him towards the bathroom mirror. Three light blue lines had appeared on his arm. They were all parallel, with the center one extending above and below the two that flanked it. More light blue lines swirled across his chest, with a flame resting over his heart. It was the same syamta Grenard had.

The Tulku smiled proudly. "It seems I was right about you."

"What do you mean?"

"I can have my mind made up on what I see in you, but the syamta only actually appear if they are meant to." He pointed to Levi's arm. "This one represents leadership. Being a leader is more than just ruling with an iron fist. It is holding a place of authority with dignity and justice while you protect your people. It is also being willing to be humble enough to truly serve your people instead of serving yourself. Leading well is a difficult balancing act. Many fall, and even among those who don't, few lead well."

Levi turned to the Tulku. "I don't want to be a leader like my father."

Grenard grabbed the boy's shoulders. "I don't expect you will be." He sighed contentedly.

The boy studied the second syamta swirling across his chest. "I thought that Hjaniyalu can only be inherited by an Alsh."

"That's true. I guess that means the syamta decided you are truly an Alsh." He squeezed Levi's shoulders. "Hjaniyalu has a meaning attached to it, more than signifying who is to lead Tulanu next. In the ancient language of this world, it roughly means to brave what you do not know with truth. In other words, it is courage. But this kind of courage stems from conviction in the depths of your soul. It will light your way even when times grow challenging and you cannot find any hope. It will serve as your armor when you are faced with difficult decisions."

Levi looked over the new lines. Aside from the strange, matte blue color, there was no mark or defect where the syamta existed. Where the lines crossed over scars, his flesh had been healed, perfected. Some of the smaller nicks had completely disappeared. It didn't make any sense. How could some ancient oil that created supernatural lines get rid of his scars? There was no medicine or procedure in Erev that could fully remove his mistakes, and yet whatever infuriatingly cold and fiery goop had turned his skin blue had also managed to cover his sins perfectly. All he had done was sit there and take it.

"What now?" Levi turned to Grenard.

"We pack."

Levi watched as Grenard stood and stretched. "That's it? What about Feyer? What about your negotiations?"

"I will give Feyer one chance tomorrow to prove he can change and be reasonable. And when that falls through, we leave."

Levi's heart skipped a beat. He could be free, free to stay by Grenard's side and free from the fear of Feyer. He hurriedly put his shirt back on and found his rucksack. There weren't many material possessions that Levi had and even fewer he cared to take with him. An extra change of clothes, the damaged recording of Anton, Grenard, and Vanyani, the book from Arden, and Levi's journal were piled into his bag. He closed his bag and brought it out to the commons area. He would be ready to bolt at a moment's notice.

The ambassador was sitting on the couch writing furiously in one of his journals. Levi set his bag on the table and plopped down next to the Tulku. He wanted to leave then and there, but if Grenard was willing to give Jake one last chance, he supposed he could do that one last service for his father.

Levi stared at the golden lines in the Tulku's fur. "Grenard, what do the rest of your syamta mean?"

The ambassador eyed the boy and sighed. He set aside his journal and slipped his shirt over his head, displaying every detail of his shimmering fur. "Words fail to portray the true depths of the concepts, but for you, my boy, I will try to explain."

Grenard took a deep breath. "I always thought of my syamta as a sort of armor that I would someday grow into. Each syamta is connected to one another, working together to form who I am called to be, and the way they are connected adds dimension, a sort of living essence, like an ecosystem of values.

"Hjaniyalu protects my heart, the most vital part of myself. Without courage, I can do nothing else I am called to. It anchors me, so I can guard others." He pointed to his back and showed Levi. "On my back is 'Protector' or 'Defender.' In many ways, it anchors Hjaniyalu. I cannot fight if I have no courage, and there is no reason to need courage if I have nothing to fight for."

He turned back around and showed the boy his arms. "I can shield others with empathy using my left hand, and with my right, be generous towards them." He touched the golden flames on his ears and grinned. "If I choose to listen, I am able to use Intuition to determine what needs to be done next, though the listening part is sometimes hard."

Levi smiled.

Grenard took a deep breath, and his grin fell. "As for the last one, it is called Vyo." He traced lines from the top of his head down the back of his neck to where the golden lines met with Hjaniyalu. His hands dropped into his lap. "It is the use of one's mind and heart to give up everything out of love."

Levi sat and thought about the Tulku's words. "Sacrifice."

Grenard smiled halfheartedly.

"Does that mean you'll die?"

"Everyone dies, son."

Levi rolled his eyes. "That's not what I mean."

Grenard grinned sorrowfully. "When we first met, I believe I told you that it was a blessing to have the syamta, though you didn't seem to believe me. Vyo is less about death than it is about purpose. We all will die when our time comes, and we all wrestle with the meaning, or lack thereof, of death. But I get to know that my death will likely have served someone somehow. It is encouraging to think that my life and my death will not have been in vain. It doesn't mean I don't fear death from time to time, but that is where courage comes into play."

Levi thought over all the Tulku had said. The ambassador had come to Erev knowing its dangers but facing them anyway for the greater good. The Tulku had defended him in the back alley. Grenard had been more generous than Levi thought he deserved and had always listened to him with empathy.

"Do you think you've grown into any of your syamta yet?"

Grenard chuckled. "Far from it, my boy."

"Do you think you'll ever fully become who you are meant to be?"

"No. That would be asking if anyone could become perfect. It is something everyone will forever be striving to attain."

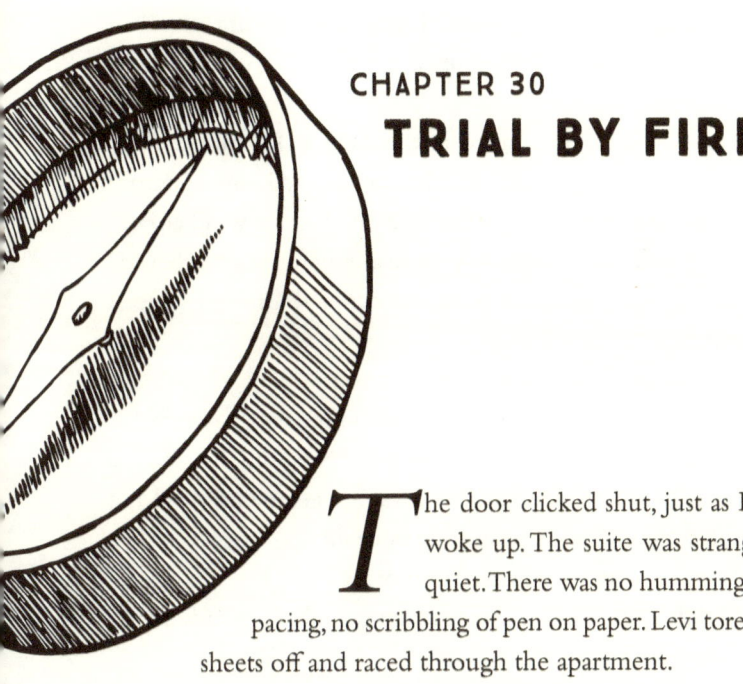

CHAPTER 30
TRIAL BY FIRE

The door clicked shut, just as Levi woke up. The suite was strangely quiet. There was no humming, no pacing, no scribbling of pen on paper. Levi tore the sheets off and raced through the apartment.

Grenard was nowhere to be found.

He opened the door and looked down the corridor. The rust-colored Tulku, dressed in his usual purple attire, was making a beeline for President Feyer's office. The soldier frowned at his sweatpants and long-sleeved shirt and groaned. There was no time to change into his uniform.

He sprinted down the hallway. "Grenard! You can't go in there! Unsavory place!"

The ambassador's ears twitched towards the boy, but the Tulku pressed forward and knocked on the large double doors before the soldier could stop him.

Levi came to a stop at Grenard's side just as Jake's voice beckoned the solicitor to enter.

Grenard eyed him. "I said I would not bring you into the crossfire, my boy." He stepped inside and closed the door behind him.

Levi stood dumbfounded in the hallway. He pulled at his hair and leaned against the wall. He should have known Grenard would pull a stunt like this. People didn't just show up at Feyer's office uninvited unless they were asking for trouble. Several minutes passed before the doors opened and Grenard stepped out calmly.

"He agreed to meet with me at noon."

Levi breathed a sigh of relief, then immediately scowled at the Tulku and pointed a finger in his face. "Next time, don't leave me behind. I understand you don't want to get me involved, but I'm still supposed to be protecting your life."

"Levi, you know you cannot protect me."

"I don't give a damn. You're saying you don't even want me to try to have your back?"

Grenard frowned. "I did not say that."

Levi crossed his arms. "Then what was the point of all the talk last night about purpose? I have a job to protect you, and it gives me purpose. And I know you're just trying to protect me, but you can't protect me from everything, just like I can't protect you from everything."

The Tulku sighed. "You have a fair point."

"Then next time you waltz into Feyer's office, I better be there with you."

"Very well."

They went back to the suite where Levi changed into his uniform, packed his sleepwear, and fixed his messy hair. Grenard sat at the table, still writing in his journal. When each page was filled, the Tulku tore it out and stacked it face-down in a pile.

The soldier resorted to pacing. The anticipation of leaving Erev forever and Grenard confronting Jake about any number of strained topics wore his nerves thin.

Time crept by at an agonizingly slow pace, but as noon neared, Grenard stilled his pen and collected himself. He donned his tyam and a royal air and waited on the soldier. Levi's palms grew sweaty, and his hands shook as he gathered the nerve to face his father one last time. He shoved his hands in his pockets and took a deep breath, following the ambassador to the president's office.

Anxiety mounted in Levi's chest with each step he took, crushing his lungs and squeezing his heart until he thought it might pop, but the ambassador gripped his shoulder reassuringly. Just one more encounter. And if he could manage to not give himself away, he would be free.

Levi opened the door and escorted the Tulkish ambassador inside. He stood as straight and tall as a pine tree, refusing to sway in the winds of his vexed emotions.

Grenard marched towards Feyer's table and bowed politely before him. "President Feyer, thank you for taking the time to meet with me."

"Please have a seat, Ambassador Alsh." Jake gestured to the chair across from him. He held his cane in his hands, twirling it back and forth. He sighed, then leaned it against the table and sat back in his chair. "I understand you wish to negotiate for the lives of the Tulku who burned down half of Trifort."

Grenard seated himself and cleared his throat. "That is one of several reasons I have come here today. Though, I might argue that half of Trifort being ablaze is a slight exaggeration after witnessing it firsthand. Shall we start with that matter, since it is already on your mind?"

Feyer glared. "Very well."

"I would like to begin by saying that I do not condone such behavior. What my fellow Tulku have done is nothing less than shameful. It is inexcusable. I do not wish for them to avoid the necessary consequences, but I would like for them to be tried in a Tulkish court—"

"And why should I trust that justice will be served if they go back to the East? Their actions, I'm sure, are being celebrated in Tulanu, yet they have caused significant damage to life and property."

"Then you forget that the Tulku are pacifists and rationalists. It is deeply ingrained in our culture and way of life. So I would ask how blatant destruction and violence against an ally aligns with either of those philosophies."

Jake sneered. "It seems you do not know your own people, ambassador, if you believe they are truly peace-loving creatures who only use logic to make decisions. My experience tells me otherwise."

"Do you take me for a fool, President Feyer?"

"Even if I did, you are rash to think I would admit that opinion out loud."

Grenard scoffed. "If you are done insulting me, I'd like to finish my thought about what the future trials might look like in order to appease your sense of justice."

Feyer's face darkened as he studied the Tulku. The corner of his mouth turned into a sneer. The stormy gaze Levi had frequently seen surfaced in his eyes, and the boy knew a sort of war was beginning.

Grenard huffed. "I would like for you and your officials to join the court and provide input. They have been interrogated here, and that information deserves to be shared. I think it would also be fair, if not necessary, for several human witnesses to provide their testimony and serve on the jury."

Feyer thought for some time, twisting the gold ring around his finger repeatedly. "Even with human input during the trial, I cannot trust that the appropriate consequences will be executed. A crime committed on Erev's soil should be tried here."

"They are not your citizens." Grenard growled. "President Feyer, you would be able to oversee that justice is indeed served. Again, I do not condone their behavior in any way and would help ensure they pay the price and make amends where possible."

"They cannot bring the dead back to life, nor can they replace the dead."

"I agree." Grenard's tail flicked at his side as he watched Feyer stew. "How many have died in the fires?"

"Seven." Feyer's dark eyes had become pitch-black.

Grenard nodded solemnly. "The loss of one life is too many, let alone seven. Might it appeal to you that the Tulkish Council come here for the trial? That would ensure that a crime committed here is still tried here, but my citizens still receive judgment from their leaders."

"Would not the members of the Tulkish Council vote in favor of their innocence?"

Grenard's ears flattened. "Why would they have reason to believe the arrested Tulku were innocent? They have willingly confessed to their own crimes. And the Council is far more pacifistic than even I. Believe me."

Feyer eyed the ambassador, clasping his hands together. "Sometimes, those in power have certain biased weaknesses that lead to poor, misguided decisions."

"President Feyer, you cannot pretend to be faultless any more than I can."

Feyer's knuckles turned white. "You are ignorant, Grenard."

"About many things, yes. But I am certainly not ignorant about the flaws that plague Tulku-kind and human-kind alike. I hope for the sake of our children that we can come to some kind of understanding."

Jake slammed his fist on the table. "My son is dead because of your people! How could you so easily forget that?"

Grenard eyed Feyer. "Forgive me. I was preoccupied with grieving the loss of my wife due to your people murdering her within a week of your son's death."

"I must ask you to leave, Ambassador Alsh."

The Tulku promptly bowed and left the room with the soldier right on his tail.

Levi looked at the Tulku as they walked back to the suite. "Do you think he'll agree to anything you propose to him?"

Grenard remained silent.

"How long are we going to wait?"

"I will give him until this evening."

Levi took a deep breath. He didn't like waiting. It gave too many things time to fall apart. But he had to trust that the Tulku knew what he was doing.

When they returned to the suite, Grenard resumed scrawling in his journal, adding to the pile of torn-out pages. Levi paced, checked his bag, and rechecked that he had packed everything he wanted to take with him for the rest of the afternoon. Eventually, the pile of papers on the table stopped growing. Grenard took them and sorted them out, neatly folding sets of them together and stashing them back in his journal.

An emphatic knock resounded at the door. Levi tensed up and slowly made his way to investigate. What if it was Feyer? What if he had found out? What if they wouldn't be able to leave tonight? The soldier opened the door, and his shoulders immediately relaxed. "General Thomason, we weren't expecting you."

The silver-haired general smiled. "Is Ambassador Alsh here?"

Grenard strode up behind Levi. "Good afternoon, General."

"I was hoping you and Levi would be interested in attending dinner this evening."

Grenard bowed. "Thank you for the invitation. We shall accept."

Levi's heart sank into the pit of his stomach.

"Excellent! Dinner will be at 6:30." Thomason clapped his hands together and bid farewell.

Levi closed the door and, after giving Thomason a few moments to make his way down the hall, let loose. "What the hell, Grenard? We're never going to get out of here at this rate."

"I'd like to keep up appearances so that no one suspects. I had no reason to say no."

Levi groaned and pulled at his hair.

As the sun lowered, Levi received a notification that Feyer wanted to see him. He complied with his summons, wondering if Feyer had made a decision regarding Grenard's suggestions.

Jake paced about his office, limping and grimacing with each step. "You said you wanted to learn about politics, boy. Tell me your thoughts on what the ambassador said earlier."

Levi shuffled from foot to foot. "I think the Tulku should still be put on trial here, sir. It is the only way to maintain control of the situation and hopefully prevent them from taking such actions again. But allowing the Tulkish Council to stay involved may be the best way to maintain peace. If we show them we are for having justice and providing a fair trial, while also showing them we are not afraid of executing consequences, that may help earn their respect while warning them that we are not to be trifled with."

Jake eyed him. "How would you maintain control over the outcome of the trial with the Tulkish Council there?"

Levi paused and thought. "I would make sure I had a convincing argument and had fair consequences that matched the extent of the crime." He looked to Jake, hopeful that he had given a reasonable answer.

Feyer chuckled. "That is not maintaining control. That's a gamble. You'd attempt to appeal to them using logic, but they are not logical creatures. How would you keep control over them?"

Levi felt his soul writhe. He ran his fingers through his hair and winced. "Ensure the jury votes that the Tulku are guilty."

"How do you control the jury?"

Levi felt his compass scream at him. "You would have to bribe them or threaten them. But that isn't honest. That wouldn't be a fair trial."

"Do you think the Tulku will choose to play fairly, Levi? They will do everything they can to gain control over the situation. I can promise you that."

Levi swallowed hard. "Then how would you maintain control over the situation, sir?"

Jake smiled cruelly. "I would do the same thing that I did to Vanyani Alsh."

The boy froze. What Feyer did... Levi's eyes grew wide. "You..."

"Welcome to the real world, boy. It is far crueler and more brutal than anyone likes to acknowledge."

Levi stumbled backwards.

Feyer eyed him. "If Ambassador Alsh would like to resume our discussion, I would like to share with him my decision on how to proceed with the Tulku's trial after dinner."

"Yes, sir."

———— ''' ————

Levi burst into the suite, wide-eyed and panting. "Grenard, Feyer killed Vanyani! He planned it all out."

The Tulku was packing his satchel and stopped to stare at the boy. "Explain yourself, my boy."

Levi took a deep breath and collected his thoughts. "When I was nine, he sent me away for about two years. When I came back, he insisted that I was his nephew instead of his son. My backstory was that Feyer's half-sister was sick and dying and needed someone to take in her son."

"I'm not following, Levi."

"The media said that I had been killed by a Tulku while out in Rylant. A week later, your wife died out of revenge for my faked death. Feyer planned it all out. He set up the faking of my death and hid me away for two years to make it convincing and gave me a backstory to cover everything up, threatening me to never deviate from the story. Then, with plenty of ammunition, he sent Anthony Pearson to kill Vanyani and claim that it was a random human who was taking revenge on the Tulku for my death."

CHAPTER 31
PRIDE COMES FIRST

Grenard burst into Feyer's office with Levi frantically chasing after him. "Is it true, Jake?"

Feyer stood from his chair and straightened his jacket. "Is what true?"

"Did you or did you not plot my wife's murder?"

Feyer glanced at the boy. "That's a serious accusation to make." He laughed, but as the Tulku's demeanor grew more grave, his smile wavered.

Grenard's fur stood on end as he towered over the president. "You framed your own son's death and blamed it on the Tulku so you could have an excuse to kill my wife."

"My son is dead because of your people!"

"No! Your son is right there." Grenard pointed at the young soldier.

Jake turned on Levi. "You lied to me! You told me you said nothing to him."

Grenard stepped in Jake's view. "He told you the truth. You forget that Vanyani and I both met him when he was too young to remember it. The four-year-old I met all those years ago is the same boy at nineteen. Did you really think I wouldn't remember him, especially after you stick me in a room with him for three months straight? No amount of calling him your nephew could cover that lie."

Jake threw his hands up in the air. "Yes! He's my son. But it was your fault that Jeda died."

"How is that my fault? I didn't make Anton poison him."

"You set him up! You were always trying to get on Anton's good side, and you turned Jeda into a scapegoat."

Grenard's ears pinned back, and his tail bristled. "That was how Vanyani and I played the game after Jeda's death. No, Jeda confronted Anton about not doing enough for you. He loved you and was fighting for you. *That's* why he died. Anton was jealous of Jeda for the attention you gave him. But you refused to honor him in his death by not taking his tyam. Your pride blinds you, Jake Feyer!"

Jake hurriedly limped to the mantle and picked up the small wooden box that lived there. "I didn't dishonor him." He opened the box and revealed green folded pieces of silky fabric embroidered in yellow. "A day doesn't go by that I don't look upon them and think of him."

Grenard frowned. "You would not have them if I did not seek to give them to you a second time."

Jake slowly deflated and closed the box. He set it back on the mantle. "Was there anything else you wished to discuss, Ambassador Alsh?" He made his way back to his chair and picked up his cane from the floor.

"Yes." Grenard took a deep breath and sat across from him. "How about we address your consistent and blatant avoidance of truth you don't want to hear? Particularly the truth about what is actually happening in Tulanu. Contrary to what Erev's media reports, none of the attacks here have been baseless. Every single one has been preceded by a worse human attack in Tulanu. For every seventeen Tulku that have been killed, only one human has died."

Jake scoffed. "Where are you getting that information?"

"I collected data on every attack on either side for the past ten years. Tell me, Jake. How many humans have died at the hands of Tulku in the past ten years?"

Jake thought for a moment. "Around three hundred."

"Two hundred ninety-four human lives have been lost. Compare that to five thousand of *my* people that have died because of *your* refusal to acknowledge reality. Five thousand!"

Jake crossed his arms. "Please inform me of the reality that I supposedly ignore, Ambassador."

Grenard eyed the president warily. "Was the arson at Trifort a few days ago really baseless?"

"Yes."

"Then why was it that when I went to Yfalo I walked past close to two hundred memorials because of a few human suicide bombers that were caught on camera from two weeks before the attack in Trifort?"

"What reason do I have to believe anything that you say?"

Grenard fists balled at his sides. "You choose to have no reason to believe me, though I have never lied to you."

"If you want me to believe you so badly, then convince me!"

"Then ask your son what he saw in Yfalo!" Grenard's flared anger fizzled as if a bucket of water had just drowned his flame. He looked at Levi, wide-eyed and terrified. "I'm so sorry, my boy."

All the blood drained from Levi's face, and his veins turned to ice. How could the ambassador do that? Grenard had promised! The Tulku had kept his word every time except the time it truly mattered. Levi stood, brokenhearted and horribly exposed.

Jake gawked at the boy. "You went to Yfalo?"

"Yes, sir." The words tumbled out before Levi could think to lie.

"You directly disobeyed my orders."

"I asked him to come with me." Grenard's ears were flat against his head. He avoided looking at either human.

Jake glared at the ambassador, intent on murder. Levi saw Feyer grab the cane and lunge forward. The soldier dashed forward and threw up his arms. The ensuing snap left Levi's arms throbbing. He grabbed the ambassador and shoved him towards the door. He opened the door and pushed Grenard out, and slammed it shut, locking it, as he caught another lash from the cane.

"Levi!" Grenard's muffled cry seeped through the door as it rattled.

Feyer grabbed Levi's uniform and dragged him across the room as the door continued to shake. He slammed him into the wall and thrust the cane under Levi's chin and leaned into the rod. "What the hell was that?"

Levi fought to keep his airway open, pushing against Jake as hard as he could. "You never told me I couldn't go to Tulanu. You only told me to keep the ambassador from harm. I'm doing what you told me to do!" Panic flooded through his mind. His composure was hanging on by a thread.

Feyer leaned harder and snarled. "You defied me, and in front of an animal. You have undermined me and sabotaged Erev's future. Everything I have worked for will be destroyed thanks to you."

Levi struggled to take in oxygen under the added pressure. He clawed at Jake's wrists, trying to pull him away. Tears slipped down his face. "Can't breathe!" He stared into his father's eyes, hoping there was one shred of sympathy left somewhere in that dark, empty soul. "Please!"

Feyer let up only to strike the boy with the cane's handle.

Levi fell to hands and knees, desperately choking in air.

"Pathetic."

Levi shook as he pushed himself up. He refused to break down and give in to weakness. He glared at the man that stood before him.

Jake had turned his back and was fiddling with various objects on his desk. "Are you or are you not my son?"

"I am, sir."

Levi questioned every aspect of his response, but his resolve could not falter. Half of his DNA belonged to Jake Feyer, and it was Feyer who had raised him, but he had never said he loved Levi. It was Grenard who said he loved him, yet even Grenard's dedication seemed to flake apart.

"Prove your loyalty to me, Levi."

"What do you want me to do, sir?"

"Kill the ambassador. If you do that, I will forgive you for disobeying my orders."

Levi's heart seized. "I don't know if I can kill him."

Feyer reeled and spat in his face. "You will kill Alsh! I don't care if you think you can or you think you can't. If you fail me, then you will suffer ten times worse than every other time I caught you defying me. Do you want to live through that again?"

The door clicked open. "President Feyer, we are expecting you." Thomason's jolly expression slid off his face as he glanced first at Levi, then at Jake. He cleared his throat. "Dinner is ready, sir. Please forgive my intrusion."

Levi could just barely make out Grenard peering over Thomason's shoulder from the hallway.

Jake kept his gaze fixed on the boy as he straightened. "Thank you, General Thomason. Will you please retrieve Ambassador Alsh?"

"Of course." The general nodded and retreated from the office only after gazing sorrowfully at the boy.

Levi longed for the general and Grenard to stay, but the door closed.

Jake tidied himself and leaned on his cane. "You will join us for dinner, but you will not sit at the table, and you will not eat until the ambassador has been dealt with."

"Yes, sir." Levi followed numbly behind Feyer. He didn't know what to think, didn't know what to feel. His moral compass felt as if it was spinning madly, trapped in a magnetite epicenter.

"Hail, Feyer!" Ten proud voices rang out.

Levi's attention snapped back to the present. The special unit stood in two neat rows in the foyer, saluting the president. Thomason had joined in the salute, but his expression was far grimmer than those of his pupils. There was something about the salute that rubbed the boy the wrong way, but he pushed it down. Now was not the time to be sorting through his jumbled feelings.

Grenard was beside the general in his formal Vey attire, staring despondently at the boy, but he did not say a word. He only trailed behind the general and the president into the dining hall.

Neither the Tulku nor the boy had anticipated such a large gathering. But Levi felt extreme relief from not being alone with Feyer any longer.

Feyer sat at the head of the table with Grenard at his left, Thomason at his right, and the special unit occupying the rest of the table. Levi posted himself a few paces away from Grenard and Jake, avoiding eye contact with everyone.

More than anything, the boy wished he could disappear, to be nonexistent for five minutes. Whatever emotional reserves he had were rapidly draining away, leaving him empty.

The silver-haired general cleared his throat as he attacked his plate. "Ambassador Alsh, how has your research been going?"

"It has certainly been an eye-opening experience. I must admit my knowledge of Erev's early history was quite lacking, but I was able to spend a fair bit of time studying the *Creed of Erev* and the *Treaty of Riyanti.*"

Thomason smiled. "Ah, yes. They are the documents Erev was founded upon. We ought to be teaching our younger generations more about them and their importance. Those laws and ideals should not be haphazardly cast aside."

Feyer set his cutlery down. "I agree. However, new times and new situations should cause careful reconsideration of some of those laws. Some things are meant to be left in bygone eras."

Grenard sighed. "Careful consideration, yes, but some laws were put in place indefinitely for very good reasons. To remove such laws would risk repeating history."

"History cannot repeat itself. There may be patterns that tend to present itself, but it can never truly happen as it happened before."

"I would disagree. Even in my lifetime, I have seen one generation act just as the generation before it. Sons become like fathers and repeat poor decisions. That is why laws are established, so as to either break the vicious cycle or to punish those who ignore the past. Neglecting well-established rules risks letting injustice seep in, just as one neglected cut may allow infection to make the entire body sick." Grenard eyed Feyer sternly.

"Leaving a cut unattended does not guarantee it will become infected."

"No, but it certainly leaves the body vulnerable."

"Or it strengthens the body's immune system, making it more resilient for when a more serious injury might present itself."

"Let us hope that we do not incur more injury. There are already more than enough open wounds to dress, and I'm afraid some are already festering. Drastic measures will need to be taken later if nothing is done now."

Thomason sputtered as he sipped from his glass. The ten young soldiers dared not breathe a word as they watched and listened.

Feyer's expression remained calm and cool. "I thought you were a pacifist, Ambassador Alsh, as all Tulku supposedly are."

"After all the years we have known each other, do you truly believe I prefer to stand on the sidelines and do nothing?"

"Then you must be a militant."

One of the soldiers dropped his silverware and mumbled an apology.

Grenard dabbed at his mouth with his napkin and set it back on the table. "War is never glamorous, but there are situations where it is necessary. I would argue that perspective makes me more of a realist than an extremist."

"What about the rationalist part of your Tulkish upbringing? Are you also suddenly opposed to logic?"

Grenard glowered at Feyer. "Rationalism only works when everyone at the table is rational. Then again, if everyone were rational, there would be no need to sit down and try to have a logical conversation to resolve conflict. Conflict would not exist if everyone was capable of thinking clearly."

Jake's brows furrowed and he cleared his throat. Feyer stood from the table, and everyone else stood to salute him. "Please, enjoy the rest of the meal without me." He grabbed his cane from the edge of the table and limped away, only stopping beside Levi. He barely spoke above a whisper. "Prove to me you aren't worthless."

"Do all fathers demand such things from their sons?"

Feyer glared at the boy. "Mine demanded sacrifice. I expect the same of you."

"Then history is stuck repeating itself."

Jake's grip on the cane tightened. He shook his head and moved on slowly and painfully. The table was seated once more. Grenard's ears had been trained on Levi, though the ambassador did not look at him. Levi only briefly glanced up and noticed Liam, the soldier with the cochlear implants, staring at him intensely, only to break his stare and return to his meal.

A few of the soldiers exchanged whispers, leading to strained, quiet conversation. Grenard kept his head down, picking at his plate. As the volume increased, the Tulku stood and approached Levi.

"You can have my place, my boy."

"I have been ordered to abstain, sir." Levi avoided Grenard's gaze.

The Tulku nodded briefly and returned to his seat. The ambassador's plate remained untouched through the rest of dinner.

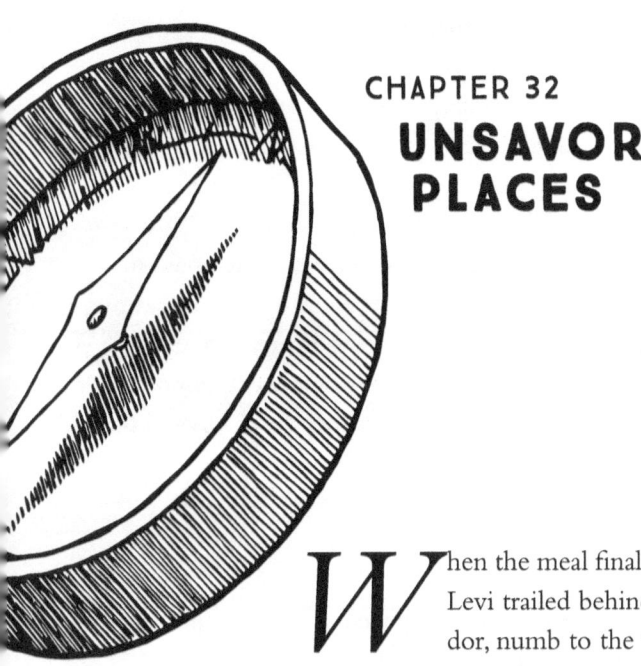

CHAPTER 32

UNSAVORY PLACES

*W*hen the meal finally wrapped up, Levi trailed behind the ambassador, numb to the world. He had been foolish to think he could run away unscathed. He was probably foolish to think that Feyer would truly forgive him for his crimes when all was fully revealed. He clicked open the door and plodded inside. He planted himself on the couch and stared blankly at the wall. Orange light smeared across the wall as the sun set over the sea.

Grenard stood at a distance from the boy. "I'm sorry, Levi. I should have guarded my tongue better."

Levi shrugged, feeling a thousand emotions pressing out on his chest, waiting for a crack to show itself. "Nothing you say will change what happened."

"I know, but that isn't the point."

"Then why apologize?"

"Because I'm not perfect."

Levi studied Grenard's remorse-filled face.

"I am broken, too, and unfortunately that has a few negative consequences that come with it. It means I cannot love you as I intend to, and I make mistakes. I know I can't undo what has already been done, but at least let me try to make amends for the damage I have caused."

Levi looked away from the ambassador and attempted to rationalize all that had fallen apart in a matter of seconds. He was angry, angry at Grenard for betraying his trust, angry at Feyer for his crimes, angry at himself for not guarding his own soul. His hope for having a better life was shot down like a bird flying for its life.

"You're bleeding."

"I'm fine."

The Tulku reached out.

Levi swatted his hand away and glared. "I said I'm fine, sir."

The Tulku pulled back. His ears fell.

A knock on the door drew Levi's attention away before he could answer. He sighed and stood. The banging sounded again, louder this time.

"I'm coming!" Levi stepped around the Tulku and went to run his fingers through his hair, but his head throbbed when he touched it. His fingers came away red. He hadn't even noticed the wound. Grenard had been right. He choked back a sob.

A broad soldier stood in the corridor, one with a scar along the back of his neck. Levi recognized him but could not place where he had seen the man. He looked Levi up and down with a sneer.

The boy glanced over his shoulder. The ambassador had disappeared into his room. Levi slid into the hallway and closed the door. He took a deep breath and stood tall, mustering all the strength and resolve that he could. "Do you have news?"

The man nodded and revealed a polished handgun.

Levi stared at the gleaming metal. "I have my own weapon."

"You will use it." There was no give, no hint of suggestion or recommendation in the soldier's voice.

Levi took the weapon. It was cold and heavy in his hands. Fear struck him as he weighed it, wondering if Feyer intended on punishing him with a faulty gun. He checked the magazine and examined every aspect to ensure it was in working order. When he was satisfied with its status, he glanced up at the soldier. "I'll only be a minute."

He turned, but the soldier held out his arm, blocking Levi's path.

"Feyer demanded a witness. That won't be a problem, will it?"

Levi's heart stopped, and he eyed the man. "No. Of course not." He smiled weakly and opened the door for the soldier.

The man posted himself just inside the doorway. Levi trudged past him, clicking the safety off. He stood by the kitchen table, desperately trying to sort out what he was doing. Something deep inside him clawed at his soul, tearing his heart. He stared down at the gun, waiting to be awakened for its created purpose.

The ambassador walked out of his room, journal in hand, writing. He looked up and stopped in his tracks. He glanced first to Levi, then to the other soldier, then to the gun. He closed his journal as fear flooded his eyes. He stared at Levi. All hope drained from his face. "What's this, my boy?"

"I was just given a new assignment, Ambassador Alsh." He took the gun and gripped it firmly in both hands. He felt his face take on the cold and cruel expression his father usually wore as a single tear silently slipped down his cheek. His heart cried out against him as he struggled to raise the weapon that suddenly weighed a hundred times more than it had only a minute ago.

Grenard dropped the journal and stepped back, bumping against the wall. "You're following through with this, aren't you?"

"I don't exactly have a choice, Grenard!" His hands shook.

"You always have a choice, son."

"Either I do this, or Feyer beats me every day for the rest of my life. I can't go through that again."

Grenard pointed to the syamta over his chest. "You always have a choice."

Courage. Levi searched deep inside himself, looking to see if it was really there.

The soldier behind Levi groaned. "Just shoot already! I don't want to be here all night."

Levi glared at the soldier. At that moment, he recognized the man as the masked figure who had tried to poison Grenard at the masquerade ball.

Levi's mind raced. Grenard was never supposed to return to Tulanu, but Levi had gotten in the way, so Feyer made him part of the plan to destroy the ambassador. The compass in the boy's heart suddenly ceased its whirling. He fired.

The soldier's eyes went wide as he thudded to the ground.

Levi's ears were filled with the ringing of the explosion. He watched as crimson blood drained from the body into a pool on the floor. He looked down at the gun in mild horror and dropped it. He stumbled backwards into Grenard. He never wanted to hold a gun again, never wanted to be forced to use one again. His heart pounded in his chest.

"Time to go, my boy. Grab your things." Grenard picked up his journal and retrieved his satchel, stuffing the book inside.

The boy still stood where the Tulku had left him.

"Levi!"

The boy started and looked at the ambassador as tears slipped down his cheeks. "I just—I—"

"I know, but we have to go, son." Grenard stooped down and picked up the gun. He held it out to the boy. "I hate to think that we might need it again."

Levi extended a shaky hand to take it. He flicked the safety on, then shoved it in his rucksack, still lying on the coffee table from the night before. He threw the bag over his shoulders and followed Grenard out into the hallway. He cast one last glance at the dead man then closed and locked the door. Grenard pulled him away.

They rushed down a back staircase and hurried outside to where Levi's car was parked, only to come to a complete standstill. Several soldiers were guarding the vehicle. Levi pushed Grenard around a corner, out of view.

"Shit." His mind raced to think of another way to escape, some way to run away. *Run!* The gate at the back of the compound he used for running was never locked and never guarded. Most people didn't even know it existed. "Come on!"

He pulled Grenard into the maze of gardens. A few other soldiers poured from the house, flashing spotlights out across the dimming landscape. Levi and Grenard ducked out of view and weaved their way to the back of the property.

An old metal gate had punched a hole through the wall that stood sentry around the mansion. It cried out in agony as its stiff hinges allowed the pair to pass into the forest. Only a sliver of one of Rufosia's moons shed any light on their path as they trekked through the trees.

Levi checked to see that no one had picked up their trail, then gazed up at the star-splattered sky. They had made it out, but he didn't know how he felt. He assumed that there would be some amount of relief, but a strange whirlpool of anxiety and hope swirled inside him.

Grenard inhaled as if to speak.

"I'm still mad at you."

"I know." The Tulku sighed.

The crack in Levi split open. He sunk to the ground and buried his face in his hands. "I'm sorry! I tried to get him to leave, but Feyer… I can't go back to that. I can't live through that again."

"I forgive you, son."

Levi glanced up and saw Grenard's outstretched hand. He took it, and the pair continued deeper into the night.

"You had asked me earlier how to know if your moral compass is pointing towards true north, and I didn't have a particularly good answer for you at the time. All of us will stray from north, but the process of apologizing and forgiving is one way to refocus on north. I believe that apologies are more for the person that did the wrong than for the person that was wronged for the sole reason that the person apologizing is, in many ways, setting themselves free. It is hard to walk away from magnetite if we cannot acknowledge that we have wandered away from north to begin with. An apology can often act like a sledgehammer to the shame that chains us to old and harmful ways."

"What about forgiveness?"

Grenard smiled. "Forgiveness is also primarily for the person with the power to forgive. Forgiveness is not saying that the pain that was caused was somehow acceptable, but it is a deliberate choice to let go of the pain and free ourselves from our anger having control over us."

Levi kicked at the ground. "I don't think I'll ever be able to forgive Feyer."

"I hope you do find a way, because living with unresolved anger doesn't only affect you; it affects everyone you interact with. Learn from someone who has made countless, avoidable mistakes because I couldn't forgive."

"If I can't forgive him, does that mean I can't follow north?"

Grenard paused, deep in thought. "It makes it far more challenging to pursue north, but I believe that anger will be confronted by North himself along the way. Seeking north is a very narrow and challenging path that requires much humility. Afterall, there is only one way to north, and that is walking north. You can't somehow end up at north if you only travel east, west, or south. But the fact that you're asking if you are pursuing what is true and what is good tells me that you are already walking in the right direction."

Levi felt his heart quiet and his breathing slow. A certain peace had settled over him as they continued north and away from the mansion until they came across a small creek. Levi turned east and began following it towards the sea. Grenard hiked silently beside him.

"How are we getting out of Erev?"

The Tulku glanced at him. "We'll have to hope Monroe is at the docks tonight."

"No one knows that you two know each other, right?"

"I would be surprised if anyone did."

"Does anyone else know you live in Lassi?"

"Jake might know. But I don't actually live in the city. Even if I did, there are a million other Tulku to sift through before you would find me."

"Okay, but how many humans live in Lassi?"

Grenard froze. "You'll have to avoid the city until Kvenu can put protective measures in place so Feyer can't find you."

Levi nodded.

Lights flashed across the trees in front of them. Levi pivoted and saw several floating beams bounce through the trees behind them. Faint shouts whispered through the trees.

"Damn it! We should run."

They peeled through the rapidly thinning trees. Levi kept Grenard in his peripheral vision at all times, doing his best to stay right at the Tulku's side when the forest allowed. Dark shapes loomed over them as they neared Rylant.

Loud pops echoed behind them. A terrifying whiz zinged past Levi's ear. His heart leapt into his throat. He reached up to touch his ear and found nothing wrong, but a sharp pain seared his side as he failed to sidestep out of a tree's way.

Grenard cried out and stumbled briefly. He picked the pace back up in a matter of seconds.

"Are you alright?"

"I'm fine!" The ambassador's voice was strained. "Into the city. We can hide there."

They veered away from the last few trees and dodged between the powerless, silent buildings. The concrete jungle was eerily quiet and empty. They twisted and turned through the streets, dodging down narrow alleys. When they could no longer hear shouts behind them, Levi and Grenard came to a halt behind a pile of boxes. The Tulku sank to the ground instantly and clutched his leg.

Levi wiped the sweat from his brow and fought to stop panting. He bent over and rested his hands on his knees. "Cramp?"

"Not quite." Grenard's pant leg was soaked in a dark liquid. "Levi, you must promise me something."

"Anything."

"Never go back to Feyer, no matter the cost. I was so foolish to wait so long. We should have left before Feyer even knew we were back from Trifort."

"Grenard…"

"I'm serious." The Tulku grimaced and gripped his leg.

Levi held out his hand. "We have to keep moving. The docks are only a few blocks away."

"I need a few more seconds." The Tulku took a few deep breaths and tried to stand. He crumpled, and Levi caught him.

The boy steadied him. "We're almost there, and then I can figure out how to heal you." His eyes watered without his permission.

"Promise me, Levi."

Shouts trickled down the street and steadily grew louder.

Grenard grabbed Levi's shoulders firmly. "Listen to me very carefully. Monroe can take you to the docks by Lassi. From there, hike south until you get to a river. If you follow the river into the mountains, you'll come up against a large waterfall. My house is just north of the waterfall. My family will take care of you and get a hold of Kvenu as soon as possible."

"Don't! Just give me your bag." Levi tightened the straps on his rucksack and took the satchel from Grenard.

"I mean it, Levi. Run and don't stop."

"No! I'm not leaving you behind."

"You have to."

"I need you!" Tears streamed down Levi's face. "We still have more unsavory places to go so I can save your stupid voluminous tail from having the shit beaten out of it."

Grenard laughed through his own tears and hugged Levi tightly.

The shouting grew considerably louder, and Levi's heart nearly stopped. "Please don't die. Don't sacrifice yourself for me."

Grenard squeezed him even harder. "I couldn't have asked for a more worthy cause to die for. Vanyalida, my son." He let go and darted out into the street.

"No!" Levi tried to grab him and pull him back, but he was gone.

Shouts and gunfire ricocheted off the brick walls of the city. Levi peered out of the small alley and saw several soldiers in uniform run away from him down another street a block away. An inhuman cry pierced the night.

Levi rushed from his hiding spot towards the sound. He crossed the street and peered around the corner of the building. Grenard was surrounded by the ten soldiers they had dined with only hours before, all with weapons trained on him. Their flashlights illuminated the fatal wound that plagued the panting Tulku.

Levi crept forward and ducked into an empty doorway, just out of sight. He pulled the satchel and rucksack off and dug through his bag, frantically pulling out the handgun. It was almost useless at this range, but it was certainly better than nothing. He flicked the safety off and trained it on the group of soldiers.

The sound of an engine came up from behind Levi, and his car rolled towards the crowd. The boy froze, hoping that whoever occupied the vehicle hadn't seen his location. It stopped, and Feyer stepped out, slamming the door shut.

Jake pulled out his own gun and pointed it in Grenard's face. He frothed at the mouth with rage. "You really thought you could get away from me, didn't you?"

Grenard straightened. "No. I always knew my fate."

Feyer scoffed. "You knew that you would die by my hand?"

"I knew I would give my life for something worth fighting for."

"What fool throws away his life like that? What is so valuable that even an animal would be willing to die for it?"

Grenard smirked as the usual mischief in his eyes returned. "You really should consider rethinking your position on history not repeating itself. After all, I'm not the first Tulku to have fought to take something away from a Feyer."

Jake dropped the barrel of his gun as the information processed in his mind. His face contorted as several emotions flashed across it. Then he aimed the gun back at the Tulku. "You won't be able to keep Levi away from me when you're dead."

"But if you kill me, you will have lost him forever, just as Anton lost you forever when he killed Jeda. He will always hate you just as you never forgave your father."

Feyer grew pale. He glanced up and down the street. "Levi! I know you're out there. Come back, and I'll let him live! I'll forgive you for everything."

Levi relaxed his own aim. Could he still save the ambassador? If he gave away his cover, was there a chance he could convince his father to let Grenard go? He started to stand.

Grenard snarled. "Why would he ever come back to you? You don't even love him."

"Of course I love him. He's my son!"

"You don't know how to love."

"I do!"

The ambassador stepped forward, tall and proud and furious. "Then why would you beat him? Tell me, Jake! What kind of man whips a little boy until he can no longer scream? What kind of man strikes his son for not wanting to dance with a girl? What kind of man threatens his child into obedience? What kind of a man are you, Jake Feyer?"

Grenard pressed into the barrel of the gun. "You're a coward. You are prideful and arrogant. You can't stand the idea of him being beyond your control. You're a parasite that gorges on his suffering. You will never be a good fath—"

An explosion echoed off the surrounding buildings.

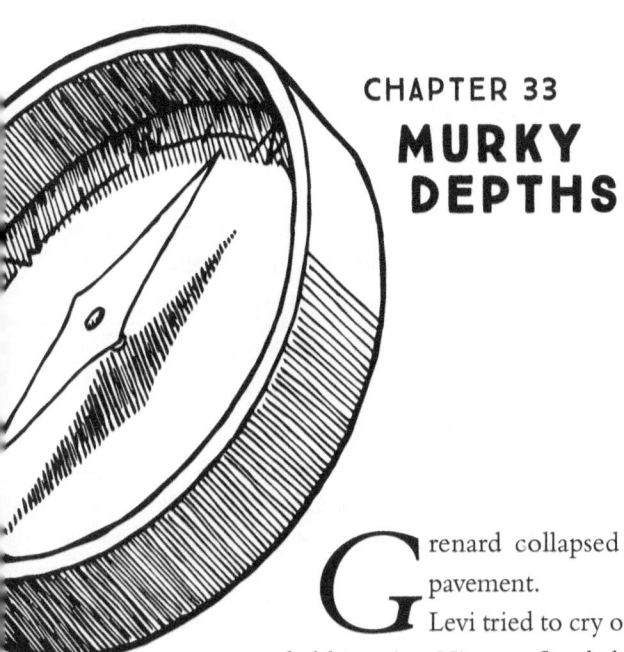

CHAPTER 33
MURKY
DEPTHS

Grenard collapsed limply on the pavement.

Levi tried to cry out, but his throat strangled his voice. His eyes flooded with tears as he watched Feyer sneer at the Tulku's corpse. A burning rage filled the young man. The gun nearly slipped from his hands, but Levi anchored himself and aimed for his father's heart. There was nothing he wanted more than to see that wretched man pay for all the suffering he had caused.

Levi pulled the trigger.

The bullet caught the edge of Feyer's jacket and ricocheted off the ground just beyond him. Jake's smug grin was wiped clean as the special unit surrounded him and escorted him back to the car. Within a matter of seconds, Feyer and the soldiers had abandoned the scene, leaving the dingy streets cold and empty and hopeless.

Levi grabbed his bags, raced from his hideout, and fell at the Tulku's side. Grenard's amber eyes were glazed over, and the rich golden lines that decorated his beautiful fur had all but disappeared. Levi bent to listen for a pulse, knowing it was futile, but still desperately hoping that there was life left in the creature he loved so dearly.

There was only silence.

Ragged sobs escaped from the boy as he closed the Tulku's eyes. "Vanyalida, Grenard. Vanyalida. I'm sorry I failed. I should have done more. I wasn't worthy! Please come back." He gasped for air and stared up into the sky. "I hate you, Feyer! I fucking hate you!"

He knew he couldn't stay, but he couldn't bring himself to leave either. He wiped the tears from his eyes and took a choppy breath. There was something deeply wrong about abandoning the creature who loved him, but Levi couldn't carry him all the way back to Tulanu. As he looked over the body, he noticed the Tulku was still wearing his tyam. Grenard's story about Ambassador G'nali and his father came to mind. He pulled the four silky strands of fabric off and stuffed them in the satchel. He had one last job to do for the Tulku.

Cold metal pressed into the back of Levi's head. He froze and slowly raised his hands.

"Don't fucking move, traitor."

"Please just let me leave. I promise I'll never come back. Feyer won't even know I'm alive. He'll never hear from me again, I swear." Levi felt panic filling his chest and making it hard to breathe.

"Dere', 'us' le' him go."

Levi glanced up and saw the blond soldier stop a few paces shy of his position.

"You're supporting the fucking animal lover? Shit, Liam. You might as well be a traitor, too."

"Then take his gun an' le' him leafe. He's no' lying."

Derek stepped towards Liam. "Who the hell put you in charge?"

"I'm no' ta'ing or'ers from you. You hafen' earne' my respec', and I doub' you efer will."

Derek roared, his gun clattering on the ground as he lunged forward.

"Run, Lefi!"

Levi bolted, and as he looked over his shoulder, Liam and Derek were sprawled on the ground fighting as another two members of Feyer's project team approached the scene, desperately trying to wrench them apart.

Levi ran for the docks and stumbled down to the end of the pier. The *Serenity* wasn't in her usual place. The boy's knees wobbled as he scouted for the boat. When she wasn't anywhere to be found, he trudged down to the beach and hid under the pier, praying Monroe would show up soon. He sat in the sand, hugging his knees to his chest. His heart ached, and his eyes had grown painfully dry. There was nothing left of himself to give.

The sound of the waves nearly rocked Levi asleep as the night dragged on, but an engine thrummed, stirring the boy. He bolted upright and rushed up onto the pier. A man in a yellow raincoat was tying up the *Serenity* under a spotlight.

Levi nearly burst in relief. "Monroe!"

The weathered man looked up from his work and grunted. "Where's Alsh?"

A new wave of guilt flooded over the boy. He choked on his emotions. "He—I couldn't—I failed, Monroe!"

The man sat him down on a bucket. "Alsh is gone?"

Levi buried his face in his hands as a new wave of tears flooded him.

Monroe took his storm-beaten hat off and wiped tears from his eyes. "Bless 'im." He sighed, then put his hat back on. "Why're ye here, boy?"

Levi's lip trembled. "He was trying to save me. He was trying to take me to Tulanu to get me away from Feyer." He took a shaky breath. "I have to find his family."

The fisherman nodded. "It'll be a long, wet ride." He untied the boat.

Levi moved to the stern of the *Serenity* and hunkered down, clinging tightly to Grenard's satchel. The boat started up with a thunderous chug and pulled away from the docks. As they left Rylant's small shallow bay, the wind picked up, and the waves became choppier, making Levi's already upset stomach churn miserably. The salty spray made the scrapes he had acquired sting terribly. Levi sank even deeper and closed his eyes, hoping his exhaustion would pull him into sleep to pass the time. But the waves never relented, and the seawater soaked him to the bone.

After an hour of nonstop bouncing, his stomach revolted against him. Levi grabbed the rail and leaned over the edge of the boat, emptying his already empty stomach into the turbulent waters. He weakly sank back onto the deck with none of his nausea relieved.

Monroe, seeing the boy's sickly state, stopped the boat and walked back to him. "We go' another 'our o' this. Ye gonna' be alright?"

Levi gave him a feeble, shivering thumbs up.

Monroe frowned and pulled something from a compartment in the bulkhead. He tossed what looked to be another raincoat at the boy.

Levi caught it and spread it over himself and the satchel.

"I can't promise th' wind'll die down, but tha' oughta keep y'a li'l drier."

"Thank you."

Monroe walked back to the bulkhead and continued guiding the *Serenity* across the Murky Sea. For the next hour, Levi stared up at the stars that peeked through the dispersed clouds, clutching his stomach. The cold seeped from his toes to his soul, numbing him. It was a relief, though not a comforting one.

"We're 'ere, boy." Monroe walked up to him and pulled him to his feet.

Levi clung to the edge of the boat to keep from falling over. The waves were negligible now, but his limbs were still stuck out at sea. He climbed onto the deck and peered into the darkness. There were no city lights, only the stars and Monroe's spotlight. Massive, pointed shadows blotted out a third of the sky.

Levi handed the jacket back to the fisherman. "Do you know how to get to Grenard's house from here?"

"Ne'er been, but the road just there goes north 'round the moun'ain t' Lassi."

"Grenard said he didn't live in town. Is there a river nearby?"

"Ay. South a dozen kilometers. Call it th' Dragon River." Monroe pointed down the coast.

"Why the Dragon River?"

The fisherman smiled. "Th' water's warm, an' it'll smell like dragon's breath."

Levi nodded then walked down the pier.

"Take care o' them, boy. Alsh's family, 'at is."

Levi turned back and saw the pain in the weathered fisherman's eyes. "I will."

"An' take care o' yerself, too." Monroe tipped his hat towards the boy and smiled sorrowfully.

Levi began the laborious trek south along the beach, only glancing back once to see the *Serenity* chugging back across the Murky Sea. A deep ache settled in his chest as he turned back to task at hand. For the next while, his boots constantly slipped on the rocks and sunk into the sand. The sliver of moons that had lit his way had slipped behind the mountains, and a dusty hint of dawn came up in the west.

As the sun just began to peer over the horizon, Levi caught a whiff of sulfur. Directly ahead of him was a river pouring into the waves. He stepped in the water and reached down. His hands were surrounded with lukewarm water.

Levi turned inland and could see the mountains slowly turning green to either side of him. The sandy banks turned into a thick carpet of moss and pine needles as he entered the forest. Dense branches overhead blocked much of the dawn as he fumbled over boulders and tree limbs. The sound of the river always stayed to his right.

The soldier managed to climb to the top of a rock outcropping and collapsed to the ground. He dropped his bags and looked out at the world. Far below him lay the sea peeking between the two mountains that hemmed him in. The forest took on a lovely green hue as the sun brought life back into the world. Levi peered upstream and saw a massive cliff looming far up the valley. He picked himself up and trekked deeper still.

The sun crept across the sky as Levi stumbled over rock and scrambled over boulder. His feet ached, and he constantly batted away sleep. With every slip, a new scrape was added to his collection. He dared not look up the valley until he found himself in deep shade.

The sound of the waterfall was overpowering from fifty meters away and deafening as Levi stepped up to the basalt cliff face. Frothing water from the top of the cliff bathed the forest below in dazzling mist. He stood in awe for a moment, letting his mind freely wander.

After a minute, he pointed himself at the cliff and stretched out his arms to hoist himself up. The rock was slick and sharp. Levi's fingers clung desperately as he pulled himself up the wall, but his arms shook violently, and his eyes refused to focus. He reached up for the next ledge, but his hand slipped. Levi watched in horror as the rock face fell away from him.

The ground met Levi with incredible force and knocked the air from his lungs. His head throbbed as he lay, panicked and exhausted.

As he stared up at the sky, a strange black shadow moved at the top of the cliff. It began quickly climbing its way down. Alarm bells went off in Levi's ringing head. He rolled onto his feet and tried to stand. He instantly fell over as the world spun around him. The shadow was almost to him.

"Wait!" The shadow morphed into a large Tulkish figure with deep brown eyes materializing out of the dark gray fur. "Let me help you."

Levi shook his head and instantly regretted it. He squeezed his eyes shut. "I'm fine."

"You're not fine." The figure's voice was deep and sonorous. He knelt beside Levi and examined his head. "You need to come with me now."

"Why?" Levi recoiled.

"My sister can help you. What's your name?"

"Levi."

The Tulku's eyes went wide. "I'm Zev."

The name rang in Levi's ears. "Have we met?"

"No, but I know who you are." Zev took Levi's arm and threw it over his shoulder and hoisted Levi to his feet.

"Is that good or bad?" Levi's mind spun as he stood and tried to walk alongside the Tulku.

"Today, it's good."

Zev half carried him along the bottom edge of the cliff, away from the waterfall. Levi struggled to get his eyes to focus on the ground in front of him. Somewhere in his rattled brain, the thought of a concussion swirled around. He didn't know how much of his state was a result from the fall, and how much was exhaustion, but he didn't really care.

The cliff face gradually tilted and flattened out, creating a tiny path that wound its way through the rubble and loose rocks. It was steep and taxing. His muscles shook as he tried to find his footing and push himself up. His shoes slipped repeatedly, and it would have brought him to his knees had Zev not caught him.

The Tulku grunted as Levi slipped again. "I'm carrying you the rest of the way."

"I can make it."

"No, you can't." Zev adjusted his grip and pulled Levi up the slope. He deposited the human at the base of a tree and frowned. As he glanced down at the satchel, a flash of recognition crossed his face. "Let me take your bags."

"No." Levi clutched Grenard's satchel and glared at the Tulku.

Zev huffed. "I'm not going to steal anything." He held out his hand.

Levi stared at the outstretched hand. His shoulders ached. "No rummaging." He took off the satchel and the rucksack and handed them over.

"I won't." Zev threw the bags on his back.

Levi had no concept of time as they trudged through the forest. They finally broke through the trees and came upon a large domed structure to one side of a broad clearing. Zev led him through a bright red door and set him on the floor.

"Beka! I need your help! Now!" Zev set the two bags beside the human and stared down at him, concerned.

Levi lay on the cold, smooth floor. It felt good on his raging head and his tired muscles. He struggled to keep his eyes open.

"You're back early." A strong, melodious voice floated through the air, one Levi felt he had heard before. "If I find you've gone and gotten yourself hurt like the others, I will be thoroughly disappointed, Zev."

Levi's view drifted from the ceiling to a tangerine Tulku with teal syamta strolling towards him. She held something in front of her face, though he couldn't decide what it was.

"I found Levi." Zev pointed down.

Beka looked up. Her ears fell as her eyes met the human's. "Levi? *The* Levi? From Ba's letters?"

The boy's gaze slipped back to the ceiling. He felt a hand against the inside of his wrist.

"Zev, I don't know anything about human anatomy...aren't any in Lassi..."

"...can't be that different, can it?"

Beka waved a blurry hand in front of Levi's face. "...get my med kit..."

Someone grabbed his hand. He tried to hold on, but his fingers barely managed to curl up.

"You're safe now... Everything is going to be alright."

No, everything would not be alright, but he was too tired to argue.